AGE OF CONSENT

The Man from Saigon
Daniel Isn't Talking
Falling Backwards
Love and Houses
Sun Dial Street
Dying Young

AGE of CONSENT

■ ■ ■ *A Novel*

Marti Leimbach

4th ESTATE · *London*

4th Estate
An imprint of HarperCollins*Publishers*
1 London Bridge Street
London SE1 9GF

www.4thEstate.co.uk

First published in Great Britain in 2016 by 4th Estate

First published in the United States by Nan A. Talese/Doubleday,
a division of Penguin Random House LLC, in 2016

1

A catalogue record for this book is
available from the British Library

The chapter 'June's Worst Day at Work' first appeared as
the short story 'Bald' in *The Harlequin*, Issue 5.

ISBN 978-0-00-730709-8

Book design by Maria Carella

Printed and bound in Great Britain by
Clays Ltd, St Ives plc

MIX
Paper from
responsible sources
FSC
www.fsc.org
FSC˚ C007454

FSC™ is a non-profit international organisation established to promote
the responsible management of the world's forests. Products carrying the
FSC label are independently certified to assure consumers that they come
from forests that are managed to meet the social, economic and
ecological needs of present and future generations,
and other controlled sources.

Find out more about HarperCollins and the environment at
www.harpercollins.co.uk/green

For Imo Rolfe

AGE OF CONSENT

THE MONEY

It was September, a weekday, a school night. She had painted her toenails, brushed on mascara, covered with matte foundation the few spots of acne that dotted her nose. She wore pale summer jeans, a shirt she'd ironed herself. She thought there might be dinner, but when Craig picked her up he drove straight to the motel, swinging into a parking space beside a delivery van that looked as though it had been parked there for a while. He turned off the ignition, then switched on the car's inside light. He reached forward, fishing for his wallet, packed in among the cassettes in the glove compartment, also for his lighter. His T-shirt clung where the vinyl seats had made his back sweat. He looked at Bobbie as though he were deciding whether to bother asking, then said, "You got any money?"

"Not much," she said.

He sighed. He rubbed his hand beneath his ball cap, red, white, and blue with a bicentennial celebration logo across the bill. "What about cigarettes?" he said. "Any of them?"

He was twenty-eight, well over six feet, while she was a little package, a ballerina-shaped girl with sun-bleached hair, newly fifteen. She watched as Craig pulled at the contents of the glove compartment, coming out with old envelopes, batteries, a bunch of menus for takeout along with important things—his car registration, his checkbook—chucking it all onto the floor. She thought if he was asking for cigarettes, it must mean he was out of rolling papers. He didn't like cigarettes and hated when she smoked. But sometimes—like now—he'd ask her for a couple. He'd tap out the tobacco in one of her Marlboros, tear off the filter, add his own leaves, then twist the ends to make a joint.

"You keep telling me to quit," she said.

"Never mind. I found something."

Cold light shone from a motel sign perched on a steel post high above them, huge and bright, with garish round letters like something from a comic book. She'd driven past this motel before, seeing it from the passenger seat of her mother's car, the sign and a strip of neon lighting the words VACANCY or NO VACANCY. She didn't know who stopped here or why. It was in the middle of the state. You'd think people would drive all the way to the city, D.C. or Baltimore, wherever they were heading. Stopping at a place like this had to be for purposes of exhaustion or drunkenness or another reason, like what they were doing here tonight.

"It's thirty bucks. And we're not even staying," he said, a trace of disgust in his voice, perhaps to show what having her in his life cost him. Then he swung shut the car door and crossed the lot, his wallet bulging in his jeans pocket. She didn't know what he kept in there that made the wallet so big. Not money, that was for sure. He'd buy her a Hostess Cherry Pie. He'd buy her a McDonald's burger. He didn't get her the things guys got their girlfriends, earrings or flowers. In her school, some of the girls wore liquid silver necklaces with nuggets of turquoise threaded at intervals, and he hadn't bought her anything like that, though she didn't know if she even wanted him to. Accepting a gift would mean something more, that she was his when she didn't want to be his. She would have liked, however, to be someone's.

She watched him disappear into the darkness beyond the streetlamps, and then reappear holding a key on a big wooden fob, the room number burned into the wood. He didn't walk all the way back to the car, but stood on the cement path and told her to get out. She followed him through a narrow passage, past an ice machine and an exit sign. He had a long-strided, swaggering walk and she had to jog every few steps to keep up.

"I need to go home soon," she said.

"I know."

"I've got a test tomorrow." Chemistry, the periodic table. She needed to have learned the shorthand symbols of the elements and, for some, their atomic weights.

He laughed. "I've got a test for you here first."

The lamps in the room were on chains connected by thick eye bolts to the floor. The dark brown curtains, folded stiffly into exaggerated pleats, zigzagged across the windowsill. Had she looked behind the curtains, she'd have seen the air freshener in its coffin-shaped plastic case. An artificial floral scent lay heavy in the room, seeping into the dark brown wood and curtains, and the carpet with its geometric pattern.

She told him she needed the bathroom and he nodded, dropping onto the bed.

He said, "Hey, you look pretty," and then watched her cross the room. "You listening? I just said you were pretty."

"I heard you."

"So what do you say when someone compliments you?"

"Thanks."

"That's better," he said. "You're welcome."

The bathroom was a space with a narrow shower and a chipped toilet. She tried not to make too much noise when she peed because she didn't want him to hear, but the walls weren't much more than strong cardboard. She flushed with embarrassment, pressing her face against the wall tiles to cool her skin while above, somewhere near her, a mosquito hummed. When she came into the room again, she found him on top of the stiff bedclothes, his shoes and T-shirt off. He was grinning at her. She could see his medallion gleaming, and the extra belly fat, and the hair.

"It's got Magic Fingers," he said, dropping a quarter into a machine on the bedside table. There was the sound of a coin dropping, then a buzz as the mattress jiggled. "You going to stand there all night? If you are, how about you turn around and spread your legs? Just kidding."

He had an erection beneath his jeans and he touched himself. She didn't turn or move.

He told her to stop staring at the wall. "Come on. I thought we were going to have a little fun here. Don't you want to have fun? Give me the matches. Get high or do something anyway."

"It's a chemistry test," she said. "I have to stay on track. No smoking pot."

"Suit yourself, Einstein. It's pretty cool what you can do with a Bunsen burner," he said, "but there's other kinds of fire."

"Don't make fun."

"I wasn't. Come here."

She looked at him, tilting her head to one side. He might have thought she was admiring him, but she was only wishing he was more tidy, had a better haircut, or a tan or something. She needed a part of him she could find handsome and focus on if she was going to do this. She looked at his hands with their broad palms and smooth fingers. The nails were healthy and he kept them trimmed.

"What are you looking at?" he said.

"You have nice hands."

He laughed. He pretended he didn't care, but she could see the edges of a smile. "I got better things for you to look at."

He made a grab for her arm, but she moved suddenly, tossing him a fresh pack of matches that had been left by the ashtray. He looked annoyed that she'd strayed from him, but he scratched up a flame anyway, lit the joint, and dragged deeply.

"Do you love me?" he said. "Do you?"

"You always ask me that."

On the far side of the room, a fleet of moths flew over and over into the ceiling light, banging into it, causing little pinging sounds when they met the shade and glass. She watched them now and wondered how they didn't knock themselves out doing that.

"So what's your answer then?" he said. "You love me or are you just messing around here?"

It seemed a nice question—do you love me?—but it wasn't. Not unless she answered quickly and as he wished. "Please," she said. She didn't know what she was asking for. She felt his anger bloom with her hesitation, and wasn't quick enough to stop it. "Please don't—"

"I asked you a question!"

"Yes," she said but she ought to have said this sooner. "Yes, I do . . . I love you." There. It hadn't been so difficult.

"Look at you, staring at bugs," he said. He stuck the joint between his lips and rose from the bed, reaching toward the light where he scooped a moth into his hand. "Up close, it's pretty ugly. You should take a look."

She didn't think it was ugly. She peered into his cupped hand and saw the moth's soft wings and the mossy texture of patterns. "Moths can smell through their feet," she said.

"Jesus, where do you learn this crap?"

"Just a fact."

Suddenly he closed his fingers into a fist, crushing the moth so that when he opened his hand once again there was nothing left of the creature except its head and two broken antennae and a scribble of legs. "Moths are made of dust," he said. "There's another fact for you." He rubbed his palm on the bedclothes, then plucked the joint from his lips, holding it out for her. "Relax," he said, an instruction. "Smoke."

She took a hit but she was worried. Not about getting caught but about whether he'd be too stoned to get her home safely and about the scent lingering on her clothes and her mother noticing. Especially that.

"How about we try something else now?" he said, his hand busy with his zipper. He was proud that his erection was so large, but it didn't do anything for her. He liked to rub his dick on her breasts and face. He liked to run it up the crack of her ass and sometimes, to her disgust, put it inside there, too, though never for very long. He always behaved as though he were giving her something she really liked. But she couldn't figure out why it was supposed to be good. It was good because he told her it was good.

"Lie down," he whispered.

She did as she was told. Sometimes she thought perhaps there really was something wrong with her because mostly sex just hurt or stung. Other times she didn't feel anything at all. He might as well be creating a soft friction on any part of her. Sex seemed a whole lot of nothing and this confused her, making her worry for the future. She was waiting for some change to occur, to acquire the taste. Like the day you finally like coffee after so often finding it bitter and undrinkable.

He turned her onto her belly and she felt the Scotchgard on the coverlet rubbing her face. She waited it out, feeling much the way she might if she were caught in a cold rain and had to march toward shelter. Just keep going, keep going, just keep going until—

Finally he finished. A few strong swipes and he rolled off her, sliding across the little puddle of sweat he left on her lower back. The bed springs creaked as he dropped onto his side. The vibration from the Magic Fingers was long gone and a stillness settled around them so that she could sense what the room would feel like after they had left—a collection of objects arranged on a rectangle of carpet.

She waited until she thought he wouldn't mind, then pulled herself away and went to the bathroom to wash. She was careful with the door, lifting it so that the lock met the catch. Once inside, she clicked on the light. She didn't trust the shower—there were rust marks along the trim and in between the plain square tiles the grout was brownish gray, like bark. She'd heard people got fungal infections from showers like these, and anyway, the water pressure would be weak. She decided to wash in the shallow sink, but even that worried her. She ran the water, then clotted a corner of the bath towel in her fist and rubbed soap along the enamel before rinsing it. The other towel she used first on her face, then between her legs, being gentle so that she didn't make herself sorer.

When she came out, he was sitting on the bed, jeans pulled up but still unzipped, his jockey shorts digging into the ruddy skin of his upper thighs. His lips were dry, and he picked at a bit of loose skin there, then stood all at once, stepping into his shoes.

"You ready?" he said.

Why did he ask her that when she was wearing only her shirt and underwear? Anyway, the room smelled like pot. She thought she should open a window, brush the ash off the tabletops, clean out the ashtray so that there were no signs of drugs. The ashtray was a blocky square of brown glass with an indentation on each side to rest a cigarette. She picked it up and took it to the bathroom, dumped ash into the toilet and flushed.

"Now what?" he said.

She could see him in the mirror's reflection, looking impatiently toward her while pinching down a loose end of a roach. She continued what she was doing, running water over the colored glass, letting the ashes slide down the sink drain. She rinsed it again, then held it up to sniff.

"Whatever you're doing in there, you don't need to," he said. A match between his teeth, a paper clip in his hand.

"I'll be just another minute." She thought about school the next morning, and how many hours between now and the bus, and that she needed to shampoo her hair before then.

"You already look good," he said. "I wouldn't be with you if you were ugly."

"I wish I had shampoo."

"Come on. I don't have all night."

Her hair was tangled with sweat. She thought, too, that he must have gotten his spit in it. She ran the ends under the faucet, tried to arrange it so that it looked okay. She heard him on the other side of the door. It was remarkable how he just pulled on his clothes and went. He didn't mind what others found, or what was suspected.

"I'm going to the car," he said. He went out, leaving the door open. A moment later, he called, "Hurry up!"

She wanted to check there was no stain on the bed, that she

didn't leave behind her comb or wristwatch or any little part of her things. She'd once read a book about how witches—not the ones from a hundred years ago but contemporary witches—could cast spells using only a few strands of a person's hair or something that had been next to their skin. She didn't want to leave anything like that behind. She didn't believe in witchcraft, but she didn't want any part of her left in this room or any room like it.

She put the pillows back under the coverlet, wadded up the used tissues and stuffed them into the little trash can by the toilet. The ashtray she returned to its place next to the Magic Fingers box. There she found a quarter, left by Craig or by someone before him. Behind it, another coin. She pocketed the coins, then looked for others. Stooping down to check the floor, she saw what looked to be a roll of paper and thought Craig had dropped a joint behind the mattress. Then she realized it wasn't a joint. It was money: a wad of bills wedged between the wall and the table. The bills were rolled loosely, held together by a fraying rubber band. Fifties. Where the lamplight hit was the west front of the Capitol and *The United States of America* in a little ribbon of letters above.

She almost called out to Craig. Her mouth dropped open, and she began to say his name but stopped herself. He was already at the car. He would not hear her.

It was difficult to say how much was there, but she knew a feeling she'd never held so much money in her hands before. It had a particular texture, a weight to it that was different from plain paper. There was dust on the side that had faced up, and a dryness to the outside fifty that told her the roll of bills had been there a long time. The rubber band had lost its spring and when she slid it off, it left gummy marks. She was alone now, the door still open so she could see the cement path outside and the glow of the big sign against the pavement. Anyone might see her but nobody was watching, and so she counted out the money.

A thousand dollars. She had never seen so much money. Wherever it came from originally, there was something wrong that it was here in the room now, and she did not think it belonged in her hand.

She decided she'd better leave it. She thought it was probably drug money and that the owners would come back at any second. She imagined the drug dealers there in the room with a gun trained on her temple. They'd say, "Lay it down," then shoot her. As quickly as that, she saw the image in her mind—the blood oozing from her temple, her body crumpled and pale, suddenly naked again on the patterned orange carpet under the dense yellow light.

And she thought, too, that money like this was always tainted, and if she were to take it, she would be tracked down, and that wherever she ran, she would be unearthed. She had learned—no, she'd not learned this but felt it inside her—that objects held power, if not in themselves then from the people who understood their meaning. This money was bad, and by taking it she was moving toward something mildly criminal. Craig gave her the same feeling. With the secrets and the drugs and the sex.

The bills had a crisper side where the light had heated one side of the roll; she could smell the special ink used at mints, a smell like nothing else. She thought money was a unique element that should be on the periodic table. N for nitrogen, M for money. She would put the money back, she decided, put it all back. But she didn't. She sat on the floor and looked up at the nightstand on which the bills now lay. Nobody had seen her enter, and if she were careful nobody would see her leave. The money was hers without consequence. It only required her to fold it into her pocket, just as she would a pack of chewing gum.

She heard the blare of the car horn now, her name being called. He would not call her Bobbie because it was a boy's name, but always Barbara, which she hated. She pressed the bills out one at a time, flattening each upon the table. Then she rolled them into two small logs. She put one log of five hundred dollars in her right front pocket, the other in her left. She checked the night table for more money, opening the drawer and searching the corners, but there was none. Strangely, she felt relieved there was no more money, no further bills she would have to hide on her person and guard. There was, however, a Gideon Bible, and a notepad and pencil, and the way they were arranged felt to her like a sign, a suggestion from outside herself. There was something more she had to do.

She took the Bible out of the drawer, noticing its gold writing and hard cover and all the crowded words inside. Then she removed one of the rolls of bills from her pocket, placing it on top of the Bible's cover. She peeled a leaf from the writing pad. She did not know to whom she was writing, some future girl in the same position in which she found herself, perhaps. She wrote, "If you need this, please take it." She put the Bible back in the drawer beside five hundred dollars of the money, a solid half of what she'd found. When she left, shutting the door quietly behind her and following the path out to the parking lot, she felt differently about the money, as though giving half of it back had removed from the remainder whatever bad spell it had once possessed.

She walked to where the beams of Craig's headlights glared into the night. She tried to look natural, like nothing unusual was happening, but it felt as though anyone could see the money straight through her thin jeans. Nobody was watching, but she imagined being seen walking out with the money. She imagined being looked at from some high, lit window. Even the night, with its warm breeze and the heat from the day still rising from the parking lot around her, felt newly alive with the threat of being discovered. She was sensitive to sounds, the buzz of the giant sign with its cold light, the whoosh of car tires overhead. On a raised section of highway above, the traffic shook the air.

"What took you so long?" Craig said. He was sitting behind the wheel, the door open, window down. The inside light shined darkly onto his face. She could see his annoyance at her, at having to wait. Gnats pulled closer to the bulb and he waved them away like smoke.

"Sorry," she said.

"You leave the key someplace?"

"On the table in front of the mirror."

"You make it all tidy and clean like you're the maid?"

She told him she was just being polite.

"That's not polite, that's stupid," he said. He was a ram, angling his horns toward her. She knew to retreat, but a contrariness planted itself inside her.

"Why are you so nasty to me?" she said.

Sometimes, just lately, she could challenge him. Talk back. But he didn't like it. He gave her a warning look. Then he said, "Stating facts isn't nasty."

"We just had sex—can't you be nice?"

"Don't call it sex. That's trashy. We made love."

HE HAD HIS own logic about when she was old enough, and she remembered how he used to stretch the elastic from her panties, peering beneath, assessing how much pubic hair she had, before declaring whether it was all right yet. The month she turned fourteen he said, yes, he believed she was old enough now. Had she not been "developed" enough they would have waited longer. And though he'd become impatient, he told her it proved he cared. She was educated into his code of ethics, shaped by his thoughts and by his steady assessment. She'd let him look.

He would pick her up from school, parking a few blocks away from the snarl of buses and the crowd of newly teenaged kids moving along the sidewalks with their notebooks and pencil cases and long swinging hair, slouching beneath the hot Maryland sun. He'd watch the procession of girls in their tank tops, their denim cutoffs. The car, an old Buick with a long bench seat in front, was hot. No air-conditioning. He'd leave the windows down and stretch out, his back against one door, his legs sprawled across the seat, and push open the passenger door with his foot when he saw her.

A year later, nothing had changed. He was still there. Not every day. Maybe once or twice a week. She'd look up through blurry sheets of hot air rising from the ground and see the Buick. She'd see him lazing in his car, the radio on, and she would stop suddenly as though she'd run out of sidewalk.

One afternoon, she saw him before he saw her. He had his head tilted at an angle and was facing away. She hoped if she kept walking, it would be possible to fade into the crowd, to hide and stay hidden. She had a load of books, her gym bag on a string, her new handbag with a separate compartment for her makeup, her pencil case, her little tube of strawberry-scented lip gloss. She scurried forward, trying to stay with the largest group. The sun was hot and she could feel her scalp going red with the beginnings of a sunburn. She allowed herself a glance back and saw him again, baking in his car like a toad in a can, unavoidable. A big wall that separated her from everything around her in one awful instant.

He wore teardrop shades, a T-shirt with the logo of the radio station where he worked across the front, baggy jeans over his heavy gut. He looked old, surrounded as he was now by the junior-high crowd. People would think he was her older brother. People would think she was related to him. People wouldn't think he was her boyfriend, never that. In the surround of junior high, in the drench of afternoon sun, it was unconscionable.

The new handbag as well as the blouse she wore were presents from her mother. She didn't want him messing them up. She had a lot of homework and he didn't understand about homework. He didn't understand about school at all. There was a lab write-up due for science and she would get detention if it was late and it *would* be late if she got in his car.

She told herself he wasn't her boyfriend. He wasn't anyone she loved. She didn't have to do what he said; she could keep on walking.

She moved along with a group of girls. Swept up in the gentle arc of students, she glided away from the car. She thought maybe he hadn't seen her, not yet. It was a risk. He mustn't know she was running from him. She hoped the group she hid within did not thin, or turn toward the car, or somehow evaporate all at once so that she was left exposed. She kept a steady gait, gradually distancing herself from where Craig waited. She ducked her head low into her books, shoulder to shoulder with the others. Part of the group splintered, lining up next to a big yellow bus. His car was behind her now, and she was blocked by the crowd. He might be distracted by the heat, by the blinding sun. He'd not seen her in the first place—surely he would not spot her now. In a swift few steps she was suddenly through the bus's closing accordion doors, and the driver prepared to pull out from the curb.

She didn't know where the bus was heading—it wasn't the bus that she normally took—but there would be no hope of getting that one. He'd be watching that one. She took a seat in back, staring down, away from the windows. If he hadn't seen her yet, she was safe. She counted backward from twenty, waiting for the bus to move onto the road, and when it did she let her breath go, then began counting again.

The bus heaved to the stop sign, took a left, everything happening slowly and with a lot of engine noise and a lot of noise from all the kids in the seats in front of her. They headed down a narrow lane that wound through a housing development, little terraced houses all crushed together behind identical rectangles of grass. She listened to the rumble of the bus, felt it glide and roll. It had come along at just the right moment; it was a magic carpet, carrying her away. She gazed out the window at the tidy circles of houses, some with bikes in the yards, some with clay pots of flowers, and thought about him, back at the school, growing more agitated in his car.

By now, the crowds of kids would have thinned to nearly nothing. He'd be sitting up, straining his neck to find her in the rearview mirror, coming up the sidewalk late. She was often late and he'd be annoyed, thinking how she was haphazard and disorganized. Eventually, he would conclude she hadn't been in school that day and he'd stew about how he was always telling her that if she wasn't going to be in school on a particular day, she should let him know and save him the drive over and sitting in the hot sun.

Once he figured out she wasn't coming, he'd begin driving to the house where he knew he was sure to find her. He'd prepare a lecture about how she should be more considerate, maybe get so pissed off he had to pull over to the side of the road and stick his bong between his knees. He'd light whatever seeds were still there, or push the flame of his Bic down on some little leftover hash pebble, take a hit to calm down. It's what she drove him to.

Out where she lived were tall, unkempt trees, the dead ones leaning on the ones still growing, and he'd stop there, searching for her mom's car or any sign of life from inside the house. If he saw the car, he'd leave, his tires crunching slowly over the gravel until he got to the main road. She'd hear from him that night or the next day by phone, worried about her. Worried angry.

It was bad enough that way, but worse if her mom's car *wasn't* there and he came looking for her, banging on the doors and windows of their split-level. He'd search for her in her bedroom closet, or the green bath of their olive-colored suite, or even under the laundry. She had hidden in all those places before, but when he found her, she would pretend she hadn't been hiding. It was the only way to keep things steady. She couldn't bear for him to be angry with her, to be disappointed. Now she was on a bus and didn't even know where it was going, or how she was going to get home, or if.

She thought maybe she could call him that night when he was on the air, when she knew he couldn't come find her right away, and say, "You can't get me at school anymore. My mom knows." She could say that her mother threatened to call the police, that she was forbidden to see him, that she was grounded. She was sorry, she'd explain, but it wasn't her fault. She was too young, nothing she could do.

The thought of her mother really finding out was too much for her. It scared her more than anything. He knew that. And because he always seemed to know when she was lying, there was little point in trying to convince him that she'd told her mother. He'd only call the house and speak to June, gauging her response. Of course, her mother would be as warm as ever to him, and then he'd know Bobbie was lying. The big problem—one of the big problems—was how much her mother liked Craig. June thought he was a kind of older brother for Bobbie, the sibling she'd never had. For this reason, and perhaps others Bobbie could not yet imagine, June would get into a conversation with him. She'd tell him exactly where Bobbie was, then hang up and feed the plants none the wiser while Craig set out on his hunt.

On the bus, she worried about what he would do if he found out she'd avoided him. It was already hot, another scorcher marking the unusual weather they would endure all summer, but it wasn't the heat that caused her to writhe and sweat and crane her neck to get more air. It was what would happen if he found out she'd run away from him. The thought was too awful, and just as she was feeling at her worst about it, even a little sick, she looked out the window and saw—she couldn't believe it—his dark gold Buick. He was following the bus, drawing up alongside it, then tucking in behind, trying to get her attention. If he was here now, he'd been here all along. He looked up through the top of his window and caught her staring down at him. He saw her, saw her right now. She could make out his words as he yelled through the windshield. She imagined how loud he was, his voice bellowing so that anyone hearing the car pass would think he was on his way to kill someone. On his way.

Sweat beaded her upper lip. She could feel her shirt growing damper. She could feel her pulse on her tongue. His face was washed in anger, his hair wet with sweat. She lip-read the swear words, feeling a rush of fear. Her throat suddenly hurt like she'd swallowed cardboard. She was trapped. She looked at the rows of covered bench seats on the bus, green nylon stretched and fraying at the corners, the aisle between them covered in a rubber mat with thinning tread. The bus windows with their latches at the top, the big square window in the rear that opened out for emergencies. She didn't know how to escape; he had her in a moving cage.

She got off with the last passengers. The road blazed with sun; she could feel the heat of the tarmac through her sandals and see the bubbles of tar erupting like tiny volcanoes across a scar in the road from last winter's pothole. He had parked behind the bus, his car angled up on the curb. He was waiting there, sure that she'd come back to him, and she did. All the way over, slinking to his car, watching that dark, steaming road cooking in the heat, she walked. She heard the school bus rumble down the road away from her. There was no one else now, just her and Craig. She pushed her feet forward, trying not to look up to where she knew she'd see him behind the windshield, glaring at her. The engine, now off, tapped out a *tickticktick* as it settled. He didn't move from the car. He was waiting for her. The door swung open. He was going to do something bad. She stopped outside the car and then felt his hand yank her wrist, pulling her inside. She dropped like a piece of fruit from a tree, falling limply into the seat beside him. There was a flash of glare from the sun, and a rise in temperature as she hit the car seat, but all she noticed was his hold, like a big claw at the base of her skull, and his words, spoken from deep in his throat. "I'm going to slap your face," he said.

All this happened last year, but she had relived the moment many times since. How she'd squeezed her eyes shut, preparing herself. How she'd thought about the machinery of the body and what can break. She had crouched beside him, readying herself for the blow, hearing a noise inside her throat and feeling the pain of his grip on the roots of her hair. It had felt as though he could at any moment push his fingers right through her bones, crushing her.

But then something else, too, something that punctured the deep awful moment before he struck her. It was a bell sound, a little jingle bell, and it was such a promising joyful sound, almost as though from another day or time, another life even. She'd opened her eyes. The bell sound was coming from outside but she couldn't turn her head to see that far; he still had her head clasped in the vise of his hand. He was ready to hit her. That hadn't changed. She looked at his face, his heavy features, full of color and pulsing with anger. He had his arm back, his grip tight; he was going to let go a swing. Staring into his readied, open hand, she felt fear in the form of acid heading north from her center. She sniffed, her nose running. Her neck felt small in his hands. She could not move away from the pressure on her head, or stop her wild staring at his open hand; she was pinned between two sides of him. She didn't think she could talk, but she did. She tried. The jingle bell was sounding and she heard it closer and closer. "There are people coming," she whispered. "I can hear them."

Two little terriers at the end of their leashes, their collar bells tinkling, guided by an elderly couple, one of whom had a walking stick. They took a long time waiting for one of the dogs to finish sniffing the ground beside the car, then to round his back and defecate. They were in no hurry, this couple, and by the time they'd moved on, Craig had eased up his hold on her, so that it only hurt a little bit.

He pushed her away.

"Goddamn! What was that, a *game?*" he'd hissed. "You better grow up, Barbara!"

She watched the couple and their dogs, now in the distance. The gray heads bobbed, the walking stick tapped, keeping with their steps. The terriers burst forward on their leashes. She wished they would come back. The sound of their shared footsteps, of the dogs' toenails on the sidewalk, the jingle bells, and the way the couple turned toward each other and away, intent on their conversation, was comforting. They seemed to carry with them everything good in life, and she'd wished they would come back or that she could follow.

BACK WHERE SHE STARTED

Thirty years later, and she is not a girl anymore.

She takes a taxi from Union Station, sitting in the hot cab with a ticking meter. Her hair feels sticky; her feet swell in her shoes. The heat envelops her so that it feels like breathing through hot wool. When she asks the taxi driver how long until the air-conditioning kicks in, he shrugs.

"Never is getting likely," he says. "It needs . . . I can't remember what. Whatever they do to AC units to make them work."

"You mean fix them?"

He nods. "Yeah, that."

The fan sounds like a jet engine, blasting warm air through the cab while the driver adjusts dials. He thumps the control with the back of his hand and says, "Looks like we're down to windows and this thing," meaning the battery-operated plastic fan clipped to his sun visor. "That's what it's like here, a D.C. summer."

Bobbie feels her skin sweat, her eyes itch. They cross block after block, the afternoon sun searing her neck and one side of her face. She thinks she has probably made a mistake to come home. Not home—she doesn't think of it as home. To come back. She might have told the driver to turn around and head for the train station, but she thinks it is probably illegal to duck out of a court hearing. Anyway, she's traveled thousands of miles—would it make any sense now to turn back?

The driver suddenly jumps a little in his seat. "Regassing!" he calls out. "That's what it's called! Thing needs regassing. Hey, you want a Coke? I keep a cooler down here." He leans toward the floor in the front passenger side of the cab, knocks the Styrofoam lid of the cooler aside, and brings out a wet can. She thanks him but says she's fine. "You want a cup, is that it? I got no cups," he says.

He is a thickset black man with carefully cut hair and a purple polo shirt, a good-looking guy. He pops the tab on his Coke and drinks diligently. When he finishes, he tosses the empty can into the cooler and says, "First time in D.C.?"

She has to raise her voice to be heard over the sound of traffic through the open windows. She tells him she was born here, that she grew up in Maryland.

"Born here? Huh," he says.

"I left when I was a teenager." All at once she recalls sitting at the wooden table in the kitchen of her childhood home chopping carrots, her math book open in front of her. She remembers the sound of crickets in the air at night, how she'd sweep her hair into a clip on top of her head, her legs with their mosquito bites. She remembers being in her mother's car on these very streets.

"Left to where?"

"California," she says. "Eventually."

"California!" the driver says. He smiles at her through the rear-view mirror. A swizzle stick rests on his lip. A gold ring anchors one eyetooth; the remaining teeth are even and perfect. "What do you do in California?"

"I own some buildings."

"Like a landlord?"

"Commercial buildings."

"That's class," the driver says. "Owning buildings."

She lets out a laugh. They swing around Dupont Circle and she looks at the buses lined up like elephants along the sidewalk, at the fountain with its three statues representing the sea, the stars, and the wind.

He says, "What brings you home, then? Family thing? Wedding?"

She considers telling him it's a family thing involving a criminal case, if only to get him to stop asking questions. But he's a talker, her cabbie. He may expect her to disclose the whole matter, and besides that she feels ashamed of being involved in such a case in the first place.

"Tell me what I should see. I never did any tourist-type stuff when I was a kid here," she says. She has no interest in being a tourist now, either, but her question gets the driver talking about the best time to see Mount Vernon and the Jefferson Memorial, the museums, the Washington Monument. His conversation carries them over the Maryland state line.

"Don't go to the White House—waste of time. Go to the Capitol, they give a tour. You like animals? We got a nice zoo." He tells her there are neighborhoods she needs to be aware of. He has a handle on the place, he explains, he's an observer. They cross the Potomac, hit some traffic, sit baking at a traffic light; all the while he is still talking: "But you aren't gonna get back into the city so easy if you're staying way the heck out there. What's that address again? That's out in the boonies, that is! Why didn't you rent a car?"

"I should have," she says. What she is thinking is how all these distances used to look so huge to her, and they don't anymore. Now it all seems so close. Baltimore used to seem so far from D.C., but in California she'd drive that far for a dinner date.

They head farther into what used to be the country, the meter clicking away. Potomac, Travilah. He hands her a cold Coke and this time she takes it, rolling the cool can across her brow before popping the tab open. They arrive at the guesthouse just as the sunset is blooming, the sky like fire. Behind a fading red-and-white barn, the wind combs a hayfield, making the grass move in waves. The hugeness of the sun dwarfs the hills and fields and everything around them as she stands in the gold light on the pebble driveway watching the shadows move. Handing her a suitcase, the driver says, "So you grew up here. What made you want to leave?"

She laughs, squinting out into the horizon. A breeze brings the swampy scent of frog spawn. "The answer to that question is exactly what I'm going to explain in court tomorrow," she says. She smiles, then gives the driver some money.

"Court! You don't look like the sort of lady that ends up in trouble with the law."

"I'm not in trouble with the law," she says. She thinks to herself, however, that she might be in for some kind of trouble.

THE ROOM IS a tidy square around an antique bed. On the table beside the bed are a pewter lamp and a mahogany stand that holds a handwritten menu for the day. For breakfast she can have "colonial style" eggs that come on a slab of brown bread made from a recipe traced back to the days of Jamestown settlers. For supper she can have peanut soup and shepherd's pie and chilled salad. There is wine and cocktails and various craft beers. It says on the menu that Maryland's state drink is milk. Plain milk, though the inn has a special cocoa they make with this milk. Bobbie finds the innkeeper in the hallway and requests supper in her room.

"The pie?" says the innkeeper brightly. Her name is Mrs. Campbell. She wears an apricot dress and a blousy apron and seems far too well turned out to be doing any actual work. But Bobbie can smell cooking downstairs and the hallway is spotless, with gleaming cherrywood floors and a brass candelabra filled with fat cranberry candles, all with fresh wicks. Every piece of furniture is polished. Even the fronds on the houseplants and the waxy tulips that fill a bowl by the front door are immaculate, shining. She hasn't seen a housekeeper and she wonders if Mrs. Campbell spends all day cleaning, and how she seems to have the only house in all of rural Maryland without a single housefly.

"There's a gazebo out back if you want to have your supper there," Mrs. Campbell says. She has a breathless, nervous way of speaking to Bobbie, the curls on her butter-blond hair rattling with her words. "We can turn on the lights. It's really quite nice—"

But Bobbie prefers to take dinner in her room. From her table by the window, her chair angled to overlook the valley, she sits, eating her dinner quietly. She detects the moon in the darkening sky. She watches the stars slip into focus. Years back, beneath this same sky, she'd lie on grass still warm from the heat of the day and watch the stars with a boy named Dan. Now Dan lives in a house with his own family, probably not far away, and she knows that had she rented a car she would find it impossible not to drive over to him, which is the one thing she must not do. Also, the only thing she wants to do.

SHE IS THE first witness tomorrow at nine in the morning. She has reviewed every aspect of her statement so it is fresh. This afternoon, on the train from New York, she had a long talk with the prosecuting attorney. The details of that conversation still swim in her mind, as does the knowledge she will see the people involved in the case over the next several days. Every single one of them.

Decades ago she told herself she would never come back, never even look back. Now here she is.

She unpacks her pumps, smeared with polish and wrapped in plastic to keep them from staining her clothes. She arranges her dress on one of the padded hangers in the antique wardrobe, a giant walnut structure with an imbedded mirror surrounded by carved leaves, inside of which is a striped Hudson's Bay blanket and a small lacy pillow stuffed with potpourri. She puts a few things into the Queen Anne–style chest of drawers, noticing they are lined with fresh paper and yet more potpourri, tiny bundles of scent sewn into silk sachets and tucked into corners.

Everywhere in the inn are sprigs of dried roses, little bonnets of flowers in vases, framed Civil War prints. The place doesn't seem real. She half expects to turn a corner and find a wax statue of General Washington in a period room roped off by velvet.

But here is something real: a phone book. It takes less than a minute to find Dan's name and the small print that lists his address. She could phone his home number easily enough. There it is, printed on the phone book's fragile paper. She could call him, hear his voice again. But she doesn't. Won't.

SHE HAS THREE different ways to fall asleep. The first, a set of single-shot bottles that tinkle like glass beads when she takes them from her suitcase and sets them out on the dresser. She's been carrying these bottles around for years because once a man seated beside her on a transatlantic flight described a cold remedy in which this particular whiskey was useful. The second method is five-milligram tablets of melatonin that she thinks will be too weak to do much but which she knows cannot hurt her. And, finally, a real sleeping pill she doesn't dare use for fear she'll be groggy in the morning or sleep through her alarm altogether.

She takes a couple of melatonin and then soaks in the tub, reading a book. She needs to remain relaxed in the little room; she needs not to think about tomorrow. The melatonin helps. When finally she peels back the layered bedclothes, slipping between the snug, ironed sheets, she hears the bed groan and imagines the whole room growing drowsy with her. She dims the light to the minimum she can read by. Moonlight edges the blinds; crickets chirp outside on the grass. She is waiting for the night to close altogether, the pages of the book she brought becoming blurry, when a knock on the door wakens her all over again.

It's Mrs. Campbell, the innkeeper. The apron is gone and now she wears a cardigan with a cameo broach by the collar. She can't be more than ten years older than Bobbie but there is something antique about her; she is a woman who attends to details—pressed flowers, starched curtains, plumped-up cushions. But Mrs. Campbell isn't here over some small matter, Bobbie can tell. There is an urgency to her voice when she whispers, "Someone is here to see you."

Bobbie is about to tell her that isn't possible, that nobody knows where she is staying except the DA's office, when from over the woman's shoulder she sees a flash of bright red hair, the glint of a gold earring, and a line of lipstick, the color of which belongs in her mind to only one person.

Bobbie's body senses her mother's presence even before she is aware that it is June who comes charging through the door. She feels herself being unfastened from adulthood and hurtled backward through time. All the decades during which they have not seen each other enter the room with her mother, with June, and it is suddenly as though Bobbie never left home at all, never grew up, or ran her own business, or bought her own house. She is again the girl who was lost, the teenage runaway, the disappeared. This happens in an instant.

June must have prepared something to say. In the car on the drive over, or earlier while checking her reflection in the mirror, even days ago, she might have spelled out in her mind a greeting for the daughter she has not seen for so long. But if this is the case, the words have vanished. June stares up at Bobbie as though it is Bobbie who has suddenly appeared in the room. Meanwhile Bobbie feels herself both here, standing on the rag rug beside the four-poster bed, and at the same time far away, watching.

Her mother is not the mother she remembers, not the image she has carried in her mind for three decades. June is no longer plump, no longer carefully "put together," either. Gone are her crisply ironed clothes, her polished nails and carefully blended, discreet makeup. She wears chunky wrist cuffs, an array of colorful rings, a flowing top that is bright and sweeping, showing a little too much flesh for a woman in her sixties, and a little too much décolletage. It is not only that June has aged—of course she has aged—but that everything about her is different. Her hair is fuzzy and short and redder than Bobbie ever remembers it. Her makeup is more daring, inexact. The look is meant to be carefree—Bobbie can see that much—and while it is not artless, it is shocking to Bobbie, who remembers her mother using safety pins to fasten her blouses so they did not bow loose between the top few buttons and reveal too much cleavage.

"Bobbie," June says, and Bobbie hears the voice of her childhood.

For a moment she wants to sink into her mother's arms, to hold this woman whose love she has cosseted in her memory—stubbornly, secretly—refusing to recognize its enduring quality, even to herself. "I don't believe it," June says, "you're finally here."

"Mom," Bobbie says. The word is so unfamiliar to her it sounds wrong from her mouth.

She is aware of a pressure in her head that comes from too much emotion, of her mother's small hand clasping her own, squeezing, then letting go. Also, of Mrs. Campbell, standing in the doorframe.

June says, "It's fine, Mary, thank you," then smiles at Mrs. Campbell, who slips through the door and disappears, her footsteps making clacking noises in the hallway.

Clearly, the two know each other. Bobbie wonders if this was why the innkeeper had seemed so nervous earlier, because she knows exactly why Bobbie is in town. She knows about the trial and that Bobbie is the other "girl" who has raised a charge against Craig Kirtz, a local celebrity whom she is testifying against. The public has mixed feelings about people like her. She has heard that a radio station conducted a phone-in on the subject, the public calling in to state how they felt about bringing charges against someone for a crime committed so many years ago and for which, as one listener correctly remarked, "there was no body." She's been called an opportunist. She's been called a "middle-aged woman with a vendetta." She has been accused of waging war against her family, especially her stepfather. For that is what Craig is now—her stepfather.

"I'll just close the door," June says, and now it is only the two of them, standing together in the small room. "Oh Bobbie—"

Bobbie can see that her mother's eyes are filling, that June is as overcome as she is. During the decades she has been away, Bobbie has wondered what it would be like to meet her mother once again. She never imagined it would be quite like this, that she would feel the connection so urgently, or that there would be so great a sorrow for all the lost time.

"You look good," she tells her mother. She thinks she ought to say this, ought to say something anyway.

"They tell me you are testifying against our Craig. I can't understand this," June says.

All at once, Bobbie feels a combination of tenderness and rage— that her mother could command such love from her, that her mother could sully that love by talking about Craig. Talking about Craig *now*. Over the years she has convinced herself that her mother had made a mistake. That was all, a simple mistake that had cost more than it ought to have. But if June's effort to track her down before the trial is about him, then it is a mistake she is still making.

"Don't say his name," she tells June.

"Don't say his *name?*" June is astonished.

Bobbie looks at her mother's left hand and sees a gold band. The sight of the ring infuriates her, as though Craig has branded her mother with an iron. "It's not my fault you married him," she says.

"What kind of thing is that to say? *It's not my fault . . .* You were invited, you know! Not that we expected you'd show up. If we'd known where you were, we'd have sent an invitation!"

"I wouldn't have come."

"Can you imagine what it was like for me, living in that house without you? Getting married without you? I told Craig then, I said to him, 'How is it a wedding without my daughter here? She should be here, with us. She should be my maid of honor.'"

Bobbie shakes her head. She thinks of her mother in a white bridal dress beside Craig. In her head is the mother she remembers, round and young with a ruddy brown bob and clear, green eyes that had the luminous quality of stained glass. In front of her this new version of her mother, with her thin over-dyed hair and the tribal jewelry, seems another person.

June says, "And now, just when Craig is recovering from this last pack of lies from that girl, you come along and accuse him? You're saying Craig *molested* you? You let thirty years pass to tell the world this?"

June smells like sour wine, Bobbie now realizes. Her mother has reached a time of day in which all the hours topping up her wineglass are showing a cumulative effect.

"*Molest* isn't one of the words I used," Bobbie says.

"But it amounts to that, doesn't it? Molested you as a child?"

"I guess so. Yes."

"Well, that is impossible! I think you are mixing things up," June says. She steps toward Bobbie. "Is that it, darling? Did something happen to you after you left home? Did someone hurt you and now you think it was Craig? Because I've heard of such cases!"

June smiles at Bobbie. She is on Bobbie's side if only Bobbie will let go of this idea that Craig—Craig, of all people—ever hurt her. She stands with her arms outstretched, inviting Bobbie to come and hug her. But there is something preposterous about the gesture. And an oddness, too, about the way June is smiling. Close up, Bobbie sees that her mother's eyes seem slightly dead, as though that part of her face is not participating. She feels a flash of concern, considering perhaps her mother has suffered a stroke. But then she detects the same unusual aspect to June's forehead, too. She sees the skin there is like smooth putty, and she knows at once it is the copious use of Botox, not a stroke, that has frozen her mother's face. She hasn't lived in California all these years without acquiring a little expertise in that area.

"My God, Mother, you can't wrinkle," she says, and touches her own forehead with her hand.

June scoffs. "Oh please, you get to this age and watch your brow line crumple."

"It doesn't look bad," Bobbie says. "But why?"

"Are you going to start on a 'love your wrinkles' campaign? Because having your daughter bring charges against your husband can cause a wrinkle or two."

Bobbie finds her jeans and pulls them on under her nightgown, doing up the fly. "I don't think you are meant to talk to me before the trial. I'll drive you home."

"Oh, please, sweetheart. I'm sorry if I've said the wrong thing."

"You're only here to convince me not to go through with it."

June says, "Don't be silly, I'm here because you're my daughter! I've barely heard from you for years. Don't you think that was unnecessary? You'd send little gifts but never make an actual appearance. Don't you think that was a little cruel?"

She might have said yes. It was cruel. Bobbie has sent birthday cards and Christmas cakes. For many years on Mother's Day she has arranged for bouquets of yellow roses to be delivered to the door. All of this, she understands, she did as much for herself as for her mother, little gestures that stemmed a tide of guilt that forever threatened to engulf her for making her mother worry, for being absent as June aged. For there is a part of her that still wants to protect her mother.

"You have no idea the kind of pain—" June is saying.

Bobbie hates making her upset. But she also doubts the woman is being honest. June's distress may only be a ploy, Bobbie thinks, and so she tries not to feel pity. Instead, she focuses on her mother's lash extensions. She hopes her mother's beauty efforts aren't all to please Craig.

"It's not legal for you to talk to me right now," Bobbie says. "It's called tampering with a witness—"

"*Legal*," June says, as though the word is a nonsense word made up by a child. "All I am asking you, sweetheart, is to *please* not do this."

"Don't tamper, Mother. Just go home."

"I will, as soon as you say you won't go through with this ridiculous trial. He's already been through one ordeal and now you want to put him through another?"

The other ordeal was in the form of a fifteen-year-old girl whose parents discovered Craig was having sex with their daughter. And even though he almost certainly had been doing just that, they'd lost the case. Bobbie takes a long breath, her eyes fastened on her mother's face. "I hope you are saying this because you think he's innocent," she says.

"Of course he's innocent!"

Bobbie shakes her head. "Do you think I made up everything I said in my statement?"

June looks at her, assessing Bobbie's tone. "I think you are confused," she says finally. "And I know you've never cared for Craig. He knows it, too, and it hurts him. But that is for another discussion. We can sort all this out as a *family.*"

"He's not my family."

"You never gave him a chance—"

"A *chance?*" Bobbie scoffs. "Has it not occurred to you that what I am telling the jury tomorrow is actually true?"

"We can discuss all of that. Of course, we can. Meanwhile, you are behaving like this crazy girl did, hurling accusations at Craig. What we need to do is come together as a family and protect one another!"

Bobbie listens as her mother describes the girl, who had been seeing a psychiatrist and who self-harmed and had no friends, who was a truant and a loiterer and a shoplifter. "You have no idea what kind of family she was from! You don't want to be linked in any way with such people," June says, shaking her head to emphasize the point. "People go after Craig because he's famous, you know. A public figure."

"He's a disc jockey, so what?"

"That is quite an achievement, don't you think? A radio announcer? A *personality?*"

"Oh Jesus," Bobbie says. The conversation is ridiculous, and so at odds with the pretty, scented room in which they find themselves. She turns to her mother now, eyeing her squarely. "I gave that statement months ago," she says. "It's already done."

"But it isn't too late to undo! The lawyer told me you could still withdraw it. Please, Bobbie, I'm begging you. I promised him I'd speak to you—"

"Did he drive you here?" Bobbie asks. "Where is he parked?" She thinks he must be outside somewhere, stewing in his car. She could imagine him there, slumped over the wheel, his temper ticking like a bomb.

June gives up and sits hard on the bed. She bends her head into her hands. She might be crying, Bobbie can't tell. She might be faking.

"If you saw this girl!" she pleads. "If you saw the parents! The mother was covered in tattoos! I am sure they put that girl up to this crazy accusation. She looks twenty-one, not fifteen. In fact, she's not fifteen anyway; she's sixteen. But she *looks* like an adult. And this thing she claims with Craig is outrageous!"

"You think so," Bobbie says flatly.

"Who told you about that case anyway? I can't believe you read *our* local papers from wherever it is you live now."

"California. And no, I don't."

"Then who told you?"

She'd heard about it from Dan. Her mother would not even remember who Dan was; he was another bit of history about which her mother appeared to recall nothing.

"You are about to make a terrible mistake!" June says. "And what if he is found guilty? Can you imagine? What if he goes to—" She stops, unable to say the word *jail*. "I'm your mother. You can't just—" Bobbie sees how bewildered her mother is, how she cannot understand why her daughter had unfastened herself from her life, had escaped and was still escaping from her. "If you'd had children of your own you would understand the pain you've caused me," she says. "I always thought that once you had your own children, you'd come back. You'd return and say you were sorry and we'd be able—"

"Oh stop it."

"But you never had children, did you? I'd know if you had. There'd be a softness—"

"You're working yourself into a state—"

"—but instead just this shelly, brittle woman with exactly the shape a woman keeps when there are no children—"

"You're doing nobody any good. Mother, really. I'll drive you."

June clenches her lips. "Fine, I'll go. But let me ask this question: Why must you take away Craig, too? You *want* him to go to jail, don't you? You want to destroy me. You *still* want to destroy me.

You've come back only because you saw an opportunity to ruin the one thing—"

Bobbie goes to the window again. This time she raises the blind and peers out to where she suspects Craig lurks, waiting for June to convince her to leave him alone in court tomorrow. She wants to shout to him that she is going to stick this out. She is not going to sit on the sidelines. She won't lie, either. Here is what she thinks as she looks out the picture window, peering into the inky sky, studded with stars reflecting blue-black grass still waving in the night breeze: She thinks testifying against him is the least she can do. That it would have been better to kill him than to let him get this far.

Meanwhile, she can still hear her mother's voice, a mixture of whining and accusation. "Why did you wait until *now*?" she says. "If he'd done something so wrong you could easily have spoken up *years* ago!"

"That's a good question," Bobbie says. When they ask her in court why she never brought a charge against Craig, why she kept quiet all these years, she might tell them that she never expected him to live this long. She might tell them that she believed—idiotically, she now understands—that she was the only girl he'd done this to. In the decades since she's last been here, she has rarely thought of him out in the world, alive. Hers is a life with deep shadows everywhere and it was easy to keep his memory in those shadows.

"Please, Bobbie, tell them you won't testify."

Bobbie sighs. "If you read my statement, then you'd certainly know why I cannot just drop it."

June shakes her head. "I haven't read the statement," she admits. Now she begins crying in earnest. "I never read the statement because it was from you, your words, and I couldn't listen to that after all these years of silence."

Bobbie feels the fight flow out of her. She wonders again if she made the right decision to come back, to get involved once again in such a mess. She would never tell June, but the reason she flew to New York first instead of flying directly into Washington was that she had wanted to have a last-minute chance to pull out of the case.

She could always stay in New York, she'd convinced herself, and blow the whole thing off. That was how close she was to abandoning the idea. But in the end, it was too much to resist. She'd ridden Amtrak out of Penn Station. She'd arrived at Union Station and found the taxi. She is aware of the enormous effect her mother has on her even now, even after years of being without her. The desire to please her, the same desire as she'd had as a child, is remarkably strong.

She is brought out of these thoughts by a metallic snapping sound and turns to see her mother has found the mini whiskey bottles and is fixing herself a drink. All the years she's carried those little bottles around just in case of insomnia and her mother dispatches one as quickly as though it is water.

"Is he really *not* out there?" Bobbie says, hooking her thumb over her shoulder.

"He who? You mean Craig?" June shakes her head. On the bedside table is a decorated tissue holder and June plucks out a few pastel tissues, then blows her nose. The little whiskey bottle is empty now. June holds up a second. "These are puny," she says.

"I'm driving you home," Bobbie says.

"No need. I'm fine. I can drive."

"No. No, you can't."

June waves a tissue at Bobbie. "I've been driving myself around for the past thirty years without you. Now you show up, telling me what to do, show up looking . . . looking like . . . you show up looking like—"

"Like *what?*"

Her mother appears stricken. The evening has gone dead wrong and all her disappointment mixes with the alcohol and with the shock of being with her daughter now for the first time in so long. "Grown up!" June sobs. "I mean I knew you would be grown up but I missed out on everything." Now she makes a sweeping gesture toward Bobbie, as though Bobbie were a large, loathsome creature taking up room where her little girl should be. "Do you realize what this sort of thing does to a person? *Do you?*"

Bobbie says, "I imagine it is painful."

"Damned right it's painful!"

Bobbie pats the air with her open palm. "Don't yell, Mother. We're not the only people in this place."

"What do you care who hears? You're willing to go to court and tell the world anything that comes into your head! You're telling a courthouse about family matters that we should be working out ourselves!"

No, Bobbie thinks. I am not talking about family matters. And no, I am not trying to work out anything at all.

ALL THE WAY back to the house, June complains about the stress of the trial. She says it has made her ill, that she does not sleep well, that her eyes do not focus as they ought to, that her heart races and sometimes she thinks she is about to have a heart attack. It's been too much, she tells Bobbie. The trial with the girl who lost, thank God, and this new one. Her life has become a giant weight she can no longer carry. "One dead husband, a runaway child, now this!"

The Chevy Impala has a dented front bumper and headlights at skewed angles. Bobbie drives steadily toward the neighborhood that was once her own, through streets that were once familiar to her. She notices the new houses that have sprung up, developments in places where there were woods, quaint little shops where there had been feed stores and gas stations. Her mother falls quiet as they approach her street and is no longer crying by the time they reach the house. Now it is Bobbie who feels emotional. She cannot bring herself to take the car all the way up the drive, to sit in her old driveway next to her childhood home. It is too much even to see through the tall conifer trees the lights in the rooms that once felt part of her. The trees have grown higher, the bushes gone wild. Buttercups have nearly taken over the lawn Bobbie used to mow.

"You're going to have to walk from here," she tells her mother.

"Come inside and talk to Craig," June pleads.

"Not on your life."

"Why don't you stay here with us? No need to go back to that old guesthouse tonight. Be *our* guest—" She stops herself. "Hell, this is your *home*."

"That's his car up there, isn't it?" She follows the Chevy's head-lights up the long dirt drive where they reflect against the plastic casing of brake lights on a low red sports car. She can see the vanity plate with Craig's initials. She can see the fat racing tires.

June sighs, then touches her forehead, feeling for a headache. "He says you hate him because he wanted some money back. Money you stole from him. I know you don't steal, so there must have been a misunderstanding. We just need to talk this out."

"No misunderstanding. There was money."

"You *stole* money?"

"Yes."

"Are you going to *say* that? In court? Oh Bobbie! You're going to *tell* them you're a thief?"

"I don't know what I'm going to tell them," Bobbie says, though this isn't the case. She knows exactly what she will tell them.

"So it is true, what he said about the money?" June says.

"I suspect not, but it doesn't matter."

"Craig says everything matters. Oh, I do wish you'd talk to him."

But she won't talk to him. June tries everything to get her into the house. She tells her that Craig will be angry if she returns with-out her, that she cannot walk and needs assistance. She tells her there is no need to bring family business into a public arena, tries to shame her into cooperating. But Bobbie isn't having it. In the end, Bobbie gets out of the car and goes around to the passenger side. It is a clear, pretty night with stars that seem to hang low in the sky. She opens her mother's door, then pulls June gently by the arm until she is standing in the night's soft glow, surrounded by the sound of crickets and the frogs that chirp (Bobbie knows) from the marshy grass behind her mother's house.

"Are you just going to leave me here?" June says, as though she is being stranded on a desert island. "And take my car?"

"I'll bring it back later."

"But darling—" Her mother doesn't move. Bobbie gets back behind the steering wheel as her mother stares in shock.

"Go to bed, Mother," Bobbie says through the open window. "Nothing is changing my mind."

"But why not? Why on earth?" June says.

She shoves the Chevy into reverse just as her mother comes toward her again with another plea. "Because," she tells June, "the man nearly killed me."

Then she reverses, driving away even as June stands, baffled by what is happening. Bobbie doesn't look at the house she has not seen since 1978, does not allow herself to think about Craig inside. She pauses a little at the very edge of the property, glancing at a specific tree that had once meant something to her. For months before she ran away from home, it hid a jam jar full of money.

CRASH

Coming out of the motel and getting into Craig's car with the money plunged deep in her pocket felt like climbing into a bull's pen. Bobbie sensed that as with a bull she must keep watch but not look at him directly. The car smelled like old bong water and burger wrappers and pot resin. His clothes, the ones he had on and every stitch he owned, carried that same green-weed smell. They drove out of the motel parking lot and she thought what she needed now, other than the newly found money folded against her thigh, was a little luck.

He said, "What were you really doing in there anyway? Smoking cigarettes, I bet."

She didn't answer and he gave her a look.

"I don't have any," she said. "I told you."

"They make you taste like an ashtray."

"I was fixing my hair."

"That was a hell of a long time for hair."

She smiled and hoped that smiling would end the discussion. He reached over and put his hand on her knee. She looked down at the cotton pocket of her blue jeans and hoped he wouldn't feel around in that area. Keeping the money from him felt like a greater betrayal than hiding from him on the school bus had been. She wondered what he would do to her if he found out about the money, other than take it off her, that is.

"What's the matter?" he said. "Are you sick?"

Not sick, she thought, but not exactly right, either. The night was inky, with a moist heat that liquefied the air. Her hair was wet at the nape, her blouse damp under her arms. No matter how many times she ran her tongue over her lips, they were dry, while the rest of her was sweating, not just from the heat. If he found the money, she would need an explanation for why she hadn't mentioned it. But she couldn't think of anything. Her brain raced like the images on a slot machine, but when she summoned it to slow down and give some answers, nothing came up. Nothing she could win with.

"I'm fine," she said. "It's that test tomorrow making me worry."

Even now, while he was driving, he moved his wide hand on her thigh, reaching higher, almost to where the money was. She held her breath and waited, waited for him to wrap his fingers around the wad of bills and then ask what in the hell was *that* in her pocket. Her head began to wag back and forth, as though saying *no, no, no* to a conversation that ran inside her mind. She better tell him, tell him now before he discovered for himself. She opened her mouth to speak but suddenly did not know what to say.

She took a long breath. She willed her heart to slow, but it would not. Meanwhile, his hand moved down to her knee and then up again, climbing her leg one finger at a time as she stiffened under his touch. She waited, and hoped, and tried not to seem as though she was hiding something. She prepared an explanation, then gave up, deciding there was no explanation. He would tell her she was selfish. He would say she was a thief. She was about to confess the whole thing when he rolled his palm away, this time toward the inside seam of her jeans, just beneath her crotch. He could not feel the money there, or where he went next, so she said nothing.

They drove a rural route, passing a farm on their right, an abandoned gas station attached to a miniature golf course, now closed

down. She wondered if there were anywhere left in the world that
didn't look like this, haggard and worn, in need of repair. For years,
the recession had caused her mother to worry she would lose her job.
When the cupboard door broke, her mother had tacked it back up
with the wrong hardware. When the dishwasher leaked, they began
using the sink to wash dishes. Now, she had five hundred dollars,
money out of the blue. If only she could get home without Craig
finding out.

He kept touching her, then looked over.

"What's the matter?" he said.

"Nothing."

She felt like a bug next to him, even more so in her thin shirt
and wooden Dr. Scholl's sandals, blocky slabs without any heel, cast-
offs from her mother who said they made her toes ache. She tucked
up, trying to hide the outline of the bills through the fraying cloth
of her jeans, and rested her head on her knee, her face turned toward
him. She hoped her expression portrayed fondness, not fear.

"You know they're still hassling me at work," he said. "That
asshole girl." He was referring to a girl who had come into the station asking after Craig and telling everyone that she knew him.
The girl was a high-school student with acne and frizzy hair. The
program director had told her to stay away from the station, but
she'd kept insisting that Craig was expecting her. "*I know Craig.
We're friends*," Craig said now, imitating the girl's light, high voice.
"Friends, bullshit. But that big shit-eating pig of a program director
makes a huge deal of it!"

He had one hand spanning the wide circle of the steering wheel,
and with the other he found her knee. He articulated his story with
little prods from his fingers. Big-*poke*-shit-*poke*-eating-*poke*-pig. He
pointed the Buick down the smaller road that led to her neighborhood, rolling the steering wheel with his thumb, all the while playing his other hand up and down her leg.

"And I don't know this girl!" he said, all innocence. "Anyway,
she's already sixteen!"

Sixteen was legal, Bobbie knew. Just as she knew she was illegal.

"And anyway, I wouldn't cheat on you," he said, then suddenly drew his attention to the radio. A song ended and he lurched forward and flicked the dial, turning it up so the sound boomed through the car. "Hang on, here comes a break!"

He was obsessed with breaks, with all performance from disc jockeys. He listened only to the station he worked for, never changing it even if he hated the song. And when he liked a song, he'd crank up the volume so high she could feel the base thumping her chest. He'd make a fist and tap the air like he was playing the drums, his expression concentrated inward, his drumming hand fastened to the rhythm, eyes half closed in concentration. She'd watch him, feeling the music pressing into her, and she'd think, *This is embarrassing.*

But the songs didn't mean much to him. They were filler; what he cared about, cared greatly as though every deep-voiced radio jock on the East Coast was in a contest with him, were the times in between songs when the DJ came in with that all-important break. That is when he'd really turn up the volume. Right now, a guy he hated who had the spot before his, a guy whose hire he'd opposed, who he'd heard had drinking problems and sleep problems, was talking over the guitar intro of a current hit, and this fact pissed him off. He listened, his face darkening as the voice ran into the song, interfering with the lyrics. Shaking his head, Craig gave Bobbie a look like *Can you believe this shit?* before moving the volume back to a normal range and returning to his conversation.

"I told that pig, I already *have* a girlfriend. And he says, 'How come I never met her?' And then, guess what? He starts asking how *old* you are."

He'd half convinced himself she was of age now, so often had he lied.

"What did you say?"

"Eighteen."

She felt her head buzz. Eighteen. That was ridiculous.

"Actually, I told him you'd be nineteen soon. But it's none of his business. What's he, your goddamned father?"

Her father was dead. Heart attack in his twenties. This made no sense to Bobbie, how someone could have a heart attack at such an age, but she'd seen the death certificate in a box in the closet alongside old wedding photos of her parents. Her mother, pregnant in a big white dress; her father, a young man in a dark suit, a gold ring on his finger.

They turned off the road and suddenly they were nearing her neighborhood, gliding beneath traffic lights suspended on wires, passing a parade of shops, what used to be a restaurant, then a dance club, now a nursing home. In a few more miles he would pull the Buick into a space at the top of her drive. She'd hear the crunch of his tires over the pebbles, see the reassuring light that shone by the front door. He'd stop some way from the house, pull up the parking brake, and turn toward her. Then he'd do something to remind her about the sex. He'd put her hand on his crotch so she could feel the outline of his dick, warm, already swelling, waiting for their next time. Then he would tell her he loved her. "I love you, babe," he'd say, just like Sonny to Cher. If she didn't say it back, he'd look at her with big eyes and keep holding on to her until she did.

Once, she had almost believed that she did love him, because he'd paid her such a lot of attention, and told her how pretty she was, and how mature. *You're different from the other girls*, he'd said. *You're wise for your years.* Those were the early days, back when he was being nice. He would take her to restaurants, pull her chair out for her, tell her to leave room for dessert. He'd sneak her into the station and let her choose records. She'd wear his headphones, talk into the microphone, hear her voice in a recording he'd play back to her. He made her feel special, clever, somehow above the pettiness of junior high in which friendship and popularity hung on such small matters as whether your hair was "good" or you had the right jeans. Then one day, he told her he wanted to marry her. *Marry me?* she'd said, stunned, terrified. He'd nodded confidently, as though that had always been the plan. He'd worked it out that they were like Romeo and Juliet, star-crossed and forbidden because of her age, but for no other reason. No legitimate reason. Plenty of guys were older than their girlfriends, he'd told her. In other countries, men older than himself married girls her age.

Who do you belong to? he would ask her, pinning her on the mattress. She'd tell him what he wanted to hear. *You*, she'd say. The thought scared her because she worried—she really did—that if it came to it, he'd get what he wanted and she would be his. His now and forever. And then all her life would have led up to marrying him. But how do you get out of such a thing? After you've had sex with a guy and told him that you loved him? And she had told him, too, more than once. It was too late to take it all back.

But it wasn't too late, she told herself now. It wasn't. They sailed down the dark street, too far out in the country for streetlamps. He sang along to the radio as they passed the elementary school. His favorite song, "Three Times a Lady," by the Commodores. She hated the Commodores. Syrupy, worse than her mother's Tom Jones. That he could even like this song bothered her. Surely she didn't have to carry on meeting him, driving with him, having sex with him. There was an out—it happened all the time. She just had to try.

She said, "I don't like that song."

He sang another line, as though she just needed to listen a little harder and she'd see how fan*fucking*tastic was this band and its number-one hit. "Number one," he reminded her, holding up a finger. "You can't argue with that!" Then he said, "So I told that prick boss of mine, that I already got a woman and not to take seriously this stupid girl and her ridiculous accusations."

Back to the program director, whatever he'd said about the girl Craig knew, or didn't know.

"I said to him, the idiot, I said, 'Are you listening to crazies off the street? Fans, oh man. They are the true head cases and a good reason to get and stay stoned!' And then you want to know what happened next? You want to hear?"

She breathed in, and he took that as a yes. He said, "I held up some weed and we went into the parking lot and got high."

He laughed out loud. Spit foamed a little at the corners of his lips. He was always complaining about dry mouth, a side effect from all the pot. It was the weed's fault but who could blame weed? He'd drink Dr Pepper or beer, or Nestlé Quik, or rum. Then he'd scream, *I'm drying up! My tongue is numb!* Like he'd never heard of water.

He said, "Reach behind my seat and see if you can find my pipe, wouldja?" His face glowed from a Mobil sign they passed, then from a restaurant's neon lights in the shape of a cactus, then from the red of the traffic light at the end of the long road.

She brought out the pipe, but it didn't feel familiar in her hands. It was a little stainless steel "L" with purple ceramic on the stem, lightweight, compact, but it wasn't his pipe. His was a red and blue one with a longer stem and a Confederate flag. This one, specked in rust, its stem clogged with oil, was so tiny you'd likely singe your lashes smoking it.

"You mean this?" she said, holding it out for him.

He nodded. "I left my good flag pipe in the head at the station and it was taken by that skinny boy-wonder piece of shit they brought in who *talks over the fucking lyrics!*" He yelled this last part straight into the radio. "I hate that little fuck. He always plays my favorite records so I can't repeat them, and now he's taken my goddamned Confederate flag pipe, the cock!"

He threw the matches at her. "Light up the bowl," he said.

She didn't want to. If they smoked in the car, she'd reek of it. "We can pull over, can't we?" she said, then remembered the money and hoped he wouldn't stop.

"No, we *can't* pull over. Jesus, you should get high. That's what is actually *wrong* with you, if ever you were wondering. The government makes shit up. Think about it. If everyone switched to weed, who would pay their fucking tax for alcohol?" He laughed, then tossed over his Bic but she dug in her purse for matches because she wouldn't burn her fingers so easily with them. That was when he saw it, saw the money making a bulge in her pocket.

"What is that?" he said, his voice suddenly slow and deliberate. He had his fingers around the roll of bills and he wasn't letting go.

"What's what?"

He jiggled his fingers, pinching the roll of bills tighter, his voice even. "In your pocket," he said.

She said, "Nothing."

"You better show me."

"It's nothing."

"Nothing is nothing. *That,*" he said, pointing, "looks like a dime bag."

"Is that what you think it is? Drugs?"

"Pot, not *drugs*! All this anti-marijuana from you, Miss Mouth, and meanwhile you've got a dime bag in your jeans!"

"It's not a dime bag!"

"Then what is it?"

"Nothing!"

Sudden commotion, her whole head in a spin. She saw the glass in front of her, then away; her vision bouncing. He stopped the car fast, swerving right as he did so, and she flew forward, her head banging the windshield, then thwacking the seat back. The car came to rest on the side of the road—dust rising, the tires cooling, the engine making its ticking noise—the whole thing settling like a big fish hauled onto shore after a long ocean chase.

He said, "You should have been wearing your seat belt."

There had been no need to stop like that. No other car or giant pothole or blown-out tire. They were off the road now, parked squarely in a bus turnout. The only reason for him jamming to a sudden halt was his temper, that old grizzly that caused him to do this kind of thing, break a bottle, hit a wall, pick a fight with some stranger in a car.

"Why did you do that?" she said.

"Do what? I only stopped the car."

She touched her legs, her face, her arms, smoothing down the goose bumps, the knots of muscles, the galloping pulse. Her nose was running but there was no blood. No blood she could see. She was about to turn on the inside light and look in the visor mirror to make sure, but he scratched up a flame on a matchbook and the fire lit his face so she could see his eyes, and that stopped her dead.

"Give me the pipe," he said. His words, their tone, and the way his eyes focused on her, made it sound like he was accusing her of stealing it.

She didn't know where the pipe was. She started to panic a little, or maybe she was already panicking. Her head felt light; she was floating. This same feeling had visited her some months back when Craig had found her talking to a boy at a public swimming pool, a boy her age. The boy and she stood waist deep in the water, leaning against the wall of the pool. They'd been laughing. She looked up and there was Craig, standing like a lion behind a little chain-link fence. He'd called her over, and just by the sound of her name in his mouth, she'd known she was in trouble. She'd been scared. She climbed out of the pool, not even taking the time to find a towel, and went to where Craig waited. She stood with her bare feet on the hot sharp grass, her face squinting into the sun, her arms together at the elbows, hands cupped on one shoulder, dripping water. He looked down on her as though he had never seen anyone so disgusting. Insects swarmed, mosquitoes, gnats, while he whispered every imaginable threat in a low voice so that others could not hear. She'd felt helpless and stupid; she'd felt she'd done something very wrong. It was the same feeling she had now, like she was in trouble, like all hell was breaking loose and somehow it was her fault. All her fault. Her head hurt. She felt a bubble of tears, but she swallowed them back and held on.

He sighed, cleared his throat, lit another match, holding it in the air. "The pipe," he said.

She willed herself to remain calm. Calm and smart—when was she going to learn that? He was about to say something more. He was about to make his point and she needed to say nothing—nothing at all—even though she wanted to run and kick out and scream. Outside, a willow leaned its tangled branches over the hood of the car and tapped in the breeze. She could climb out and shimmy up its leafy fronds. She could throw the door open and tear down the road. But she couldn't, and she knew it. She felt her blouse wet down the length of her back, and a headache blooming between her eyes, and the pain in her face, right in the middle of her face, was like a target. She thought of all the times she'd found herself saying, *I want to kill myself*, found herself recently saying exactly these words, and she hadn't known why. But this had been why.

"Barbara," he said, drawing out her name. "I want that pipe."

She knelt on the mat of carpet in front of the seat, keeping her eyes on him as she did so. The floor mats were full of grit and twigs and dust. There was no air that wasn't tainted with a bitter dampness, with spilled bong water, stale beer, soured milk, puke. She didn't care. She scrambled on the floor in the dark. It was time to find the pipe, find it now. She groped around on the floor, her hands moving across the carpet like little windup toys, jerky and erratic. She squeezed her hands into fists and then released them again, trying to steady herself.

She worried maybe there was a time limit for finding the pipe, like he had her on a timer and she'd taken too long already. She was in trouble. She felt it deeply, as though she'd already heard a *ding!* But then—thank holy Jesus—her palm moved over a bump in the carpet. It was the bowl, like a little marble of gold, and for the first time in what felt like a long while she let out her breath.

"Don't get angry," she said, bringing the pipe up to him.

"I ask you a question! A simple question, like 'What is in your pocket?', and you give me all this shit, then tell *me* not to get angry!" He was exploding; he was orbital. But there was her friend, the clock on his dashboard, moving toward midnight when he had to be at the radio station, sitting in the big swivel chair in the center of the studio. Midnight to five a.m., he was on the air. He didn't have much time to go crazy. His crazy time was confined as she was confined.

"What do I have to do to get a straight answer out of you, Barbara?"

She rubbed the pipe clean, tried to get him to take it from her, but he acted like he didn't want it now. She pressed it toward him and he pushed it away. Finally she gave up, placing the pipe on the seat between them.

"If I ask you a question, answer the question."

"Okay," she said, patting the air. "No reason to get us killed."

She regretted saying this. Right away, she regretted it. His anger ignited freshly, and she felt his grip as he grabbed the top of her belt, hauling her up like a bucket, then tunneling his hand deep into her pocket for the money before shoving her back onto the seat again. She felt a scrape on her hip from his wristwatch. She felt her pocket empty of its treasure.

Now he turned on the light. She stayed as he had dropped her, curled like a shrimp, her limbs pulled toward her center. She watched his face unfasten its anger, then bloom with surprise, even wonder. For a moment it was like seeing a boy with a magnifying glass examining the complicated wings of a flying insect, enthralled and amazed, as though he could not believe his luck to live on this earth with such a thing as he held in his hand.

"What the hell?" He leafed through the fifties. Taking one, he flipped it over and back again, holding it up to the yellow bulb in the car's roof. "Jesus," he said, inhaling carefully, counting the bills in time with his breath. He turned them over, counted them again. For a long minute, he stared at the money, as though searching for a message in the stout face of Ulysses S. Grant. In a low, serious voice, he said, "Where did you get this?"

She couldn't speak.

"It is a simple question."

She heard her words—silly, girlish—as she tried to explain that she hadn't been looking for anything, certainly not for money, and how the bills were dusty and had clearly been there for a long while. "So I took it. That was the wrong thing to do, but I took it."

"From the motel room? Money was just sitting there in the room?"

"Yes, and I should have told you, okay? But I was worried. I mean, who leaves a thousand dollars in a motel except maybe a drug dealer? I would have told you. But I didn't know what you'd think—"

He didn't register her apology. He was looking at the money, counting all over again. He pinched the wad in his hand, squinted at it as though measuring its thickness. Then he said, "You say a *thousand*." He spoke very slowly, and far more seriously than she had ever before heard. "So where's the other five hundred?"

HE WAS ON the air in just over an hour, but they were heading away from the station. He had to get back to the motel, find the rest of the money, then get out again. The car burned through seventy, eighty, ninety on the straightaways, him screaming at her, asking why in hell's name had she left five hundred dollars behind? He could not be late to his midnight spot. Could *not*! She had fucked everything up, fucked it clean up, and why was he always making up for her incompetence?

She tried to read him, to figure out where the flying ball of his rant would land. She had to appear not too casual but not too wary, either. Whatever else, not scared, because that always made him worse. Slanted on the bench seat of the Buick, shoulder against the window, she stayed as far from him as she could without being accused of sulking, holding on to the seat with one hand, the door with the other. She didn't want him to know she was worried by how fast he was driving so she held on lightly, as though her hands just happened to rest there. Meanwhile she watched the short distance between the car bumper and everything else in front of them. She tried to look up at the moon, a tonic of white stillness in the slate sky, to set all her thoughts there and ignore the speed of the trees and bushes and telephone poles flying past.

Out on the highway, he skirted the traffic. "You better hope we don't meet a cop!" he said. Always her fault, always. He glared hard at her, as though she were the reason for all his ills and every trouble in his otherwise tidy life.

They skimmed the bed of a big semi, so close to its wheels she felt the suck of a vacuum pulling the side of the Buick. The shadow of the truck bed fell over them, the darkness covering her lap. A weight of gravity pushed against her shoulder, and she thought for one clear moment that her life was done now, that she would be taken by the truck as a field mouse is taken by an eagle.

Craig jerked the Buick into the next lane. She breathed out hard as he pressed down the accelerator. She felt her stomach burn as he swerved into a third lane, then skirted up two cars and over once more.

Now the highway dipped downward, with a long tongue of road ahead. The car rolled faster and faster. It was exactly as though they had no brakes because he did not use brakes. His response to everything—bends and bumps in the road, other cars—was *forward, forward*.

"What made you think I didn't need the whole grand?" he said. As though the money—all of it—was already his.

After a moment she said, "I didn't want to draw suspicion."

"*What?*"

Louder this time, so that her voice carried over the road noise, "I said I didn't want to draw suspicion!"

He slapped the steering wheel in exasperation, then punched the accelerator at the belly of the highway's slope, and she swore they went airborne. He said, "Who was *watching you*? How can it be 'suspicious' when there is nobody to *see*?"

With the word *suspicious* he took both hands off the wheel to draw little quotation marks in the air. Air quotes while topping a hundred. He said, "That's just *retarded*! You find money, it's *yours*! That's how it is with money. And other stuff, besides. Not car keys, okay. You can't take someone's fucking keys!" He spoke angrily, as though she'd done just that, taken a whole ring of keys off an innocent bystander. "Only a pussy takes someone's keys!" he shouted.

She tried to think of a way of distracting herself. She started counting in threes: three, six, nine, twelve . . .

"And not clothes, either—that's personal! And not even money once it's in someone's pocket—*that* would be stealing. But loose money is like air. It's for whoever happens along. Do I ask if it is okay to breathe the air near you? Do I say, 'Barbara, mind if I have a little whiff of your air?' Well, *do I?*"

Thirty-six, thirty-nine. She opened her eyes to see the cars beside them becoming dangerously close as he teetered toward the next lane. She heard the sound of a car horn over the music and Craig's bellowing voice.

"Come on! Answer me when I ask you a question, Barbara! Do I or do I *not* ask if it is okay to breathe the air near you?"

She hadn't realized he expected an answer. "No," she muttered. *Forty-two, forty-five . . .*

"No, I fucking well don't and why *should* I? Same with loose money." He glanced at her from across the car, a low, sorrowful look as though he was concerned about her intellect. "You need to understand some things," he said. He checked the road briefly, then whipped his head back to her once again. "Would you agree that you need to understand some things?"

"Yes," she offered. *Fifty-one, fifty-four . . .*

"Quite a few things?"

She nodded.

"Because you don't know anything yet. Tell me one goddamn thing that you think you know."

She had no idea what he was talking about, or why she had to answer, or how. "Fifty-one isn't a prime number," she said. "You'd think it would be. It sounds prime."

He shook his head. "You're completely insane. A total nutbucket," he said.

"It's true. If you had five and one together it's six and therefore divisible by three," she said.

He glared at her. "That's the kind of stupid shit nobody cares about."

"Three times seventeen." She knew he didn't care. That nobody cared. She was talking nonsense. She was scared to death.

"What is wrong with your brain that you are doing math in my car? You need to get your *shit* together, Barbara. You need to pay attention to the University of *Life*."

She told herself if she got out of this car alive she would never get back in. This was the last night of the last day, the very last time she would ever see him. She didn't care what it took to rid herself of him. Let him scream and shout. Let him tell her mother. It made no difference. She was done.

But she nodded in agreement that she needed to get her shit together—oh yes, oh yes, get her shit . . .

"Okay," she said. "I agree." Her admission satisfied Craig, who liked to seem sage and intelligent. He liked to teach her. He'd once explained why blood did not belong to one person but to everyone, and how if he were in charge of stuff, he'd stop blood-supply shortages by requiring hospitals to drain the blood of patients who died, but only a few minutes after they died so that it was still good, the blood. It wasn't rotten or anything. Then there was the guy he worked with who was born without thumbs. Craig had explained that the worst thing about missing thumbs was how it made it so the guy couldn't work a bong. And this was a shame because bongs gave you a better, cleaner, and more complete high. He was sure of this. He believed that one day science would find ways of measuring such things.

He veered onto an exit ramp, the motel sign a great beacon of light, then put the car in neutral as a way of saving fuel, a habit she never liked because traveling the slope of the road at high speed always made the car feel light and out of control. They rounded the curve of the exit, the car swerving and swooping along the contours of the road like an osprey tracking the air above the ocean's swells and surf. They were fast; they were flying. He was smiling now, singing along to a tune on the radio. He didn't care how fast they went; he was hunting. He was about to get his money. It was waiting for him there by the big bright sign.

———

SHE'D LEFT THE key in the room, so they had to get the manager's keys to get inside. She followed Craig through a glass door with a strap of bells attached, then into a little square room lit from above by strips of humming, cold light. He rang a bell on the desk and called out "Hey, anyone here?" loud enough so if you were there you'd come running. That, or hide.

The countertop had neat piles of leaflets, a rubber plant, and a desk calendar with curled corners and a photograph of the motel on it. The night manager, or whoever he was, must have still been around because he'd left half a cup of coffee in a blue enamel mug, and a coffee pot roasting dry on an electric ring above the filing cabinet.

"You ever seen so deserted a place as this?" Craig said, thwacking the bell with his palm. "Hey, anyone here?!"

There were fishing rods in one corner, a trash can, an old sign. Craig called again and still no reply.

"What the fuck is the matter with this place," he said. He stamped his foot, banged the bell with his fist, called out again. The hum from the fluorescent ceiling lights annoyed him. "Someone shut that damned tube off," he said, as though to the staff. He took a broom from its place by the door, tossed it up and grabbed the brush end. He whacked it on the light fixture so that it blinked and swayed before resuming its noise. Now he grew red with impatience, paced the length of the counter, slapped the top of it, sounded the bell over and over again before finally throwing it against a wall. Then he went over to the bells tacked on the door and shook them like he was trying to get a coconut out of a tree.

"Hey!" he shouted. He was wearing the bicentennial ball cap. His untucked T-shirt billowed over his front, where a loose swatch of leather from his belt wagged with his steps. "Hey! I need some attention here!"

His voice boomed toward the back of the room where there were some closets and an exit door. Nothing happened. He flipped up a section of the counter that allowed him through to the manager's area, then opened cupboards until, at last, he found where the keys were stored on pegs. The one he wanted wasn't there and he searched the rack then looked on the desk, yanked open a drawer and swept his hand through, scattering paper clips, an ink pad, a calculator. A log of staples fell to the floor and broke into sections he then stepped on, turning abruptly when the phone began to ring. "You gonna answer that?" he said to Bobbie, sarcastically. The white light flashed on one of the extensions and the phone rang and rang. They both looked at it. "This is all your fault," he told her. "Making us come back."

Then he told her to get out, go back to the car and wait there.

She left him in the motel office and stepped into the night, wishing she were home already. Her house had a screened porch and she'd used paper clips to fix some extra mesh over the holes in the screen so bugs could not get through. She would sleep out there on nights like this, lying on a little camp bed beside a long section of screen, watching the moon through the trees. It was what she'd done the night before, quietly drifting into sleep in the silky warmth of the night. She had woken at dawn, feeling part of the trees and woods around her, part of the songbirds and squirrels and night animals.

She could still hear Craig calling for the manager. She had eight hours until she had to be at the bus stop for school and she'd better have washed her hair. It was sticky and stiff, hanging in her eyes. Sleep would be good, too. There had been times recently when she nodded off in class and the teachers behaved as though this was deliberate rudeness on her part. Her geography teacher once woke her, saying, *Do you have a problem I can help you with?* She'd shaken her head, stifled a yawn, endured the laughter in the classroom. No, he couldn't help her. She had a lot of problems he couldn't help her with. Her problem right now is she has to wait for Craig to get the money and get her home. Who could help her with that?

The motel sign was reflected in long bars of light on the Buick's gold hood and in colorful splashes on the window. When she approached she saw her own shadow, angular and dark. Then she stopped. Somebody was behind her. She could see plainly enough in the window's reflection. He was moving along the little cement path that led to the front of the motel. The night manager. He disappeared from view as she got into the car. She rolled the window down and listened. Crickets, the whirring of the ice machine, traffic in the distance. She smelled freshly cut grass and the fecund, growing greenery, and she breathed this in and tried to relax. Don't worry, she told herself. Craig would get the key and get the money and then drive to the station. In a matter of hours the whole awful night would be over. She pulled her knees up and hugged them. "Don't worry," she said out loud. But when she heard the door of the reception area bang shut, upsetting the bells, she felt like a fuse had been lit somewhere in the distance and soon everything would blow.

She saw Craig walking quickly down the path, the wooden fob in his hand, his head bent in the direction of the room. He turned in to the path that led to the motel's interior, then down the step to the little path that led to the room. A motion sensor clicked into action and produced a sudden, gauzy light that draped over him like a cape. He disappeared into the light and she could see no farther.

She opened the glove compartment, searching for cigarettes just in case Craig had missed them. Crushed in the corner was a single stale Marlboro with a tear in it, which she fished out carefully and tried to straighten. The filter had specks of loose tobacco and she was busy picking those off when she heard her name and looked up. Craig was standing on the bank of grass, blue in the neon light, his ball cap in his hand, his hands on his hips.

"Barbara, get in here and help me!" he said.

She poked her head through the open car window. "Help you how?"

"Don't ask me how! Move!"

How could he *not* find the money? It was in a drawer on top of a Bible with a note. She'd already told him that. It was impossible to miss. She wondered if she'd made a mistake and the money wasn't there. Maybe she was remembering incorrectly. Maybe she put it somewhere else. Finding the roll of cash, fishing it out from behind the night table—all that felt as though it had happened long ago. She could no longer think straight; she was tired, her thoughts agitated. She wanted to lie down, but she pushed open the door instead.

Her Dr. Scholl's clip-clopped along the cement path and she was aware of the noise and the likelihood of disturbing people. But she couldn't figure out how to tiptoe in such inflexible shoes and he pulled her along so quickly she had no choice but to clomp down the path. They reached the room and he pushed the door open, then stood in the yellow light taking up a good deal of the small space where they'd been all those hours ago and said, "Find the fucking money."

The room looked burgled. The bed still had the brown coverlet but he'd been through the drawers and they stood open, some now with broken handles, some pulled off their runners so they lay at angles across the floor. The dresser drawers were only made of flimsy plywood and the back of one had come off and now sat inside the three remaining sides. In another she could see the print of Craig's shoe across the lining paper. The curtain was drawn back so the light from outdoors shined onto the bed, which was still tidy, still as she'd left it, except two of the curtain hooks had flown onto it and gleamed there like pieces of jewelry left behind by a guest.

She went to the bedside table. He'd already pulled the drawer out, leaving it open at an angle. The Bible was there, the pages open beneath the book's spine.

"We could have had it already!" he said. He was stripping the bed, pulling up the mattress, digging inside the pillows. "We were here! In this same fucking room! And you had the money in your *hand.*"

She felt his anger radiating toward her. "I'm looking!" she said, but when she pulled out the Bible, which was facing down on its open pages, there was no money inside it. She shook the pages so they waved beneath the hard cover like a swatch of hair, but nothing came out. No money, no note. She kneeled down and looked under the night table's squat legs, but found only cobwebs and a stray pack of matches. In the space against the wall was an electrical cord and a socket. She could not see the money no matter how much she willed it to be there, and she could not leave until it was found.

"Stupid!" Craig said, about her or about the situation or maybe both.

For a moment she thought she saw it and gave a sudden shout.

Craig looked up. "You got the money?"

But it was only the note she'd written, which she threw back to the floor now. She dropped lower, scouting close to the carpet, her nose to the ply, looking crossways over the room. The contents of the drawers were all over the place: a pen with a crack in it, a phone book, some brochures.

Craig looked at her. "Fucking stupid," he said.

There were footsteps outside. She heard them and froze. Both of them did, Craig standing with a corner of the mattress leaning on the wall by his ear, her on all fours with her head cocked to one side like a dog. The footsteps grew louder and Craig said, "Get to the bathroom!"

She ran, stubbing her toe on the edge of the bed, then stepping out of her sandals and hopping barefoot, so that she all but fell onto the bathroom floor. She switched on the light and heard Craig yell, "Off!," so she switched it off again and sat on the toilet, perched on the edge of the rim, arms folded on the tops of her thighs, forehead against her knees. She felt a slushy sourness in the pit of her belly and listened as whoever it was came into the motel room. She thought it must have been the manager. She heard the shock in his voice from seeing the place so torn up and Craig there with a bedsheet in his hands.

The guy said, "What the hell?," and then Craig started shouting at him that he was looking for his money.

"What money?" she heard the other man say.

"What I left here!" Craig's voice. "What you took!"

"I never took any money! I'm calling the police!" The guy's voice went falsetto at the word *police* and then she heard something snap and a kind of slapping sound and a heavy object fall. She heard the

manager saying, "That's it, I'm definitely calling the police, man!,"
and then Craig's voice booming as though from a megaphone. He
had a deep, thundering voice with a lot of reverb, and when he
shouted it was as though there were ten men inside of him.

"Call the police and tell them you stole my money, you fucking
coward!" Craig bellowed. She heard a dull wet thud, and something scraping the window, and finally a boom so the whole room
shuddered. Now the guy was screaming. She heard a whooshing
sound and the guy yelping in pain. Craig was still shouting about
his money and being robbed. The motel manager was crying out
"Please stop!," and she didn't want to open the door, but she had to
look.

There was Craig with the antennae from the TV in his hand,
slender long metal twins, jagged at the broken ends. He was using
them like rapiers, or not like rapiers exactly because he did not
thrust the ends of the antennae into the guy but sat astride his chest,
beating the metal whips across his face as he was down on the floor,
his head pinned in place by Craig's knee on his neck.

"Tell me where my fucking money is!" Craig was shouting.

They were angled into the corner, the motel manager making
the most awful crying and begging noises. She'd never seen two men
actually fighting but she realized now that it was nothing like what
you saw on television. There was no sport to it. They did not size
each other up and take honest swings. The man on the floor being
whipped in the face cried out in a high-pitched voice while Craig
kneeled on him, lashing his cheeks and forehead and nose until the
man gave up and howled, animal-like, lying on the ground, and still
Craig did not stop.

There was the open door leading out to the dark inviting night,
and all she could think was to run, but her legs were shaky. She'd
left behind the stupid wooden sandals and her naked feet did not
feel sturdy or even under her command. She didn't dare run, but
instead crawled on her hands and knees, down on the floor where she
hoped she would not be seen. She kept hearing the manager's cries;
imagined the sting of the antennae against his neck and shoulders,

heard his garbled answers that he did not know where the money was, that he didn't know about *any* money.

She watched as the mattress suddenly fell onto the night table, which itself tipped over, sending the drawer flying out toward her head. She rolled into a ball, squeezing her eyes shut as it missed her by inches and hit the floor. She forced herself to stay still, to think clearly. She needed to get out the door and run. The men were still in battle; nobody would see her. She needed to keep moving. She opened her eyes, crawled forward once more. She only had to make another twelve feet or so, but the men were there, legs flailing, the long sweep of the metal rods stinging the air. She crouched forward and suddenly in front of her—she felt dizzy seeing it—*there was the money.*

The bills were in a roll just as she'd left them. They had been stuck or pinned or behind something—she could not imagine how the money ended up beside her, but there it was. She could hear the beating continue. She thought maybe she should call out, *The money is here, goddamn it, leave the guy alone!* But Craig would kill her if she let anybody know she was in the room. Being underage was another of her many faults. Her job was to stay hidden. People weren't allowed to see her. And certainly not in a motel room.

She heard the man yell out, then form a sentence. This comforted her, that he wasn't so hurt that he couldn't talk. He said he did not know about money but if it meant so much, why not go to the office and rob the cash register?

"There's tons of money in there!" the guy told Craig. "If you want money, go *take it*!"

"I'm not a fucking thief!" shouted Craig. "I'm not some lowly criminal who robs a fucking cash register, you cunt!" He kept hitting the manager as he spoke, punctuating his words with swipes from the antennae. "I'm only after what's *mine*!"

She closed her fingers over the wad of bills. She measured the distance between herself and the open door that led into the night. And then, in a moment she thought she might regret, she held tight to the five hundred in her closed fist, and she ran.

It was not that easy to get away. She didn't have any shoes. She didn't have any idea where to run now that she was out of the room. The security light flicked on as she passed, but she did not stop. The men in the room did notice, of course. The light meant someone was coming and this paused them.

She ran down the path, skirted the turn, crossing the parking lot with its rough surface and sharp pebbles. She moved in high leaping steps as her feet stung, climbed a bank of grass, cool and lumpy on her naked soles. Now she was beside a road that paralleled the bank of highway that rumbled above. She stopped, bending forward and resting her hands on her knees, looking out at the motel as she tried to regulate her breathing. She wanted water. Water and a bicycle, or at least a pair of shoes.

She was ready to give up. If there had been a phone booth, she would have called her mother and explained what happened. Or not explained but said, *Please help me. Please, I need you.* And her mother would get that serious tone in her voice and say, *Bobbie, where are you? Can you see a road sign? Can you see the name of a store or a restaurant or anything near you?* Her mother would tell her to stay put and that she'd come. But her mother was not at home. She wasn't sure where she was. Bobbie didn't even have a number to call because by now her mother would be driving home, arriving sometime in the middle of the night, exhausted from the road.

So there was no one. She would walk, she decided. How far could it be? Ten miles, twelve? She'd won a National Fitness Award last year in school. She was a good walker. But it was the shoes. That was her problem. And she wasn't too sure about directions.

Even so, the night was pleasant and dry, the temperature comfortable. She thought about finding a place to lie down here on the bank between roads, here in the grass. How bad could that be? Hadn't people slept outside hundreds of years ago? Or if not hundreds, then thousands of years ago? In the summer, no less? With darkness to cloak them and the serenity of the stars? Hadn't she read a poem like that in school? And who could see her out here? She dropped to her knees, then curled her legs under her. Her mind was cluttered with images of Craig and the manager and those awful metal antennae. She pushed them from her thoughts. She was so tired. Surely it was all right to lie down now? She lowered herself into the tall grass; if she stayed on her back nobody would see her. She closed her eyes and let her mind swim toward sleep. She told herself she was surely hidden. Not even the moon could find her shadow.

CAR HEADLIGHTS SPRAYED light on her face, and she was tossed from sleep into the night she now detested and wished away. She was blind and chilly and footsore, and she was scared. Even so, her first thought was that somehow her mother had figured out where she was and had come for her. The stopped car meant she was safe now. Rescued. She realized that this was what she'd longed for all night, to be rescued. Though it was impossible, and part of her knew it was impossible, in her dreamlike state and the suddenness of her awakening she believed that the greatness of her need had defied all physics and made itself known across miles and time to her mother.

The night air was pricked with dampness, as though the rain that gathered did so from beneath the ground. She sat up, hugging herself, wet from the grass. The sudden waking had jarred a place inside her stomach where she now felt a sour pinching. She shielded her eyes with one hand as someone threw open the car door. She could not see properly—the headlights were too bright—but she could see it was not her mother; it was a man. She could tell it was a man by the force of the door and how he left it open, and his outline in the beam of headlights, large and wide and tall. She thought perhaps it was the police, but then she saw exactly who it was, still wearing his ball cap, and engulfed even now—oh, she could hardly believe this—in the same fierce anger that had possessed him back at the motel.

On the car radio, turned up loud, A Taste of Honey was singing "Boogie Oogie Oogie," a harmless teen song that seemed directly at odds with the glaring lights. The force of headlights had temporarily jarred her vision. Everything in front of her was halos and drifting clouds of color and great gobs of blackness through which she could see nothing, even after she pushed her palms into her eyes and blinked. She got to her knees. She felt weak and heavy, held down by the light, as though it was a weight that pinned her.

"Barbara!" His voice was booming and deep and full. "What do you think you are doing!"

She would have loved to have an answer. Instead, she sat down on the grass once more.

"Get up," he snapped.

She stood. She thought about running and would have done so, but for the no shoes.

"Well, come on! What do I have to do? Pull you up off the ground and carry you to the car? I have a job to get to, you know."

Her sleep, which had lasted less than twenty minutes, seemed to have been much longer. And now her mind filled with images of the snapped-off antennae and that man on the floor with his hands in front of him, trying to ward off Craig. She wondered how Craig had found her but then she saw the obvious trail she'd made through the wet grass. She might as well have put out signs.

Suddenly the headlights were off. She could hear the DJ on the car radio talking over the long exit of a record, and when she turned around she saw Craig peeing on a spot of ground just in front of the car.

"Let's move!" he said, doing up his fly.

She got back into the car and Steely Dan started playing, and Craig said "Finally!," though she didn't know if he meant finally she was in the car or finally there was a decent song on the playlist.

He put his pipe between his teeth and wheeled the car around getaway-style, his head bent over one shoulder.

He said, "I'm going to be late and it's your fault. That money— how the fuck did you leave it behind? I mean that is just stupid. Don't tell me you're sorry because—"

"I'm not sorry," she interrupted.

"Good God, do you do *nothing* but argue?" he said. He drew his hand up as though to hit her but didn't. "One day, Barbara, someone is going to kick the shit out of you, acting like you do."

And now, into her vision came the antennae from the motel TV. He'd taken them with him. There they were, lying across the top of the dash like the stems of headless flowers. She thought, *If he touches me with them I'll . . .* But she had no idea what she'd do. She couldn't think clearly with the wind blowing through the windows and the cloud of traffic noise. It felt like being out on an airport runway or fixed into the engine of a helicopter. Her brain couldn't work with all the noise.

"If I had my pipe instead of this Mickey Mouse toy shit of a pipe, I'd be a lot happier," he said, then tossed the pipe in her direction. "Fix me up a bowl."

The sandwich bag of pot was lodged in the ashtray. She took a pinch of grass, rolling her fingers to feel for the seeds and separate them out, letting them drop. She bent down, avoiding the ceaseless wind driving through the car's open windows, and tamped the leaves so they would catch when she brought a match to them, which she did now. Lighting the bowl was the next thing he was going to ask of her so she might as well.

"Thank Christ for reefer," he said, and turned up the volume button on the radio. He took the pipe from her and drew in a long toke. "I wouldn't need to smoke so much if things were less fucked up in this world, but you can see how it is, can't you?"

"Are you taking me home?" she said, her voice raised in order to be heard over the wind.

"No time. You can sleep in the car at the station," Craig said.

"I don't want to sleep in the car. I want to go home and take a shower."

"You should have thought about that before you *made us so damned late!*"

This was the end. She wasn't going to get home tonight. Her mother would arrive to an empty house and go crazy. And even if her mother didn't check the bedroom to see that she was there, the fact was that Bobbie would miss her morning shower. There would be no time to wash her hair. She'd have to go to school in these clothes and without her books. She'd arrive for a chemistry test without her calculator, fail the test, get detention. Worse yet, she didn't have any shoes.

"I have to go home before school starts," she said. "I don't have any shoes."

"You left your goddamned shoes? How could you have done that!"

"I couldn't walk in them—"

"People walk in *shoes,* Barbara. All the fucking time."

"I couldn't run, I mean."

"You think you're so smart—who leaves their shoes behind?"

"I don't think I'm so smart—"

"Yes you do! You think because you get good grades that makes you smart. Well, it doesn't mean anything, Barbara. You got that? It doesn't mean dick."

All at once she felt a fury course through her. She wanted to kick out, or break up the car. Instead, she did the one thing that she knew would get to him. She reached forward and punched a button on the radio, changing the station. That did it.

"Hey! Jesus CHRIST!" It was as though she'd done something awful to him, actual physical damage, changing the radio like that. His music suddenly gone, his station gone. That station was *his,* the songs on it were the soundtrack to his *life.* But coming through the car's immensely overpowered speakers now was Doris Day. Doris Day singing "It's Magic," her voice clear and slow and melodic. It sent Craig into a fit of pain. He started thwacking at the radio, trying to stop the ballad, but Doris played on: "How else can I explain those rainbows when there is no rain? It's magic!"

He looked pissed, like someone was trying to harm him—out of nothing, for no good reason—injecting this "music" into his ears. The pipe fell from his lips, dropping onto the floor as he lurched as though in pain, thumping the radio dial again. It went off this time and now there was silence, except for the rushing wind, and she could no longer hear Doris Day's voice moving skyward, nor the violins creating that celestial air. "*Sonovabitch!* Why in HELL did you do that!"

She said nothing at first. She didn't really know. Every once in a while she got brave. Every so often, a well of defiance rose up inside her. It had been building for months now and if she tapped into it, she was capable of anything.

"It's her birthday," Bobbie said quietly.

"*Whose* birthday?"

"Doris Day's."

"No it isn't!"

"Yes it is. It's her birthday and that was her greatest song. Put it back on."

"It isn't her fucking birthday. Jesus, how did you get to be such a . . ." His voice trailed off as though it was hardly worth finishing the thought.

There was a beat of silence and then Bobbie said, "It *is* her birthday! I'm a member of Doris Day's fan club and I got a card in the mail—"

"You didn't get any card," he said.

"You don't know that!" She was following a stream of anger that led to a river that led to an ocean. She was sailing now.

"I know it isn't Doris fucking Day's birthday."

She was up on her knees, balancing on the bench seat, leaning toward him. With her voice as loud as she could make it, her face close to his ear, she shouted, "You don't know *shit* about Doris Day!"

A silence. For a moment nothing, then Craig said, "Who cares? Who the hell cares?"

Bobbie dropped back into the seat and said, "She just happens to be my mother's favorite, okay?"

He looked like he halfway heard this and that in some other universe somebody could understand why this fact mattered, but what he said was, "Find that pipe that fell on the floor before we light the car on fire."

"It *is* her birthday."

"Okay, fine. Happy birthday, Doris. Now get the pipe. I can smell it burning a hole."

But she didn't get the pipe. She thought how she was going to listen to the rest of that song now—why not? She'd half convinced herself that it *was* Doris Day's birthday and that this was enough reason to insist she get her way. She put her bare foot on the dashboard, trying to look confident, then reached to switch the radio back on.

"Don't fucking touch that!" he bellowed.

"Don't whack my hand!"

"I'm warning you."

"Back off! That's my favorite song!"

"It is not."

"Yes it is! And you wouldn't know. My favorite song is *what then*? If you are so sure it isn't that one?"

He rolled his eyes. "Fine," he said, "do what you want."

She got the radio on and back to the right channel, but it was too late for "It's Magic." There was only the last lingering sad note, and the rising and falling of the dying violins and the DJ's voice coming on to say, "That was the incredible Doris Day!" before Craig slapped the dial once more.

"There!" he said, sending it back to his own station where the Village People sang "Macho Man": "Macho, macho man . . . !"

"Oh, yes, this is much better," said Bobbie. As loudly as she could, she sang along: "Macho, macho man . . . I want to be a macho man—!"

"Shut up!" he shouted. He made a grunting sound like someone was standing on his foot, then said, "What is that little turdball playing?" He punched the dash so hard the tuner button spun off like a saucer. He swore and writhed in his seat and shouted at her. "Why on earth are *you* singing!"

He was truly insane now, shifting in his seat, hitting his car, screaming at the radio, the seat bouncing with his weight, the car drifting into another lane, so she stopped singing. She was sorry that she'd argued with him, sorry about wanting to go home, about the radio station, about everything. They were going to crash. He twisted in his seat, the cords of his neck showing like ribs; he was facing her now and howling, *"Fix this fucking thing!"*

She realized the problem. The tuner button, having flown off, was now missing. He couldn't escape the Village People. She scrambled to find the button on the floor, then brought it up and aligned it with the little stick of metal on the radio to get it working again. She let him find a station he wanted and didn't flinch when he yelled, directly into her ear, "Get! The! God! Damned! Pipe!" His voice was huge, even with the tearing sound of the wind through the car and the tires rumbling over the road and all the other cars' engines, and the pumped-up speakers that shot the music in four directions all at once. Nothing was bigger than his voice. It was massive, like a weather cloud. She did what she was told.

"Light the fucking thing!" he barked at her, and she tried. If he smoked enough, he'd get mellow. He might even get sleepy. God, she wished he'd smoke himself into a stupor.

They turned off the highway and moved down a long, near-deserted stretch of road, heading toward the station at a speed that would land them in prison. She no longer dared look at the speedometer but focused on keeping the pot flowing. The pot would calm him down. She took the bowl and dumped the charred contents out the window, her hair flying in sheets around her head. She lit a new match to start the bowl, kneeling in the passenger's seat and leaning low toward the floor, trying to keep the wind out of the bowl, trying not to light her hair on fire.

"Oh for fucksake!" he said, pissed off by how incompetent she was, not being able to light a bowl, and how he was going to have to roll up his window, what a pain in the ass.

She thought she should roll up the window on her side, too. Normally, she didn't dare touch the windows, the seat position, the radio. These things belonged to him. But she cranked the lever from her bent position, angled on the floor, her elbow taking the strain.

With the windows up, she could get a bit of a spark and then slowly, after a few short sucks, some embers kindled. She passed the bowl carefully across to him and he drew in the smoke and held it.

"Finally," he croaked, holding his breath. He exhaled and said, "There's countries where it's legal to hit a wife who won't obey."

"I'm not your wife," she said. But she shouldn't have said anything and knew it.

He said, "You're spoiled because you're pretty and people do things for pretty girls."

She didn't know what he meant. First, about being pretty. Her legs were pink and white like a plucked chicken. Her eyes were invisible behind blond lashes. The only good feature she could identify was her hair, which right now felt like dried-out cotton and was so snarled and ruined that she thought she'd have to cut the tangles out.

"But one day you won't be so pretty," he continued, "and then you'll be very truly fucked, just so you know." He took a toke from the bowl, but it went dark. He sucked the pipe and got nothing. "Jesus Christ, it's out again! What a rip-off fucking no-smoke goddamned pipe! This is *not* my reefer's fault."

She wasn't so sure. The draw on the pipe was weak, but the grass was young and it made a lot of smoke and wouldn't keep a light anyway. She took the bowl once again, added some fresh leaves, and relit it, handing it to him like medicine. But it was out in ten seconds and he groaned in frustration and shoved it back in her direction, saying, "Fix this fucking thing."

"How?"

He leaned forward and took one of the antennae off the dash and said, "Break this up and poke it down there and get out all the shit."

Remarkably, she knew what he meant. The pipe was bunged up with resin that needed clearing. But she didn't want to touch the antennae, which seemed to her as lethal as a gun. Anyway, she could not easily break them in two. He suddenly swerved the car to the left, passing a driver who wasn't traveling at a hundred the way they were, and she felt a sloshing inside her guts as they moved sideways all at once like that. The antennae dropped to the floor and landed, sharp side up, bent in her direction as though pointing.

"God, Craig," she said.

"Give it to me," he said.

"What?"

"The TV thing, *that*, what's next to you, on the floor. Jesus, Barbara."

She thought of the motel manager all over again. She wished Craig hadn't brought the antennae. "What happened with that guy in the room. Is he all right?" she said.

"He's five hundred of my dollars richer, is what he is."

And then she remembered: the money.

It was rolled into a log in her back pocket. She almost reached into her pocket to make sure it was still there but stopped herself. Instead, she put some weight onto her right buttock, trying to feel if there was a lump there. Slowly, secretly, she moved just enough to tell if there was some tiny resistance from the roll of bills. If he found out she had the money, he'd go wild. She could not risk that he'd find it. Could not risk it.

"But you *have* the money," she said weakly.

"I have *this*!" he said, and pulled out a flattened stack of bills, wadding it into the ashtray next to the grass like it was an oil rag. "But my *other* five hundred is fucking disappeared."

"But the guy—"

"What about him?"

"He's not—" She didn't know how to say it, how to ask if the guy was dead.

"He's a fucking fairy!"

"But . . . alive, right?"

Now he laughed. He laughed and told her he was hungry and to watch out for the golden arches because he needed a drive-through. Then he picked up the antennae in his non-driving hand and broke them against his knee, which made the car jerk to the shoulder. She held the dash and watched him as he poked around the pipe and pointed the car toward a turnoff that led to a stretch of road where the radio station would eventually be found. It was already midnight and she did not understand why he wasn't tearing his hair out, then heard the DJ on the radio say he was playing an album, which meant Craig had another half hour or so before he'd have to be sitting in the studio.

"He's playing an album, Craig, did you hear that?"

"So what?"

"So you can relax," she said, meaning he could go a little slower.

"That only gives me so much time." He pinched the air to show her how little time. "And I'm hungry."

HE PULLED INTO a McDonald's, circled into the drive-through, and leaned toward the microphoned clown. He said he'd need two Big Macs, large fries, and a Coke, plus a milk shake. That was for her, the milk shake.

"I'm not hungry," she said.

"Yes, you are."

They drove around to the window and a young guy in eyeglasses and a brown nylon uniform stood waiting for the money, the paper bags beside him and the cardboard drink-holder, too, plus all the napkins and straws and plastic pouches of ketchup and slim packets of salt, assembled in a messy pile like a salad.

The guy told Craig it would be three dollars and something and he said, "Fuck that's a lot for a couple of burgers," and then looked at Bobbie for the money.

"What?" she said.

He held out a hand. "We need four bucks."

"Three seventy-five," the McDonald's guy said. He had a tag on his lapel that read Dan and curly hair that spiraled around the cap on his head.

"I don't have enough money," she told Craig. These words seemed dangerous to her. She wondered if this was a trick, that he knew she had the other five hundred and this was his way of showing her he knew she had it. One of his little tests.

"You left the house with *nothing*?" He didn't move. He didn't look in his own pockets or in the glove compartment, only at her. His eyes were slits of pink and his mouth hung open like he was caught mid-chew.

She said, "Not four dollars."

He shook his head slowly, like he was at the end. At the very end. He had no time for this. "Give me some money, Barbara, so we can *eat*! People need to *eat*, you know."

Again, she wondered if this was a trick, like she was supposed to hand over the five hundred now. Why else would he have stopped at a McDonald's when he was already supposed to be on the air? Why else would he demand that she pay for his food? She didn't even understand how he'd lucked into having the DJ before him play a whole album as his last record. Craig must have called him from the motel and told him he was going to be late. It was the only explanation, and suddenly the whole thing felt like it had been staged. He must know she had the five hundred. On the other hand, she'd had a few tokes while lighting his pipe and maybe she was paranoid. She always got paranoid when she smoked pot. It was one of the reasons she didn't like getting high.

"I don't have any—"

"Bullshit!" He was furious now. It was over. She would give the money to him, give him all the money. She didn't want it anymore. She couldn't remember why she had taken it in the first place. It had rolled its way up to her, right up to her face, that was why.

A story came to mind, one Craig had once told her about the Hope Diamond. He'd said everyone who had the large and beautiful gem came to a terrible end. It was cursed. She concluded now that the money she'd found in the motel was cursed, like the diamond. He could have the cursed money, every last dollar. She reached into her pocket to get it. She couldn't wait to hand it over and have this done with. She wished that after she gave him the money she could get out of the car. All at once, this seemed a fair exchange. He got the money, and she walked free. Free from him not just now but always. It was a bargain. She felt the roll, a sense of immense relief filling her heart. But just as she took it in her hand, everything changed. Craig pulled up the emergency brake, gave a great groan of impatience, and now she watched in confusion as he pushed his body toward her, then over the back of her seat. She pressed the money toward him but he knocked into her again, reaching his arm to the seat behind where her handbag rested. He grabbed the handbag and threw it at her, threw it at her face, so the buckle slapped her teeth, the strap stung her eye.

"Get some money!" he shouted.

"Sir, we can take a check if that helps," the McDonald's guy said. But nobody was listening to him.

Craig's eyes were fully on her now. "You think I'm so stupid I don't know your mother will not let you out of the house without cash?"

"My mother wasn't home—"

"Shut up! Shut the fuck up."

She still had the fist of bills, but he didn't notice. He grabbed the steering wheel with both hands as though steadying himself on the ropes of a boxing ring, then he said, "You're a trial, Barbara. Do you know that? It makes no difference what I do with you! You have to make everything difficult."

She closed her fingers over the five hundred, hid it deep into her palm, then dug into her purse and found some change, mostly dimes. In her lipstick case she kept an emergency dollar. But she couldn't make it four dollars without handing over one of the fifties.

"Sir, if you don't mind me saying," the MacDonald's guy began. He was stuck in his little brick-and-glass box; he was a head in a square of glass. His hair curled against the dull uniform and you could see the reflection of sweat on his chin. His name tag, Dan, seemed like something a small child would wear.

Craig whipped his head around to the McDonald's guy. "WHAT?" he said.

"If you don't mind me saying—" The guy suddenly stopped. He was nervous, was young himself, only sixteen, seventeen at a stretch. His beard looked like stray hair that needed plucking. His hair had a hedge shape of tight curls. "In the car there I can see quite a bit of cash. More than three dollars seventy-five. Just there, sir. In your ashtray."

Craig glanced down at the roll of bills in the ashtray, then at Bobbie, then at the McDonald's guy again.

"What is this all about!" he yelled, as though the two of them—Bobbie and Dan the McDonald's guy—were working together to swindle him. "*Everyone*, his dog, and his uncle, wants to separate me from my goddamned money!" He pointed into the ashtray with a single strong shake of his arm as though trying to hurl his index finger into the pot of cash. "That's mine, son! You got that? Nobody is touching this money! Now here, take *this*!"

It was Bobbie's money. She watched as Craig handed it up to the boy, who nodded and thanked him. She waited as he counted.

"You going to give us our burgers, man?" Craig said to Dan. "Or are you going to stand there with our money *and* our food, working out how to wipe me clean of every red cent?"

The boy finished counting, then looked unsteadily at Craig. Bobbie could see the reflection of the car in the windowed booth and Craig's face snarled in the yellow-and-red lights that pricked the glass.

"Sir—" The boy looked distressed now, truly distressed. He stood on one foot, then another. He opened his mouth to speak and stuttered out the words, "This is . . . this is only three twenty-five."

"Oh. Fuck. You," said Craig, like he was tired now, wiped out with all the bullshit this kid was giving him. "Come on, sunshine, give us our burgers!"

The boy licked his lips. His shoulders were thin and sharp. He had a hollow chest, long arms, bony wrists, slender fingers, and you could see every pore on his face in the fierce laboratory-bright light. He leaned on his arms and sunk his head into his neck, then looked over his shoulder and back at Craig, and spoke again, this time in a voice that sounded even younger, "I'll ask my manager. Maybe he could do something—"

She felt Craig flinch and the colossal spear of his approaching anger. She saw how he fixed his eyes on the boy and knew what this meant. It was impossible to keep silent. The idea that Craig would hurt the boy filled her mind completely. It didn't matter that there was a window and, in fact, an entire wall between the car and the boy. Her mind was stuck on the memory of the motel manager, the sight of him down on the carpet, his face bent ninety degrees from center so the side of his nose pressed against the floor, mouth contorted, eyes squeezed shut, hands raised, swatting at the antennae as Craig pinned and beat him. It was all she could think about. From where she sat stiffly in her seat, she now leaned forward and caught the boy's gaze and motioned with her head in small, fractional side-to-side movements. *No*, she told him silently, wagging her head almost imperceptibly, so that Craig would not see. *Do not get the manager.*

She saw the subtle change in the boy's expression and heard him say, "Never mind," and she nearly collapsed with relief. "This is fine," the boy said. He tried to smile, but it didn't look like a smile. He handed the bag of burgers, the cardboard tray of drinks, all the straws and slim packets of extra salt, and the napkins through the McDonald's window. Reaching toward Craig's open window with the bag, moving as carefully as he could with shaky hands, he delivered the whole thing down to Craig, who passed it all to Bobbie in a swift movement and then told the boy he was a peckerhead.

"You're a peckerhead," he said to the boy. "Do you know that?"

The boy said nothing. He stared at Craig, swallowing hard.

"Say it!" demanded Craig. "Say, *I'm a peckerhead!*"

He waited until the boy did as he was told. "I'm a . . ." The boy was trembling. "I'm a peckerhead?" he said, his eyes fixed and staring.

"Yes, you are!" Craig laughed, then put the car into gear and they got the hell out of there.

———

THEY LEFT MCDONALD'S and sailed forward, the car now filled with the smell of burgers. It was midnight and she was caught in the cloud of noise from the radio and the road and him saying, "Take the wheel while I unclog this thing," meaning the pipe. She scooted over and sat close to him, her head pulled back away from the spear of the antenna as he held the pipe in his mouth and poked the sharp end inside, then took it out and examined the bowl in the passing glare of streetlamps. Her fingers were locked around the steering wheel and she tried to watch the road out ahead the way he had instructed her many times before, not allowing herself to focus on the bleached cement that fed itself under the car just in front of the hood, which was where she naturally looked.

The road was straight, banked occasionally by leafy birch trees with bark that peeled in silvery paper upon their trunks. Above them was heat lightning and a faraway storm, but also the silent, sure flight of a jetliner aiming for the airport. If she weren't having to concentrate so hard on keeping the car on the road, if she didn't have to *drive*, she might have leaned against the door and stretched her vision up to the pretty halo around the moon, then tracked the plane's red-and-white lights across the map of sky.

"Keep her steady," he said.

"Next year I can get my license." She squinted ahead, shifting her legs so they unstuck from the sweaty seat.

"Don't remind me. You can already see it happening. Girls change. You're already argumentative and pissy. You'll be finished by sixteen."

"I'm not *pissy*," she said. She wondered what he meant by *finished*. "Am I driving okay?"

"Fourteen is optimal. I liked you better then. And I thought you'd turn out better than you did, too. Stay a bit straighter. Here," he said, and pushed the wheel with his thumb.

"How far ahead should I be looking? Like a hundred feet or fifty feet or ten?"

"I'm not saying I don't love you. But you were nicer then. Much.

You had promise. I've seen this happen before. A nice girl one minute, then they hit fifteen, sixteen, and suddenly they turn into little bitches."

"I'm not a bitch."

She felt the weight of his disappointment in her, but she had to concentrate on the road. She had to be careful. She could get hypnotized by the road immediately in front of the car. It looked like what the arcade games looked like when you put in quarters and got to pretend you were a race-car driver. The car was tricky. Its headlights weren't aligned and the beams turned in on each other so she was driving into a cone of light. Meanwhile Craig was cleaning out the pipe bowl with the broken antenna. He took a few tokes, leaning back and sucking the pipe, poking it with the antenna every now and again to get a better draw. "That's good," he said.

He seemed like he might fall asleep, resting on the nylon seat, so she said, "You're not sleepy, are you? Don't forget you're the one with the brakes."

He said, "Can't you tell we're going a steady sixty?"

"I'm just saying."

"How could we be doing sixty like this if I weren't doing my part with the gas pedal?"

"Okay, sorry."

"See what I mean? Now you're telling me how to drive. You don't even have a damned license yet but you're the expert." He pinched some grass and held it above the bowl, talking all the while. But he looked like it was too much trouble to get mad at her. "Remember last year when we'd go down to the quarry and swim and have a good time?" He sighed. "You were sweet then." He stirred around the leaves with the end of the antenna, then told her again to keep the damned car in a line so he didn't get seasick. "*Steer*," he said, exasperated.

She hooked her fingers tighter around the wheel and said, "I'm doing my best."

"Make your best a little better, then."

She said, "Please hurry. This is hard, keeping it straight when I'm sitting at an angle."

"It's not hard. I'll show you hard."

He took one of her hands from the wheel and she nearly screamed. He laughed, and put her fingers between his legs. She was already too short for the seat and had to lean over, and now she was one-handed, and he expected her to keep the car steady.

"Please," she said.

"I got no time for you anyway," he said. "I'm already late as hell."

She thought for a moment, then said, "Is there any chance of me getting home?" She didn't want to bring it up again, but she didn't want to sleep in the car while he did his show, either. She'd done that back in March and it hadn't gone well. He'd found it funny when he got back to the car and discovered her huddled under a blanket, a thin glazing of ice on the windows. She'd been unable to sleep for the cold and she begged him for the hot coffee that steamed in a paper cup held in his hand. Her mother had been in New Jersey that night, too, working one of the trade shows and sleeping in a Marriott. She'd phoned Bobbie to say she was bringing her some chocolate coins they sold in the gift shop and something else, too, that was going to be a surprise, and Bobbie had been so groggy she could barely say thank you.

But now, as she steered the car with Craig beside her with his matches and his pipe, she noticed the branches to the left of the road became unsettled and suddenly, as though out of a fairy tale, there sprang an enormous deer in a graceful arc before them, its legs folding and unfolding, its back stretching and unstretching. From the veil of forest, it landed for an instant upon the road much like a bird lands momentarily upon the bare ground, awkward in stillness, its eyes toward the approaching car. In the blaze of headlights, she saw the stag's bright golden pelt, the overlong legs, the elegant neck. She saw the antlers, angled and strong and fixed on its broad head, and she was mesmerized by the dark eyes, and the deer's steady gaze. The car was still coming fast, the brakes untouched, the tires rolling dumbly toward the deer. She called out to Craig as the animal took in the car with its bold, soft eyes. It did not turn away but waited on the road, framed in the headlights, the colors of its coat filling her vision, planted before them as though it had been searching for death all evening.

Craig did not brake, or at least he did not brake early enough. He'd said he was doing his part with the gas pedal, but it hadn't been true. She turned from the deer and the car became a missile, aiming for the trees. White sparks flashed against battered trunks as the whole of the woods charged toward them. She felt the tires blow out, the rims banging, and a terrible dropping as though her body were suddenly reduced to nothing but her head. Her head rolling like a ball in the dark of the car.

The accident seemed to go on forever, the car dying slowly as it looked for a landing among the forest, the trees falling, breaking, and bending, with tremendous cracks and jolts that came from all sides, all at once, even under them. They had passed the area of hardwoods and come off the road's shoulder into a section of farmed Christmas pines with their bushy fans of needled branches and scaly bark, all precisely planted. They'd been driving so fast the car had hit the weak line of wire fencing and somehow gone up, climbing the wire, snapping the posts at their bases, and flattening the fence so that it lay on the ground like a tarpaulin. The pines were immature, the sound of their breaking trunks like that of guns firing. She heard great explosions of wood, then a blast of glass as the rear window crumbled. A cape of branches flowed over the car and then she saw nothing at all. She smelled burning rubber. She smelled an oily cedar scent and gas fumes and blood. Her nose was bleeding. She hadn't been wearing a seat belt and had flown downward into the well of the floor in front of the passenger's seat where she had stayed until at last the car stopped moving and the explosion of wood ceased to echo in her ears.

She felt herself roll out of consciousness, and then her mind sprang forward as a current of sensations and images flooded her. It was like dreaming with a broken brain, all these sharp little thoughts firing inside her skull. She threw up hard, her chest heaving to bring in air that was suddenly in short supply. She was a rag doll, weightless on the floor. She thought she was dying, then threw up again.

It was as though they'd entered a cave with a blackness so complete she could not tell if her eyes were open or shut. The space of the car seemed to have transformed around her. She banged her head as she lifted herself from under the dash, feeling for the seat behind her, filled now with broken branches and bark scrapings. The whole car consumed by the forest, stuffed with wood and branches and great shavings of bark so that she was poked by their jagged ends coming through from the open window beside her.

She tried the door but it was stuck, the car wedged at an angle. It was possible the door was so damaged it might not work in any case, even if she managed to clear the pressing branches. The headlights were punched out, the engine silent. She touched the window and it suddenly disintegrated into broken glass. It was difficult to believe the car had been perfectly functioning along the open road only moments before. She pushed all her weight against the door but it sprang back just as hard. She felt for the inside light and switched it on and looked at Craig next to her, understanding at once that he was dead.

She thought about climbing out the window on his side, which meant climbing over him, but she saw his face and immediately felt the bile erupting into her throat and mouth, until she tipped her chin and retched. The antenna he'd used to beat the manager, and later to root through the bunged-up pipe so he could smoke cleanly, was now lodged inside his right eye. She could not see the whole of his face but only his profile, unnaturally bent, the blood washing over his cheek below the speared eye, and the sight of him sent her into a shivery panic. She bounced in her seat, screaming and sobbing, the muscles in every part of her clenched so hard she felt she'd pass out from the strain of breathing.

She called his name and he did not answer. She could not bring herself to touch him. She thought, *I must get help*. She thought, *It's too late. Everything is too late.* In a feverish confusion she used her shoulder like a weapon on the door, banging against it again and again. She could not stay trapped in the car, caged in by the battered metal and the broken wood around her. It felt like she had been lowered into the ground with a dead man. Even the sounds outside were muted, as though they were underground. But no matter how hard she pushed, the door bounced back at her, never giving more than few inches, until at last she gave up and sat quietly, and hoped that nothing started to burn.

There was a red box from a Big Mac crushed next to the windshield, which was shattered but intact, with thousands of pieces of glass fitted together like a puzzle, so that the glass was opaque. The burger wrapper put her in mind of the boy at McDonald's and then, with a start, she remembered the money. Craig's half, the wad he'd stuffed into the ashtray.

There it was, exactly as he'd left it, pinned by the little door of the tray on the dash. She took out the bills and held them to her face. She breathed in the scent of ink and dust, inhaling because they smelled like the world outside the car and the forest. She put them in her pocket along with the other rolled-up bills and she did not know what to do next.

The backseat was the only way out. There was a hole in the rear window and it could serve as an escape hatch. She told herself that the leaning, uneven half wall of shattered window could be easily pushed aside, the little cubes of broken glass no threat at all. *You will not get cut from that window*, she told herself sternly. *Or not seriously.*

She used to read books about adventures and terrible physical tests but none of them were the least bit like the real thing, which was slow and uncertain and tormenting. The pain—even little flecks of pain that she felt now—was enough to send you into a fear so solid that the only positive outcome was a full-scale rescue of the sort in which you lie belly-up and pray.

But Craig was there with a metal stick in his eye and she wasn't waiting however many hours it would take for help to arrive.

She knelt on the front seat, then pulled herself toward the back of the car, gliding carefully over broken branches and shards of bark, one hand shielding her eyes, the other reaching like a probe. She felt for jagged ends and sharp points. The yellow light was enough to guide her but not enough to see fully the contents of the backseat, an assortment of loose branches and pebbles of glass glistening on the upholstery and all over the floor, like thousands of eyes. She could not risk stepping onto the glass with bare feet. She could not stay in the car. She perched on the rolled ledge of the front seat like a big cat hugging a high rock, and then slowly slid to the left, guiding herself out of the rear window, and sliding roughly along a mesh of branches before dropping slowly to the ground below.

She landed on her side and looked up. Still, she could not see the sky. A broken tree was canopied above her. Crawling through the branches she at last reached an open section of forest perhaps ten feet away and she looked up at the stars and cried out for help. Her voice was weak and she became aware of a thirst unlike any she'd had before. She felt her tongue thickly in her mouth, her eyes dry beneath their lids. Her skin stung everywhere as though she'd been burned, and for a moment she thrashed upon the ground in a kind of contained hysteria, before getting to her feet and squinting through the night to find a path.

Her feet were alive with pain, her steps mincing and tentative, and sometimes after another agonizing spike from a pebble or thorn pressed itself on her soles she dropped to her knees, feeling the ground for sharpness. At times, she let herself cry out freely. At other moments, she held her breath and raced through and over whatever was in her path.

The trees were set in tidy rows as though sewn in place by a giant machine. Once she got far enough from the crash, her path to the road was clear, spelled out in moonlight and the shadowed brush of pine beside her. As she walked, the Christmas trees became smaller and weaker, so that she could see through and above them and it was like walking as a giant through the land. She stopped when she reached a wire fence that banked the road and walled her from it.

Her head was heavy. A buzzing worked itself furiously toward its center and she stooped on the dry ground and clutched her forehead, pressing against both temples to contain the ache. She did not know how long she walked the line of fence—up on her tiptoes or with her weight on her heels or, just as cautiously, on the full flat surface of her stinging feet. She wanted to lie down and sleep. She would have slept, but the only way she could contain the events of the night, to keep them separate from the part of her life she still wished to preserve, was to escape from the crash and these woods.

She wanted to go home, to enter the porch through the swinging screen door and find the key beneath the stone tortoise, a garden ornament that had been on the porch's brick floor as long as she could remember. She wanted to sit behind a locked door in the kitchen and reassemble herself, to decide what to do next, for there would be things she had to do. Go to the police, for example. But she did not want to go to the police. They would ask her questions. *What happened? Who was driving? How did you know this man? Why did you leave him there?*

She thought of herself at the police station, sitting in a hard chair at a steel desk in a room with no windows and no way of leaving.

The policeman might ask her, *Don't you know to call for help when you need it?*

But who could she call? And with what phone? She walked the fence, feeling pain everywhere, especially in her right hip and her bare, bleeding feet. The thought of a police station made her feel sick with terror. She was old enough to be left on her own but would they say her mother had neglected her? Her mother had never neglected her, but that is what they would think. The police are trained to think like that, that every bad thing that happens is someone's fault.

And the drugs. Good God, what would the police say about the pot? If she owned up to having been in a car with marijuana and all that paraphernalia, it would be the end of her education. She would never get into college. She would never become anyone.

She came across a clearing and there she saw a reflection of eyes gleaming in the moonlight like stones in a stream. It was a herd of deer, trapped in the same way she was behind the mesh of fence and the empty road that divided the woods. She did not want to startle them, to frighten them into scaling the treacherous wire where they could so easily get their legs or antlers caught.

She thought of the stag they had nearly hit. In her mind's eye she could see again the unquiet bushes, the moment the stag entered the road, and how her vision was transformed with its sudden presence. She'd controlled the wheel, Craig the brakes. Had he been in control of their direction they might not have crashed through the woods but, instead, held their course and hoped the stag leaped forward and that its appearance in their journey became just another in the long string of near misses that followed Craig's life.

But she had turned the wheel. The stag, so wonderfully perfect in the headlight's bright observance, had disappeared in a fraction of a second as she veered toward the side of the road. They had not hit it, that was one thing she was sure of, and for that small blessing she was grateful. Now she squatted by the clearing and watched the rest of the herd beneath the gauzy moon, their ears flickering. She thought it best to back away from them, but could not bring herself to take even a single retreating step, as getting this far on the stubbly ground had been so hard-won. So she waited until at last one of the larger deer drew its weight back upon its haunches and turned, dissolving through a dark patch of pine, followed then by another, and another.

The clearing was empty now and she entered it without worry, eyeing the fence with its lattice of unforgiving wire. It had been such a struggle to walk, and now she had to climb. With her bare feet and bad light and an unsteady head. Something flashed in her mind: the inevitability that her mother would find out. No matter what she did now, one day, her mother would know. She could not afford to think about such a thing; it dragged her down to imagine that soon, perhaps in a matter of hours even, her mother would find out about the crash, about Craig, about the sex. She couldn't live with that, with her mother knowing. So she thought instead about the fence in front of her. She reached for the top of a post with both hands, and with the light of the moon as her guide, she pushed against the post and stood up on the wire.

JUNE'S WORST DAY AT WORK

Bobbie had been wrong. It wasn't a matter of hours, or of days, or even of months before her mother found out about Craig. Decades later, June still doesn't know what happened on that night in September. She has never considered whether her daughter was in Craig's car, or what transpired between them.

On a Saturday afternoon a lawyer shows up at the department store where she works. June knows nothing about an arrest, nothing about lawyers. She looks up from wiping the glass countertop and sees someone she thinks is a man checking out the makeup testers. Then she realizes it is not a man at all but a woman in her forties with a bald head, completely smooth, shining in the spotlights of the counter. She has no eyebrows or lashes, no hair on her forearms. The woman looks back at June and she sees a question on the woman's face.

June thinks cancer, definitely cancer, but the woman looks healthy enough. Her skin is fresh and unblemished. Her eyes are clear, and she has a warm energy. She smiles at June, showing big glossy teeth with a playful irregularity to the front incisors. It is charming, the smile, and the way she speaks. Leaning over the counter the woman explains to June that she has come this afternoon because she needs to talk to her. The way she speaks, so lightly, so engagingly, makes it possible to believe that she has brought June good news, or (at the very least) the challenge of beautifying an extraordinary woman with a bald head.

"Of course!" June says, and looks at the woman. Without any hair, the face is wholly exposed. There could be no mistakes with foundation, no hard lines that might otherwise have remained hidden in a hairline. Everything had to be perfect. The thought of working on the woman energizes her. "I've got some ideas that should make a difference!" she says. "Never underestimate the power of excellent makeup."

"Makeup?" The woman sounds confused.

June says, "I'm thinking eyeliner to begin with. Have you tried eyeliner before?"

The bald woman seems surprised. "As it happens, I have a lot of trouble with eyeliner," she admits.

"Let me guess," says June. "You're using a drugstore brand that drips down your face the minute you blink your eyes."

The woman laughs. "It runs in thirty seconds and I look like a mime. But that's really not the reason I'm here."

June studies the woman's face. In order to frame her eyes, the woman would have to pencil a coal color on the edges of her eyelids, just above where her lashes should have been, but were not. To be effective, she needed to use quite a bit of the stuff.

"Actually, I'm here about another matter—"

"Hang on, let's sort this one out first!" June says. The woman wears a light foundation and a L'Oréal lipstick. June recognizes the lipstick because she is wearing it too. She tries not to notice the exact angle of the woman's ears, so exposed on the bare skull, or the subtle division in skin where forehead meets scalp. She looks instead at the carved nose, the slightly asymmetrical lips, the open inviting eyes. At a beauty school in Newark, she was once trained to recognize skin hues and face shapes and she tries now to think about these things and not about hair. Or lack of hair. The bald woman's complexion has undertones of blue, with small pores that would take foundation well. June studies the face with its big cheekbones and small chin, deciding it is a diamond.

"I'd go with Chanel," June says. "The chocolate liner, not pure black, not with your"—she was about to say *hair*. What was the matter with her?—"coloring," she adds quickly. She tries to fasten onto another part of the woman's appearance, unrelated to the head. The woman has a long neck, a long torso. Strapped around her middle—twice—is a thick belt in fake rattlesnake skin. June tells herself to look at the snake, not the head. Think about skin, not about hair.

"Really, it doesn't matter," the woman says. She is smiling, but two little frown lines appear between her large eyes. "There's something else I've come to discuss—"

"Oh, but it does!" June says. "It does matter when you don't have—" Oh God, she'd nearly done it again, nearly said the word *hair*! "—when you don't have the right product. But you're going to *love* this," June says, uncapping the tester pencil. She draws a little arc on the back of her hand, softening it immediately with a few swipes from a wedge of sponge. She waits, then rubs the line with her finger before raising her hand to show how it has not lost its soft, perfect shape. "Impressive, huh?" June says.

The woman stares, a look on her face as though she's just witnessed a magic trick. "That's a good pencil!"

"Shall I ring it up for you?"

"Well, perhaps we'll get to that in a moment. It's just that I have another problem—"

June knows all about the problem: baldness. "Let's do something about the eyes first, dear," she says.

"Do I really look *that* bad?" The woman smiles as though there is something funny about June's assessment of her.

"Not at all—" June begins. What surprises June most is that the woman's appearance, taken as a whole, is not altogether marred by her baldness. She has beautiful skin with a kind of luminosity as though whichever way she turns, she is looking into the sumptuous glow of a flattering lamp. It was possible to see the baldness as amplifying her beauty, as water, passing over decorative stones, causes them to shimmer and enlarge. "You're a peach!" June says. "And you'll love this pencil! I'm not just saying that. You really—"

she was about to say *need it*. Oh God! She was about to tell the woman, *You really need it!* "You should always buy the best," she says, "especially when it's near the eye."

The woman touches the corner of her eye and smiles. June admires what she has achieved, adding back in makeup and jewelry and clothes what the lack of hair has taken away. It is as though she has designed herself, painting a self-portrait onto a blank canvas. The look is impressive, and not only because of the artistry involved but because, as June imagines, there is a recurring despair that needs to be overcome in order to begin afresh each morning.

"I'm not really here for eyeliner," the woman says.

Now June very much wants the woman to have the liner. She grabs a bag from behind the counter. "Don't make a decision today!" she announces brightly. "Give some thought to the liner. Let me give you some freebies. You won't believe what I've got back here!"

The woman looks surprised as June fills the glossy black bag with samples of moisturizer, of toner, of exfoliating pearls and day cream. She begins to protest but June insists, adding tiny vials of perfume, a travel lipstick, a sachet of night cream, and an oval blusher the size of a fifty-cent piece.

"You can do a lot with a matte brown powder," June says, still moving. "I've got a sample here and it comes with its own brush." She rummages further, finds a compact containing a trio of gold tones from Estée Lauder, and flashes it at the woman like an ID card. "Nice, huh? And look, some mini Dior . . ."

These last items aren't strictly speaking free samples. They are testers, designed to be fitted into their respective places on the counter display for anyone to try. You weren't supposed to give testers away, but June had a lot of them cluttering the drawers. And she feels such a strong urge to contribute to the effort the bald woman has made. It is as though she is cheering on a marathon runner, that she is an essential voice calling from the sideline.

"I couldn't," the woman says.

"It's no trouble!" June says and then, secretly, in a gesture to which she gives little consideration, she tosses the eyeliner into the sample bag as well.

The woman holds up her hand, refusing the bag. "It's just that I have another reason for being here. An additional reason." The woman has grown quiet, and quietly serious. She is looking directly at June as though trying to make a decision. Not about makeup but about June.

"Yes?" June says. She takes the bag, replete with product, and hands it to the bald woman, who reluctantly accepts it, smiling a thank-you.

The woman says, "I want to know something about your husband."

It is the last thing June expects to hear. "My husband," she says. "Why do you want to know about my husband?"

"I am sure you were relieved when he was acquitted," the woman says.

With the word *acquitted* a barrage of images fills June's mind. Of meetings in law offices and policemen at the door. She is about to tell the woman to turn around and get the hell out of the store, when she hears: "But I've been asked to be his defense attorney in this new trial."

The words seem to blur in June's mind. *"What?"* she says helplessly. "A new trial? We just finished with the other one."

"This is off the record. I'm sure you already know that as Craig's wife you cannot be made to testify if we should ever get as far as the courtroom. But I'd like to know if we can talk sometime, privately. I need to know everything that can be known—" The woman stops, pausing to study June's face. She leans toward her, a breath of hesitation on her lips. "I thought as much," she says. "He hasn't told you, has he?"

June stares. "Told me? Told me what?"

There was the pretty smile again. "Mrs. Kirtz, you need to know that your husband, Craig, has been accused of a third-degree sexual offense."

"Sexual offense?"

The woman nods. "And I am his counsel."

June has already been through the awful ordeal with another girl (her name was kept out of the press, even though Craig's was dragged through every local paper), who rang the radio station one night in order to request a song. She claimed that Craig got into a conversation with her and arranged to meet after his show. The girl eventually told her parents this, and confessed to them, too, that he was having regular sex with her.

June hadn't known anything about the girl. To her relief, that trial had come to an abrupt close. Craig had been left alone.

"Obviously, the more information I can get," the bald woman is saying, but June cannot follow. Her stomach is buzzing; her mind is chaos. June thinks the woman is from the police and all she can focus on is how there is eyeliner at the bottom of the bag in the woman's hand, shielded by the wealth of samples June has provided. She has broken the law. This woman—police or lawyer or whatever she is—will soon know. June decides she will claim it was an accident. She will say it was a slip. Because the woman had scared her with these accusations against Craig and not identified herself with a badge or anything.

"I have no idea what you are talking about," June says. "This is all crazy."

"I thought he might have already discussed this with you—"

"Are you the police?" June says.

"I'm a lawyer. Your husband's lawyer." The woman puts her hand out and touches June's arm. "We will talk later. Meanwhile, you should call your husband."

"Call my husband," June repeats. She knows she is acting strange. She steps back from the counter, crossing her arms in front of her, and is relieved when the woman takes this as a signal.

"It was wrong of me to come like this," she says.

"Craig hasn't done *anything*," June says. "He is innocent."

The woman smiles again, that big reassuring smile. "I'm sure he is." She tells June she had better go now. "We'll talk again soon," she says. She steps away and then turns again to June, holding up the bag. "Thank you for this."

June watches as the woman moves off, the bag looped over her elbow. The words *third-degree sexual offense* burn in her mind.

The woman passes through perfumes, her scalp reflecting the ceiling lights like a mirror. All the way down the aisle, the woman walks in a relaxed manner while June, watching, grows increasingly anxious. She is confused about who this woman is, whether she is going to help Craig or hurt him. She feels a swell of anxiety that seems to go in all directions. Third-degree sexual assault. What was that? She clutches herself with both arms, craning her neck toward the ceiling, then back to the woman, who moves with punishing slowness along the glossy aisles away from her.

She needs the woman to leave, to leave now. The woman bends over her handbag, removing a pair of sunglasses with big dark lenses, and June is glad for the sunglasses, for the fact that the woman is hiding herself from the scrutiny of other shoppers, from the onlookers who seem all at once in abundance. She can't bear this woman being in her store. It is painful—to June it is painful. For a moment, she considers pulling the fire alarm so that the store will be evacuated quickly, ending at once the awful encounter, the accusations against Craig, and the chance, however slim, that there is a security tag on the liner box which would cause an alarm of a different sort at any moment.

The woman begins moving again, floating through the aisles and reaching the exit, her naked head held aloft, tilted back, the sidepieces of the sunglasses slashed across her pale temples. June thinks at last she is leaving, but then, out of the dark recesses of men's coats, arrives a security guard.

He is wearing a dark blue jacket, a navy tie. His shirt is perfectly ironed and his stride, so determined, makes him seem taller than he is. June feels a thud in her belly as though a rock has landed there. She knows what will happen next. She has seen it before with those who, deliberately or by sheer oversight, reach the threshold of the store's big glass doors with unpaid goods and are stopped by this same guard. She cannot bear to watch as the woman is asked to open her bag and produce a receipt, nor the inevitable scene that will follow.

She does not know what to do. She wills herself to rush out to the woman and declare with great apology that she has made a mistake with the bag. She can see herself standing beside the guard, laughing and shaking her head. She really needs to be more careful. *I really need to be more careful!* she would say. But she does not move. When it comes right down to it, she has no guts.

She busies herself with a spray she uses on the glass counter-tops. Bending down, she rubs like mad the clear surface, all the while telling herself to do something to help the woman, do some-thing *now*. Her husband has been accused of a sexual offense; she has planted stolen eyeliner on his lawyer. The woman will be arrested and she is doing nothing about it. Not one thing.

Finally, because she can bear it no longer, she gathers up her courage and opens her mouth to shout out to the security guard. But just as she is about to speak, she realizes he is no longer there. He has vanished. She searches the store and sees him finally off in a corner, checking his watch. She looks for the bald woman and finds her at last, moving through the exit doors, leaving the store. Noth-ing has happened. The guard is now waiting for his lunch break. The woman is on her way out with the bag.

June stares at the woman, at her insouciance, at her confidence. Nobody was ever going to stop her. And this woman has never been afraid of one damned thing, while June has been afraid all her life, it seems. Looking at her now, June sees the sunglasses that she'd imagined as a means of camouflage are not on the woman's nose. They are not hiding the bare eyes, the brow bone without eyebrows. She has placed them high on her forehead to adorn the skull, con-cealing nothing.

June had forgotten, or possibly she had never understood, that there are people in the world who are this confident, this sure of things, and who drift through life in a regal fashion, winning at everything. She sees at once the power of this woman, and the fact that if Craig aligns himself with her, chances are that he will come to no harm.

Suddenly, June rushes from her station at the makeup counter, walking, then running out of the store after the woman, who has disappeared through the glass doors.

The stabbing afternoon heat meets her abruptly as she exits the store, her throat feeling full as she shuffles across the parking lot. She catches up with the woman just as she is settling into the driver's seat of her sports car.

"Yes?" the woman says, surprised.

June leans against the car, but the metal is hot and she lurches back from the stinging burn, still trying to get her breath. "Tell me what the charges are again," she says.

The woman sighs. "Inappropriate sexual contact with a girl under fifteen."

The girl's age glides into June like splintering glass. She looks around to see if anyone is within hearing distance. But the parking lot is nearly empty, its white grid of divided bays like a giant fish skeleton baking in the inordinate sunshine. "I can't believe that," she says. "Craig would never—"

The woman hesitates, then adds, "Mrs. Kirtz, this is your daughter we are talking about."

"My daughter? My daughter is forty-five years old!"

"In the state of Maryland there is no statutory limit to child sex crimes."

"What does that mean, statutory limit?"

"It means that alleged crimes from even years back can be tried as though they happened today. If your daughter convinces a judge that she was the victim of a sexual crime when she was under the age of consent, it will be as if that crime took place today. Well, almost. I'm giving you a very general account and . . ."

The lawyer is still talking but June can make no sense of what she says. Why is she speaking of her Bobbie? She has not seen Bobbie for thirty years. What would she have to do with any of this?

"We can only hope there isn't enough evidence that your daughter—"

"Bobbie hasn't lived with us since she was a teenager! She hasn't even visited. And I have no idea where she lives—"

"I think that is the point, Mrs. Kirtz," the woman says evenly. "She *was* a teenager—"

"No."

"If it happened at all."

"It didn't!"

"She claims that she left home for this reason—"

"That is ridiculous!" June can't hear one more word.

The woman gets out of the car. She stands in front of June, almost a foot taller, looking at her with her large eyes. "I'm sorry. I hate being the one to tell you this. I did try to call you but the phone was never answered."

"Craig doesn't like the phone. He worries fans will find him at home so we don't answer it. And there has been such a lot of trouble since the last crazy girl accused him—"

"I need to ask you about something. It could really help us. Your daughter says—"

"You've been talking with my daughter?"

"She gave a statement. She claims she was in a car accident in September 1978 in which Craig was driving. Do you know about this?"

"About the accident, yes. Of course I do. He lost his eye."

"And your daughter was with him? She'd have been fifteen."

That was impossible. How could Bobbie say such a thing? How could she expect to be believed?

"My daughter would be dead if she'd been in that car!" June says. "So that is a lie."

She notices how the woman looks at her, how she seems suddenly to question her judgment, perhaps because she has just called her own daughter a liar.

"I think the court will agree with you that it is unlikely she was in the car, which would perhaps discredit her. If there isn't enough evidence, the judge may not even hear the case in the first place. Just to be clear. You don't remember her being involved in any sort of accident?"

"Absolutely not."

"She wasn't in the car?"

"I know she wasn't."

The attorney raises her eyebrows. "How do you *know*? This is important."

"Because I was at the hospital hours after the accident. Craig was brought in and no other person was in the car or at the scene. The police were very thorough. It was—what do you call it?—a pivotal moment in my life. I'll never forget."

The lawyer gives June her dazzling smile. "Like I said, if we can discredit her on the car crash, we can discredit her altogether. She was at home at the time of the crash?"

"Yes, she was."

"You can testify she had no injuries? That she was home at the time?"

June nods.

"There's a date, September seventh. And you say you remember where you were on that date?"

"I do. I remember everything! It was hotter than Hades, just like today. I was driving home. Bobbie was waiting for me. She wasn't with Craig at all."

"Normally, a wife does not have to testify, but what you are saying could help him."

She shakes her head. It feels as though she is saving Craig. Saving him from drowning. "Then I'll testify."

"Good," the lawyer says. "You may just win his case for him."

CRASH NIGHT:

WHAT JUNE REMEMBERS

It was the hottest day of the year, no rain for weeks, the tail end of a scorching season. These health-and-beauty trade shows used to excite June, back in the days when staying at a hotel, even a Howard Johnson's, felt special. But now shows were little more than long, solid days on her feet and a lot of extra hours. She wanted to go home, take a bath, sleep in her own bed. She had planned to start driving earlier, she didn't like leaving Bobbie at home on her own, but her car had no air-conditioning and the heat sat heavily on the whole of the East Coast, so that the dust and humidity found her even in the shade, the forecast declaring record temperatures. Due to an engine fault she was reliant on movement to keep the car's fan in operation, and she worried what would happen if she was stuck in traffic. She'd be stranded on four lanes of concrete, cooking.

By three o'clock, the heat had risen further. The radio reported schools, newly opened for the academic year, canceling their afternoon sports activities. Local TV stations chattered about the importance of hydration, symptoms of heat stroke, risks to the elderly. She'd already checked out of the hotel; she wanted to go home. But when she reached her car, its sauna interior unchanged even with the doors open, she turned on the radio and heard that there was a pileup on the parkway. She realized now she could hear ambulance sirens, the noise seeming to mix with the broiling sun.

The waiting and the heat and the sirens made her anxious, so she went back to the hotel and bought cupcakes from the little gift shop inside, fooling herself into believing she was buying them for Bobbie. Some minutes later, she discovered that the turnpike also had major problems and now there was no choice but to remain in the cramped hotel lobby—her room key long returned to the desk, her car motionless in the parking lot amid shivering rises of heat—for God knows how many hours.

The cupcakes were in a pretty box with a ribbon. She reached for them, then diverted herself by arranging the collection of magazines on the square glass table into a concertina. She managed a few more minutes, thumbing through the pages of the hotel's travel magazine, the cupcakes untouched, until at last she gave in and plucked the colorful ribbon from the smooth white box. There they were, six perfectly shaped cakes, all different flavors, all laden with creamy frosting and sparkling sugar sprinkles. It was the anxiety and boredom that caused the cupcakes to disappear as, one by one, she plunged her tongue into their whipped frosting. The calories, she knew, were astronomical, and she despaired once more that everything good in life came at so high a price.

At last, the big orange sun lowered itself in the sky and the traffic report brightened. She pressed through the springy automatic doors of the hotel, meeting at once a wall of fuzzy warmth and a cloud of insects that might have been waiting for her all these hours. She looked across the parking lot and saw she'd left her passenger-side door wide open. She trotted in her heels across the asphalt, hoping there was still charge in the battery.

The seats were no longer red hot as they had been hours earlier but warm like wet towels, even inviting. She hoped that she'd be home by midnight. If all went well, Bobbie might still be awake. She would set up a fan beside her daughter's bed, and another next to her own, curl up in the cool sheets, and get the sleep she now longed for and which would come, she knew, as soon as she closed her eyes.

But the journey was a disaster, the roads a mess, and her stomach rumbled beneath her flowery blouse from all the sugar with which she'd poisoned herself. Yes, she admitted, poisoned herself, wrecking yet another diet day, this time with the unconquerable cupcakes—six of them in total—not because she'd been that hungry but because they came in a box of six. She was ready to check herself into a fat farm, chain a leg to a vegetable patch, eat only what she could hoe. It was past time for a change, she told herself. Way past time.

She thought about men, about the way they looked with their shirts off, their chest hair, long torsos, the way they felt and smelled. It had been a long while since she'd been with a man and she couldn't see how she would attract one if she stayed at this weight, which she saw as the great drawback to her life, the reason for everything being amiss. But she had been here before, having this same little talk with herself, and in some ways she was at home with such desperation.

She pawed at her stomach, untucking her blouse, creased and in need of laundering, then hiked her skirt above her knees to make driving easier. It was too tight, the skirt, and she recalled the days when it had hung comfortably, wondering what had happened between then and now. Cupcakes, that's what had happened, and all their irresistible cousins: brownies, doughnuts, baked goods in general. She thumbed loose the skirt's button, then notched down the zipper a few inches. There was no law against undressing while driving, none that she knew of anyway, and while truckers might see a little too much leg from their high vantage points, it was unlikely they'd look at her leg, which had its own defense mechanism against voyeurism, being round as a Labrador and a shade of bluish white normally associated with recovered bodies.

She tried not to think about this, nor the condition of her Plymouth sedan, and especially not the new Dorothy Hamill haircut that she felt made her round face rounder and had done nothing whatsoever to lengthen her neck, despite promises by the stylist at the salon. The haircut mistake happened, she knew, because it took no effort to change hair, while bodies took longer, possibly forever. If she'd been in any doubt of this, some unkind bastard at her weekly weigh-in had reminded her of the fact a few weeks earlier by saying that shoes and hair were the only thing fat women could control, which is why they did it.

Did what? she'd asked. She'd been standing by the buffet table, wearing a freshly ironed dress and new patent leather pumps. She'd curled her hair and polished her earrings before clipping them on. It had all been part of a new image she was trying to cultivate, to look more stylish, sophisticated.

Fuss with the hair. Buy every damned shoe, the man had said.

The weekly meeting took place in a church. On the wall above his head was a crucifix and posters of Scripture. Vases of carnations left over from Sunday wilted on tables. She ought to have said something sharp to the man, something cruel, but instead she'd asked him whether he'd ever stooped so low in his pursuit of a thinner self that he'd found himself actually envying Christ's trim figure on the cross.

As she said this, she noticed the man widen his eyes at her. She took this as a sign of interest. She continued, explaining that she'd occasionally looked up at the image of Jesus on the cross, ignoring the bleeding feet, the pierced palms, the bloodied brow, and instead admired only his leanness. It made her think she was more desperate than others, and she wondered if it was a common thought, and whether, indeed, he'd ever felt the same.

Jesus, he'd said.

Yes. He's always portrayed as very thin.

I meant, Jesus what a crazy thing to say.

He stared at her as though she was foul. He was not a handsome man, not someone who would normally intimidate her. He had the swollen belly of a drunk, a hernia sticking out under his shirt like the stem of a pumpkin, a pink can of Tab in his stout hand. The first time June had noticed him there—one of the few men who attended the weekly weigh-ins—she'd imagined him to be a warm, avuncular member of the group, but she been wildly mistaken.

I was only being honest, June said. She wanted him to change tone, to tell her he was sorry and he hadn't meant it that way. *I was being honest about how I feel,* she continued. She smiled broadly at him. She'd taken to wearing red lipstick—true red and not pink—as part of her effort to appear more chic. The smile ought to have softened him, but it had the opposite effect.

I bet you have a whole closet of shoes, he'd said coldly.

She couldn't think of a reasonable retort. She kept imagining that a man like him, whose back was round with fat, whose neck had long disappeared into his shoulders, whose stomach would make it awkward to drive a car, let alone to walk a mile, was only so vicious because he, himself, was wounded.

Actually, I don't have a lot of shoes, she said gently.

He looked at her directly, licking his upper lip, then his bottom lip, as though sharpening a pair of knives. *I don't believe you,* he said, like he'd been in her closet already and taken an inventory, knew exactly how many slingbacks and ankle boots and clogs and open-toed sandals and mules; every color—yes, she did keep them in order by color—and the succession of long boots that her calves had outgrown, extra wide, and then extra extra wide, and the heels she could no longer balance in.

Well, it's true, she managed, before having to get away from him, away from the meeting, the other people, including the slim figure of Christ dying. She pushed past the man, rushing outside to her car, where she climbed into the driver's seat, put the key into the ignition, and waited to stop shaking so she could drive home.

She thought about the guy now because, beside her, sitting high up in an eighteen-wheeler, was someone who looked just like him, staring down at her with an expression that may have been intrigue or disgust. She couldn't tell if he disapproved of her driving or he'd figured out that she had unfastened her body from the control-top panty hose and the great harness of a bra that kept her shape. She did not like being so untidy. She *was* precise with her clothes. To be seen as she was now, even by the truck driver, pained her. But she could not afford to distract herself when the traffic was so fierce. No hard shoulder, crazy speeds, radio full of static. For hours, she had been wedged between cars on her left and a metal fence on her right, so close it was within touching distance.

And so she plunged on through the night, through the gritty air that smelled of exhaust fumes. Her eyes itched. Somewhere during the journey, another car had hit a pigeon and feathers exploded all over the road—and now there were tufts of white down stuck on June's windshield, though she'd done everything she could with her wipers. All of this—the cupcakes, the unpleasant man at her weigh-in, the truck driver, the feathers—was what made it so important that she find her radio station as soon as possible. Her favorite radio station, like her own bed and bath, brought her peace. As she drove toward the sphere of its signal, the all-important wave range that would bring the midnight show clearly through the car's speakers, she thumbed the dial, hearing the static lessen with each mile she traveled, and was relieved. She watched the clock for the minute when Craig Kirtz would burst on the air.

He always started the show with a cool hello, as though he'd been waiting in a hotel bar all evening for his listeners to arrive. She tuned in to him most nights, his voice alighting like a nocturnal creature across the night sky. It wasn't the music he played that lured her—sometimes she didn't even like the songs—but the way he spoke, the tenor of his voice. Whenever he introduced a love song, a slow song, a ballad, he made a kind of direct address to the audience, as though he had someone special in mind. He had a deep, velvety voice that floated across the airwaves, and while she imagined there was probably nothing sincere in his seductive murmurings, no live, actual woman to whom he was speaking, and certainly not her (why could she not remember this?), she pretended that it was she who was the object of his longing. She remembered such language of love, of desire, of a special harmony from years ago, before Bobbie's father had died. And while the voice could never take the place of a husband's voice, it felt intimate and thrilling.

Craig Kirtz. She wondered if it was his real name.

She admitted the little crush only to herself, how the sound of his name seemed to separate from all the words that preceded it and all those that followed. Even when she met someone else with that same name, Craig, she was suddenly wrenched into attention, as though the name held a tiny charge that freshly lit all her senses.

Nobody else knew how she felt about him, but she was embarrassed anyway. Craig was many years younger, a disc jockey (was there a sexier profession?), handsome, and tall, probably surrounded by girls. And while she waited nightly for his show to come on, feeling a rising anticipation, she also loathed herself for holding out— she had to admit this—a wincing hope that by some miracle he might one day turn his attention to her. It was not entirely out of the question—not strictly a hundred percent impossible, that is. Because among the unlikely events that defined her life so far, June had in fact made a friend of Craig Kirtz, or near enough a friend. The thing that made Craig special to her, aside from the way he cooed into the microphone in whatever distant room he occupied at the station, was the fact she had seen him in person—several times, in fact—and that he not only knew her name but had even been to her house.

She'd met him the first time as he stood by the radio station's van, giving away bumper stickers. She'd come out of the Safeway with Bobbie and there he was, telling everyone to come over and enter a drawing for a record album, pick up a bumper sticker, maybe win a shirt. She'd allowed Bobbie to enter the raffle and later, incredibly, discovered she'd won the album. To their amazement Craig dropped by the house to bring her the prize. He wore Levi's and boots, a braided leather belt. Handsome, and so very kind to her, sitting in her kitchen. She'd offered him a Coke, then on second thought dug out a couple of Budweisers from the far reaches of her fridge. *How sweet that you made the trip out here yourself,* June had said.

I remembered you and your lovely daughter, Craig replied. *How could I forget?*

It was this last remark that stuck in her mind, and the way he'd said it so sweetly: *How could I forget?*

Then one day she ran into him at the Department of Motor Vehicles. She'd been there to renew her license and had come into the building and seen him sitting in one of the terrible hard seats in the main area, looking bored, tapping his thigh rhythmically with his thumb as though playing the drums. His mood, she later came to understand, was set permanently on rock 'n' roll and he seemed oblivious to where he was or the people around him who made it clear they did not like his "dinging" sounds or how he hissed when, in his mind's eye, he'd hit the snare.

He'd been wearing a duck-down jacket and those same leather boots that put him up around six three, his eyes hidden behind sunglasses. She didn't quite understand why he was wearing the sunglasses indoors like that, but he was a minor celebrity, she supposed, and did not want to be recognized. She'd spotted him right away. Once she'd distracted him from the song inside his head, it hadn't taken long to get into conversation.

Do you remember me? she'd asked him.

You've got a girl, don't you? A daughter. Nice kid.

So he had remembered her. It seemed impossible, but it was true. She tried to breathe easily, to think of him as a friend, just a friend like anyone else.

Does your family live out this way? she asked him.

Foster family, but that was back in Maine, and they've kind of moved on, he said.

Foster family, she repeated, the words rolling in her mouth. She'd wondered whether that meant they'd just looked after his physical needs or whether that meant real family. The way he said *that was back in Maine* made her feel like she'd missed an important fact stated earlier about his life and childhood and where he'd found himself through the years. Also, she wondered what *moved on* meant. Moved on to another place, or perhaps another child now that he was grown?

Are you going back for Thanksgiving? she asked.

Back where?

Again, she'd felt that she'd missed a vital aspect of the discussion, that she ought to understand more than she did.

You could come to us! she'd offered. *It's only Bobbie and me. Informal. I mean, you don't have to decide right now—*

She knew he would say no; of course he would say no. Why on earth would a celebrity spend Thanksgiving in the quiet of her home? He probably had parties to go to, any number of invitations. She'd waited for him to tell her he was spending Thanksgiving with his girlfriend, but he looked at her without replying, until she could no longer hold his eyes. Then he was called to the counter.

She pulled a pen from her bag and wrote her phone number hurriedly on the back of a receipt, then pushed it into his hand. *There you go!* she'd said, and watched as he closed his fist over the note and walked to the counter.

She'd felt ridiculous, inviting him the way she had. She would have raced to the ladies' room to hide, except her number was coming up and she didn't want to miss her turn. She was still in the same place when Craig finished at the counter. He marched across the waiting room without even looking at her while she pressed her knees together and forced herself to not speak or move or turn or wave. It was a great relief—a blessing—when at the door he turned and nodded his head goodbye.

She was sure that was the end of the matter, that she would never see him again. But then, the day before Thanksgiving, the phone rang and there he was, his voice in her ear.

Thanksgiving still on? You and your daughter? he'd said with that same soft caressing tone to his words, a dark, low rumbling like the deep purr of a lion. *I'd like to come along if you're still asking.*

Yes! Yes, of course! She hadn't even bothered hiding her enthusiasm. For the next twenty-four hours, she planned her outfit, prepared recipes, tried different styles for her hair, arranged the table with various centerpieces, all the while attending to the dreadful persistent thought that either Craig would not come at all or that he'd not come alone. He'd bring a girlfriend, June imagined, a despairing thought that made it difficult for her to look forward to the dinner as much as she would have liked. She worried she would be forced to entertain the two of them right there in her own house, that her affection for Craig would be obvious and shame her. She could not ask if he planned to bring a girlfriend, either, because to do so would be to suggest that he ought to. She tried to put it from her mind but by the time Thanksgiving dinner was in the oven, she was so sure he'd arrive with a girlfriend that she'd almost put out an extra place setting.

A few hours later, she watched his car roll down her street, then the door opened and he got out. He wore a corduroy jacket and had combed his hair back. She waited for the other door to open and for a long-legged, glamorous woman to emerge from inside the Buick. But no woman came. He walked to the steps by himself, just him, all alone, and she nearly leaped at the sight.

He'd brought a couple of T-shirts from the station as gifts. Throughout dinner, he told them all about what it was like to work in radio. June watched the way Bobbie tensed in fascination, her face shining toward Craig, the beautiful child mixing now with the teenage girl she'd newly become. Bobbie had been entranced by Craig. He told her stories of where he'd worked, of the famous disc jockeys he'd known. He talked about band members he knew personally. He did an impression of Casey Kasem. June was grateful, if a little jealous, when Craig promised to let Bobbie come to the station and see it in real life.

That would be fun, wouldn't it? he'd asked her, and Bobbie had nodded, unsure how to accept so great an offer. To be inside a real radio station was an unimaginable treat.

At the end of the evening, June said, *You'll have dinner again with us, won't you?* She couldn't bring herself to say *have dinner with me.* It felt too unlikely, even preposterous. She knew she still needed to lose some weight; she needed to wear better clothes, to do *something.*

All she had been able to offer—for the moment—was the appeal of a home-cooked family meal. Weak bait, but maybe Craig was a hungry fish?

Sure, he had said. And for a little while he'd come have supper with her and Bobbie. He'd astound them both with his knowledge of records and hit charts. He'd reel off the Top 10, even sometimes the Top 20, for any year in a decade. He could tell you whether a years-old album was gold, silver, or platinum without pausing for thought. Bobbie adored him—that was obvious—and hugged him at the door as he was leaving.

She's fond of you, June had said.

She's some girl.

It was nice of you to remember her birthday.

He'd brought her several record albums and a big box of chocolate for her fourteenth.

Least I could do.

But then, just as it had appeared he and June were establishing something, he'd disappeared. She resigned herself to the fact he was not attracted to her, not interested in *that way*. Even so, she listened to him on the radio and sometimes sent him a note. *You played my favorite song today!* she would write, though that might not be true. Once, he'd dedicated a song to "the little lady in the house surrounded by woods," and she'd thought for sure, or at least perhaps, he'd meant her.

All these thoughts sifted through June's mind as she drove. After the awful heat wave and the hours of fierce traffic, and the tired remaining last hour of the journey, his voice was the tonic she needed. When he did not begin his show, she wondered what had happened. She thought perhaps her car's clock was fast, but when she checked her wristwatch, she saw that it was well past midnight and still no greeting to the listeners from Craig, nor any explanation. Songs played, one after the other, and the music felt to June like silence, each song like another three-minute block of empty time.

Something was wrong. Twenty past midnight and Craig still

hadn't arrived on the air. It was a terrible thought that he could disappear from the airwaves and that such an important part of her life could conclude so abruptly. She wondered if something had *happened* to him. The station sounded unmanned, just a parade of songs, one following another, and it seemed ominous, a sure sign that Craig was either injured or dead. She now felt certain that something bad *had* happened; Craig was gone.

This notion that he was physically injured was so powerful that she finally pulled into a gas station. She teetered in her heels over the broken cement to a phone booth in order to call the station. Why not? she reasoned. She was a devoted fan. The station should be grateful for listeners who cared so much. But standing in the booth, enveloped in the smell of beer and urine, looking through the glass door mottled with dead gnats, and seeing stars peeking through a veil of purple sky, she considered that the people at the station would not be grateful. They would see straight through her, spy the inane, hopeless crush she had on Craig, and dismiss her completely. Nevertheless, she continued. Under the halo of a yellow lamp, in a cloud of stinging insects, she dropped her coins through the slot and waited. But the station didn't answer. He probably had dozens of women calling him nightly. Too many like her.

Back in the car she decided she was just man-starved. That was her trouble. Whenever she left home for a period of time, a more adventuresome spirit took hold and she did things like buy a new dress or get her hair restyled or call a man. At home, in the normal routine of her days, it was possible to live in a closed, sexless world. She sold makeup to women—who are you going to meet in a job like that? Women, that's who. She wanted a man, or at least his voice, and now she had nothing. She told herself there were any number of reasons Craig was off the air now. He could be recording commercials or creating voice-overs. There was little reason for her to worry. Even so, a little while later, when Craig still hadn't arrived on the air, she pulled into a rest station, already reaching for her purse.

The phone was next to the bathroom door and she hoped nobody flushed while she was talking. She dialed the number, then listened to the phone ring and ring. She was tired; the phone seemed heavy in her hand. She'd almost decided to hang up when she heard a click and someone's voice. "Hello?" she said, cautiously. "Is this—?" She heard music in the background. It was, indeed, the station. She did not ask if Craig was there. She said, "I am a friend of Craig Kirtz. Can you tell me why he is not on the air now?"

She was surprised by how she came across, not like a silly, lurking fan but businesslike, concerned. The person on the other end of the phone, the screener—a young man by the sound of his voice— treated her accordingly. Craig was now forty-five minutes late, he explained. She heard the sigh at the end of the line. "We don't know why."

"Shouldn't you check the hospitals?" she said.

"Check hospitals?" The man sounded alarmed. "Lady, I've got to get his show filled."

SHE DROVE TO a hospital—in the early hours after midnight, at a time when reason sleeps, it seemed a sensible thing to do. She parked the car, then made her way across the lot toward the main building, with its blocky wards and tiny squares of lit windows that gave it an all-night feel. She entered the wide doors at the front of the emergency room, hearing the whoosh of them opening and feeling the sudden chill of air-conditioning within. It seemed to June she'd been ebbing toward this hospital all night, but with no clear reason why she had come. A young man had gone a little AWOL—it did not mean he was in the hospital and it certainly did not mean he was in *this* hospital. She'd taken her fantasy of Craig too far, not only half believing that it could be she to whom he was speaking words of affection when introducing love songs but now that it might be she who came to his aid at the time of his greatest need. She was pathetic, she decided. She wanted to leave the hospital, the state, the nation. She wanted to never be seen again. But she had come this far.

She went to the desk and asked after Craig, explaining he was a radio celebrity, expected right now at the station, and that everyone was concerned about him.

"We are asking hospitals all around the capital if he has been admitted," June said seriously, as though this were a reasonable thing to do. If the receptionist—or whoever she was—mistakenly believed she was from the station, that was okay by June.

"Who would have brought him in?" the receptionist asked. She had corn-yellow hair with dark roots. Her eyeliner had filled the creases beneath her eyes, and she wore an expression as though she'd been hounded all night by crazy people and June was just another.

"I don't know," said June.

"What I mean is do you know if it was an ambulance? Do you have a reason to think he's at this hospital?"

"No. Yes. I don't know."

The receptionist took a sharp breath. June told her what he looked like, his age, height, a guess at his weight. The receptionist checked through a clipboard full of admission sheets, pausing finally and looking up at June.

"Wait here," she said, then disappeared behind a curtain for a few minutes. When she returned, she went to the corner of the desk and made a phone call. Then she approached June with a curious expression as though she wasn't quite sure what to say. Yes, a person of that description had been brought in.

"Oh!" June said. She was horrified. She felt she had created this scenario somehow. That the power of her imagination had caused Craig to be in this hospital, in pain.

"His first name is Craig but his last name . . . well, he has his radio name but his actual last name is . . . uh . . ." She wondered how long she could stall. If she really knew the man, she'd know his real name.

"We've got Kirtz," the receptionist offered. "Hang on a second." The receptionist held up a finger.

June watched as she went back to the phone and punched some numbers. The woman was turned away from June, having dragged the receiver as far from the desk as the cord would allow. Another woman, a black nurse with a stethoscope and a crisp white trouser suit, arrived a few minutes later from behind a curtain and told June she was not allowed to discuss patients with anyone except relatives.

"Are you a relative, ma'am?" She had a thin flat face with a wide nose, deep lines beneath her straightened bangs. Her eyelids hung heavily, like two weighted curtains, and she looked serious, even angry, or it may have been that after so many years of organizing patients and staff, an air of exasperated bossiness had become her natural state. Typed out on a badge above her shirt pocket was the biblical name Esther.

"Oh . . . yes. Yes, I am a relative," June said.

"You his wife?" Esther asked.

"Not his wife, no."

"Then who are you?"

She thought for a moment. "His wife."

Esther gave her a look, then shook her head slowly from side to side, as though everything about June was difficult. "He had a car accident," she began. There was an explanation about how he'd been retrieved, and that he had not been conscious when they brought him in, and how there had been no number in his wallet so they hadn't notified his next of kin.

"Next of kin," June repeated and wondered if he was dead. When her real husband had died, had been found dead, in fact, it had taken three of the staff just to cope with her. And she wondered if it was her apparent calm now that made this nurse doubt who she was. "How bad is it?"

"He broke his arm—"

"That's it, his arm?"

"And a head injury and . . . are you *really* his wife?"

"We've been married for three years," June heard herself say. As she said the words she began almost to believe them. "We have a daughter," she added, then felt a shiver of panic and a deeper voice calling to her from inside herself, asking, *Have you lost your damned mind?*

She sensed a subtle shift in tone in the nurse, who came out from behind the desk and took her to one side, huddling beside a fire extinguisher mounted on the wall and a big stainless-steel table on legs. June was told it was serious but that he was stable. No, he could not be seen now. She could go home or she could wait.

June searched out a chair in the waiting room, joining a few other people with their newspapers and bandages and kiddies in strollers. The seat was hard plastic, linked by the arm to the one next to it. Across the aisle was a family—a mother and father with their little girl whose lap was filled with a large, gaudy pink teddy bear, and her foot wrapped in ice. The foot was swollen so that it looked like a paddle, the toes bluish. The girl did not look especially unhappy. Like many of the injured, she had an almost giddy response to her accident. She bounced the teddy bear on her knee, then pretended to feed it some of a Hershey's bar she was eating. June did not worry for the family; the worst was over for them and now only good things would happen. The foot would be x-rayed, then set in a cast. They would go home with the feeling of near escape. She was not even that worried about Craig. He was alive; she was here waiting for him. The doctors would fix him. Every bad thing about the day—the long drive, the dust of the road, the sun's uncomfortable heat—was over now. She could relax in the waiting room as these others around her were doing, with a sense that within the labyrinthine corridors of the massive hospital, and all its privacy curtains and examining rooms and surgical suites, good was being done for those who needed it.

COURT BEGINS

She doesn't understand much about criminal court hearings, but Bobbie is pretty sure she can't be seen driving her mother's car, or admit to speaking with June last night when she'd arrived into her bedroom like an aged Thumbelina. There are strict laws about trying to persuade witnesses. June could be held in contempt of court, Bobbie worries. And then she thinks how she's only been back in her mother's life for a matter of hours and is already trying to protect her.

She parks the Impala a mile from the courthouse, locks the door, and leaves the keys on the front wheel. She's going to walk the rest of the way. The traffic is heavy, with sudden explosions from car horns that unnerve her on this raw morning, but it is better to walk and clear her head and not have to answer any questions about why she is driving her mother's car.

The courthouse looks like a college library, set back from the road with fat pillars and impressive stairs, a concrete fortress that scares her. She can't bear the thought of climbing the stairs to the entrance. She wishes she was going anywhere but through the massive doors and into the entrance hall, which has the official feel of a municipal building and a worrying coldness to it as though the law is there to frighten people, not to keep them safe. The only people she is allowed to talk to right now are from the district attorney's office and she tries to find the conference room where she is to meet with them before the hearing. She has been told that everywhere else, and everyone else, is off-limits.

"Hello, hello!" she hears, and there is the assistant district attorney, a young man named Dreyer, in a tailored suit and crimson tie. He has pink cheeks, a receding blond hairline. He looks like he's fresh out of law school but has, in fact, been litigating for years. He tells Bobbie this is a nice judge and an outstanding jury. "They will like you!" He smiles, as though he is about to introduce her to his parents. "And here's coffee!" He holds out a paper cup. She notices his cuff links, two little white-gold squares, and his wedding ring, a fat band on his young hand.

"I hope you take it with milk," he says.

As they go into a side room next to the courtroom she says, "Am I going to be humiliated in there?"

"Absolutely not," he says. "I wouldn't let that happen."

She wants to ask him about Craig but doesn't want to risk hearing something that will upset her. Dreyer must sense this in her because he says, "He's not going to talk to you. He may *look* at you, but so what? He's the one on trial, not you."

"He doesn't worry me."

She knows he doesn't believe her. He says, "Don't direct your answers at him when you testify. Look at the jury. And if you can't look at them, look at me."

"My mother—"

"Your mother won't be in court until after you testify. She's a defense witness. You won't even see her."

"I'm afraid she's going to try to, you know, disrupt things."

Dreyer looks at her sharply, his eyebrows knitting together. "What makes you say that?"

"I think she's gone a little nuts. She showed up in my room last night. She practically climbed through the window."

"Showed up at your *hotel* room? Does anybody else know this?"

"The woman who let her in, I guess."

"You didn't talk to her about the case?"

"I didn't talk to her at all. I drove her home."

"You haven't spoken to any other witnesses?"

"No."

"Not to Daniel Gregory?"

Dan. Absolutely not. "No," she said. "I haven't."

"Not even on the phone?"

She hadn't called him, though she'd wanted to. When she'd returned to the room, having dropped her mother off, she'd found his number in the book. She'd even written it down. But she hadn't called him, mostly because by then it was too late at night to phone a man you haven't spoken to in decades. "No," she says to Dreyer. "The last I heard from Dan was when he told me about the girl, the one who said Craig had been having sex with her. The one whose case got messed up."

Dreyer says, "Then stop worrying. Relax. This morning is easy. You are talking to me. We're just going to have a chat while you are on the witness stand. You know all the questions and you know all the answers."

His words are designed to reassure her but she cannot help feeling as though she has done the wrong, that it is she who is the defendant. There is something discomforting about bringing this charge—in this court, at this time—over a matter that happened decades ago. Even she asks herself the question that is on everyone's mind: Why bring it all up *now*?

She glances into the courtroom as they pass, noticing the wooden benches set out like church pews, the judge's seat like an altar, the jury seats to the side as though they are a choir stall, and it seems to her as close to Judgment Day as mankind can create. She wishes for the hundredth time she had never given a statement. She wishes she'd never responded to the e-mail from Dan, or opened the attachment that revealed a scanned copy of a recent article about Craig, reporting that he'd been acquitted of a statutory rape charge. There had been a mistake made during the trial, some sort of technical error that Bobbie didn't entirely understand. What she did understand was the girl's age: fourteen. The girl had even gone to her same junior high.

She waits with Dreyer in a small room to the side of the court. She tries to remember the last time she was this nervous, the last time she felt so exposed. If she thought about it long enough she'd bring herself right back to when she was a young teenager, loaded to the breaking point with anxiety about Craig.

"Five things I want you to remember when the defense attorney questions you," Dreyer says. He holds his palm up, his fingers in the air. "Number one, listen carefully to the question." Down goes a finger. "Number two, answer only the question being asked." Another finger down. "What's number three?"

"If I don't understand the question, I ask them to repeat it, or to rephrase it."

"Exactly."

"And four?" She can't remember four.

"Four is you answer in as few words as possible. Lastly, don't worry if she makes you answer yes or no. That's what she's going to do. She wants to reduce every answer to yes or no. Go with it. We'll fix everything up on redirect."

Redirect is when Dreyer speaks to her on the stand again. He will come along after the cross-examination and ask questions that will allow her to expand on her answers and present them more favorably.

"Do you know what time it is?" he says.

There is a clock on the wall and she glances toward it but is stopped by Dreyer, who places his hand on her arm, then shakes his head in a mild scold. "Try again. Listen to the question, answer *only* the question." He studies her, his eyes fixed on her eyes. "Now, do you *know* what time it is?" His eyebrows are raised, his lips parted. He leans forward, waiting.

"No," she says finally.

He lets out a long breath. "Perfect. You are correct. You don't know."

She can hear the swing of the doors and the shuffling of people as they cram onto the courtroom seats. She hears the bailiff settling everyone down for the proceedings and the judge entering. She imagines the packed room, the reporters in the wings, the court reporter with the tiny steno machine, the clerk with his Bible.

"When do you go in?" she asks Dreyer.

"In a minute."

She wonders who will watch the hearing. The parents of the girl who accused Craig of statutory rape will be there; members of the public who know him from the radio, of course. Plenty of journalists, a number of his fans.

The air-conditioning is weak; the room has no windows and is hot. She imagines the temperature of the courtroom elevating by the minute. She imagines her mother somewhere in the building. She thinks of Dan, considering what he looks like after so many years. She cannot stop herself thinking about Craig. He will sit with his long legs, his big frame taking up a lot of room. He will be wearing a suit and tie, a handsome middle-aged man, a man of the community whom she fears the jury may love.

"I'm going to leave you here for a little while. You'll be brought in shortly," Dreyer says. "We're going to take it from the day you met him, then forward up until the car accident. If you need a recess, say so. Or just gesture. Do this." He makes a little movement with his finger. "Okay?"

"Okay."

"We need to recount as many of the separate times he had sex with you as we can. Just like we've gone over before, but this time you'll be saying it in front of the court and that will be more difficult. Just follow the program. Exactly as we've practiced."

She nods.

"And of course we will slow down and really focus on how you came through that accident in such good condition," Dreyer says.

"I didn't."

"I mean, that you lived."

"Oh, yes, well there's that."

"The defense is going to ask why you didn't go for help."

"I didn't want my mother knowing," she says, the beginning of an answer she has already rehearsed with Dreyer.

"You are going to have to explain how you got home, having walked all night, without your mother suspecting anything."

Bobbie nods. "My mother was with *him* that night," she says. "From that night forward she was always with him."

"I know, but you need to say that. And you need to say—"

"That she didn't find out because by the time she got home, she would have believed I was at school."

"Good," Dreyer says. She has answered the way she is meant to. He wants it all down pat. No errors. No surprises. "One more thing. Do you know how many miles you walked that night?" he asks.

"From the accident, you mean?" She tries to remember the miles; it was noted in a document Dreyer had given her months previously.

Dreyer answers the question for her. "Seven miles barefoot after a near-fatal collision," he says. "That may be difficult for a jury to believe. Describe it the way you did in your statement. In detail. They are going to want to know how you managed it, a kid of fifteen."

She almost laughs. "Well, that's exactly how I managed. Because I was fifteen. I wish I was as tough now." She could hear the murmurings of conversation in the courtroom next door, the bailiff making announcements.

"Even so, review your testimony," Dreyer says with a serious, almost grave expression. "I know you are ready, but be extra ready. Think about that night and exactly what you did. Every footstep if you can."

"Okay," she promises.

"And when I press you for why you didn't ask for help, for why you were able to walk so far after such a collision, remember that I am only speaking like that because the defense is going to ask you anyway. We have our chance early on to set it in the jury's mind that the whole thing makes sense."

She nods. She reminds herself that she always knew this would be hard.

"She will try to discredit you during cross-examination, first by trying to convince the jury you weren't in that car. Second by claiming your hatred of Craig as an intrusion in your childhood is what brought you here today and not anything he did to you directly. But it won't be easy for her, believe me."

"Why won't it be easy for her?" Bobbie asks meekly.

Dreyer smiles. She loves how confident he is. She wonders what magic pill people take that allows them this measure of confidence. He says, "Because she knows that if she treats you badly and the verdict goes against him in the end, the sentencing will bear that out. He'll get slammed with more time."

He snaps his briefcase shut. He pulls it forward and she hears the leather scrape against the table. Then he stands in front of her, shoulders back. His expression is full of appreciation, as though she is doing a special favor for him. "Hey, feel good about yourself," he says. "You're doing right."

She watches him leave. She sips her coffee alone in the windowless room. There is nothing to do but recall the crash all those years ago, what she can tell the jury, what she can remember. She recalls the terrifying collision that seemed to go on forever. And the awful march through the night that followed.

WALKING OUT

▪ ▪ ▪ 1978

The smell of burned rubber and new sap followed Bobbie as she walked from the crash, out of the woods, and
onto the road. She stubbed a toe early on and kept re-stubbing it
for miles afterward, wincing each time she did so. She peeled dried
blood from her lips, picked a clot of blood from one nostril, squinted
into the night with gritty eyes. She'd already been tired when she
started and now she was more tired still, following a road she didn't
know to another road she didn't know.

She would do anything to see her mother's car, to be bundled
into its comfort and whisked home. In truth, however, had she seen
her mother's car, she'd have hidden. How could she explain what
had happened? To imagine everything about her life being suddenly
laid open, suddenly exposed, was an injury greater than the cuts, the
bruises, the pounding head, the hurt feet.

At last she saw lampposts, appearing like candles of light ahead,
and what appeared to be a shopping mall, set between vacant slopes
of abandoned farmland. It was a new build, still white with fresh
plaster, planted with saplings clothed in wire to protect them from
deer. Outside the mall, a spotlight illuminated flowering shrubs in
a circle of lawn at the entrance, and when finally she reached it, she
arranged her body in a comma around the base of the spotlight,

careful to avoid the black insulated cables. The shrubs bordering the circle were high enough so that they had shielded her from sight, the grass shorn so she did not become sodden with dew.

She slept only for a few hours, no more, and when she woke, she had no idea where she was. The image of Craig's face came to mind, the awful stillness, and the metal rod that balanced in his eye socket. She wrapped her arms around her head and rocked herself, imagining what would come next: police and jail and terrible shame.

The hard ground had made her stiff. A muscle spasm meant she could not turn her chin toward her right shoulder. She did not dare look at the feet but stared at her scabby arms, her hands latticed with dried blood, allowing herself to peer down the length of her ruined jeans to her feet only after she'd picked out the worst of the imbedded dirt and hard crusts of blood there. Deep scratches and a ball of dark blood swelled beneath the skin by her knee, and something else, too. Tree sap, she suspected, stuck between her fingers and under her nails.

She wiped her feet and arms and hands on the wet grass, straightened, then tested herself on her ragged soles. She stepped delicately to the edge of the parking lot where there was some taller, wetter grass with which she tried to wash her face. When that didn't work, she got on her knees, pressing her cheek to the lawn and rubbing back and forth, feeling the dew on her skin. She picked her way across the mall parking lot and knelt between two parked cars, then angled a side mirror her direction.

Overnight her face had gone from white and pink to a dull sienna. There was a bluish-red cast across her nose, a swelling there, ripening beneath the skin. The dirt and bits of bark in her hair made it look as though someone had poured coffee grounds over her head, and she tried to rub off the dirt and blood using spit and the bottom of her shirt. When she ran her fingers through her hair she was stopped by tangles and something sticky—tree sap, mixing with her blood where a scab was forming.

She had the urge to cut all her hair off. Cut it at the base with scissors. She thought how much she'd like a sink of warm water right now, how much she'd like a bath. First to drink the water, then to soak. For long minutes she sat on the ground with her head on her bent knees, her temples throbbing. She felt the sun pressing on her. She felt her spine, one painful piece all the way up to her neck, and her stomach, begging for food. Her clothes revealed a story she did not want to tell. She had to find new ones.

The mall was new. Not all the vacancies were yet rented, but she saw a uniformed man with a bored expression and a fist of keys unlock a set of glass doors at the far end of a Kmart. She watched from a distance until he'd gone, then set out across the parking lot, up on her toes on the rough asphalt, running like a bird trying to take flight. As she neared the entrance, she slowed down, dropping back onto her heels. She forced herself to breathe slower, to walk casually, to appear as though she was in no hurry. At the very least she needed to appear *unreportable*. Stepping through the doors into the air-conditioned store, her feet connected at last with the linoleum. The smooth surface against the painful skin on her feet was a cool balm, almost medicinal; she wanted to skate on it.

In the front of the store a row of windows, silver with light, were being scrubbed by a man in coveralls. Register five was the only one with its light on and there sat a large woman with a big bosom, staring into a compact, applying lipstick. None of them even noticed Bobbie, not the guy polishing the windows, not the cashier, not the man with keys who had disappeared from view. She began to feel hopeful. She would get new clothes; she would go home. And here was the best part: She had money. She pressed her pocket, feeling for the carefully rolled cylinders of cash, and she found them against her thigh, the relief nearly sending her to her knees.

And then she remembered, as though she could ever forget, Craig and the accident and the hideous metal rod. His face was right *there*, hanging in the air in front of her as though on a black cord from the sky.

She walked deeper into the Kmart, a giant, narrow rectangle, with low-slung tiles on the ceiling, and the feel of a warehouse about it. As long as she stayed focused, and nobody tapped her shoulder and asked why she was so dirty and scraped up and not in school, she'd be all right. Her lips were chapping, the corners caked with salt. In her nervous state, her hunger had vanished but she was thirstier than ever. What she really wanted, even more than clean clothes, was a water fountain, a faucet, a bucket, anything. She craned her neck, peering over the clothing displays and lit cases of cheap jewelry and big dump bins full of socks and headbands, searching for a vending machine to buy a drink. Then she remembered she had no change, only bills.

She headed down the rows of clothes. At the end of each aisle were mirrors but she did not look at the mirrors. Hiding behind racks of dresses and blouses, she peered through the garments to see if anyone was noticing. She reached out to take a hanger from the rack. Then, trying to affect an air of casual concentration as though this was an ordinary shopping trip, she studied a shirt for a few seconds before putting it back quickly, in a panic, realizing she was in the maternity section.

She needed jeans and a shirt, long sleeves to cover up. She needed socks. Socks were easy. They came in packs of three. She got lucky with shoes, finding some knock-off desert boots with gummy soles and yellow webs for laces.

She bought a hairbrush, a pink handbag-size one. And then she remembered: her handbag! It was still in the car. What would happen when the police searched the car? But she had no ID in the handbag, she now realized. No wallet, not even a set of house keys. Nothing in the bag could identify her. Even so, she worried. She'd left him there. He was dead, but she'd left him.

By the registers was a revolving tree of sunglasses from which she plucked some mirrored shades. Last thing was gum, taken from a rack behind the conveyer belt where she placed all her purchases. Gum instead of a toothbrush. Hairbrush instead of shampoo. Somewhere around here would be a bathroom and that was where she was going next, to clean herself and put on her new purchases. She only had to get past the cashier.

There was no one else waiting, so she went to the checkout area. The cashier took notice of her, darting her eyes at her, then away, then straight back again as though noticing for the first time the wild-looking girl in dirty clothes. Bobbie placed her purchases on the counter. She watched the cashier reach for the tags, then punch some numbers on the register.

She didn't dare look at the woman, didn't want to give any excuse for conversation. She felt the clotted dry interior of her throat. She wasn't even sure she could speak, had not practiced since waking and now worried she would be unable to utter a sound if she were called upon to talk. She felt a rush of panic, brought to bay by a sudden stinging of salt from the road in a cut on her toe. She shifted her focus down to the gratings of skin that surrounded her toenail and winced uneasily at the sight of blood on the polished floor. When she looked up again, she saw the cashier staring directly at her, studying the shirt Bobbie wore, splattered with blood and dirt and stinking as though she'd been living in it for days. Her thin jeans had a big tear in the back, and a back pocket torn at one end, wagging by her hip. The jeans were a disaster, looking like something that had been dragged through a field, and meanwhile another bubble of fresh blood spilled over the edge of her broken toenail onto the floor, so that Bobbie moved the pad of her foot to cover the splotch of red.

"Are you all right?" the woman asked. She gave Bobbie a pitying look, then punched more buttons on the machine and let the numbers tally.

"Yes," Bobbie managed. But her voice was wrong; her words croaked out as though it was unnatural for her to speak. She thought about water again. "Of course."

But she wasn't all right. She heard a buzzing in her head. The Kmart felt completely foreign to her, as though it was from another world and not the kind of place where she and her mother shopped all the time. She curled her fingers into her palms. She felt like she no longer belonged among those who shopped at stores and bought what they needed and raised their children and fed themselves at a table each evening.

The cashier took a moment to look closely at Bobbie before saying, "Cash or charge?"

Bobbie touched the money in her jeans. She was amazed that even through all the drama of the night, the money had somehow remained with her. She was going to have to get some out now to pay for the clothes and the thought terrified her. Her vision seemed to separate from her body and float up among the ceiling tiles, so that she was now peering down onto herself, on a filthy girl being looked at suspiciously by a round, kindly checkout woman with a mint-colored V-neck. She thought, *Craig is dead now*, and felt a fire of panic inside her chest.

The cashier leaned forward from her chair. "You able to pay?" she whispered.

She remembered how she'd left him. She had not brushed the dirt from his face, nor the little splinters of glass that sparkled like salt against his lips, nor allowed her gaze to rest on the spear of metal through his eye. There had been no moment of regret, no goodbye, spoken or unspoken. In her mind she saw his corpse all over again, and it was several moments before she realized that she was still staring at the cashier, who was waiting for an answer.

"What?" Bobbie said.

"Can you *pay?*" the cashier asked again.

Bobbie nodded. But she was genuinely afraid to show her one of the fifties. It was as though the money had on it the written testimony of the night's awful events: the image of Craig's destroyed eye and the skewered face embedded in the bills just as indelibly as the Capitol. She felt a knot of pressure between her eyes, but then she remembered all over again how Craig had refused to pay the boy at McDonald's, and how unkind he was, not just last night but often. He would tell her he loved her, sure. He would listen when she voiced her fears over pop quizzes and science labs. But there were things he did not understand about her body. He hurt her. He yelled at her for no reason. She remembered the day at the swimming pool when she stood on the scorched grass, her wet hair flat on her head, the August sun beating down, and how he'd threatened to tell her mother all about her, about the things she did with him, if she ever humiliated him like that again, flirting with another guy.

"Hang on a moment," she said to the cashier, then hunched her shoulders and leaned into her pocket, separating one of the fifties from its roll, bringing it up slowly, so that none of the others would come with it, and handed it to the cashier.

The cashier looked at the bill carefully, angling it above her head and tilting it from side to side under the ceiling lights. Then she looked at Bobbie. "I'm supposed to get the manager for anything over a twenty," she said.

Bobbie waited. She wondered if the bills were counterfeit. She wondered if Craig had beaten a man half to death last night over fake money.

"You on your own?" the cashier said. Her voice was light, even kind, like she wasn't meaning any harm.

"My mother's working."

"Uh-huh."

"She sent me to get some clothes; she didn't want me going around like this," Bobbie said, hardly breathing now, allowing the woman to take her into her vision and draw her conclusions.

The cashier nodded slowly. "Okay, then."

She thought she saw in the woman's dark eyes a mixture of disapproval and pity, and a scrutinizing intelligence, too. She almost expected to hear the woman say, *Where did you get this?*, and then to watch helplessly as she signaled security, turning Bobbie over to the guard with the keys who had opened the doors. He had worn a uniform. He might even have a gun.

Instead, the cashier sniffed, then looked at Bobbie directly. Then she ran her finger over the security thread on the bill, a little vertical strip embedded into the paper, opened the drawer on the register, and placed the fifty beneath the tray. Bobbie swallowed. She tried to act naturally, breathe easily, as though paying for the clothes had been nothing unusual, and there was no particular reason for the tremble in her hands as she accepted her change.

ANY PERSON WHOSOEVER

The defense counsel, Craig's lawyer, the lean and hairless Ms. Elstree, sourced and subsidized by a pool of radio-station owners, turns out to be one of the most beautiful women Bobbie has ever seen. Over six feet in her heels, she looks to Bobbie like a runway model for Burberry in her navy blue suit and stout, square diamond earrings. She might have been too beautiful for the courtroom. She might not have been taken seriously by some of the less evolved male jurors or even inspired envy among the female ones, except for one fact: She had no hair, not a single strand. She is tall and she is bald, a raw truth she does nothing to hide. Confident, elegant, big in every way, Elstree has such presence that when she leaves her seat at the defense table and steps toward Bobbie, it is like seeing a lion sprung from its cage.

"Good morning!" Elstree says. Her greeting is as fresh as though everyone has convened in the courtroom just this minute, not hours ago. Bobbie has already explained her story in total, every excruciating detail, as Dreyer led her through a long series of questions. She'd done well with her direct testimony, she thinks. But here is Elstree, filled with a kind of urgency, as though the jury should pay special attention now as the real story unfolds.

Meanwhile Craig sits right in front of Bobbie in his own private hell, glaring just as he has from the moment she walked into the room. His expression had hardened when she gave her testimony to Dreyer. His face had changed color. But she told the story truly, just as she'd practiced with Dreyer, and ignored Craig.

Now Elstree. She has none of the emotions of Craig. She is breezy, confident. She is as comfortable as if the courtroom were her home.

"Just a few questions," she begins, cozying up to the stand for cross-examination. Her first questions are so reasonable and matter-of-fact they might not even be leveled from the defense. "You told the jury you were thirteen when you met Mr. Kirtz?" Elstree begins. She is giving a show for the jury, encouraging everyone to trust in her sense of fairness and respect for the witness, Bobbie. "And that you were with your mother, who is now married to Mr. Kirtz. Correct?"

"Yes," Bobbie says, a bag of anxiety next to Elstree's pleasant confidence. Meanwhile, she just can't help it; she keeps noticing Craig, wondering how on earth he has the nerve to stare at her as he does. Then she remembers that the one thing about the man is that he is all nerve.

"Okay," Elstree says, as though they'd just come to a tacit agreement and all is right between them. The bald head gives Elstree a mystical appearance; the ceiling lights reflecting on her scalp make her seem almost to glow. She pauses a moment, eyeing Bobbie like a puzzle she is trying to figure out. Then she continues. "You've already told us that nobody saw you enter the motel the first time, nor when you returned for the rest of the money. Is that the case?"

"Yes," Bobbie says.

"So you entered twice and you exited twice, but in neither case did any person *whosoever* see you, is that correct?"

"Yes."

"Even though there were plenty of people around, I presume?"

"I didn't see anyone."

"What about the motel night manager, Mr. Williams? Did you see him?"

"I didn't know his name, but I know who you mean. Yes, I saw him."

"The motel room is where you saw the alleged fight take place between Mr. Kirtz and Mr. Williams, correct?"

Bobbie is trying not to look at Craig, who keeps glaring at her. It takes every bit of concentration to give a simple answer. "Yes," she says.

"In your testimony with the DA, however, you claimed that Mr. Williams did not see you?"

Bobbie pauses. "I don't think he did, no."

"So nobody saw you at the motel, not even a man who was in the same room as you. Is that correct?"

"That is correct. Nobody saw me."

"You stated earlier that you returned to the room in order to help Mr. Kirtz look for the money, is that right?"

"Yes."

"You've already told the court that Mr. Williams entered the motel room after you were inside, is that right?"

"Yes."

"But you also say he didn't see you, correct?"

"Yes."

"Well, I'm a bit confused," Elstree says. "Were you both in the motel room at the same time?"

"Yes, but—"

"And *you* saw *him*, correct?"

"Yes."

"Thank you. You told us earlier that you were frightened. Is that the case?"

"Yes."

Elstree says, "Even though you were frightened, you did not call for help?"

The judge, a black woman in her sixties with a wise face and graying hair and long flowing robes, a figure that awes Bobbie, breathes in a long breath as Bobbie says no, she did not call for help.

Elstree tilts her head as though she is genuinely trying to see it from Bobbie's point of view. Finally she makes a clucking sound as though, despite all her efforts, she just isn't buying it. She shakes her head and Bobbie is again drawn to the shining scalp.

"You told the jury earlier that you sprinted across the room and out the door in your bare feet. Is that correct?"

Bobbie watches Craig shift in his chair. She stares into the courtroom, straight across to the opposite wall, and answers the question. "Yes."

"You have also said that you hid in the bathroom while the fight in the motel room took place, is that correct?"

"Yes."

"And that you ran from the bathroom out the door without being seen?"

"Yes."

"But not so fast you couldn't put hundreds of dollars in your pocket? Is that correct?"

Bobbie thinks about the way she'd crawled along the floor of the room, how she'd suddenly seen the money, and then put it in her pocket.

"I didn't run the whole time. I crept along the floor and then dashed out."

"You've said you ran, but now you say you did not run. I am confused. How could you both run and not run?"

"I crept along the floor first. Then I ran."

"Once you got the money?"

Bobbie hesitates. "I ran with the money, yes," she says finally.

"You told us earlier this morning that you were very scared, correct?"

"Yes."

"You used the word *terrified*?"

"I was terrified, yes."

"But you got the money. You weren't so scared that you didn't have the wherewithal to pocket that. Correct?"

Bobbie says nothing. Elstree does not say this but Bobbie imagines her saying, *You were scared but you didn't call for help. You ran but stopped long enough to take half a grand out from beneath the noses of two men in the same room without being seen. Who can believe you? Nobody can believe you . . .*

Meanwhile, there is Craig, sitting like an angry Buddha at the defense table, with his wide, wide chest and his unmoving face, staring. Remarkably, he seems to have two eyes. Two perfect eyes. And because he looks at her so unceasingly, it is difficult for her to tell which one is real. A flash of memory—the antenna in his right eye, the reflection of moonlight against its silver—and she knows that it is the left eye that is his own.

"How much money did you say you picked up on your way out?" says Elstree.

"Five hundred dollars."

"You knew it was five hundred dollars?"

"Yes."

"So you had time to count it?"

"No—"

"You ran, you didn't run. You know how much money it was. You don't know how much it was," says Elstree. Bobbie looks down. "A big noisy fight and nobody came to see what was happening?"

"No."

"You are a kid in the middle of all this chaos and you don't cry out?"

"No."

"No calling, no yelling, you apparently aren't even visible—"

"I was visible. No one saw me."

"Except at a McDonald's, where the attendant who served you *did* see you."

"Yes."

"A Mr. Daniel Gregory with whom you had a sexual relationship—"

"We didn't have a sexual relationship at that time," says Bobbie. "I didn't even know him then. And it was more romantic than sexual when we were . . . you know . . . together."

"More romantic than sexual," Elstree repeats, as though trying to understand what Bobbie could possibly mean. "An interesting distinction." Dreyer objects and the judge gives Elstree a warning. Elstree paces a little, then stands close to Bobbie.

"Was it sexual?"

"It was . . ." Bobbie hesitates and Elstree begins again.

"Do you know what I mean when I say sexual?"

"Yes."

"You may not remember exactly."

"I do remember."

Elstree looks down at her notes as though she'd been scribbling Bobbie's answers there, though she has not been. "More romantic than sexual," she says, repeating Bobbie's words. "You aren't answering the question."

"Yes, it was sexual."

Elstree sighs. "Thank you," she says, as though at least they can now move on. "From what you've said to counsel this morning, in the entire fourteen-month period during which you claim Mr. Kirtz had sex with you on a regular basis, nobody ever saw anything. Right?"

"I don't know—"

"No one saw him at your school?"

"No."

"Nor at your house?"

"Yes. I mean, he came to the house for dinner—"

"And from your testimony we know that your mother was with you during these meetings at your house, correct?"

"Yes."

"And as far as you are aware, your mother did not witness any behavior toward you from Mr. Kirtz that was of a sexual nature?"

"I don't think so."

"Did anyone other than your mother see you with Mr. Kirtz outside of the home in which you lived with your mother?"

Bobbie thinks hard. She says, "I think someone may have seen me at his work."

"Who would that be?"

"I can't remember."

"But you *can* remember that nobody at all saw you on September seventh when you walked away from a near-fatal automobile collision. Nobody saw you, then. Is that correct?"

Bobbie sighs. "That's correct," she manages to say.

Elstree steps gracefully toward the jury. In the manner of a hostess asking them all to raise a glass and toast the witness stand, she invites them now to look at the monitors in front of them where they will see photographs taken at the scene in 1978, showing the condition of Mr. Kirtz's car after the accident.

"Do you recognize this vehicle?" she asks Bobbie.

The images are old, the quality poor, but Bobbie sees the battered car, like a broken dinosaur unearthed and in pieces, and knows exactly what she is looking at. "That's Craig's car," she says. She watches as Craig responds to his name from her mouth.

"Correct," Elstree says. She begins reading the forensics report aloud, describing the damage to the car, which had been so destroyed that it had been taken out in two pieces. The state of Mr. Kirtz, she explains, whose pelvis had been broken by the vehicle's steering column, his right arm shattered, not to mention the substantial head injuries, had been understood as in keeping with the type of injuries likely to be sustained in such a collision. Expert opinion was that any passenger in the vehicle would have also sustained serious injury.

Now Elstree turns to Bobbie. "But you walked away from this wreck," she says. "Walked miles in your bare feet, you tell us. Is that correct?"

"Yes, I did."

"How many miles, do you recall?"

Bobbie tells her exactly. It is a number that Dreyer and she have discussed. "Seven," she says.

"Boy, that's something," Elstree says, as though genuinely impressed. "You must have been some kid. Do you do any extreme sports now?" The courtroom fills with half-suppressed laughter as the judge glares at Elstree, who bows her head and puts her hand up, accepting the caution. It doesn't matter that the judge disapproves; the effect is clear on the faces of the jury.

"I believe we have the route you took," Elstree says. A map shows on the bank of computer monitors. Bobbie is shown the same.

"Is that about right?"

"I think so."

"You passed a phone booth just here, at the corner of these two roads. Did you call for help?"

"No," Bobbie says.

"And here is an all-night gas station. Did you go inside and ask for help?"

Bobbie shakes her head.

"Into the microphone, please."

"No," she says.

"Were you aware there was a police station just here, not far from where you were?"

"No."

"See here?" Elstree says, and indicates an area with her pencil. "There were houses all along here, with people inside who would have helped you. Did you ask for help?"

"No."

"You say you were barefoot? That must have been difficult to walk all night on a road with no shoes. But you didn't ask for help?"

"No," says Bobbie, feeling defeated, exhausted, wrung out.

"So you never cry out, you never ask for help, your mother doesn't know, and the only one who ever saw you with Mr. Kirtz other than your mother, Mrs. Kirtz, is Daniel Gregory, with whom you later happened to have a sexual relationship?"

"Yes," Bobbie says after some time. She had been warned by Dreyer that the cross-examination would be exhausting, but she hadn't expected this.

"Maybe a little recess?" Elstree asks Bobbie, as though she wants to do something nice for her, a little act of charity.

DAN THE MCDONALD'S BOY

O utside the mall, Bobbie had two problems. The first was how to get home. The other was hunger. Past a set of traffic lights, she could see an Arthur Treacher's Fish and Chips, newly cut into the earth. Baby trees, caged from deer, edged the restaurant's recently laid parking lot. But the lot was empty and she was pretty sure the banner pinned across the building would read OPENING SOON. Other than that, nothing but industrial buildings between vacant lots of wild overgrowth, and beyond, the highway with its dual streams of cars.

On the road in front of the mall was a new bus stop with the route map bolted to a pole and a metal slab that served as a bench seat, so she went there. Staring at the map with its spiderweb of colored lines connecting in places marked with O's, she realized she had no idea where she was. None of the names were familiar. If her house or street was anywhere on that map, or near the dozens of stops, she couldn't tell. She didn't know even which side of the road to stand on. She decided to ask the drivers of the buses that came along if they were heading anywhere near her neighborhood and figure it out from there. The heat was back, not much past nine a.m. and already hitting the upper eighties.

Meanwhile, another annoyance. A teenage kid leaning against

the entrance of the bus stop with his school knapsack was watching her. Without turning her head, she could see the black teeth of a hair comb lodged in his back pocket and a silver sleeve of Pop-Tarts in his hand. She felt her stomach rumble as he tore through the packaging with his teeth, then slid out one of the strawberry Pop-Tarts. Its colorful sugar crystals were embedded in pink icing, and she wanted to reach across the air and grab it.

She looked away quickly but he'd noticed her already and now he smiled, then took another bite of the Pop-Tart and cleared his throat all at once, preparing some kind of greeting. She steeled herself and waited. He said, "Didn't you come through McDonald's last night?" Another bite, then, "It's kind of weird, me seeing you again."

He had a soft, polite voice and as soon as he spoke she knew exactly who he was: Dan from the drive-through booth, Dan the McDonald's boy. She looked at the place where he'd worn the name tag last night, though of course it was gone now, and his eyeglasses were newly clean, washed of burger grease. She recognized his curlicue hair, his freckled nose, the long arms and long legs, the angular chin that made a shadow on his neck. She remembered how his skin had gleamed under the close, fluorescent tube at the drive-through, and how he'd been scared when Craig started on him, and how she'd been scared, too.

She shrugged like she did not recall any of this while a full-alarm, run-for-cover siren screeched inside her head, all the facts ringing out: being seen with Craig the very hour of the crash, the money in full sight right there in the ashtray, the smell of pot in the reeking car. Dan would be able to recount all of this to the police. There had been a witness. The word echoed in her head: *witness.*

She thought of all the dreadful effort—fighting her way out of the car, forcing herself forward on sore feet, sleeping on the ground—all of it had been a waste. Once Craig's body was found, the police would call for information and Dan would come forward. Of course he would. He was a pleasant citizen, a member of the public, a kid whose schoolbooks filled to bursting every corner of his knapsack and who worked a part-time job while at high school. He'd come forward responsibly, he might even feel very important, saying he had seen the car that night, seen her in it. He would explain how she'd later appeared mysteriously at the bus stop outside the mall and then the woman at Kmart would testify that she'd bought a change of clothes. They would assume the worst of her: that she'd murdered Craig.

Dan said, "Last night, you came by the drive-through with that, uh, guy, right? Wasn't that you?"

She felt sick inside, but she opened her mouth in a little smile, then shook her head like she thought it was funny that he could imagine such a thing.

"I don't know what you're talking about," she said, making a face.

He dropped onto the bench, allowing the knapsack to slide off his shoulder onto the cement floor. "It sure looked like you."

"Not me," she said.

He indicated a bruise or mark or scratch; she wasn't sure. "What happened there?" he said, and touched the air in front of his face.

"I don't know what you mean." She scowled as though she thought it ridiculous for him to make such a remark, that she thought it very uncool. "Is there something *wrong* with my face? Is that what you're telling me?"

"No, no. I didn't mean that. Just that it looks almost like you broke your nose."

"Oh," she said, flustered. She wondered if her nose really were broken. She felt a swelling there and a band of numbness across the tip. "I did that a while ago. Fell off my bike."

She thought that might be the end of it. She kept him in the corner of her vision, noticing his white skin, his shining hair, the long smooth fingers of his hands. He seemed startlingly clean by comparison to her. The pads of her soles felt worn through as though she'd been walking on bone all night. She couldn't let him see her limp. She couldn't let him see her bleed, either, and hoped the toe cut didn't seep blood through her new shoes.

Meanwhile, the Pop-Tart was torture. She wished she could take it from him, lick the strawberry glaze, bite deep into the pastry. The thought of food set her stomach in motion, and she felt another low grumble of hunger even before she heard it. Pressing her belly with her palm made no difference and now the noise of her stomach drifted into the still air between her and the boy, who looked as though he was still puzzling over something.

"You want one?" he said, holding out the foil pack.

Though she was becoming shaky with hunger, she said, "I just ate. I ate at home."

He took another hefty bite and her stomach pinged and gurgled while he chewed. "Are you sure?" he said.

"Positive." She looked away. "I had toast—two pieces—and cereal." The glass bus stop was like a greenhouse and she wished she had her own Pop-Tarts and that she had water. Her body was acting strange. Her hands shook; her armpits pricked with sweat; she shivered, then felt okay, then dizzy. One thing for sure: She could not *think*. Closing her eyes, she listened to the crinkly sound of the Pop-Tart packet, imagining Dan biting into the second one. She wished a bus would come—any bus, it didn't matter—and that this kid lived somewhere other than right here, where she'd happened to turn up. In the distance was a hill of little yellow houses with green, hedged lawns, part of a new development, and she imagined he lived in one of those. She leaned her head against the glass wall. And then some vibration in the air made her realize a bus was arriving. She jumped up, scrambling to the edge of the sidewalk and through the accordion doors into the bus's pale interior, asking for a transfer ticket she had no idea how to use.

The bus was largely empty and she went to its center, dropping into a window seat behind the second set of doors. She heard Dan behind her, getting change from the driver. She tried not to take too much notice of him as he passed. The bus heaved forward and they traveled for a few miles. She heard nothing from Dan during this time and she thought maybe he was done with her. A few miles more and she saw a high school—not her school, not even one she knew—and she heard Dan's footsteps again, and those of some other passengers. She stared at her knees, waiting for him to get off the bus. He walked to where she sat and she heard the crinkling sound of the foil pack—the lone Pop-Tart, the one he'd been willing to give to her. She glanced up, and he handed her the Pop-Tart, smiling as he did so. She knew he meant her no harm, but in her head he was already identifying her in a lineup.

"What's this?" she said.

"Nothing."

"I told you I already had breakfast."

"Take it anyway."

She took the foil pack from him, then watched as he walked through the doors, drawing a little wave in the air as he entered the street. Despite how young he was, how thin and full of angles, he had a confidence she admired. This feeling deepened when she removed the Pop-Tart from the sleeve and saw, folded into quarters within, a 3 x 5 file card on which Dan had written the words, *Stay away from that guy.* He had signed it with his name and a smiley face. She looked out the window and saw Dan there, saw his handsome young face, then she looked at the note again.

Suddenly, she was out of her seat. The doors had already closed, the bus readying to set out, but she launched herself down the steps, slapping at the doors with her open palms until at last the driver told her to quit and that he'd open them again if she'd just step back. She pushed herself away and waited as the doors sprang on their hinges, then spilled out onto the sidewalk toward Dan, who had watched the commotion at the door and looked stricken by the sight of her, with her bruises and messy straw-colored hair and the way she hurled herself at him, grabbing his arm and pulling him to the side, away from the few other students who were also arriving late to school that day.

"I don't know where I am," she said urgently.

He looked confused. "You don't go to school here?"

She shook her head. She was suddenly appalled at herself. She stood back, her hands in the air as though she'd touched wet paint. "I'm sorry!" she said. "Forget it! Forget what I said!"

He began to speak but she heard nothing he was saying until, at last, he stepped toward her and she felt his cool hand against the skin on her forehead. With that, it was as though the sound had been turned back on, and she understood the last snatches of a sentence including *very pale* and *drink some water.*

He shepherded her toward the school's entrance, its wide doors ajar to catch any breeze that might come up. She felt the cooler temperatures inside where fans whirred. He led her to a drinking fountain humming beside a trophy case, then pressed his thumb against a button until an arc of water leaped up in front of her.

"Drink," he instructed. She was scared to be seen here, scared to be found out. Being in a school that wasn't your own was somehow fraudulent—she could get in trouble just for that, she thought. But she was thirsty and Dan stood over her as she drank from the fountain. Between long, solid swallows she whispered, "I have to go!," and he nodded and told her they would go, but please calm down. "You have to get to class," she added.

"I haven't signed in yet. Nobody knows I'm here," he said. "You should call your folks."

"No!" She felt the adrenaline rising inside her. The thought of Dan somehow persuading her to call her mother alarmed her freshly and without any thought she shot out of the school, down the sidewalk, across the hot grass, and through the fierce, whitening sun, thinking now what a mistake it had been to talk to Dan, what a disaster she'd set herself up for. When she got to the bus stop, she wheeled around and saw him there, trailing behind her.

"What's wrong?" he said.

She told him that under no circumstances—*none*—would she call her mother. "That's rule number one," she said.

"But you have to get home," he said gently.

"Yeah, and I don't know *where* I am, not even which county, or the day or time, or how to *get* home. It's like I'm on Mars—"

He let out a sigh. "Montgomery County," he said quietly. "Friday." She sensed Dan's steady, willing nature, exactly the same as the night before when he had encouraged crazy Craig to look for the money he owed in the wad of cash in the ashtray. "It's just after ten in the morning. Does that help? And I'll help get you home," he said. "Don't worry about that."

THEY RODE TOGETHER, changed buses twice, then stopped at a deli and ordered pastrami sandwiches that came in wax paper and made a mess of mustard and sauerkraut in their laps no matter how carefully they ate them. She drank two ginger ales in a row and still wanted more, so he pulled another from the deli's cooler and gave the cashier money he fished from his jeans pocket, even though she kept saying, "No, really, I can pay."

She didn't tell him about the fifties. If she thought too much about having nearly a thousand dollars in her pocket it made her paranoid, as though she were holding drug money, which she may well be, she concluded.

Outside, the buses were slow, the schedules shot. Waiting for the third bus, their backs pushed up against an oak tree, their bellies now full, she fell asleep. Falling asleep had not been a gradual thing, not a drifting off but a plowing under. She felt something pulling her, almost like she was drowning, and then *lights out*; she was gone.

Waking up was just as abrupt. She was wrenched out of sleep and into the solid heat of midday by the hum of cars passing and the stiff tufts of gnarled grass not yet killed by the sun digging into her skin. Lying on her side, her arm over her eyes, her head on Dan's knee, she felt like she'd been tossed here, thrown from the sky. When she spoke it sounded strange inside her head, as though her skull were a vacuum and the words trapped inside.

"My head hurts." Her stomach contracted and she wished she could spit somewhere. "How long was I asleep?"

"Maybe fifteen minutes."

How could sleep be a poison like that? She stretched the muscles in her calves, feeling the heat like a warm cocoon around her, the bones of Dan's knee beneath her cheek, and then, inevitably, the tender, pained muscles of her body—every single one of them—

groaning into action. She wrenched herself up in jerky movements. The evil nap had made her more tired. She wondered if this was the way it would be now: sleep, an exhausting, terrible mission from which she returned feeling buggy and depleted. She wondered if she had a concussion—what were the symptoms for that?

"You talked in your sleep," Dan said.

"What did I say?"

"Not actual words, but it all sounds bad. And you twitched; I think you were dreaming. I thought maybe you were crying, so that's why I woke you up."

"You woke me?" She'd had no idea.

"Yes, you were somewhere very bad in your head and I didn't think it was a good idea to leave you there."

She smiled. "Thank you."

"I want to say something. Are you okay for me to say something about last night?"

No, she wasn't. Not now, with the pastrami sandwich doing wheelies in her stomach, but also not ever. "Does it have to be this minute?"

Apparently, it didn't. Whatever Dan was about to say, he swallowed it back. His face was still bright, with a soft energy and eagerness that drew her. When he smiled instead of speaking she was so relieved, she said, "Go ahead then."

"It's nothing, really," he began. "Only that last night I was worried that guy was going to do something. That he might hurt you. I thought about it afterward. I hadn't gotten the plate number and I thought how stupid I'd been not to call the police. Now here you are asleep on my leg. This can't be a coincidence."

"Yes, it is," she said. "It's a coincidence. That's exactly what it is."

"I feel like it was fate. Do you believe in God?"

"Less and less."

Dan was waiting for her to say something more, but she didn't. What she was thinking was that it would have been better for Dan if he hadn't met her. And if there were a God, he should protect people like Dan from meeting people like her.

"Are you a friend of that guy?" he asked. "I wondered if you were being kidnapped."

"Craig," she said, then realized how much she hated saying his name out loud. "Not really friends, no." She realized she was talking about Craig as though he were still alive and that it felt like he was alive, too. She remembered his face, both before and after the accident, and she smelled all over again the burning tires, the blown engine, the blood.

"I feel like he did something to you last night. But you don't have to tell me."

He meant like rape her. She could see it on his face. "Not what you think," she said. He looked away, embarrassed as she continued. "He didn't do anything. It was me. What I did."

All the while they'd been talking, she'd been trying to force her legs to bend against the sore muscles and scraped skin. She'd gotten one of her ankles to twist a little so she could sit cross-legged, but the other was too grieved to bend, so she gave up, and stuck her legs out straight, leaning onto the bromegrass with her open palms, which were also sore, she now realized.

"You have a lot of marks on you, is all," Dan said.

"You're imagining stuff," she said. There was an awkward silence, both of them embarrassed. "When is this bus coming?"

"It was supposed to be here already."

She asked him how he was going to get back, and he said it was easy and he'd been hopping on and off buses all his life. The rural routes were unreliable, the timetables a joke, but the buses did run and were cheap. He had a lot of older siblings who'd taught him how to get around and he'd been riding buses in and out of the capital since he was twelve.

"When we moved into that house there wasn't even a supermarket within ten miles," he said. "But I'm saving for a car. I already have a license. If I go to a college that allows cars, I'll buy one. Otherwise, I'll buy one when I graduate."

She didn't want to think about cars or driver's licenses anymore. There was a time when she couldn't wait to get her license but all that was ruined for her now. The police would find her. Of course they would. She put her head in her hands. She wanted to wipe away the whole mess but couldn't.

She said, "You think you want an exciting life and then you find out that you don't."

"I want an exciting life," Dan said. "Everywhere I'm applying to college is way out of state."

She looked up at Dan and tried to think of something normal to say to him, something that would make her seem like any other teenager. "Like where?" she said finally. "Where are you applying?"

"New York, Boston, California," he said. "I don't want to stay here. My parents are making me apply to Hopkins—and I know it's good. But I don't want to be in Maryland."

"I wish . . ." she said, then wasn't even sure what she wished for. She wished she, too, could go away, go somewhere else, to a new place and a new life, somewhere she could begin afresh. "If I tell you what happened last night it will be bad," she said. "Bad for you, I mean."

"How can it be bad for me?"

There was a puzzle. She wasn't sure how to explain it. "I can't say why, but it will be."

He shook his head. He looked so confident, unmarked, and fine. He looked almost regal, as though he could go anywhere in the world and set up his life as a prince. If he had any sense he'd get up and leave her there on the grass, never speak to her again. The thought came to her once more: Last night she'd killed a man. It was too great, the weight of it. "I'm going to be in so much trouble," she said.

"I don't understand," Dan said. *"Why?"*

It would make her feel better to tell another person, but she was scared. He saw that fear and told her not to worry and asked her, not for the first time since they boarded the buses, if it would be a good idea to call her mother.

"No, she's at work. But anyway, no."

She did tell him. Not then, under the oak tree, but after the third and final bus ride before they said goodbye. It wasn't because she knew he'd read about it in the newspapers, though later she told herself this was the reason. It was because he rode with her all that way in the heat, because he bought her the sandwich and the ginger ales and waited with her for all those late buses. Because he'd missed school for her, even before he knew her name. So she said, "After Craig, the man I was with, bought the burgers, he wanted to get more stoned. He was driving, so I held the wheel for him while he did that."

She explained how she steered and he messed around with the pipe and that they'd gone off the road.

"A deer," she said, "but we didn't hit it." She didn't want to think about the trees and the exploding sound they made and how the tires blew up like bombs.

"So a deer jumped out into the road," Dan said. "That doesn't sound like your fault." His eyes were busy taking her in, gauging her, maybe deciding if she was telling the truth or if she was dangerous. She thought all of this at once; she thought she might be going a little crazy.

She sighed. "The deer wasn't my fault," she agreed, "but I left him there, you know? And he was—" She didn't want to tell him about the state of Craig, nor how she'd almost crawled over his body, trying to get out. Not once, not even for a moment, had she considered calling help for him. She didn't want Dan to think of her as someone who had so little compassion for another human being. But there it was, all her humiliating indifference laid bare for him to see.

"But it wasn't anyone's fault, the deer. You didn't kill him."

"I was steering—"

"That doesn't matter."

"It *does*," she said. This next admission was harder. "And I didn't call for help. I didn't let anyone know he was still, you know—"

"But he was already dead, wasn't he?" Dan said. "What were you supposed to do?"

"Ambulance, I think." She wasn't sure she was doing the right thing telling him all this but he seemed so solidly on her side. Now there was no turning back and he might tell others. He might tell the police. She felt herself tear up at the thought of this, of him whispering the truth to his parents and taking their sage advice to tell what he knew to the police, and how the officers would write it all down and then have him sign a paper. She thought about how her mother would find out, not only about the accident but everything before it. After all this time, she would be discovered. Everyone would know about her.

"I don't feel good," she said. A flat statement a child might make before vomiting. Dan was speaking again, but she could hardly focus on his words until, at the very tail end of a sentence, he said, "I guess, okay, it would have been better if you hadn't left the scene—"

Left the scene. She knew there would be a law—there had to be—but she hadn't known until now what it was. Leaving the scene. That was her crime. She looked to her right and saw a line of yellowing hedges. She marched herself over to the hedges and waited to be sick, but nothing happened.

"Is that against the law?" she called over her shoulder.

"If you'd been in *another* car and hit him, yes, but in this case you were in the accident, so . . ."

She was desperate to hear him tell her no, she'd not broken the law. Instead, he said, "I don't know, but ask yourself this. Are there people—I mean, really—who go to jail for getting out of a car they weren't even driving?"

"I was *steering.*"

"Okay, but you didn't have control of the brakes right? You weren't even in the driver's seat so how—"

He stopped. Someone else was approaching the bus stop, so they went whispering together around the side of the library, a brick box only open twice a week. It was beside a bike rack and a Dumpster, the kind of place where kids hung out to smoke and drink illegally. They stood near discarded bottles and broken glass, the stale gray smell of ash baking in the sun around them. Dan leaned toward her and said, "Who else saw you with him last night?" He whispered his question cautiously and she realized that he would never tell anyone about the accident. He would keep her secret; indeed, he had entered into it and made it his own. An A student with a father who was a doctor and a mother who made her own curtains, a boy with a pile of finished college applications from around the country sitting on the desk in his tidy bedroom surrounded by books and posters, he had made a decision in her direction and very probably at his own cost.

"Just you," she said. "But there is something more. Something you aren't going to like."

"Tell me."

She shook her head. "I can't."

"Then don't tell me now. Tell me later, when you're able to."

She leaned into him and he put his arms around her. She liked that she could feel the bones and muscles through his skin, that he was sinewy and angular and so very young. He was like her, and he fit with her. He felt nothing like Craig. He didn't grope her or pull at her. He held her carefully, even uneasily, and it was his awkwardness and gentleness that she liked best. She said, "I've got almost a thousand dollars in my pocket."

She felt his body tense, then his slow release. She knew the risk she'd taken; she knew she should be afraid. But for one widening moment she was not afraid but free. "Don't worry," she whispered. "I didn't steal it."

YOU'D HAVE TO ASK JUNE

Before she ever laid eyes on the packed court, on the formidable judge on the raised bench, or on Craig sitting at the defense table, Bobbie had waited in an ancillary room in quiet solitude while Diana Elstree, the most bewitching of criminal defense attorneys, a woman who made it her life's work to ensure that no innocent person be locked up, turned to the jury and delivered in her opening statement a perfectly rehearsed, critical message.

"Ladies and gentlemen," she began, "our justice system tells us that if you have a reasonable doubt then you cannot find a defendant guilty. That's the law. It's not a special favor to this man that reasonable doubt means he cannot in these United States be convicted, it is the way in which our judicial system works, a system all of us in this room are sworn to abide by. But you already know that. The honorable judge has already explained to you that this man must be presumed innocent until proven guilty.

"I will show you that Mr. Kirtz is innocent, but I want you to know that innocence is not what you are deciding. You are deciding whether the evidence proves he is guilty. You are going to hear a lot of things in this courtroom about what allegedly took place thirty years ago. The prosecution is asking you to declare that these historic acts took place and to make that declaration without any reasonable doubt in your mind. That is a big ask. Especially, as I will show you, because there is not one piece of physical evidence against my client.

"Not only no physical evidence—there is no circumstantial evidence, and absolutely no witnesses to the alleged sexual offenses, either. That piece of furniture over there we call a witness stand will only be used for character witnesses in this hearing. None of the witnesses for the prosecution actually *saw* anything.

"With no evidence against him, my client nonetheless took a polygraph test. Voluntarily. You can read the polygraph report yourselves, but shall I tell you what it says? It's inconclusive. It says nothing. After thirty years of silence, a woman has taken it upon herself to accuse Mr. Kirtz—her stepfather—of a historic crime nobody saw, with evidence nobody can produce. And while it may be true that in the state of Maryland there is no statute of limitations on sex crimes against children, there is still the requirement of a burden of proof."

A lesser lawyer than Elstree might have leaned harder on the historic nature of the case, but what Elstree set out to do was chip away at the fragile evidence, then convince the jury that to convict a man on so little proof was unethical. Elstree was a showman, but even stronger than her presence in the courtroom and her ability to charm a jury was that she was a principled professional with a long-held belief of her own, one handed down by the second president of the United States, John Adams, whom she quoted as she finished her opening statement. Walking over to the jury, she leaned on the railing in front of them, and as though reciting the Lord's Prayer, she said, "It is more important that innocence be protected than it is that guilt be punished."

Closed up in the ancillary room, unaware of anything taking place in the courtroom, Bobbie heard none of this. If Elstree had been warned by the judge not to argue the law, Bobbie did not hear. If she'd been stopped midway and asked not to make closing arguments during her opening statement, Bobbie did not hear. Nor did she see the jury warming to the defense. She did not notice the one juror who nodded as Elstree finished her remarks. But somehow, even before she stepped onto the stand, Bobbie knew the defense counsel had won over jurors. Equally she knew that the man on trial was not innocent. Craig had done exactly as she described, and more. Bobbie reminds herself of the facts when the recess is over and she returns to the witness stand to continue the cross-examination with Elstree. As the questions begin, she tries to keep herself focused, in control of her emotions, and absolutely solid in her testimony. She's good for a while, but as time drags on, Elstree digs into her, and she feels the case sliding south.

"So after the crash, you thought Mr. Kirtz was dead, is that correct?"

"Yes," Bobbie says.

"Did he have a pulse?" Elstree says.

"I don't know," says Bobbie. "I didn't check."

"You didn't feel for a pulse?"

"No."

"Did you listen to his heart?"

"No."

"Did you check that he was breathing?"

Bobbie thinks about the fact that she did not even check such a simple thing. Then she says, "No."

"What did you do, then, to determine that he was dead?"

She ought to have done something, she knows, but she can't recall touching his body. She remembers wishing she could bring herself to crawl over it to get out the window. But this, she understands, is nothing she should admit. "I don't know," she says.

"Is it fair to say you don't remember?"

The courtroom is silent. Bobbie's head is pounding. She feels a tingling in her arms, too, another stress response that she can do nothing to control. Meanwhile, Elstree continues, "This is a pretty important fact—a man being dead or not. And you can't remember this?"

Bobbie feels she is being cornered. "I didn't know if he was dead or not," she says.

"Is it possible that you don't remember because you were not there?"

"No."

"That you imagined you were in that car because it played such an important part in what happened next, when your mother devoted herself to Mr. Kirtz?"

Dreyer objects, Elstree withdraws. The judge seems to agree with Dreyer but Bobbie answers the question anyway, saying, "I did not imagine it."

"After the crash, am I correct in saying your mother became very involved with Mr. Kirtz?"

"Yes."

"Caring for him, taking care of his bills while he healed, even moving him into the family home?"

"Yes."

"And that before the car accident none of this had transpired?"

Bobbie understands where Elstree is going with this line of questioning but is at a loss, as she has been so many times today, to stop her. "Yes," she admits.

"Suddenly, all this attention to Mr. Kirtz. Did you want Mr. Kirtz to live with your mother? Yes or no?"

She knows that Elstree wants the jury to imagine her as jealous and misguided, a lonesome teen who grew into a resentful woman, now coming to testify against a man just because she hates him. But she is helpless to prevent the picture coming into view. "Well, given what he'd been doing to me, you can imagine I didn't like it."

"So, your answer is no?"

Bobbie hesitates. "That's correct," she agrees.

The room is silent as Elstree says, "You say he had sex with you around the time of your fourteenth birthday. Is that correct?"

"Yes."

Elstree does her best to describe what is meant by sex, an excruciating explanation that nonetheless seems to put a favorable gloss on it.

"From what you told the DA, there were no witnesses, correct?"

"I explained that. I knew it would get Craig in trouble—"

"I am not asking you about that. I'm asking you to name a person who saw any sign of sex taking place between your and Mr. Kirtz."

Bobbie says, "Daniel Gregory knew."

"Did he or anyone else *see* anything that would suggest that Mr. Kirtz was having sex with you?"

"Objection!" Dreyer's voice again. "Irrelevant."

The judge overrules and Elstree continues, saying, "So nobody saw any sign of attraction. To your knowledge, did anyone ever see you and Mr. Kirtz together without the presence of your mother or another supervisory adult?"

Bobbie wants to tell her that she hadn't wanted to be seen, that she was terrified of being seen. Also, that she has already said as much to the court. She explained all this first thing this morning, when Dreyer asked her to describe what had happened. But she understands she is supposed to answer yes or no, even though neither of these words are adequate. "No adults," she says finally.

"Does that mean that nobody saw you alone with Mr. Kirtz?"

"Daniel Gregory did," Bobbie says quietly.

"Yes," says Elstree, and then thumbs through some notes on her table. "You had a romantic relationship with him, correct?"

"Yes."

"Any other person you can name right now ever see you alone with Mr. Kirtz?"

Bobbie shakes her head, then stumbles through an explanation. But all it amounts to is that no, nobody saw a thing. She hates to admit this. She is aware of the jury watching her, of the judge beside her in all her robes and splendor. She feels puny, sitting in the witness stand. And she feels wrong.

Elstree says, "During the time that this sexual relationship was allegedly taking place, did you tell your mother about it?"

She hadn't. She has so often wished she'd said something, anything, no matter how difficult that might have been, but she had said nothing.

"No," she says.

"And nobody saw any such event take place?"

"Objection, asked and answered," says Dreyer.

She does not want to answer this question again but the judge, remarkably, rules against the objection and requests her to do so.

"Can you answer into the microphone?" Elstree asks.

"No, nobody saw," says Bobbie.

"At the time, did you tell your mother your wishes that Mr. Kirtz *not* live with you?"

"Yes," says Bobbie. "Yes, I did."

"But your mother allowed him to live with you anyway?"

"Yes."

"Did your mother ever explain *why* she asked Mr. Kirtz to live with her? Did she tell you that she loved him, for example?"

"No."

"Did she tell you that he brought in a substantial income that would help the family, and help you?"

"No, absolutely not."

"Are you aware of this income?"

Bobbie shakes her head. "No," she says.

"So you had no idea why it might be a good thing for your mother and, perhaps, even for you if Mr. Kirtz came to live with you in the family home?"

Bobbie says no, she did not. She feels demoralized, humiliated. Why would it have been a good thing for Craig to live with them? "I can't recall *any* good reason," she says. In fact, she could never figure out why her mother even *liked* Craig, let alone why she loved him. He was rude and intrusive and filthy and rank, and yet June seemed to take in none of this. Every once in a while he'd make a gesture—a dinner out, a bouquet of flowers—but these were only moments and did not deserve the great importance June placed on them. Her mother was crazy about him—isn't that the expression, crazy about a person? "You'd have to ask June."

WHY SHE LOVED HIM

Because June wanted to be part of something, of someone *else*. Because she didn't want to be alone at night,
to go to bed with her mug of Lipton tea and a book in her hand,
shut the door and feel as though she was kenneling herself until
morning. Because her bedroom had become exactly that, a confin-
ing four walls that no number of scented candles, ruffled pillows,
or thick colorful quilts could change. Because she wanted more and
better and regular sex, not with men generally—she could have sex
if she wanted, she supposed, she could have *men*—but with *a* man.
A singular man. Because she fussed over her face each morning,
smoothing and creaming and powdering—the collective term was
applying—all this damned makeup. That was why she went—daily,
religiously—to the hospital to see Craig, anchored in bed by needles taped to his skin as though his body was no longer human but
something that was adhered to and hung upon, stuck into, bound,
moved, rotated, and sewn.

"I'm here, darling," she would say when he was asleep, closed off
from the world, unable to hear the word *darling* from her lips nor
see the claim she made on him, her fingers softly resting against his
hand as though they were lovers.

They'd done surgery on his face and his arm, which was full of
metal rods and plates, a long line of stitches winching it together.

They'd transfused blood, cleaned up the other wounds, kept him sedated, pouring medication by the hour through IV drips. Head trauma, an arm in pieces, a fractured pelvis. He was dependent upon the long wall of machinery, all those flickering dials and red-lit numbers banked beside him. The machines were a kind of standing army that protected his body. She sat among them.

When he was awake she did not touch him but stayed at a respectful distance and tried to imagine what she could do to help. He was quiet, and quietly monitored, immobilized in the efficient room where he seemed too large, too dense with muscle, too wide in girth to belong. Big joints, big knobby feet, he was not suited for so slim a mattress. If he turned over he'd fall on the floor, except he couldn't turn over, not deliberately, nor by accident, nor by any means at all except with help from others who attended to him in abundance. Even so, regulations meant they'd erected safety bars at the sides of the bed, metal gates that flipped up and locked into place to keep him in. Later, when he could speak, he would refer to these as "baby bars."

She was there through the awful purgatory of his recovery as he lay on the high bed with its thin starchy sheets branded with the hospital's name. A chair angled beside the bed allowed visitors to sit in relative comfort. She spent hours in that chair, staring into the swathings of sheets and gauze and tape. There was a drip on his left wrist, another in his leg. A smaller line, taped to his face, allowed a slow drain of pink to leak from the site of the dreadful injury to his eye. It drained into a bag strapped to the bed, the collection of fluids measured twice daily. By her knees was another line that coiled under the thin cover and took care of his urine. This, too, was measured. His head was solid with bandages except where breathing tubes entered his nose. His arm was in a sling above him, hanging like a piece of meat at the butcher. If she came close enough, she could smell his daily perspiration that they could not yet entirely wash away beneath the scent of iodine, fresh plaster, and blood.

Sometimes she approached his massive, bandaged head and could see his lips drying in the hospital's thirsty air, the skin flaking, the corners of his mouth crusted with salt. She dabbed at his lips with a wet cloth, smoothed back his hair. Part of her nurtured the hope he'd wake up just as she was ministering to him and that they'd share a moment. This never happened.

What she'd heard was true: They'd removed the eye. In another part of his skull they'd drilled to relieve the pressure on his swelling brain. He was remarkably unharmed by these procedures; so far, all his neurological tests had checked out. But the splintering fracture that had turned his arm to mush was tricky, pieced together as it was with rods and metal fastenings. At suppertime one night it swelled in the cast and they had to saw that one off and put on another while he screamed. She wasn't in the room at the time but outside in the corridor, and she could hear him. She came back later in the quiet of evening, as he lay slumbering on pain meds, and she promised him that it was over now, the pain, and not to worry.

But the arm was determined to break free. It swelled all over again as though it refused to be encased, modified, or healed. They sawed the plaster a little more to ease the pain, allowing the ballooning tissue room to expand, but it wasn't enough. He cried out, pumping the morphine button with his good hand, giving himself as many doses as was allowed. Another cast was set and still the arm was bad. They took more X-rays. There was talk of amputation. The doctors arrived in white coats, always traveling in pairs, June noticed, like police.

There were real police, too, hovering somewhere on the periphery, waiting until the patient—waiting until Craig—was able to talk to them. The doctors protected him from their questions, for now. No interference, they insisted.

"Will his arm get better?" June asked them anxiously. What she meant was will they cut it off.

"We hope so," came the reply. "We think we see some improvement." But they had to add in more drugs to keep him from thrashing, from ripping out the tubes, from unlocking his arm from the canopy above, disrupting all those balanced ties, and wrecking the room. Even on the maximum doses, he lashed out and cried out and kept them all hopping. He was not an easy patient, not a cooperator.

JUNE WOULD SIT with him through it all, the groaning of his discomfort, the quiet dozing, the awful moments when a team of nurses would come in, their cloddy shoes squeaking on the lemon-colored tiles. They would surround his bed like a pack of wolves, then put him through the agony of turning his body. During the worst of procedures, she stood behind the screen, clutching the blue, flimsy material in her fist and counting backward from a hundred, unable to tune out the awful cries and how he cursed. Cursed every damned one of them. She sometimes wondered why there was no mother or sister or brother or father or *someone* anyway for Craig. Why was he so alone? Because he *was* alone—she could see that. Solitary, sequestered here in the hospital, unable to move.

Secretly, of course, she was grateful that it was just Craig and her. She liked to think they had forged a special union, that she meant something in his life. She'd imagined all sorts of scenarios, of him waking and finding her there late in the evening, reaching out and taking her hand. In her imagination, a story unfolded: She would learn he always listened for her voice and hoped she was beside him. Especially at the worst moments, or late at night, when he was unable to sleep for the pain. Thank you, he said to her, in her imagination. Thank you for looking after me.

In real life, she'd been nowhere near him when he first gained consciousness and as far as she was aware, he hadn't said anything by way of gratitude to a soul since that moment. He lay wrapped in his bandages, looking dead when he was asleep, tense and still when awake. She did not know whether or not he realized he had only one eye (now *there* was a conversation starter), and she dared not tell him. He had taken an awful lot. His body was a robust piece of hardware, but any human has limitations, and so she forgave him for ignoring her except to make single-word demands: "water," "bedpan," "food."

One evening, the drugs lifting, his condition more promising, they finally had that longed-for first conversation, or near enough.

She was sitting in the chair with a copy of *Cosmo* and coffee in a Styrofoam cup. It had become her regular place, this chair, an evening destination, a kind of waiting room for her life. She had one leg hooked over the low arm, a pillow under her shoulder.

She hadn't even realized he was awake, so the last thing she expected—the last thing in the world—was to hear his voice, lucid and strong, when all she'd heard for days was his silence or pain during these late hours.

"What happened to Barbara?" he croaked out.

She jumped, spilling coffee over her hand.

"What?" she said, leaning closer. She had to get right up next to him, but she could hear him now, that same voice she'd heard months ago when she'd invited him to the house, that same voice on the radio that she'd looked forward to nightly. All those times she'd stayed up, switching to his station at midnight, and now the voice was beside her.

"Is Barbara okay?" he asked. It took effort to get the words out. He sounded pained. She thought he needed water.

"Bobbie? Of course! Bobbie is fine. She's at home," she said. She thought he must be delirious. Too many painkillers, anti-inflammatories, antibiotics, anti-nausea pills, sleeping pills. She wondered how often he'd been awake when she thought he was sleeping, listening when she thought he heard nothing. She was suddenly aware of how she looked, her skin a little sweaty in the warm hospital, her lipstick chewed off hours ago, her eyes bloodshot in the harsh ceiling lights. She was aware, too, of being very close to him, practically on top of him, as he spoke into her ear as though it were a microphone. She moved back in her chair, listening to the little farting noise the cushion always made, which embarrassed her now. She was grateful when he began to cough.

Then, as though hoisted by a derrick, he suddenly heaved from the bed. "God damn *you*!" he said directly to his arm, floating above him on a traction bar. The arm did not look like an arm. It hung unnaturally, seeming detached, out of place, suspended from above, large and imposing, reminding June of the installation of the blue whale in D.C.'s famous Museum of Natural History. "God damn *yoooou*!" he called at it.

The arm remained silent and unmoving as he called it a fucker, an asshole, as he called the arm a piece of shit.

"Don't say that," June whispered. She offered him water through a straw.

He slurped at the water, spilling it onto his chin from where it dripped down his neck, then he started swearing again as she tried to dab his face with a cloth, swatting at her hand. She told herself he was tired of being at the mercy of everyone, unable to even wipe his own face. That was why he was so angry. She told herself she would behave the same under such conditions. Worse, maybe. She wouldn't want a single other person to look at her in such a state. To think that everything about him now—his food, his pain, his waste—was managed by others. No wonder he was always in a temper.

"She buy anything good with the cash?" he said angrily.

June didn't understand. She said, "Barbara . . . Bobbie? You are asking if *Bobbie* bought anything?"

He'd exhausted himself already and lay weakly in the bed. He began to say something and June got down close to his face so she could hear him. His mouth smelled sour, like pus. Or maybe that was the rest of him, his head, his eye.

"All that money," he muttered.

She did not know what he meant. What money? She might have asked him but he looked so tired. He closed his eye, exhausted. He seemed to be getting paler, weaker, as though a tide of illness was drawing near. He coughed and moaned loudly. "Get my head out of this fucking oven," he said.

He coughed again, touching his good hand against his chest, which rumbled like a car engine trying to start but did not clear. She gave him some water and he drank it, then threw it all up in a fit of hard coughing. His lips were turning purple, his face a strawberry color. She thought he might be choking and she grabbed for the call button, a little red dial encased in beige plastic that hovered over the bed like a spider. She had to get out of the way in a hurry on instructions from the nurse, Esther, who charged into the room, her rubber soles slapping the hard floor, yelling "Get the hell up, mister!" when he leaned over the bed, almost falling. "I'm not lifting you again, that's for sure. They'll have to call in a crane!"

Standing at the door, she watched as Esther pushed one side of him, trying to protect the lines taped onto his skin. She pressed the buzzer again and another nurse came in, a young one with blond hair piled on her head, flying past June so that she had to press her back to the wall.

"You might want to come back another time," Esther said, her tone making it clear this was not a suggestion but an order. June stood at the door, frozen, horrified, but grateful to the women who worked on Craig. One of the machines was making a bell sound and she wondered if the alarm meant something bad was happening, that he wasn't getting enough air or that his heart was stopping. He didn't look like his heart was stopping. He was flailing, coughing, his lungs rumbling inside his chest, while the nurses hauled him back onto the mattress and told him to stay there, *stay there now!* She wanted to explain to Esther that he couldn't get up easily, couldn't move or see, now apparently he couldn't even breathe, and that she should be more careful with him; after all, he was in *pain*. But she backed out of the room as she had been instructed, calling out that she would wait in the hallway and not to worry. He couldn't hear her anyway. He was yelling at the blond-haired nurse that she was a motherfucker while Esther untangled his IV and shouted back that he better shut his mouth or else she would let him die.

IT WAS PNEUMONIA. The fever was high and they removed some of the bandages, placing cold packs on his forehead to cool him. His scalp flaked dramatically, with clots of dandruff and sore areas where there was some irritation from the trapped sweat. Where they'd shaved his hair were tidy stitches and pebbles of dried black blood, the surrounding skin orange with Betadine. Over his empty eye socket, wedged between the bones, was a thick pad of bandages held in place by a constellation of surgical tape. He was more alert now that the drugs were working.

What they called "hospital pneumonia" was a consuming, fever-ish illness that lasted for days. Even on IV antibiotics, he was baking; a 102 degree temperature made him shiver in the stiff bedsheets, his face slanted toward her, watching her there in the blocky chair with its sweaty upholstery, a cushioned orange nylon. He coughed, then winced, then coughed again. Sometimes he coughed so much that he gasped for breath. One time, after a violent bout of this, he whis-pered, "I guess my body would rather suffocate than drown." She asked the nurses for an oxygen mask, but they said he didn't need it.

"He ain't drowning," Esther said. "He's bullshitting."

But he wasn't bullshitting, June thought. He had to concentrate hard just to keep his lungs working; he had to think about breath-ing. For days he communicated very little, but gradually the illness seemed to draw back, receding so that he was no longer as fragile. She could almost feel the weight of the pneumonia vanishing into the hospital air, drifting like a ghost to another patient, or perhaps disappearing altogether. One day he was desperately ill, the next he was a man recuperating in the narrow bed beside her chair, able to respond when she spoke to him.

"Are you watching me?" she teased. "Think I'm going to pull a fast one?"

He smiled, just a little. "I hope so," he whispered.

It was a strange, one-sided courtship. She prepared for him each evening, her makeup bag growing ever bulkier in her purse. After work, she would drive to the hospital parking lot, bend over a lighted mirror, and wash off the day's stress with a moistened towelette, dabbing foundation under her eyes to hide the shadows there. She considered herself an artist, and like an artist she allowed her whim to take over. She drew feathery sweeps across her eyebrows to make them higher and fuller, brushing them smooth to blend the marks. She plumped up her mascara, first with one wand, then another. She drew on a fresh line of lipstick, after penciling the line of her lips in a raspberry shade. Sometimes she left a laundered blouse in the car so she could change from her work clothes and go to him directly from the store. Sometimes she went home and took a shower, putting on a pressed skirt and blouse, spraying the air around her with perfume before she went out, as though on a date.

"You look good," Craig told her one evening as he took her into his vision. He was much better now. There was a newly ignited masculinity in him; she felt it in the way he looked at her. He watched her unabashedly, looking at her neck and breasts, straining down to take in her thighs. In any other situation, it would have unnerved her, but not here. Over the days, then weeks, the room had started to feel like their own. She brought in a flowering plant, a pillow for the chair. She left a few *Cosmo*s around to read during the hours that he slept, and (she admitted only to herself) because she wanted anyone who entered the room to see that a woman had been there.

He asked her about Bobbie, what she was up to, who she hung out with. It was kind, how he took an interest. And sitting with him was pleasant. They listened to the sounds from the nurses outside, their purposeful footsteps, the buzz and wallop of the machines, the breathy swish of the elevator. The silence of the room was punctured by the clank of gurneys rolling, knocking through the swinging double doors that separated the wards outside. He'd say, "Another body," as though there were corpses being wheeled in, and she would laugh.

"Get me a radio," he said one night, and she bought one at Radio Shack and made a present of it the next day.

He listened to the station where he worked, always that one station. But when he slept, she listened to the classical station, or to one that often played show tunes, because why listen to Craig's station when Craig wasn't on the air? Whenever he woke, she switched it over as he preferred so that he didn't have to hear any of "her" music. He didn't like "old lady music." He didn't like jazz, either. Too depressing, too old, and sometimes no lyrics at all. He liked rock: Lynyrd Skynyrd, Jackson Browne, Bob Seger, the Stones.

"Oh me too!" she told him. She tried to think of other artists he might like. She told him she liked Linda Ronstadt. "Do you like her, too?"

"Yeah, I'd like to fuck her," he said. Or at least, this is what June thought he'd said.

Esther was in the room at the time, writing a note on a clipboard hung at the end of his bed. She moved like a whip toward him, brought her hand back and threatened to slap him on the mouth.

"Hey!" he shouted.

"Next time you say something dirty in my presence, I'll make a fist and you *will* feel it!"

"Someone should fire you," he said.

"Somebody might," she snapped back. She flicked her finger against the IV on his hand, looked at the saline bag on its metal pole, and waited until she saw it drip. "But I'm here now and if you talk filth, you'll get beat."

"I think it's the medication making him cranky," June said. She smiled an apology at Esther.

Esther widened her eyes and stared down her nose at June. "You think it's the medication?" she said. "Oh girl, you better think again." To Craig she said, "I wish that arm would stabilize so they'd send you home."

"They should have cut it off at the shoulder," he said. "So I could be a one-eyed, one-armed monster."

June shook her head. The conversation seemed wild to her. Profanity and threats of slapping; now violent thoughts of mutilation. She gave Craig a pleading look. "You don't mean that," she said.

In private, away from Craig, June asked Esther if the police had been back. She'd seen them a few times and wondered if they had been in to see Craig.

"You mean to question him about drugs in his car?"

"That, yes," June said. "Or anything."

"You want to know if the police are after your man?"

June blushed. She liked the sound of that, *your man.* "They wouldn't be *after* him," she said.

"Dunno," said Esther. "He got in a fistfight with some guy before getting wasted and driving his car into the trees, or so it's being told. He's going from here to the courthouse, I imagine. Boy, they can have him."

That day he'd sworn at the Jell-O, calling it a green mound of butt fat. And he'd demanded a second dinner after eating only the meat out of the stew of the first one. June wished he wouldn't do such things, but a courthouse? She couldn't believe it would ever come to that. He was a public figure, after all, practically a celebrity. In her mind, she'd imagined that he would soon be discharged from the hospital, and they would begin dating, and everything would blossom from there. She tried to sound reasonable now to Esther. "He's just a little rough around the edges, plus all this pain he's in. What he wants is a little love, I think."

Esther breathed out a long sigh. She had four clipboards under one arm and an assortment of plastic tubs in another. "Oh honey, you got that wrong," she said. "He wants jailing and then some."

JUNE WOULD BRING him cold cans of cola, chunky crab salad sandwiches, brownies she'd baked, but then Craig would talk about marijuana as though she'd missed an important part of the menu.

"You got any weed?" he'd asked.

"Weeds?"

"Pot, marijuana. Don't tell me you never heard of it. You can put some in these brownies next time you come. Would you do that for me, babe? Add a little reefer?"

June hesitated. "Oh, I don't know," she said.

"Hash? Hell, I'll take some Lebanese if that's all there is, but bring something to kill a bit of the reality around here." He made a gesture toward the room, then looked at her pleadingly.

"I'll bring beer," she said, though she knew alcohol was forbidden, possibly even dangerous with his medications.

"That's a start. But I could give you a phone number to call—"

No numbers, no buying drugs. He gave up after a few tries with her, the expression on his face as though he'd been trying to teach a dog to ride a bicycle.

She decided his behavior was all because of his painkillers. She'd spent an afternoon in the library, looking up the effects of certain analgesics and barbiturates on the brain; she'd read the fine print on the drugs he'd been prescribed. The warnings included dementia, mood swings, all sorts of antisocial behavior, not to mention various physical problems. You couldn't expect him to act "normal" when he was taking all these drugs. And anyway, sometimes he was very sweet.

"You tell Bobbie I'm thinking of her," he said. "She's a nice girl."

"Oh, she is," agreed June. "I couldn't have asked for a nicer daughter."

"And *so* resourceful."

June thought about that. "Yes, that is true. She makes dinner most evenings these days. And does the laundry, too."

"You pay her for that?"

"Pay her? What, like an allowance?"

"She might need some cash. You ever ask her? Whether she's got enough *cash*? I've got a feeling that girl would be good with money if she had some. Ask her if she has any money."

The way he said these things made June wonder if he were passing judgment on her mothering skills. It was true that she hadn't recently asked Bobbie anything about money or what her needs might be, and she realized now that this had been an oversight. A teenage girl had to have money for clothes and makeup and that sort of thing. It was kind of Craig to point this out.

"I guess I ought to bring up the subject," she said.

"Yeah, tell her I was wondering how she was getting on with

money—that I was *concerned*. And that at some point maybe we should talk about it."

June couldn't think why he'd want to talk to Bobbie about money. And she couldn't understand the way his mood seemed to plunge even as his body healed. But she did what she was told and asked Bobbie whether she thought she had enough money.

"Enough *money*?" Bobbie said, as though June had asked if she were planning to rob a bank. "Who wants to know?"

"Craig wants to know," June answered. "I think he's worried that you don't get an allowance."

ONE NIGHT, DURING the last minutes of visiting hours, he said, "You look forward to coming here, don't you?"

June was gathering her car keys, slipping her feet back into her pumps, readying to leave. She thought he'd been asleep and had been moving as quietly as she could when she heard his voice. "All the damned day long this is what you think about," he continued.

She looked at him, unable to contradict him but refusing to agree.

He said, "You can't wait to get here every day, sit yourself down next to me."

She made a sound like a laugh, but she wasn't laughing. She didn't understand why he was reducing her caring for him to some kind of obsession. But perhaps he had it right. Call it weakness, call it loneliness, call it the need for distraction, she'd grown to love the routine of visiting him at the hospital. Her nightly visits were the closest thing she'd had to a romance in many years and she felt like a girl again, walking beneath the banks of umbrella lamps in the parking lot, her heels making clicks on the lighted sidewalks, coming through the great glass entrance of the hospital with its atmosphere of quiet urgency, taking the elevator to his floor. It felt important, like going to an office, except there was more to it. A romantic edge that made her eager. It gave her something, she didn't know what.

"What you're thinking about is getting here," Craig said now. "The whole day long, in your mind, you're always on your way."

She shook her head. "No," she said. But it was true. From the moment she rose, showering and washing and dressing, she was thinking about what would happen at the other end of the day. Through all the hours at the store, serving customers, sorting stock, counting out the register, while driving back in the car, scrubbing off the pencil lines and powdered shadows from the backs of her hands where she'd demonstrated to customers the difference between matte rose and frosted rose, or sepia compared to dark rust, she was an arrow searching for a target, flying through the hours until at last she could land at the hospital, at his bedside.

"Believe it or not, I'm a very busy lady," she said, smiling at him with her eyes.

His response was immediate and damning. "But you don't care about all that," he said.

"I do!" she said, but it sounded unconvincing. Weekends, tidying the house, handwashing her dresses, hanging damp stockings over doorknobs, bleaching her yellowing bras. She'd sit in the bathroom with an angled hair-dye brush, dabbing Clairol onto her roots, looking at her face that seemed with each passing summer a little more overcooked. Weekdays, the mad rush to work, the endless standing and stooping and smiling behind the showcases of cosmetics. She sweated in the heat from the spot lamps above. She hid her freckles and the pockmarks of her acne beneath Gold Beige (44) or Natural Buff (60), her stomach swaddled in her skirt, the glint of her earrings reflected in the countertop glass. She was always smiling, always inviting, always ready, and she did not know any longer for what, if not seeing Craig at the end of the day.

"You better be quiet now or I won't come tomorrow," she said.

"Oh, you'll come," he said, rolling his tongue over his gums.

He reached to touch her. It seemed almost as though he were trying to touch her chest, but she intercepted, taking his fingers in her palm and stroking them.

"Not if you talk to me like that." She was trying to gain some

ground, give him a gentle scolding without discouraging him altogether. "I won't come back if you're going to talk to me like that,
no sir," she said, but she was smiling, trying to make it better. His
fingers were thick and warm, filling her palm. Surely he wanted
her here with him at the hospital. She couldn't have been mistaken
about that.

"Talk to you like what?" he said slowly. His one eye blinked at
her. "I'm only making an observation."

"But you shouldn't say—"

"I already did."

She looked down at the floor. He was really very rude, she
thought. She wondered why she was so glad he held her hand, but
she *was* glad. It thrilled her, even though it was so little a gesture
after all her greater ones. She accepted it, cherished it, knowing all
the while that she gave it greater importance than she ought to.

"Close the curtain there," he instructed. He meant the cotton
blind across the wall of windows on one side of the room. The blind
had a coating like a shower curtain and was made from material
that did not hang like cloth. It was a flimsy covering that was meant
to offer a degree of modesty to the patient or perhaps only to block
the lights of the hall.

"Don't the nurses usually do that?"

He shook his head. "Go. Do it. Nobody will care."

She rose, watching his face. He wasn't angry, not exactly, not yet.
She got the feeling that the things he asked her to do were a kind of
test to see if she cared about him. To see where her loyalties lay. She
went to the window that faced into the corridor. Outside, a few feet
away, was the nurses station: a desk, a lamp, a standing fan, a blond
nurse currently on the telephone. She saw, too, that the nurse was
not alone. There was an orderly, leaning on one end of the long desk,
drinking coffee and watching the nurse as she spoke with the caller.
Evidently the orderly had brought the nurse coffee, too, because it
steamed on the ledge above the desk. Most of the ceiling lights had
been switched off for the night and the desk was now lit by a lamp.
June watched the nurse take a sip of coffee, then finish the phone

call. She watched the orderly waiting, his face registering an attraction that the nurse, too, had taken in. June could see the way the nurse smiled at him, and the kind of composed anticipation that the orderly returned. Locked into each other, they had no interest in what was happening in Craig's room or in even glancing her way as she stood stiffly at the window, unsure of what Craig was asking of her, or why he wanted the curtain drawn.

"Go on, close it," he said.

She pushed the curtain together. She could feel Craig's gaze on her, on her legs, on her ass. She sensed he had a plan, and that she mustn't interfere with that plan. She understood, too, that the moony persistence that the orderly displayed toward his nurse was of a different type to that of Craig, who she heard moving in the bed, adjusting his position. She wanted to turn around, to deflect whatever was starting between them, but she didn't dare.

She heard him now, the deep, slow voice, the determined instruction. "Take off your blouse," he said.

She could not say a word, not to protest, not to agree.

She heard Craig speak again. "Undo the front," he said. "Unbutton it."

Her lips were dry, her palms wet. She felt a bead of perspiration run down her side. She had never before taken off a stitch of clothing in public. It wasn't the sort of thing she did.

"Nobody can see."

"Even so—"

"Please," he said.

She did not know why he was choosing this moment. She wondered if the crash, the near-death experience, had altered Craig's views on such matters. Maybe he needed to feel attractive. Maybe he needed confirmation that she saw him as vital and desirable. She thought about his eye. She thought about the hole drilled in his head. She undid the first few buttons of her blouse. There were things she wanted to discuss with Craig; their age difference, for one. He must be aware that she was in her mid-thirties—she had a fifteen-year-old daughter, after all. But she didn't know exactly how old he was, and surely they should talk about that before sex got started. Which was now, apparently.

The remaining buttons were now undone and the folds of her blouse hung loosely at her sides.

She heard Craig again, his voice low. "Turn around," he said.

She glanced at her watch; it was a quarter to eleven. If anyone walked in, they would know what was going on. She looked down at her chest, at the freckled sternum, the plain white bra. If she turned now there was no going back. He would see her naked, or half naked, and this would be the new expectation every time they met. Did that matter? Did she expect they'd keep seeing each other after he was discharged from the hospital if there was no sex? Anyway, she'd wanted sex, hadn't she? But she'd wanted, at the very least, to kiss him first.

She breathed in and out slowly. She did not want to do what she was about to do. Nobody was forcing her. Nobody could make her do a thing. And yet here she was, as though her body did not belong to her, as though she had no will at all. She had watched herself do as Craig asked, unbuttoning the blouse, and now she crossed her hands in front of her and swung toward him, as he had directed.

He was sitting up, his legs apart. She could see how he stared at her breasts, his face hard with concentration. It had been a long time since she'd been with a man. She'd forgotten the energy that came with desire, the flush on the skin, the intensity in the man's eyes, the muscles, flexed and waiting. She opened her mouth and a little breath escaped, she felt a charge move up her spine.

"Move your hands," he said.

She didn't know if she could. She pleaded with herself to do as he asked but she wished that if they had to do this—to do this right now—she could lie down and let him move over her and be somewhere private. She didn't think she should undress so close to the window. She didn't think she should be so brazen.

"Craig, I don't know if—"

"Pull up your bra."

It was too much. She almost said so. It wouldn't be difficult to get her blouse straight, grab her handbag, and leave, would it? What could he do? If he yelled at her, he would have the nurses to contend with. Esther would set him straight. *Put that thing away*, she'd say. *And keep your hands to yourself in my hospital!* That was the kind of scolding he needed. But she was not Esther, and he would not be interested in her if she were. She looked at him, his bandaged head poking toward her, his good eye fixed on her chest. She wasn't a small-breasted woman. The breasts were certainly more impressive in their bra, shaped, blooming proudly outward instead of flopping down. If she lifted them out of the bra cups, they would dangle unnaturally unless she removed her bra altogether, which she did not want to do now, right here, just feet from the orderly and nurse on the other side of the glass, whose own lovemaking was so far confined to words and glances.

But she did not want to lose that expression on Craig's face, his longing for her, his attention. All her life she'd craved just this kind of smoldering look from a man, this raw desire. Yes, she had wanted other things, too: friendship, security, a home. But at the heart of it all, at the very center, she needed to feel as though she fulfilled this very necessary, authentic desire.

She drew the straps of her bra down her shoulders a few inches, caught in the embrace of his stare. Now he could see her full breasts. Uncaged from the bra they were strangely shaped, with nobbly areas around the nipples, and wide, dark areolas. The angle of her nipples was low, facing down; a disappointment, perhaps. It would have been so much better for him not to see her breasts like this, in the unforgiving hospital light, with the humming of machines and the silent dripping IVs and the people just outside. But here they were, and nothing could be more clear than the promise of her naked breasts, and her willingness to disrobe at his request.

"Touch yourself," he said.

She wondered if he were only joking, that at any moment he would relax his gaze and tell her that he was sorry and had been wrong to say anything like that. Maybe he'd explain that he'd gotten carried away because he found her sexy, holding his apology up like a bouquet of roses. Button up and give me a hug, he might say. Wouldn't any decent man say that? *Button up and give me a hug, if you can find a way of doing that with all these tubes.*

But that wasn't what he said, though she longed for these words, as well as for his embrace. She knew that with the arm in traction and the crack in the pelvis, and the way his head was bandaged and unmovable, there wasn't much chance she'd be able to hug him, but those facts didn't stop her wishing for it. She wanted him to stand beside her, lean and tall and fully able once again, and for her to reach up and bury her face in his neck, to feel the heat of his body against her own, to press into the architecture of his bones and muscles, and to feel him press into her. But she needed all this to take place in privacy.

"Put your fingers on your nipples," he said.

"I don't think I can—"

"Yes, you can. Do it. Do it for me."

She stared down at her breasts. The fluorescent light caught the blueness of the veins that crisscrossed and all the little imperfections of her skin. They were enormous, her breasts, but they'd taken on a lot of the extra calories she'd been storing and the weight caused them to hang like skirts above her stomach. Still, she imagined that was a turn-on for a man. Big breasts, that was a plus, surely? Even so, she couldn't bear to touch them, to pretend that touching herself that way gave her pleasure. She was already imagining how in the future she would remember this moment, standing on the cold linoleum tiles, exposing herself. She decided a good compromise would be to hold her breasts, covering them as she did so, but in a manner that might fool Craig into thinking she was getting some pleasure from it. She thought she could manage that much.

She cupped each one in a hand, then slowly lifted them up. She did not dare look at Craig, fearing his disapproval. There were secrets to men she had never understood. What had moved him to insist that she show her breasts in so unromantic a setting? And why would he want her to fondle herself, as though his touch was wholly unnecessary? There was the question, too, of where exactly she was meant to focus her gaze. Was she meant to look down, as though admiring her own breasts? Or watch her fingers and pretend they were another's? Was she supposed to look at Craig, as though catching him in the web of erotic play between them? It was hard to tell, so she closed her eyes. That proved quite useful and she managed to do as he wanted for several minutes before opening her eyes once again, blinking into the opaque brightness of the hospital room.

She saw at once that he was in a kind of trance, watching her, his bandaged head rolled back, his mouth open. She wasn't sure what was going on—it was difficult to work out his expression under all those bandages. She could see the look of concentration, how his mouth opened and closed in vague little gasps like a caught fish. For a second she wondered if he was in pain, wondered if he'd suffered some kind of seizure, but then she glanced south to what he was doing with his good hand, how it was moving under the bedsheets. Even with the injured arm in traction and the pelvis aligned in a rigid splint to keep him from aggravating the fracture there, even though he was using only a single eye to stare at her breasts, he was able to masturbate, sending the sheet springing up with every pump.

"Oh my God," she said.

"Baby . . ."

She wanted him to stop, to stop right now. But it was too late; she saw his hand suddenly freeze, his face grimace, the muscles in his arm relax and be still. What he'd done, what he'd done right there in front of her, that *act*, reminded her of an awful trip to the monkey house at the National Zoo. Like those animals, Craig seemed untroubled by his body's demands, whatever those demands might be. Now she was going to have to say something, but she didn't know what. She waited for him to call her over but he said nothing. And so she turned to one side, lowering her shoulders in an attempt to cover herself as she placed her breasts once more into the bra, tugging her blouse around her and fastening the buttons down the front.

She had crossed a line; *they* had crossed a line. And now there was a sudden emptying of hope. It was as though the dream of a burgeoning love had been punctured by some nasty doppelgänger dream, a raw, evil version of their relationship that now substituted for what she'd been wishing for, what she'd been imagining the past many weeks.

She straightened her clothes, combed her hair behind her ears with her fingers, then wiped her palms on her skirt. She still felt exposed. She remembered with relief that she'd brought a jacket. She thought surely he would say something to her, as she was standing next to the bed, inches from him. But his head was tipped away.

She wasn't sure how to behave in such circumstances. She felt the way she did after stopping at a gas station and buying a Hershey bar and a Snickers, then eating them both all at once so quickly that she didn't even enjoy it. After such an event, she wanted to pretend nothing had happened, or that it did not count or did not matter. But such trickery was impossible with someone else involved. She thought she would say something to him now, but did not know what to say. She stared at the floor. It felt such a burden to look up. Finally she picked her handbag off the floor and whispered, "Good night."

She thought he'd at least say good night back to her, but he did not. He said nothing. She wondered if he expected her to just shuttle out, dismissed from the room. Surely nobody could be that cold. She stared at him, and now she realized that he was not moving. The awful fear floated toward her: Perhaps because of the excitement and strain on his heart, he had died.

A little gasp sprang from her, and a sudden, overwhelming horror. She cried out. Her legs wobbled, unable to balance her. She collapsed forward onto the bed, the handbag dropping to the floor, its contents spilling. A lipstick flew across the linoleum like a hockey puck; her hands sprang to break her fall, one on the mattress, the other on the hard frame of his pelvic brace. Her mind could not hold the cascade of thoughts and feelings that flooded into her, that seemed to swirl around her. He was dead; she was falling. The awfulness of it was overwhelming until she finally felt him shudder and cry out and tell her to get the hell off him. Get the hell off him now!

"What?" She sprang back. She might have dropped onto the floor but the chair caught her. "I thought you were—"

"Asleep!" he said. "I was asleep!"

She could see his face creased with anger, smell the yeasty heat of his drying wounds, the sharp scent of Betadine and dressings. He was alive all right—how could she have imagined otherwise?

He did not speak again, not to ask what time it was, nor to tell her, as he normally did before she left each night, to hold the plastic cup and straw for him to sip water. She stayed in the chair just as she had fallen, her legs splayed, one of her shoes missing, her jacket flopping unbuttoned around her. She saw now that her hairbrush had slid under the bed, and that all the items from her handbag littered the floor: tissues, the pink paper casing of a tampon, pens, lipstick, coins. She was going to have to crawl under the bed and fetch all these things, and she hoped that she would not run her stockings in the process. It was late. She did not have to look at the clock to know that. And it seemed such an awful lot of trouble right now to get down on that floor. She envied Craig, who dropped so easily back to sleep while she waited, stunned and floating, in the aftermath of an encounter she fought to believe was not humiliating. Humiliating for her.

She heard through the hospital window the faint blare of an ambulance and focused on that noise as it increased, louder and louder. She could worry about anything, she realized now, how she looked in a certain light, whether or not certain people would catch her doing the wrong thing, or what was being said or not being said about her. Meanwhile, there were ambulances emptying themselves of those who had real troubles, who could not breathe or move, who could be dying. She should look outward, she told herself, and think of them. She should focus on what is important. What did she need off the floor, what did she need right now? Her wallet and car keys, that's all. Would it be so awful to leave the other things? Was she obligated to mop up life's every little mess? She scooped her keys into her palm, fished out her wallet with her toe. She would go now; he was asleep and so what was the point of waiting for him to talk to her, to care for her, to tell her something that would make what they had done feel good? She got up from the chair. He did not move. She adjusted her clothes, ran her fingers through her hair. He slept with his mouth open; she could see his pale pink tongue. She wished he would wake and smile at her, and hold her hand. Never mind, she'd go home now. That was all. She'd collect the rest of her things tomorrow.

BECAUSE SHE WOULDN'T MARRY HIM

Bobbie cannot eat the club sandwich she is given for lunch. She cannot drink the coffee. She can drink water; she can play with the wedge of lemon in the glass. She does not want to think or to talk to anyone.

She keeps watching for Dan. He is next in the line of witnesses for the prosecution. He is here in the building, somewhere. She isn't sure whether she wants to see him or not. She is sure, however, that she doesn't want to see anyone else.

When she gets back into the courtroom, she searches her bag for some lip gloss or ChapStick or anything that can soothe her dry lips. She feels inside the bag, but instead of finding the lip gloss, she feels a stiff piece of paper. She looks down and there, in her handbag, beside her makeup and notebook and keys and papers, she sees a page from a yellow legal pad folded into thirds, waiting for her. Her name, written in strange, blocky handwriting, blazes on the front of it. She knows at once that the letter is from Craig and that he has disguised his handwriting.

So nothing has changed for him. She feels a freezing in her chest, a sudden unsteadiness. Even now, he is able to do whatever he likes—in front of a judge and jury, in front of his own counsel. She believes the brazen manner with which he would write her a letter—at all, but especially here in court—is because he thinks he has done nothing wrong.

She recalls freshly how he would invent his own moral world, deciding in his mind the rightness or wrongness of an act. He had rules. He had notions of conduct. He would watch pornography before having sex with her, for instance, making a point that she should not see it. She was too young for that, he'd explained. She was not old enough yet to "handle porn." Watching alone, then calling her into the bedroom with him, made it okay because he wasn't letting her see what he called "the ugly side of sex." He was shielding her from that which he found unsavory.

And so she would wait somewhere else. If his housemates were away she would stay in the kitchen while he watched a video, the curtains drawn, the only light coming from the TV screen. Sitting on a kitchen stool, waiting for him to call her, she might have been blowing bubbles in milk with a straw or dividing her M&M's by color. Then she'd hear her name, put those things away, and walk like a zombie through the open door of the bedroom. Her eyes adjusted to the dim light and there it was: his arousal, abrupt and unconcealed. No matter how often she'd been exposed to him, naked and erect, the suddenness of seeing him on the bed, running his palm over his erection as though polishing a stone, the video still frozen on the screen, felt newly alarming.

She thinks to herself now, *He is still the same.* And the notion that such a man has continued unstopped, continued through days and years and decades while she covered her face with her hands and saw none of it because it was so much easier to do nothing, makes her feel a different sort of shame. She might have prevented it happening to other girls. She might have stopped him dead.

She imagines that the letter he has somehow slipped into her bag is supposed to prove to her that she was never entirely outside of his grasp, and that nobody can take away his freedom. He can reach inside any part of her he wishes. Hasn't that always been the case? Not that he, specifically, over the years had been able to reach into her, to hurt her, but that his memory had done so. Hasn't his mark upon her been as constant as though he'd been there all along, darkening the stain he made on her all those years ago?

She wheels around and sees him there at the defense table, engaged in a conversation with Elstree. His broad face is cross-hatched by an enormous frown line that runs the length of his forehead. He wears a pair of narrow black-framed eyeglasses with lenses that go from light to dark in different light conditions. Somehow in the last too-many years he's managed to lose his eyebrows. She isn't sure how a person can cause their eyebrows to suddenly disappear but she sees plainly where they used to be but are no longer. Maybe he burned them off smoking from short bongs. He'd once singed off all his eyelashes doing just that.

She thinks she should rip up the note but considers that perhaps it could be used as evidence. She can't decide whether to read it or to show it to Dreyer. Perhaps she will do neither, just throw the paper into the trash as though she had only noticed that it didn't belong to her. She stares down at it as though it is a zoo animal that might come crashing through the cage bars, and tells herself that nothing he writes to her can touch her. The risk from such an action is for himself. He should be more careful.

Despite herself, she opens the letter. It is only a single sentence, formed in the blocky letters that will make it impossible to identify as his. It reads, *I married her because you would not let me marry you.*

Marry. When she was fourteen he'd made the promise to marry her one day. He stated this plainly, with confidence, as though it were inevitable. The thought used to terrify her, as though having sex with him meant that, eventually, she had to marry him. Refusal to marry him when she was doing all *that* with him would be a terrible reflection on her character. She felt bound to him, the same feeling she often had that obligated her to get into his car when he opened the door, and to say nothing as he drove her out somewhere private. The same sense of obligation that meant she let him assess her body, turning her in front of him like the mechanical ballerina in a music box, checking her hips and breasts and ass. To marry him was only a continuation of that same hold he'd had on her. One more step in a process she'd seemed helpless to end.

I will stop you from hurting others, she thinks. The declaration rings with bravado and she knows it is unlikely. It helps her, however, to believe that there is rightness to her actions, just as it had helped him all those years ago to make declarations of love or marriage. Such promises served in Craig's mind to legitimize everything he'd done—luring her, fixing her in place, convincing her to stay. She understood this in a way she could not have as a girl. He was convinced he loved her, and this fact, if it were a fact, made whatever he did acceptable to him. He could feel like a good guy because he offered marriage, as though that made up for it all.

She looks at him now. In his version of their story, he has loved long and deeply. He has risked everything for this one dark passion. His girl, his Barbara. How can it be imaginable to him now, at this late date, that she loves him or ever had loved him? *I married her because you would not let me marry you.* She watches him at the defense table and he suddenly turns toward her, as though he'd known all along that she was watching him. He stares at her, smiling. The note is still in her hand. She wishes she hadn't read it. He is so pleased, she thinks, that once again she has taken his bait.

From the right, Dreyer approaches the stand and now obstructs her sightline. "You ready?" he says. "We're going to fix everything up again."

He means the cross-examination with Elstree that went so wrong. He means that he is going to put her back on the stand and ask her to clarify why she said nothing, why she did not ask for help, and why she had not been seen. These are the essential questions upon which everything rests.

If she is going to show him the letter, now is the time.

"There is a letter," she says.

Dreyer waits for the hum of conversation to begin again before pushing Bobbie for an answer. "What letter?"

Everything is in motion once more; the judge is arriving, they are being told to all rise.

"Never mind," she whispers.

"Tell me."

She thinks of the letter in her bag. What is the point of showing it to anyone? Who would believe he'd written such a thing and stuck it in her bag? She'd only be accused of writing it herself. "A long time ago," she tells him. "From Craig. But it doesn't matter now."

Years ago, Craig had scrawled a similar note on a piece of hospital stationery in what looked like a child's hand. She remembers how she'd come home from school and found the letter in the mailbox. That letter had served as the one in her bag did now, to unsettle her, to make her feel as though her life would forever be haunted by him.

HOSPITAL LETTER

All those weeks, head wound in so many bandages he couldn't angle it to rest, face half covered, tubes everywhere, bruises and needles, and a permanent throb deep in his right hip that kept him up most nights. He'd never been so fucked up. His body was a painful storehouse of organs and bones; he couldn't make it do anything more than fart. Finally he was feeling better and would they connect a phone in his room? Would they, hell! No phones were allowed in this particular room, this *treatment room*, they said, as though he was getting any decent treatment here.

"That being on whose say-so?" he asked.

"That being the rules," one of the clan of nurses told him. They were all in cahoots, these nurses—tribal, sisterly. This one was into her forties, a give-up-on-looks kind of a woman who was getting fat and letting her hair go gray, which would be all right if at least she'd be kind and motherly, which she was not.

"What the hell sort of rules stops you using a *phone*?" he said.

The nurse shrugged and wrote something on his chart.

"What are you writing there?"

"Nil by mouth."

"Oh ha ha. You gonna starve me, too? Starve me in this phoneless prison? Watch me through the window like a goldfish in a bowl?"

He wanted to tell the nurse how once he'd seen an actual, real goldfish sick in a tank with something called "swim bladder" disease. The fish swam pathetically upside down, making slow circles with its one working fin, and that he was like that fish now. On his back, unable to use all his limbs, floating through his days. But would she care? No, she wouldn't care that he was sick like a fish. He'd been shut down, made to comply by virtue of his body that stank and itched under the bandages and didn't do one damned thing he asked.

"A phone is a basic necessity," he insisted. "You could allow me that much."

The nurse gave him a sideways glance. "You want me to wire it in myself?" she said. "With my phone wires and all my workman tools that I keep right here on my person?"

She was wicked, he decided, another ugly one past her prime. She was looking at him with that superior look he hated so much. It didn't seem right that an ugly woman could act so haughty. "Who you want to call anyway?" she said.

"*Who you want to call*," he said in a singsong voice, mocking her.

When finally—at last—the arm was cut loose, he was at least allowed paper and pen, so he tried writing a letter. By then, he was desperate for some pot and had the feeling of a castaway scrawling a help message in his own blood and hoping the bottle is found before fresh water runs out. He needed Bobbie—needed her right now—to bring him weed or else he really would go crazy in the glaring desert of this hospital and all its nasty nurses, many of whom he would have found difficult to cope with straight even at the best of times, let alone when he couldn't stand up to pee.

Using his bent knee as a surface, he started the letter in messy left-handed scrawl, the best he could do with his right arm mummified. He hated the plaster cast that housed his broken arm, and lately he'd been hating the arm, too. It itched and stank and hurt and made him want to bash the plaster off and gnaw away the bone at the shoulder. His left arm was pretty useless, too. It was like a weak, emaciated twin that couldn't even hold a pen at a useful angle.

He did his best, pissed off at how long it took and how sore his hand was from the effort and from all the needle holes and bruises and gummy areas where tape had been ripped off and reapplied. His left hand was being abused here at the hospital. No wonder it didn't write well.

He pressed the call button at his bedside. "Someone gonna come help me with this thing?" he called out. "Someone going to give me a little *help* here?" But all that happened was a nurse stared at him through the window, saw what he was doing, and walked away. Was he surprised? No. They seemed to enjoy taunting him. They probably liked watching him struggle with the letter.

Writing it was hard, but folding was worse. Folding was a bastard. It turned out you needed two hands to fold a letter. He struggled, stuffing the letter into an envelope, and spending extra time on the address so it was legible. Task completed, it was only a matter of convincing one of the nurses to help him mail it. He got a hold of a weekend staffer who didn't know him and told her that the letter was for his mother. Could she get a stamp for him and post it? His old mother, dying in Kentucky of emphysema, smoking those Salems—could she be a nice girl and post this letter to the dying old woman?

"Emphysema, huh?" the nurse said. She had one of those whiny sympathetic voices that spoke every sentence with pain and reluctance, as though all of life's communications were bad news. He thought she should quit her job as a nurse and work in a mortuary. With her long face and big teeth, she looked half vampire; a mortuary job would suit a girl like this.

"You'd be good with the dead," he said. It just came out like that before he had time to think. She squinted at him and showed the big teeth again, so he said, "I meant the dying."

"Oh, thank you!" She smiled. She had a yellow incisor that reminded him of a rat's tooth.

"My mother would love you," he said. "She's dying."

"Your poor mom, emphysema is just a nasty one, huh?" she

said, drawing back at the word *emphysema* as though at spiders in a garden shed.

He said, "Oh yeah, hell on earth. Coughing all the time, spluttering, nearly drowning in her own spit—"

"Oh dear!"

"That's how my old mother spends her time. She should call it a day—it's that terrible—but she wants to carry on, to struggle through all the terrible pain. Bravery? Madness? You decide. What's your name tag say there? Cheryl. That's sweet, Cheryl. A pretty name for a pretty girl."

Cheryl blushed, then said, "I think she sounds brave. Very brave, bless her."

"Maybe, but it isn't as though she is doing it willingly, is it? She didn't stare into the face of hideous disease and say, 'I'll take that on!' So how is that brave?"

"I don't know, Mr. Kirtz—"

"Craig. You call me Craig, sweetheart. And I'll tell you what, you wouldn't find me gurgling away like that at her age, my lungs full of water. She's tough, that's for sure. I wanted to be with her at the end, but look at me." He nodded down at his body with all its plaster and bandages. "Not much use to her, am I? Woman reaches an age when she needs to rely on her grown son, her only child, and look at this. Damned shame, isn't it?"

The girl looked sad now and he regretted that he'd caused her to put on a sad face because she looked even more like a rodent with her mouth twisted down like that.

"Don't go crying on me," he said. He knew he'd overstepped the mark. Not by inventing a mother, or even a dying mother, but by describing the loneliness of the old and the dying. Nobody wanted to hear about that, not even him. Not even when it wasn't true.

"Oh, no. It's just that . . ." the girl began, her buck teeth resting on the dry ledge of her lower lip, her eyes seeming suddenly larger and wetter than before. She was one of those hugely tall girls, a kind he especially did not like, stretched out like Gumby, with a narrow oval face and a helmet of bobbed hair. Hard to imagine a woman like that had tits, he thought, but he'd seen it—and this was true— women exactly as ugly as this with nice tits, some with real nice ones, though admittedly you wouldn't ever think it. "I wish there was something I could do," she said, finally.

"Well, there *is* one thing, if you don't mind," he said. He nudged the envelope her direction. "I have a birthday card here for her. Would you mail that for me, Cheryl?" he said. "Cheryl, would you do me that favor?"

"Of course I will." She took the envelope from him. It was only a slim half sheet of paper, with none of the size or bulk of a birthday card, and he watched as she felt it carefully in her fingers. He sensed her confusion at how light it was, almost as though the envelope were empty.

"I couldn't get out to buy her a real card," he said, looking ashamed. "So I drew her a picture."

"Oh." The girl was holding the envelope carefully, as though it were the envelope they use to announce the Miss America pageant winner. She looked down at it, then at Craig, her face earnest. "Well, that will mean even more to her," she said finally, though he sensed the strain in her voice. She didn't really think his pretty picture would please his mother at all. Surely Cheryl was lying.

"Do you think so? Really?" he said.

"Oh yes. Mothers love their children's drawings."

It was too much; he almost laughed out loud. "Even though I'm fully grown?" he managed.

She hesitated, but then said, "I think so, yes."

"And it was done with my left hand, which to be quite truthful, is hardly good for writing my own name."

He watched her face carefully and saw some doubt, either that an incompetent drawing by an adult son in plaster might be so welcome, or that he was fully lying to her. He opened his mouth in a small gasp. "It's not good enough, is it?" he said, as though this possibility had just occurred to him and was crushing.

"I'm sure it is fine," Cheryl said, recovering quickly. "Better than fine."

He needed to get her out of the room before he cracked up. But he couldn't resist, no he could not. Suddenly he lunged toward the letter. "No, no it's no good!" he cried out. "Give it back to me. Give it here!"

But she clasped the letter against her belly. "No, let me post it for you. I want to. It would be my privilege," she said.

He gave her a smile, or as much as he could smile given all the bandages on his face. He thought how his head was like a monster's head, and his smile was a monster's smile. "And maybe bring me back a beer?" he said, knowing that she would. "Just a little one. A Michelob, maybe? A Bud?"

She looked sternly at him, so he winked at her. Winked with the one eye, and it kind of freaked her out. "Well, okay," she said, "but just the one."

"Thank you," he whispered. "There's a thirty-two-ounce bottle at 7-Eleven. You'll see them there at the bottom of the cooler. Grab one of those big boys for me, darling, okay? You can do it on your break time. I'll wait."

She nodded, then backed away hesitantly.

The envelope didn't even have Kentucky in the address. It was marked with the local zip code, and she could have looked down at any time and called his bluff. In fact, he was kind of hoping she *would* notice that it was a local letter. He liked the thought of confusing her. If she came back and asked why it was for Maryland and not Kentucky, he'd fuck with her mind and say it *had been* addressed to Kentucky. It had said Kentucky right there on the envelope, couldn't she read? That would blow her away, make her think she was taking too many drugs, although she probably wasn't taking any drugs and that, certainly, was among her problems. He imagined her standing at the blue-and-silver U.S. postal box, the one tacked onto the wall at the entrance of the hospital, sucking on her tooth and being confused by the address, and it made him laugh just thinking about it.

"Thank you," he said as she slid out the door. And then, wistfully, he added, "I wish I could meet a girl like you."

HE KNEW IT was Bobbie, not June, who got the mail every afternoon from the little silver-and-red mailbox at the end of the drive. The pleading note was to persuade her to come to the hospital in the morning instead of going to school. That, or she could leave school quick at the bell and come to the hospital by four o'clock. He needed her here, then out, before her mother arrived. And he needed some pot.

He thought she owed him at least that much—a little visit and his weed. But nothing happened. He waited for her to turn up but she failed to arrive, day after day, until it began to piss him off, the way she made him wait around for her. She thought she could do anything she liked with him now that he was in the hospital, and that was an insult if he'd ever heard one. It made him so angry that by the end of the week he began growling, actually growling like a dog there in his hospital bed, whenever Bobbie's face sprang into his mind. He'd been so sweet in his letter, telling her he loved her. He *loved* her. He'd written it the fuck down and asked—no begged— for his pot. Did he get anything out of all his efforts? Hell no. And now his mood was on permanent pissed off. A few days later, when the rat-toothed girl poked her head through the door and asked if his mother had liked his drawing, he told her to go to hell. Her chin whipped up, as though someone had slapped her on the ass, and she said, "I beg your pardon!"

"She died before she got it," he said.

"Oh!"

"Sorry I swore. I didn't mean it. It's all the drugs." But Rat Tooth didn't come around again even though he'd apologized and his mother had died and his body was a like a chest of broken toys.

So he worked on a different one, a candy striper, some do-gooding volunteer, to lend him five bucks in quarters and park him next to the phone where he could get something done.

"I need to call my mother. She's in Kentucky, dying of lung cancer," he said. For some reason, mention of dying mothers was surprisingly effective, a master key that turned every lock in a woman's heart. It got them to break hospital rules, which was surprising because people died all over hospitals and you'd think the employees would get used to it. The candy striper took the bait and said she'd be back in ten minutes, and she was, too, with an orderly in tow. The orderly unfastened him from the machines, slapping the brakes off the bed. She was a good woman, the little candy striper, a volunteer from the high school, still young enough to be unbitchy. She wheeled him through the hall to the pay phone, his lap full of quarters, and he said, "You make me feel so good!"

"Glad to help," she said.

"I feel just like one of those little handicapped kids being taken to the state fair!"

Her face changed at this remark. "Oh," she said.

He rang Bobbie on a weekday, just about the time she would walk into the house from the school bus. He could picture her there in the kitchen, its windows darkened by the heavy autumn foliage outside. He imagined the slam of the porch door, then the sound of the metal doorknob and the rattling of the back door as she came in. She'd think the phone was her mother and grab it before thinking.

But just when the phone began to ring, one of the nurses showed up, asking what he was doing in the hall, and he was pulled from his reverie.

"I'm waiting for the orderly to bring me to X-ray," he said.

It was another of the bitch nurses, not the normal heifer-shaped variety but a slender brunette about his age with a nice face and way too much attitude. "I'm going to check that," she said, angling her hip away from him and launching her comment over her shoulder.

He watched her walk away. "Is a man not allowed to make a phone call in this place? It isn't the morgue, is it? You think you're working in the morgue? We're still alive up here, you know!"

"No beds in the hall," she said.

"What do you think? I *flew* here? I wheeled over with my two strong arms? Listen, sunshine, one of *your* side put me here. *That's* how I got here!"

"And that's how you'll get back, too," she said, flicking her hair, smacking her lips, big bows of pink recently doused with lipstick. She was so confident with that agile body, leaning into the double doors, glancing only briefly at him, looking down her nose. He watched her push through the doors.

"Oh, you are so *pretty,*" he called, forming the word so that it came out hard. "Pritt-*ee,*" he said, menacingly.

She held up her hand, fingers outstretched. "I'm coming in *five* minutes for you."

By now his reputation had swept through the team of nurses; they all knew about him and gave him a hard time. Ballbusters, the bunch of them, taking advantage of the fact he couldn't walk. It was the fault of that Esther, with her hard metal face and skinny estrogen-deprived frame, those dirty white stockings on her bark-colored legs, *she'd* done this to him. Set them all against him.

"Bunch of lesbians!" he called at the nurse. But the nurse didn't turn around, which was typical, which was *exactly* what he had learned to expect. "Sadists!" he yelled. Still no reply. Then he remembered he still had the phone in his hand. If Bobbie had answered, she'd have hung up by now. He slammed it back onto the receiver and dug though his pile of coins, dialing all over again. He hung on anxiously as it rang and rang. He made a bitter sound, feeling the vibration deep in his throat. If all he had was five minutes, he'd let it ring for five minutes. But Bobbie didn't pick up. He waited and waited, until finally the lesbian nurse came through the double doors with an orderly, a look on her face like she meant business.

"We're rolling," she said, and despite all his protests, they wheeled him back to the room.

He tried a bunch of other times, whenever he could convince someone to move him. But it was as though Bobbie were avoiding him. This he could not understand. What had he done to her? She'd driven them into a goddamned forest and gotten away with it—he was the one who should be pissed off.

He thought he would have to resign himself to living un-stoned in the hell that was the hospital, but then, one day while the nurses were ignoring him, preoccupied with some old fart who broke his hip falling on pickle juice in his kitchen, June came to see him and it suddenly occurred to him—June! Why hadn't he thought of her in the first place? She could disconnect him from all the machines they leashed him to, push out the clunky, horrible bed, and park him next to the phone. All he had to do was distract her for a few minutes afterward, send her on a mission somewhere, and he'd have time to get Bobbie on the phone.

"Hey babe, unhook me here, will you?" he said casually, as though this was a routine thing he'd been doing right along.

"You mean, from all the *monitors*?" she said, as though he were asking for death itself.

"Yeah, it's easy. I do it all the time."

"But I don't know how," June said. He watched her brow furrow, then a nervous licking of lips. He wished she wouldn't do that thing with her tongue.

"I'll talk you through it," he said gently. "Unhooking is the easy part. It's the re-stabbing that sucks. We'll leave that to the death squad."

She unplugged him, at first cautiously, as though she thought the machines breathed for him, then with more confidence. He talked her through how to prop open the double doors and then, while the staff was preoccupied with the pickle-juice man, June wheeled him into the hall. "How about you call the radio station and give them a progress report for me, will you?" he said. "And use a different phone—I need this one right now. Use one on another floor. And then, how about getting some Burger King takeout? We need some decent food in here. This place is all soup and fruit and shit."

He watched her walk off. She was so padded out she looked like a piece of furniture you could sit on, but she was very useful, he had to admit. A useful, nice lady who didn't mean him any harm. Given this, he thought he might grow used to how fat she was. He watched her waddle down the hall and he felt honest gratitude. At least she didn't give him shit like all the others. She was patient, maternal. She brought him cake instead of kicking him in the ass like the nurses always did.

He dialed the phone, keeping watch on the activities of the nurses on the other side of the ward as he did so. He felt a tide of luck moving his way and, sure enough, Bobbie answered on the third ring. She probably thought it was her mother.

"So I guess you made it home okay," he said. "You going to ask how I've been? Go on, say it. Say, 'How have you been, Craig?'"

She didn't say anything and so he said, "Don't you want to know what it is like being stuck in this hole with tubes everywhere, even in my pecker?"

Still no answer. For a second he thought she'd hung up. Then he heard, "Mom says you're fine. And that a lot of those tubes are gone."

"She mention that I'm blind now?"

"Half," she said.

"Is that not enough for you?" He felt a fury in him, that big panting angry wolf that followed him around. Sometimes he could almost feel it hovering. But he needed to focus. He needed some pot and Bobbie was his only hope. "Look, you going to give me some help here, babe? I'm all broken to pieces, so maybe you can see it in your heart?"

"Don't you have doctors?"

"Doctors, fuck. What I need is you to take some of *my money* that you've got—I'm giving permission now to use some of *my money*, do you hear? And you're going to get a taxi to my house and tell whoever answers the door that you need to get me some clothes, okay? You're going to get me the stuff I need, then come back here to the hospital."

She didn't say anything, and he imagined her standing by the back door in her kitchen, the cord winding around her middle, or crossing her breasts, or curling around her long sun-blushed arms. He'd liked her better when she was younger and he could circle her white belly easily with two hands and when the whole of her breast fit into his mouth, but he liked her now, too.

"I'm not hearing 'Glad to help you out, Craig, after all you've been through.' Why is that? Why don't you want to make up to me after ditching me in the car like that? I didn't tell on you, you know. The police are around here all the time, but I haven't snitched."

She took a long breath and he waited for that and then, finally, heard her say, "I can't go to your house. I'm not allowed to be seen there, remember?"

"You can *this* time. I'm saying you can. Because it isn't like I'm *with* you. You're just being the postman, picking up a package, so what? What I need is the reefer that's in my closet. It's in the lining of my winter coat. Bring it here quick. That's all I'm asking, bring me the coat. Also, my radio. I'm being soft-rocked to death in this damned hospital and the crappy transistor your mother bought me is a piece of shit."

"I can't go to your house. They'll see me."

"Oh Christ, don't be so dumb! It doesn't matter who sees what—"

"I don't want to get in trouble."

"It's just clothes—"

"But the pot—"

"Cut me some *slack*! It's a coat as far as you know, okay? The pot is in the *lining*, about which you officially know *nada*. It's in the lining because I have to hide it from my roommates. They always steal my good bud. It's hidden, see? Nobody will know a damned thing."

"But *they'll* see me. Whoever answers the door—"

"—won't care! They won't ask anything. They're assholes. They can *not* think."

"I can't get there. The police might come."

"What police? There are no police. I said you could use some of my money. Get a *taxi*!"

"I don't have any of *your* money."

His heart was pounding; he wanted to yell. He listened as the phone beeped a warning that he was almost out of credit. *Please insert coins if you wish to continue, please insert coins . . .* "Hang on!" he shouted, then wrenched himself up, causing his pelvis to hurt like hell, and pushed in a couple of quarters.

He heard her say she had to go. "No, don't!" he yelled, a little louder than he ought to have. "For fucksake, Barbara, use the money to get a taxicab, you know what a taxicab is, don't you?" He imagined her with his money, buying all the stupid bullshit she liked—pastel T-shirts and makeup and toe socks, or pet fucking rocks—God, he hoped she hadn't blown half of it already. "I'm not pissed off, okay? I respect what you did; it was almost professional. But you got caught. I caught you. If you want to steal from me, you've got to kill me. And try as you did to make it so, I. AM. NOT. DEAD."

"I didn't try to kill you!"

"Then I hate to think of what would happen if you *had* tried!" he said. He thought about what to say next, what would scare her. She'd always moaned about who might see them and what she should say and how she should act. She'd always worried about being in trouble that way. Well, he'd show her some trouble. "Listen, missy, you're lucky I'm not talking to the cops—yet—because they *do* want to talk to me," he said. "I'm not going to tell them you tried to kill me, but I know it, and you know it."

He paused, letting that sink in. She'd be going crazy with the thought she might be arrested for attempted murder. "It's really very simple. I want the pot—I mean coat—and I want my money, but you can use some of my money for transportation. Isn't that simple? Isn't that easy? So how about it? We'll call it quits after that, no more arguing about you trying to kill me. No point staying mad at each other."

She didn't say anything and he felt it again, that anger, charging up from inside him. "Oh come on!" He wondered if she'd hung up, actually hung up on him. She couldn't possibly hang up on him; he was the *victim*, the one in the hospital, institutionalized among an army of vicious nurses and remote, untalkative doctors who sleepwalked through their rounds. Besides, she'd never before done anything of the sort. He yelled into the phone, "Goddamn it, answer me! It's not too late for me to go to the police, you know!"

And then he looked up, and there were the two cops that he'd seen before, almost as though he'd summoned them. He had no idea how long they'd been watching him barking orders at Bobbie about drugs, his hand curled so hard around the phone there were sweat marks on the plastic so that he even looked like a junkie. He'd seen these cops before, lurking in the hospital, staring at him through the window of his room: a freckled young Irish-looking one in a crisp dark blazer and a black guy with an open-neck shirt and acne.

"Are you for real, Salt and Pepper?" he said. Though he'd been avoiding them for some time by feigning sleep whenever they came around, he wasn't entirely sure if he'd invented these two. Back when he'd first been admitted to the hospital, when he hadn't really understood what was going on and people were sticking him with needles and prying through his skull and wheeling him down hallways to darker and smaller rooms, attaching him to machines, he'd seen them—or thought he'd seen them. His brain hadn't been operating smoothly for quite some while. He had to admit that he was in an advanced state of fucked up. There had been times over the past week when he would forget words. Not dictionary words but common, ordinary words, words like *pee*, for example. He'd get only so far in a sentence, *I need to . . .* , and then draw a blank and finish the sentence with *you know!* A nurse would then race from the room to find a doctor, who blared a penlight in his eye and asked questions like whether he knew his own name and what the hell day it was, and he never knew the answer to that one because every day was the same to him now. It could be Tuesday seven times in a row—what the hell difference did it make?

He narrowed his vision on the cops now. "If you *are* real, are you looking for me?" he asked. He hadn't been a hundred percent on that, either, whether the police were seeking him specifically, or whether for some reason they just hung around hospitals. Perhaps they were present in the wards all the time, like fuzzy dice hanging on the rearview mirrors of roadsters. It was hard to tell because time jumbled in his mind so that a day could be super-elastic and last forever or disappear altogether, plucked from his life without his ever having being informed, taken from him as his eye had been.

For days, he wasn't sure about the eye—had it really been removed? It had been, he'd finally understood, just as he understood now, as the police came toward him, that these cops were real.

"Hey, can you hang that up for me and call a nurse? I think I'm going to throw up," he said. Since the removal of his eye there was always something draining into the back of his throat and it could be relied upon to provide a kind of emergency vomiting situation if needed. Leaning over the mattress, he moaned and writhed, making it appear that only the weight of his broken arm anchored him in the bed. Like this, he hawked up a sizable dollop of fluid; it made an impressive splat on the floor.

Sure enough, the head honcho, Esther, came rushing. She told the cops they needed to wait somewhere else. That she needed to attend to him now.

"Thank you, Nurse Esther," Craig said. "I'm about to throw up again. I need my machines. These good folks will have to go away now."

"Oh, please!" Esther scolded.

"*What?*" He let out a long moan, farted loudly, then began breathing in a shallow irregular way. He was actually very good at this, he decided. He was beginning to feel nauseous and light-headed. Now he really did feel terrible, his skin hot and cold at the same time. He could feel the sweat beneath his bandages, the deep ache low in his right buttock where he'd broken his pelvis. "I'm going out!" he called.

Esther let out a long breath, then turned to the police, seeming positively apologetic that she had to ask them to leave. "I would love for you to arrest him and take him away," she sighed, "but I got to get him on a drip now. If he loses consciousness we have to revive him. That's just rules."

"But he is *faking*," the black cop said.

Esther smiled. "I know."

The police would eventually speak to him, of course, but he couldn't figure out why that would matter. What was the great crime anyway? He'd driven his car off a road, nearly killed himself, but he hadn't hurt anybody else. Altercation at a motel? The manager had stolen from him. And he couldn't even remember who threw the first punch. Pot in the car? There was some pot in the car, but not much. Someone left it there, you know the radio biz. The porn in the trunk was legal. What the hell had he done wrong? Not a damned thing, so let them ask what they liked.

HOW ARE YOU, BARBARA?

■ ■ ■ *1978*

He called three weeks after the accident. Even before she got off the school bus, hauling a stack of books and a PE kit from which she'd purposely lost the shorts, keeping her scabby legs hidden in sweatpants, she'd felt a dull warning inside her. This internal alarm had proven correct in the past, and she was not surprised when she walked into the house and heard the phone.

It was him. And while she knew it was impossible, the noise of the phone seemed personal to her and had a forbidding, accusatory feel. It may as well have been his voice, shouting at her from inside the house, calling her name louder and louder until at last she gave in, and came to where he ordered her, and stood before him. The ringing phone meant he was here in her life once more, just as she'd known he would eventually be, and the days between the crash and now collapsed at once, so that he was again present— inside her, even—like a monstrous second head that directed her every thought. *Pick up the damned phone, Barbara*, his voice said. *You don't even know for sure it's me.*

The next time he called, she was in her bedroom, sitting by the record player, trying to get an earring to go back in. The ear piercing had gone wrong despite being done by the jeweler. He had used something resembling a staple gun, shooting a gold post cleanly through the lobe. She still recalled how he had scowled into the measuring device, so close she could smell his face and his hairy little mustache, and then declared she had very small lobes and that this was a problem, the lobes. Now there was a hot swelling and a persistent localized infection in both ears. She wanted the little gold studs so badly, however, that she dabbed alcohol onto the weeping holes where the posts rested and hoped a scab would form, and that she would soon look like the other girls who seemed to take no notice of their earrings at all, not even when they knocked the dangling ones by accident as they brushed back their hair.

The phone rang again, but she didn't answer this second time, either. Instead she held her breath, her heart ballooning inside her chest, the sound of Elton John on her little stereo unable to drown out the noise of the ringing. She twisted an earring post into her ear, feeling it stick against the dried blood, and the small, pinching sting knocked her thoughts away from Craig a fraction. He was probably seething at the other end, thinking how she would not pick up the phone, would not do one goddamned thing he wanted. She could imagine how he'd sound if she were to answer, his breath heavy in the phone. *How are you, Barbara?* he'd say, the greeting sounding more like a curse.

And that was as it always had been, him hating her at the same time as wanting her. If she answered now she could pretend she'd been out when he rang before, but if she didn't answer this time— this critical second time—he would know she was avoiding him.

She might have answered if it would have put a stop to whatever dark attraction was developing between him and her mother, but she knew already that it was too late. Craig was the prize her mother had set her sights on. And so, as the phone rang downstairs, Bobbie stayed in her room, sang along to the record, tried to worry less, to sing louder, shouting out the lyrics. *And butterflies are free to fly, fly away, high away, bye, bye!*

It happened again toward evening, the sound of the phone splitting the air with urgency. By now, she'd gathered some courage. "Not on your life," she told the phone.

She imagined his response: *Why are you being so mean to me, Barbara? What have I ever done to you?*

She didn't feel mean, not exactly, but she did feel as though she were breaking rules. She paced the kitchen. With every ring, her steps quickened, her heart beat faster. She glared at the phone, telling herself she could not know for sure it was him. But it *was* him; she would not be fooled. She stared at the receiver, a slim wall-mounted aqua push-button. "Scream your head off, for all I care," she said.

She counted twenty-five rings, then a brief silence, long enough for someone to dial again, then another five minutes of ringing. She could imagine Craig at his end, the phone cocked up on his head, the fury in his face, punching at the plate of numbers. His body was a stored battery of pain. His injuries had been described in detail to her many times by her mother, who explained how the pelvis meant he could not walk, and the single eye meant he'd lost his depth perception, which would make him extra unsteady once he was on his feet. What she couldn't understand was how he managed to get to a phone in the first place. She thought of him on a gurney in the hospital struggling with the sticking numbers on the metal keypad, and listening helplessly to the lonely ringing on the other end. Growing angry, his fury making him sweat in his backless gown, he would plan a revenge she could not imagine and dared not think about.

"You are a peckerhead," she told the phone. "Say it. Say, 'I am a peckerhead.'"

She imagined her mother had never seen *that* side of Craig, the one that terrified Dan at McDonald's, the one that drove a car as though they were inside a pinball machine and could bounce off trucks the way a pinball bounces off paddles, the one that spread her legs and wiped spit on himself before plunging inside her.

"Nobody is home," she told the phone. But she could hear his voice inside her head, as though he were planted there with direct access to her brain. *Grow up, Barbara!* she heard him say. *Pick up the goddamned telephone!* And with that voice came all his stored hatred, all his resentment. If only she would follow his logic; if only she would come to see his reason. That was what all the fights were about. His problem, he had often explained, was that he was smarter than other people. That was how he saw himself. He had a set of questions to which there were exact answers and she was supposed to agree to these answers because he had already thought it all through, thought of everything.

She walked outside, letting the porch door slam and holding her ears against the phone's shrill echo. The sky was closed and dark, the moon hidden behind clouds. She remembered how when she was a very young child, before she'd even gone to school, she'd come out on a night like this and seen her father, a flashlight balanced on a tree stump, the wooden stem of a rake in his hand, gathering bits of bark and slivers of wood around the chopping block where he worked. He'd always been doing chores. He chopped logs and dug up the lawn when burst drainpipes caused a flood, laying new clay ones. She remembers him sitting in the living room with a cup of coffee while she watched cartoons, waving to her as she went off to bed in her flowery pajamas.

She felt a raindrop splash on the part in her hair, another on her shoulder. She listened for the phone but everything was quiet now. "I'd better go inside," she said aloud, as though her father were there in front of her.

LATER SHE TOLD Dan about what had happened—how the phone had rung and she'd known it was Craig and had not answered it.

"Maybe he'll give up now," he said. But neither of them believed Craig would give up. There was no stopping him. He was a bull on a slow charge, but he was on his way.

"From now on, when you call me, let it ring twice, then hang up," Bobbie said. "I'll call you back."

"Okay."

"It wasn't you, was it?" She was sitting on the floor in the kitchen, the cord looped around her legs, a tall glass of Coke on the floor beside her.

"No."

She sighed. "Maybe he'll die after all."

"I doubt it."

"Or have some other problem." She kept hoping something would happen to Craig, that a medical mix-up would cause total amnesia and he'd forget all about her. Or that he'd need to go out of state for rehabilitation and decide never to return.

But the damage to his arm was healing and she'd heard from her mother that he was regaining feeling in the numb areas. His wrist was better, too. The pelvic fracture turned out not to be unstable—just a slab of broken-off bone they had to retrieve surgically. It wouldn't be long before he was able to walk.

"Unfortunately, every passing day brings more good news," she told Dan. "The best I can hope for now is a hospital fire."

She heard Dan's laughter through the phone. She imagined him in his house. He always called from his father's office, a boxy room with a mahogany desk and fat medical books stuffed into the shelves. He'd described it to her just like that, and she pictured him sitting in the wingback chair, his long legs tucked beneath the desk, the phone in his hand. In her mind's eye there was an antique clock and eggshell blue walls, an atmosphere of enduring calm like a membrane that held everything in place. She thought of him there in that room and the image of him in her mind was like a talisman, a good luck charm.

"Maybe you can feed him underdone chicken?" Dan said. "Or some poisonous mushrooms?"

She repositioned herself on the floor, leaning against the kitchen wall with its splashy pattern of flowers climbing above her head. She took a long slug of Coke and said, "He'd make me taste it first."

"My father once told me it is easy to slip poison into strong drinks."

"Your *father* told you that?"

"Doctors know this kind of stuff. I'm surprised there aren't more cases of murder in the profession."

He made her laugh. That was the first thing. With Dan she did not have to explain all the things she felt, nor the crazy way she'd become entwined with such a man as Craig, nor how difficult it was now to extract herself. Nor did she have to lie.

They understood the problem; they did not talk about the problem. They did not discuss what had happened or had not happened with Craig. They did not talk about the sex. She did not tell him all the things she'd done, about how she'd been pushed always that little bit further, or about the shame. It was as though they agreed that life before the day they met was a prehistory not worth mentioning. They liked to kiss and hold each other. They liked to lie face-to-face wherever they could find soft ground: on the clay banks that cradled a creek, on a cushion of grass in a field bordered by brambles. He would touch her cheeks and stroke her hair while she stretched out against the length of him. She'd touch the swell of muscles at his shoulder, smooth a finger over the great ledge of his collarbone. His hands went to her back, then to her breasts, his lips following. She knew him by scent and touch and voice. It was enough for them. And here was the surprise she could never have imagined: that with Dan it all felt new.

Another thing. They did not try to tease out a reason why Craig had set his gaze on Bobbie, or what to do about it. They couldn't know why, or fathom the logic of a man like Craig, and hadn't any notion what to do, in any case. The one good thing about June's obsession with Craig, the one liberating aspect for which Bobbie was grateful, was that when June ran off to the hospital it freed Bobbie to talk on the telephone to Dan. They spoke almost nightly, and their random chatter become a blanket under which she hid.

"Okay, I love you," she said one night, whispering into the phone.

"You already know I love you," he told her, as though he'd said it thousands of times already, and not this first time.

"Say it again—"

"I love you."

"No, but really—"

"I love you."

SOMETIMES THEY STUDIED together, finishing a piece of homework and then phoning the other as a reward. Sometimes they watched TV—that is, he watched from his house and she from hers, and they stayed on the phone without speaking until the commercials.

"Do you think that actress is very beautiful?" she might say. On the screen was Jane Fonda or Farrah Fawcett Majors or Sophia Loren.

Dan took some time to answer. Finally, a hesitant "Yes," as though he'd needed to consider the question.

"But she has brown hair and I have blond hair. So how can you say that?"

"You're right. She's not you. She can't be pretty."

"What about that one?"

"Oh yes, she's very pretty."

"But she is very tall while I'm short. Again, we're hardly alike."

"Hmm, I see. I'm understanding now that she isn't you, either."

They had a strange way of teasing each other, a language of their own. Bobbie would speak in a low, serious tone as though she did not want to hurt his feelings, but that there was something she had to tell him, however much it pained her.

"You are fat," she'd tell Dan, whose scooped-out stomach and angular shoulders and backside that hid beneath the pockets of his Levi's meant that every waistband was cinched by a belt and every collar hung loose around his neck.

"I know. But what can I do?" he'd say. "I've tried dieting but nothing works."

"Lock yourself in your bedroom and don't come out until you can fit *under the door.*" They'd started the teasing about weight because June was now pulling out all the stops on her own diet. She would arrange a chopped tomato on a plate, cover it in sprouts, and call it dinner; she'd try on clothes from years past, using them as a way of seeing how close she was to becoming the slender woman she'd once been. Bobbie understood these things just as she understood why June kept a tape measure by the bathroom sink and a weight chart on the inside of the cupboard door, and why she sprouted cress in plastic tubs on the windowsill. It was all part of the Great Effort, the campaign to win Craig. She wanted to be thin, to be beautiful, to make the house more inviting, and all of this for him.

"Come and see me," Dan would say, so full of emotion that only these few words could escape.

"Okay, okay, I'm on my way."

Traversing the physical distance between them was awkward and time consuming. They each took a set of different buses, meeting at a midway point between their two houses. Outside, as the autumn winds grew cold and the leaves swept into crunching piles, they stood close enough that their breath mingled. They hugged through their wool jackets, held each other's chilly hands. In some ways, they were like any young couple, two kids whose discovery of each other was made all the more exciting by the concurrent discovery of attraction itself, that appetite that signals the end of childhood. But there was a part of Bobbie that sometimes "fled the scene," or at least that was how she described it. Every so often, when they were at their closest, she felt herself lifting away from Dan. It was as though she were still tainted by Craig, and when Dan unbuttoned her sweater, or put his hand up the back of her blouse, the part of her that Craig had spoiled sent her running in her mind, sent her flying.

"Relax, don't move," he whispered to her one night. He hovered over her, running his fingers slowly over her cheeks, then her forehead, then across her brow. He had large, dark green eyes, a brow of curls.

"You can't say 'relax' and expect me to actually relax," she said, pretending to be exasperated.

He carried on silently, touching her lips, tracing her jawline. One minute, then another, for as long as she would allow him to look at her with all the longing that she returned. "Are you still with me?" he asked finally, and she nodded, because she was.

"Mmm, progress." He smiled.

AND WHAT DID he say on the stand in court all those years later? As much as Bobbie wished to know, she did not stay for the session. While Dan was sworn in, while he fielded questions and answered yes or no at cross-examination, she waited at a coffeehouse, remembering how Dan had been like a tonic to her all those years ago. She remembered how they had kissed so often amid the slow, roaring movement of buses that the smell of fumes became part of it, part of the union. And that they laughed while they kissed, as though there was something terribly funny. They sometimes grew quiet, falling into lengthy, intense silences that made them both uncertain. They would lie side by side—even on wet grass, even on cold earth—and listen to the sounds around them, listen to their heartbeats.

"This is how it should be. How it should have been," she had told him. Autumn 1978, while Craig was in the hospital.

"How what should have been?" he said.

"You know."

He'd pretended he had no idea. He played dumb because in his love for her everything that had happened before was not worth recalling. This is what she understood.

Sometimes she would mimic Dan's mother, whom she had never met and refused to meet, imagining her as a perfect and beautiful lady.

"Is she like this?" she'd ask, taking a pose. "Or is she more like this?" He told her to stop, please, because he did not want to think of his mother and Bobbie at the same time.

"But tell me!" she'd insisted. She was teasing, of course. He shook his head, drew her close. In all the years since no man had held her as completely as this skinny kid.

"You will meet her one day and then you'll know," he'd said.

She did not mention his doctor father, whose specialty, internal medicine, sounded vast and mysterious. It wasn't that she had taken a dislike to his father, who she also had refused to meet, but almost as though she could not fathom him.

"My father used to fix things and he used to chop logs," she said.

"Hmm, wow," Dan said. "Do you miss him?"

Bobbie thought about this. "I miss remembering him," she said. "My mother misses him. Or used to."

They had been walking together, navigating a stony path into a darkening woods, the temperature dropping noticeably with the coming of a rainstorm. The sun had long since faded; the wind was picking up. She walked in front, holding a bike light that later, when the woods were completely dark, would blaze a yellow trail they could follow. He had on his down jacket and work boots and heavy jeans. She wore a stocking cap and duffel coat and sneakers.

"My dad's nice," Dan said. He stopped and she turned to look at him. Behind his shoulder, a canopy of bare branches broke up the deep blue of evening. She could not read his face in the half-light but she could hear the urgency in his voice, the bewilderment, too. "He would like you," he pleaded. "They both would."

"No, no," she said, answering the question that he no longer asked outright about whether she would come over for dinner, meet his parents, be with him openly in the house instead of all this sneaking around. He was proud of her—couldn't she see that?

"Why not? There's no reason not to," he said.

"I can't be like other people," was her reply. Really she did not know why this was the case, only that she was certain that her judgment was correct and that she needed to stay away from his parents, or from anyone who might look too closely at her.

"Meaning what?" he said. "You can't meet strangers like other people? You can't eat dinner like other people? They are my parents, not strangers. And they have this thing we will soon really need."

"What thing?"

"Electricity. Central heating, shelter from rain . . . the collective term is a house." When she said nothing, he asked, "Why does it all have to be so hard? What are you worried about?"

What was she worried about? Sometimes it was so great, the constant anxiety, that it was impossible to tease out a single worry and name it. But she tried—she did. Because Dan had asked her.

"It's like I've got an enormous secret," she said, turning toward him. "And every new person I trick into thinking I don't makes the secret bigger."

He thought about this. "But it's not a secret," he said. "Not really. A secret is something that you ought to tell, that you owe it to someone to tell. And you don't owe anyone."

But she did. That was the thing. She just didn't know who.

"And it's over," Dan insisted. "What more can he do to you now?"

"I don't know. But it's like he's getting closer," she said.

"Closer to who? Not to you."

"To my life."

"Everything with that guy is over," Dan said.

But it wasn't, and she knew it.

JUNE ON THE STAND

The defense rests and the following morning, June is called to the stand.

She has worn her best dress, warm colors, a soft neckline, an abstract design. She had thought the dress flattered her but here in court, surrounded by the somber attorneys in navy and charcoal, she feels silly. She is reminded—this is awful—of TV cop shows in which a plainclothesman arrests a hooker, and the girl arrives at the station wearing an outfit that announces to any passerby exactly what she is. What does June's dress announce? That she is uneducated and small-town. That she is not sophisticated. It's a terrible failure, the dress, and now she hates it. Hates the dress and how hard she has tried: semipermanent eye makeup, glue-on nails, a two-hour hair appointment the day before. Why did she go to the trouble when all that is happening is that she is sitting before an audience that thinks she is a bad mother?

Bobbie is in the courtroom, but far back in a recess where June can barely see her. It seems to June that her daughter has spent a lifetime hiding from her and she has no idea why. The courtroom is packed. The bench seats are already gone and they are setting up folding chairs in the spaces between rows. The air-conditioning is inadequate and people are fanning themselves with their notepads and handbags. She is mildly alarmed by the armed bailiffs, whose guns look bigger than strictly required to control a courtroom and who scurry about, rearranging people and issuing loud warnings about fire regulations. Even more disturbing is the imposing woman judge in her endless dark robes, presiding in thick tortoiseshell eyeglasses and with an air of constant disapproval. She looks, in turns, bored, angry, bemused. She scolds the attorneys as though they are reckless schoolchildren. Even Craig's glamorous defense attorney bows in deference to this judge, who sometimes appears as though she'd like to put them all away, everyone involved with the case, lock them all up.

The witness stand is a terrible place to be, like a set of colonial stocks in which the whole community sees you. The only person for whom the humiliation is worse is Craig, who sits glumly at the defense table in front of her, and before everyone assembled, absorbing all of their disapproval. She wants Craig to be proud of how she handles being a witness; she wants him to see her as his powerful ally.

She does well with Elstree, because she knows what to expect. Elstree takes her through how she'd met Craig, how their friendship had developed, the accident, the courtship. But here is Dreyer and he worries her. His questions are much more difficult than the ones that Elstree had asked, which were designed to put her in the best light. Dreyer leans over her, studying her as she speaks. She thinks about asking the judge to tell him to step back, but of course that would mean talking to the person of whom she is most afraid.

"Before Mr. Kirtz moved into your house, were you aware of your daughter ever being in his presence without you being there?" he asks her.

"No," June says. "Bobbie was a little girl and she was always with me."

Dreyer frowns, as though her answer is disappointing. He says, "Did you know your daughter was with Mr. Kirtz at the radio station where he worked just weeks after having Thanksgiving at your house in 1976?"

"Oh, yes, but that was different. There were lots of other people at the station."

"Were *you* at the station with her that night?"

June tries not to appear annoyed at the manner of this question. He already knows she was not there. And now he wants her to inform everyone in the court that she left her little girl alone with a strange man. She wishes she didn't have to answer the question, but the judge sits above her like an evil gargoyle and so she has to admit that she was not there.

"How many other people were in the studio with Mr. Kirtz and your daughter, who I'd like to remind the court was thirteen years old at the time?"

"How many?"

"Yes. How many people?"

"I don't know." This is true, but how could she have known if she wasn't there? "How could I know if I wasn't there?" June says, annoyed.

"Thank you," Dreyer says, in a manner that means *be quiet, please.* He turns from her now, his hands in his pocket, and continues. "In 1977 and 1978, did anyone supervise your daughter as she went to and from school?"

"Supervise? No. She just went to school like all the other children."

"Was there any way you could know whether your daughter was on the bus every afternoon after school?"

"Well, she must have been because she got home okay."

"Let me rephrase the question. Were you there when Bobbie arrived from the bus? Please answer yes or no."

She does not like to be taken to task like this. "No," she says, a little miffed. "I was at work. I was a widow, you'll recall." She crosses her legs, looking away. She wishes her silly dress had pockets so she would have somewhere to put her hands.

"Was there a tracking system or any true way of knowing?"

"Of course not," she says. "And you already know that."

"Did Bobbie telephone you when she arrived home?"

"No, there was no need. I didn't have to *spy* on her."

"Mrs. Kirtz, did you always know where your daughter was when she was not in school?"

Did she always know where she was? "At home," she says. "Or babysitting."

"Did you *know* where she was on September 7, 1978, the night of Mr. Kirtz's accident?"

"She was at home."

"And where were you?"

"I was working."

"Where were you exactly?"

"Orange, New Jersey. There was an event I had to attend."

"If you were in Orange, how do you know that your daughter was at home?"

"She didn't tell me she was going anywhere. And she always told me."

"Did you telephone her at home?"

He knows she did not but she wonders whether he can prove it. She is tempted to tell him that yes, she'd telephoned Bobbie, and that Bobbie had been brushing her teeth, preparing for bed, and that the child had given her all the details of her school day: how she had eaten the lasagna that June had left for her, how she'd been to the library and borrowed a new book, how she'd sat next to a friend on the bus. But she worries her lies will be unveiled. She doesn't know how this would happen, but the worry is like a weight she cannot lift and so she says that no, she had not phoned Bobbie that night. Though she'd thought of doing so. Several times, she'd nearly called her. "No," she admits sullenly. "I did not call."

"Did you have any contact with her whatsoever that night?"

"I was driving," she states flatly. But then she sees the look on Dreyer's face, warning her to please answer as simply as possible, and says, "No."

"Did you check to see if your daughter was in her bed at home when you arrived?"

She hadn't. She'd come back from the hospital so tired that she'd dropped onto the sofa, removed her shoes, and fallen asleep right there. She looks now at the faces of the jury; their expressions tell her that they already know the answer. She did not check on her daughter when she came in. She did not even look in the bedroom.

"Into the microphone, please. The court needs to hear your answer aloud."

She wishes so much she had looked into Bobbie's room that night. If she had, she'd have seen Bobbie asleep beneath the sheets, the veiled moonlight through the bedroom curtains glowing on her pale hair. She'd be able to testify that this was what she had seen: a naked foot that had escaped the bedclothes, the wing of a shoulder above the loose neck of Bobbie's nightgown, her daughter asleep in bed, safe, as she'd always been safe. She'd glanced into that same room countless late nights and seen Bobbie asleep just so. Undoubtedly the same had been true that night in 1978. If only she could say yes, that she had looked into the room, the case would be over. Their lives would not be disrupted and damaged and slandered. If they put Craig away, everything she has worked for and put up with will have been a waste. And why would they put Craig away, when he'd done nothing?

There is the other unfairness, too, not spoken of in the ordered courtroom: that she is on trial as well. For being a bad mother, for failing to protect her daughter. But hadn't she protected Bobbie? Had she not allowed her to dream in bed as she, herself, had stayed up late, dusting shelves, making packed lunches, bleaching mold from grouting, hauling laundry in the old brown basket with the rupturing weave? That young woman who had all those years ago taken Bobbie to have her feet measured, her teeth checked, buying pink tops and beach balls and tickets for the merry-go-round, who was always by herself, scrubbing the kitchen table, washing out dresses in the sink, had she not been good enough?

She tells herself it does not matter. She has already been tried and found guilty years ago when Bobbie left wordlessly into the night, leaving no trace. What can they do to her here on this witness stand that is worse than what she has already endured? For months, the police believed Bobbie was dead. And then arrived the first of Bobbie's infrequent letters, telling June that she was fine and alive but did not wish to have any contact—yet. Those letters, posted every few months from different states across the country, kept June sane until, at last, the force of her love was drowned through misery, her heart a landmark and no longer a living place. Now they want her to testify, defend herself, aid the process of justice. And why should she?

"Mrs. Kirtz, would you like me to repeat the question?" Dreyer says. "Please tell the court if you checked to see if your daughter was in bed when you came home the night of September seventh." Dreyer glares down at her with his angular face and small, piercing eyes. He is like a bird standing above her, taking what is left of her dying body. He is a vulture eating her before she is even properly dead.

She decides she will lie. She will tell them she came home that night and saw Bobbie in bed. Why should she be honest when they want so much to disgrace her? It would be easy to lie and she knows, too, how much Craig wants her to do exactly this. He has instructed her to say yes, she had seen Bobbie in bed. She looks at him now. She wants so much to please him. Never in all the years they've been together has he blamed her for Bobbie running away. He has always said that she did the best she could but that some kids are headstrong. Some kids just go their own way. She longs to reward him for his allegiance by saying that yes, she saw Bobbie in bed when she came home. She begins to open her mouth, but eyes the judge above her, and the line of jurors, and suddenly she is afraid. She mouths the word "no," and immediately she feels a great wave of regret. Whether the regret is about not looking into the bedroom for Bobbie that night in 1978, or about what would come to pass because of her answer today in the courtroom, she isn't sure. She is angry at herself for saying no, for missing an opportunity. When Dreyer asks her the next question she is determined to answer in a way that helps put an end to the preposterous notion that Craig had been sexually involved with her daughter.

But Dreyer doesn't ask another question. He asks the same question, as though she'd said nothing. Apparently, her answer had not been heard.

"Mrs. Kirtz, we need to hear your answer. For the jury, please," Dreyer says. He clears his throat. She thinks he looks so smug in his fancy suit, his thick silk tie, all that blond hair he's swept back. Very slowly, he says, "Is it correct that on the night of the crash, the night that your daughter has stated she was in the car with Mr. Kirtz, and you were *not* with your daughter, *not* in the same state even, that you did *not* check on your daughter to see if she was in her bedroom?"

She can't let him debase her like this, or allow him to judge her. All her life, she has been cooperative, been nice, made peace, given of herself even when so tired she was on her knees. But not today. She opens her mouth and what comes out has little to do with the night of Craig's crash, nor with Bobbie. It's about what is taking place right now between this young man and herself. He wants her to tell the world she was a bad mother and she will not allow it.

"I checked," she says, her voice changing with the lie. Everything has become different with this simple declaration; she feels the lie breaking into her mind, eclipsing her thoughts so that she cannot imagine what she will say next. Yes, she was there that night. Yes, she saw her daughter. She looks at the judge, believing that she will find the woman scowling down at her with the full knowledge that she has lied under oath. She looks at Dreyer, thinking that he will laugh at her for believing she can fool him. But both the judge and Dreyer appear unable to detect what is happening. The judge gives a little cough, then reaches for a box of tissues on her table. Dreyer takes a step back, as though needing to rebalance himself after this unexpected news.

Dreyer is genuinely surprised. June can see this. And she realizes that for the first time in a long while, she's done something of significance. She's done something that matters. He says, "Are you stating, Mrs. Kirtz, that on the night of September seventh you checked on your daughter, Bobbie, and that she was at home?" He looks confused, and it gives June some pleasure to see him so.

This is the new truth. She saw Bobbie in bed. She was home that night. There is no turning back. She knows she must maintain these new facts all the way to the end no matter what is asked of her next, or how much pressure they exert upon her. She dares not look at Elstree; she is not sure whether she will be cross at her for altering her testimony or pleased that she is being so helpful for Craig's defense. The problem—if there is one—is that before this moment June has never claimed to have actually *seen* Bobbie at home in bed. She has only ever stated that she believed her daughter to be at home. This new information will come as a surprise to everyone, not least Elstree, who has warned June that she does not like surprises. But she cannot worry about that now. Dreyer is glaring at her, waiting for her answer. June opens her mouth to speak and now the words glide effortlessly, lie after lie, slithering into the air. "I saw that she was in bed. I didn't wake her," she tells the court.

Dreyer nearly stomps the ground in anger. "You've stated previously that you did *not* check on her," he says.

"I didn't check her on the night of the seventh because I wasn't home until after midnight. *That* is what I said previously," she says, nearly spitting the words at him. "But the seventh becomes the eighth at midnight, does it not?"

"You are stating that when you came home, you did check?"

"Yes. When I came home she was there."

Dreyer touches his brow, concentrating. "What time was that?" he says.

"I don't remember."

"Where was your daughter when you saw her."

"Asleep. In bed."

"What day was this?"

"After the crash."

"You mean the next day? The morning of September eighth? Or the night of September eighth?"

"I don't remember. After the crash."

"Mrs. Kirtz, it seems you cannot recall exactly when you checked on your daughter."

"I just told you it was after the crash."

"Okay, but from what you've said, you *might* have looked in at some point to see how your daughter was, but it could easily have been at any time after the crash. A day or two later, for example."

"Objection," says Elstree. "Ask a question, counselor."

Dreyer looks hard at June. "May I remind you that you are under oath?"

June looks over at Craig, who shines his approval at her. The way he looks at her strengthens her. Makes her realize she does not have to do what this man, Dreyer, wants her to do, to confess to being a negligent mother when she was not one. "I think I know that," June says.

There is silence in the courtroom. Dreyer takes a few steps away from her, his hands crossed in front of his chest, chin down, wrapped in thought.

"Did your daughter ever express any concern over Mr. Kirtz coming to live with you?" he says all at once.

"No concern at all," she says, another lie. She panics a little in her seat, realizing that this is how witnesses get caught out. One lie, another, and then they lose track. Under all the pressure and with everyone watching, they fall apart.

"Did she *want* him to come live with you?"

An objection from Elstree, something about speculation. June has no understanding about why she doesn't have to answer, or why it even matters. She'd only have said she did not know.

Dreyer continues. "Did your daughter ever tell you she did *not* want Craig Kirtz to come live with you?"

"She may have," June says, then immediately regrets saying anything that might put Craig in a bad light.

"She may have?"

"It was a long time ago. I can't recall."

"Think back. Did your daughter ask that Mr. Kirtz *not* live in the house?"

"No," June says, hearing the word as false, and as though someone else has spoken it. She can't imagine how she will continue to lie in this fashion without it becoming obvious to Dreyer, obvious to everyone. And then there is the fact that she *is* lying. That she remembers all too well how Bobbie had felt about Craig coming to live with them. Bobbie had pleaded with June, with her face full of emotion that June refused to take into consideration, with words she refused to hear.

A BAD DAY IN COURT

Dreyer offers Bobbie a ride. She thanks him, but explains that she does not want to take him out of his way and that she'll get a taxi. He insists, and she wonders if perhaps because it went so badly with June on the stand, he is trying to make it up somehow. As they walk through the parking lot, he seems preoccupied and closed off, a side of Dreyer she hasn't seen until today.

"That didn't go particularly well, did it?" she says.

He unlocks his car, drops his heavy case into the backseat with what seems like more force than is necessary, and says, "No."

His car is a boxy Audi diesel that chugs comfortably. Outside, a breeze clears away the heat and dust of the afternoon. In a different mood, Bobbie might have enjoyed the drive, the calm roads, the landscape on this pretty evening not so different from when she was a child. Nearly dinnertime, the sun is settling low in the sky, the temperature perfect for sitting outside. If she were here on a vacation she might unwind beneath the pergola at the inn with its manicured lawns and perfumed gardens, but her day has been a turmoil and she is not in a holiday mood. Her mind is alight with one thought: Her mother lied on the stand.

"Tell me again what happened," Dreyer says.

"You already know."

"Yes, but there may be a detail, however small, that will help."

She tells Dreyer once again the history with Craig, with the crash, with its aftermath. She reminds him of the chain of events—not her mother's version but her own. She feels doubt on Dreyer's part, as though he may no longer be quite as willing to take her at her word. He doesn't say anything to convey this, however. He nods as she speaks, driving assiduously along rural roads unfamiliar to him, relying on his GPS, never stating outright that he believes her or does not believe her. She watches him, eyes forward to the road, both hands on the wheel, his mouth clamped shut. She imagines him telling himself that it doesn't matter what really happened but what he can win with.

"I'm telling you the truth," she says. She wants him to say, *I believe you*, but all he does is nod. Suddenly she wants all the people in court—the judge and jury and everyone else—to say that they believe her. For years she has consoled herself with the notion that one day the truth would reveal itself, and now that the day has arrived she discovers the truth is not enough.

"It seems easy to get away with lying in court," she says.

"It's not easy," Dreyer says. "And it's not over."

She hopes he will say something about how he sees the case going forward, but all he says is, "When there is no evidence and no other witnesses, lying outright is a good strategy for a witness. That is, if they've got the stomach for it."

"I don't have the stomach for lying," she says, all the anger deflating within her, turning into a slosh of other emotions, bewilderment, despair. She feels an unworthy opponent to Craig, who would always lie, and now to her mother, who had made lying look easy. "I can only tell the truth."

"That's okay." Dreyer's tone conveys that he wants to end the conversation. Maybe he wants to distance himself from her. Maybe he is feeling a puncture in his professional pride. "That is all that is required of you," he says.

"I'm finding that difficult to believe right now."

Dreyer says, "You mustn't come to any conclusions just yet. Your mother is back on the stand tomorrow. We get a second shot."

"Okay."

"Do you want me to get you in the morning?"

"I don't think so," she says. "I may not go at all. I don't want to watch as she perjures herself. God knows what she'll make up next."

"She may find it challenging to keep track of what she's said. That's what we hope anyway."

"In which case she'll get in all sorts of other trouble, and I'm not sure I want to watch that, either."

Dreyer takes in a breath, then blows it out slowly. "She's taken a very specific position that is not in your favor," he says.

"She wasn't always like this, you know," Bobbie says. She recalls her mother as she was so many years ago. She kept recipes in card files, ironed the pleats in her skirts, instructed Bobbie not to slur her words, not to slump in her chair at dinner, not to lie. Ever. "But then, Craig came along."

Dreyer nods. "Well, he's sweating now," he says.

She thought of Craig in the courtroom. His height and size gave him such presence and he seemed completely in control today, solid in his chair. No matter what was said of him, good or bad, he did not show any sign of his own feelings. He did not speak, except to occasionally whisper to Elstree. He did not fidget or even shift in his seat. "He doesn't look like he's sweating," Bobbie says.

"Of course not," Dreyer says. "He's a criminal."

It occurs to her all of a sudden that she has never heard anyone say that about Craig, that he was a criminal. It feels like an enormous release, as though a latch has finally been unlocked, a door opened, allowing light to pour in. A criminal, she thinks. She almost laughs out loud. Of course he is.

They pull into Mrs. Campbell's driveway and she can hear the crunch and pop of pebbles beneath the Audi's fat tires. In the next moment, the inn with its pale painted timber and large sash windows, its borders of flowers that spill onto the flagstone path, comes into view. With the sun setting spectacularly in the field beyond, the colors reflecting in the windows, the house appears to glow.

Dreyer says, "Get some rest. Don't talk to your mother. I don't care what she tries, even if she sets up a ladder and crawls through the window—"

"I won't talk to her," Bobbie says. "There's nothing to say. We are done. We were done a long time ago, but now . . ." What she realizes, even as she declares its end, is how she'd always thought that her mother loved her, and how much she longed for that love.

He takes a moment to study her. "I'm worried about you," he says. "Should I be?"

She thinks it is sweet that he should be concerned. And maybe he should be worried about her. "I'm fine," she tells him. "I'm tougher than I look."

"Actually, you look pretty tough. But assuming your mother lied—"

"She did."

"Okay, so assuming that's the case, she lied in the weirdest direction. Parents will lie in favor of their children all the time. But not against. That must be hard."

And there it is, a simple observation that sums up everything that is wrong now. She says, "It's Craig's influence. He gets people to do what he wants. I've never understood how."

Dreyer shakes his head slowly back and forth. He looks more relaxed than he has all day, but tired, too. "How did he persuade your mother to let him come and live with you guys in the first place?"

"How did he *persuade* her?" Bobbie repeats. She almost laughs. "It wasn't like that." She smiles at Dreyer. He's a sweet man, she thinks, and far less worldly than one might expect of a trial lawyer. "He didn't even need to ask."

HE COMES TO STAY

Six weeks after the accident, June drove to the hospital after work as usual, touching up her makeup in the car, then trying to fix her hair so it didn't hang so straight. She wasn't expecting anything special to happen tonight. She was thinking about hair spray. Maybe, too, she was wishing she had eaten just a little bit less the day before. It didn't show yet, but there had been an infraction, a chunk of almond nougat that she'd found irresistible. In secret, she'd eaten a big piece of it, so much nougat that she'd actually felt sick afterward, yet still wanted more.

Walking through the hospital's automatic sliding doors, she had considered taking the stairs to his ward in order to burn calories, then decided against the idea as it would only rumple her clothes and she didn't want to risk appearing untidy. The hospital was too hot anyway, and hotter still as she rose in the elevator. By the time she was walking the corridor, she could feel the perspiration on her lip. In Craig's ward, beds were being stripped, the mattresses up on their sides. She had a sense that something was changing, had changed. And yet everything was as it had been the day before. The same trolley of newspapers and magazines stopped and started from room to room, making the rounds. The same nurses she had grown to think of as friends hovered here and there along their station. Two physios were helping a man with a broken leg work out how to use crutches, and there was an old guy in a wheelchair waiting to be taken for a shower. This was all normal.

Finally she saw Craig. Sitting up in bed, his arm with its boxy white cast, wearing what looked like a button-down shirt. That was the first difference she noticed. Street clothes, and how he sat stiffly and as though he'd been waiting for her. He turned fully toward her as she entered the room and she saw immediately that the bandages on his eye were gone, exposing the raw, pale flesh of his brow, the bones of the socket surrounding an angry oval of orangey-red, rubbery flesh. The overhead light shone on his face in a manner that seemed almost improper, drawing out the degree of bruising and scarring and the precarious thinness of the remaining folds of skin around the socket where his eye had once been.

She didn't know what to do. She made a little hello wave that seemed weak. She had to discipline herself not to look away. She had expected a gash, a hole, some great monstrous portrait of agony. She hadn't known what to expect. Somehow she'd invented the idea that she would be present when they unwrapped his face. She'd imagined a doctor taking them through the experience. She had the idea that the doctor would speak of all the great improvements that would come with a prosthetic eye, and how the sagging skin that hung down was left there on purpose to be used later when the new eye was fitted. This was how she'd imagined it. But instead here was Craig's face with its grotesque, bruised concavity, the absent window of the eye, the wattle of ruddy, hanging skin.

She felt a shortness of breath and a heat rising from within. She tried to walk toward Craig, but her legs had become uncoordinated, her balance all wrong. She knew she should not react like this. She should be matter-of-fact; *supportive* was the word that came to mind. She thought of all the weeks she had arrived diligently at the hospital, the long nights she'd sat quietly while he slept. She thought about the night he'd asked her to undress, and about other nights in which the same sort of thing had occurred. All of the progress she had made with Craig would be ruined now in an instant if she reacted wrongly to his face.

She could see his good eye—his only eye—tracking her response. The swimming-pool-blue cornea was large and full and clear.

He spoke slowly, loudly. "Don't say a word," he said. His arm, out of traction, lay across his body.

"You look fine—"

"Not a fucking word."

She sat down. She didn't know what to do. She looked out the window.

She wanted to answer all these concerns, explain how she could help him, how she wanted to help. That he would adjust to seeing with one eye, that his pelvis would mend—was already mending—and that if he hadn't broken his arm, he'd already be on crutches. "You're going to be fine," she said.

"I can't get to work."

"I'll drive you."

He took in a long breath. "The station is still only offering me the midnight-to-five slot."

"That's okay."

She thought about his voice with its smooth beauty. She imagined taking him to work, collecting him in the early hours of the day, perhaps having breakfast with him, escorting him through the process of healing. Did he not already understand that she expected to do as much, that she'd counted on it, in fact? "You can stay with me, with Bobbie and me. You can stay with us."

There, it was out.

He pursed his lips, considering this. She rode through the long minutes wondering if he was appalled at the idea, wondering if he'd laugh in her face.

"Stay with you," he said finally. "But why?"

"Why not?"

She thought briefly about the police, about the assault-and-battery accusation. But she told herself that celebrities were easy targets, and anyway no arrest had taken place. She wanted to protect him from the police, from all that wrongful inquiry. Perhaps it was because of that sense of wanting to protect him that she blurted out the next thing. "Because I love you," she added. Craig seemed unmoved by her declaration and she felt a rope of panic weaving itself across her middle. She tried again with a slightly different tack. "We love you, Bobbie and me," she said. "We think the world of you."

He exhaled. "Huh," he said. And then, as though he were suddenly awakened from a daydream, he said, "You're special, you know that? You're kind of special, June."

She listened to her name said in his beautiful voice, and thought how he found her special, and that for that moment she was.

"I give you a hard time once in a while, but you still pull through," he said.

She smiled. It had all been worth it. Every minute. "You'll stay with us," she said. "We'll look after you."

She promised him. She did not ask him how long this would be for, or think about Bobbie, whether or not her daughter would want him there. In fact, through some kind of magnificent oversight, she had forgotten to tell Bobbie at all.

BOBBIE HAD SUSPECTED her mother would arrange some complicated care scheme for Craig, maybe get a crowd of his friends on a rotation system to visit, arrange to bring him a few hot dinners. It hadn't occurred to her until she opened the porch door and smelled the sweet, grassy scent of marijuana, then noticed the closed blind and the general presence of another person in the house, that he would come here, to them, to *live* with them. She was unprepared, so much so that at first she felt confused, as though she had walked through the wrong door. In her mind, he belonged in the hospital now; he was part of the low ceilings and buzzing fluorescent lights and the pale, flecked tiles of the ward where they kept him.

"Hi babe," he called. "It's been a long time."

She'd nearly dropped the books she'd been carrying, had in fact begun to drop them but clutched them back. She wondered where he was in the house; she did not need to ask how he got here; she knew at once how. He had connived to persuade her mother to invite him. He'd used all his usual trickery. It was possible that it hadn't taken much persuasion on his part. Women like her mother—who could not see what was before them, or had no experience, or no memory, or did not believe—required little effort. In all likelihood, June had offered for him to stay. All he'd had to do was say yes.

"Aren't you gonna ask how I am?" he said.

She went into the living room, his voice following her like the pot smoke. "A bit goddamned lonely is how I am," he said. "Why didn't you come see me in the hospital? Every day, I waited for you."

She wondered where her mother was. She moved back to the hall and began climbing the stairs, searching the house, looking for June. She wouldn't leave him here and not tell her, surely.

"I still love you, Barbara," she heard him call. "You still love me, babe?"

And with that sentence she knew her mother wasn't home. She'd left her stranded with him; she'd gone to work. Through the window in the landing she saw the empty carport; June's car was gone.

"You going to come say hi?" he called out, his voice snaking through the house. She told herself to be brave, hold on. She told herself to make an excuse and get the hell out.

"Not even going to answer me? Not even going to say hello?"

She imagined his mocking smile and could picture his face as though he were right there in front of her. A recess where the eye had been, a recess at the mouth.

"Hello," she said, her chin angled over her shoulder, speaking into the empty hall.

"I can't hear you! Really, babe, I just want to talk to you." He sounded confused, as though her failing to come see him was genuinely hurtful and he couldn't see why she was so cagey around him, couldn't understand, no.

"Hello!" she said, louder this time.

"Barbara, get in here! What's the matter with you anyway? You think this is contagious? How would you like it if I treated you this way?"

"It's not that," she said. "It's not your—" She couldn't bring herself to say the word *eye*. She walked slowly down the steps again. She knew where he was now, in the dining room. She came closer. She could hear him in there. She could sense his presence and there was another thing, too, a kind of animal smell coming from the room mixing with the grass.

"I'm a cripple," she heard him say. "Cut me some slack, okay? I've been through hell. Can't you see I'm being *nice?*"

The kitchen and dining room were divided by louvered saloon-style doors that snapped behind her as she pushed her way gently between them. She stopped on the other side, feeling the doors tap her bottom. What had been the dining room was now a bedroom, except it was filled with stagnant clouds of smoky haze, lit only by the bar of light coming through the top of the blind. In place of the dining-room table was Craig's bed with a quilt and a number of fluffy white pillows. Next to the bed was a card table, a cloth covering the worn corners, a stick lamp with a frilly shade. June had put tissues in a china holder made to look like a lemon cake and positioned a phone so he could reach it.

Craig was sitting up, his face dipped, the good eye fastened on her. It seemed to pin her in place. She could feel her heart scratching her ribs, her throat filling with a weight that made it difficult to speak.

"Okay," she said. The room had a toilet smell that she decided to ignore. "I'm here."

He searched her face. "You're looking good," he said.

She tried not to look at the empty socket beside his remaining eye, the dark clouds of bruising below and above, the lid that hung heavy and red like a theater curtain.

He let his gaze lower and she felt him taking in the shape of her breasts. "All grown up. Aren't you going to say anything?"

Say what, exactly? "Hi," she said.

He waved. "Hi over there," he said. "W*aaa*y over there."

He wore a pair of pajamas her mother had bought him, unbuttoned so that his stomach showed. A lavender-colored bong rested against his belly, a pack of matches balanced between his thumb and forefinger. Beside him, a can of Mountain Dew and an ashtray rested on a slab of encyclopedia. It was her encyclopedia, volume one, Aardvark to Amazon. If he'd opened it he'd have seen her name there on the bookplate and the date that she'd received it on her tenth birthday.

"I guess someone found you some drugs," she said.

"Not drugs, pot. Jesus!"

"It wasn't my mother, I hope."

He shook his head. "Shit, no. Not June."

"Well, you enjoy yourself, then," she said, and made to leave.

"What do you think I'm going to do to you, anyway? I'm stuck in a damned bed, can't hardly move. I don't see why you have to act like this when you're the one walking around. Two good legs, two good eyes—"

"I'm not acting like anything," she said.

"Yes, you are. Like I'm going to bite your head off. That just pisses me off. I keep trying to be nice to you, Barbara, to fix all the shit that happened. And you're the one who hurt me, remember? That was some driving."

"That was a *deer*," she said.

"A deer you could very well have steered around."

She wanted to resist him, but part of her believed he was right, that she was to blame. And right, too, that she was afraid. Within his friendly tone she sensed a deeper craziness that she had not seen from him before. It was almost as though the accident had loosened something inside him. Anything could happen now.

"You're still my Barbara," he said.

She shook her head slowly. If ever he'd been able to make that statement, he no longer could. Sometime during the slow trawl through adolescence, in the shedding of old skin, she had changed, leaving him behind. He was summoning her back. But she could hold her ground now. "No, I'm not," she said.

He put his finger to his temple, then flicked it away to indicate he didn't understand her, that she must have grown stupid. His hair was longer now and pushed behind his ears in stiff, dirty planks that reminded her of the jutting-out feathers on the faces of certain owls. Unadorned by a patch or bandages, his absent eye appeared like scorched earth against the rest of his face. He no longer cared, it seemed, how ugly he'd become. Let him be ugly, it made no difference. He'd be ugly; she'd be stupid.

"Smell that?" he said.

There was the smell of marijuana that surrounded him, yes, but more overwhelming, the smell of human excrement. Somewhere in the room, she already knew, was his shit. She didn't want to come upon it unexpectedly but she didn't dare look for it, either. And now that he was talking about it, the smell embarrassed her even more. Her thoughts moved only to that smell, and the smell overwhelmed all thinking.

"What's the matter, babe?" he said.

She couldn't speak of it, just as she couldn't speak of so much. And the fact that she was unable to mention the smell made her feel again those other things about which she was so ashamed. The things he had done to her over the past many months, or what he understood they had done together, had formed her, molded her, shaped her into who she was now. The specific sex acts—all the various ways—would float away from her readily when she wasn't in his presence but always settled back onto her once again when he appeared. All the hiding and the lies she had to remember, the great burden of secrets like a garden that needed tending.

"You can't shoo me out of your life," he said.

She wanted to tell him she could do anything she liked. If only she could tell him once and for all that she did not love him, had never loved him, and in fact hated him (*I hate you*, she would say), she might feel his anger clench into one final, suffocating grip before releasing, possibly forever. But she could not. She was silent, and it was that silence that connected them now.

He said, "You can't just dump me like that."

What had she done to etch their union in stone, where had she signed?

From the heavy knot in her throat burst a sound, a kind of cry, and then the words, "My mother—"

"What about her?"

"What are you doing with her?"

"I'm not doing anything."

"That's not true."

"It's you, Barbara."

"No, you're lying. You're . . . fuck—" She interrupted herself, clasping her palm over her mouth.

He laughed. "You can't even say it. That's what I love about you, Barbara. You're sweet."

"No—"

"And you're the one I want. Always have been. It's always just been you."

"I don't have to . . . I don't have to put up with . . . with you . . . I don't have—" The stutter of a statement that, itself, surprised her. She hadn't thought she could speak and there was her voice suddenly high and loud around them.

He watched her. "I'm not done with you yet," he said.

She nodded slowly, then with more force. She could see a little chink of light, a little hope. "Yes, you are," she said.

He began to laugh. He laughed and seemed to enjoy it.

She felt her moment of power leave her, felt weaker for all her effort. He coughed, then angled the bong toward his face, filling it with a tangle of pot. "You must be high," he said, and lifted his bong as though raising a wineglass to toast her.

"You're not funny," she said, finally. She saw in his face a shadow of disapproval. "And I'm not yours."

His expression changed. He fastened his gaze upon her as though she had failed to follow a command, then set about arranging his bong hit, tamping the bowl lightly, pinching a slim match between the bulbs of his fingertips, his fingers moving expertly and with some urgency, as though loading a gun.

He swooped the match across the back of the book and held the flame at the base of the bowl. He sucked at the rim of the bong, drawing the fire down onto the leaves, his gaze never leaving her face. When finally he had a promising glow, he turned his head, exhaled audibly, then pressed his mouth against the plastic rim once more. His lips stretched inside the bong. Water bubbled in the bowl. He lit another match, the flame bowing into the leaves, an opaque cloud of smoke growing in the tube, and at last the smoke disappeared into his mouth all at once, like a ghost passing between walls.

He held the hit firmly in his lungs. "I hear you got a boyfriend," he croaked. "What's his name?"

She shook her head.

"You fucking him?" He exhaled, let out a little hiccup. "Of course you are," he said, his voice scorched.

"No," she said.

He looked at her. "He like it when you suck his dick?"

"Shut up," she said. "Shut the hell—" She sounded like a little kid trying to cuss and getting it all wrong.

"What did you say? Did you just say shut up? Did you, babe? I find out you're fucking someone behind my back and you tell *me* to shut up? That's rich. That's really rich."

She took a step away, leaning into the swinging doors. The doors creaked on their hinges; he stared at her and she froze. She didn't want to look at his face, but she could not turn away and it was as if she saw his brain moving inside his skull, applying his poisonous mathematics, working out a solution. How to deal with her, how to manage her, how to get her to do what he wanted.

"Stop," he said. "Don't move. Let me tell you something. You know why I'm here, don't you? The only reason?" A little cough. "It's not because of your damned mother, that's for sure. I'm here because I don't have any *money* to go anywhere else."

That wasn't it, of course. Not it at all. She wished her mother were home so she could ask her why he was here and when he was leaving.

"If you give me back my *money*, I could go." He used the burned match to stir the bowl, then got a new one and lit it all over again. "You know the money I'm talking about. A thousand bucks, you'll recall."

She felt her heart pumping. "I never had a thousand," she said.

"Yeah, you did. I finally figured it out. That five hundred we couldn't find in the motel room was in your goddamned pocket, wasn't it? Or somewhere. You had money hidden the whole time but you let me drive like a fucking lunatic anyway. You let me get in a fight trying to get it back."

"That's not true!" she said, but she sounded like she'd been rumbled. She sounded like a liar.

He shook his head, making a *tsk-tsk* noise. "Now listen up, Barbara. I want my money. I don't give a shit what you're doing with this little cocksucking teenage boy but I want my money."

She smelled the grassy smoke as the bowl was lit once more, its orange embers glowing, the seeds popping upward into the stagnant air with its dull light. She would run away if it came to it, and she was aware that with nearly a thousand dollars, it would be easy to run, and safer, too. Without it, impossible.

"I see you there, considering your options," Craig said. "So don't you tell me you don't have the money. I can see little dollar signs right through your skull. I know you've probably spent some of it on stupid things, but you have most of it, nearly all of it, don't you? You're a responsible girl, not a waste case. You've got it all tucked away neatly, pressed into a book like flowers." He smiled. He took the next hit in a quick gulp, then held out the bong for her to take. "Clean it," he said. "I'm a lot nicer when I'm high. I think you already know that."

She couldn't deny it. Once, so stoned his eyes were like slivers of red meat in his skull, Craig had gone to Safeway and bought six different flavors of ice cream, a bag of unsalted ground peanuts, whipped cream and bananas and chocolate sauce and maraschino cherries, all so he could make her the best banana split ever. Another time, he'd let her choose all the records on his show for a whole hour and even played "Mellow Yellow," despite the fact his program director would go nuts (or so he said).

She wanted him to smoke more. It might calm him down. So she stepped toward the bed, her hand outstretched for the bong. The smell of shit was stronger here. She felt a turn in her stomach. He held out the bong and said, "Stop being such a wimp and take it."

She reached out to grasp the bong's chamber, a lavender tube almost a foot long, angled thirty degrees from its base. From this close she could smell the resin and charred embers, the oily residues of smoking, mixed in with the toilet smell that filled the room.

She knew he wanted her to say something about the smell so that he could be suitably offended that she thought he stank. He wanted to get good and mad. But she wasn't giving in. She would say nothing. She held her breath, and felt the bong in her hands, its warm plastic, still alive with smoke.

He grabbed her wrist and she nearly screamed, his face suddenly close to hers. She saw the hanging skin surrounding his eye socket, the discoloration, the shine of scalp from his temple where he was beginning to lose his hair. She closed her eyes and focused on the pain around her wrist. He wanted her to moan, but she wouldn't do that. Nor would she give him the money.

"Do you know how many lies I've had to tell for you! To *protect* you? Nobody knows that you stole the money! Nobody knows you crashed the car! You walked away from the scene of an accident. That's a serious charge, Barbara. Do you know that? That's prison time!"

She felt herself splitting, as though her bones were coming through her skin. The piercing pain at her wrist was the locus of it, but she felt this shedding of her skin, her face, everything that identified her as herself, as Bobbie. She heard an awful ghostly mewing sound and realized the sound came from within her. He held even tighter and she cried out. He was right up against her; she could have reached over and socked him in the gut but she couldn't move and she didn't dare. Now she felt her legs giving out and a sudden urge to kneel down under the pressure of his hold, and all the awful humiliation. She dropped slowly to the floor, the caps of her knees making a quiet knocking sound against the wood. Her wrist felt like it might snap in two. The smell of him—of whatever he'd put in some corner of the room—rose into her nostrils so that she might throw up under the force of the pressure on her wrist and the curtain of stink.

"Empty that," he said.

She could not tell what he meant. He eased his hold slightly and she opened her eyes. There, on the floor beneath the bed frame, was a bedpan, the sort they used in hospitals, its contents coldly staring back at her, next to a wad of used toilet paper.

"Take that away," he said. "Then come back with my money."

JUNE MAKES A DECISION

■ ■ ■ *2008*

A ll night long June is disturbed by thoughts of lying in court. When finally she falls asleep she dreams about being in the courtroom again, speaking into the stemmed microphone from her place at the witness stand with its blond wood and uncomfortable chair. In the dream she tells unimaginable tales to the judge: that Bobbie had tried to kill her, that Bobbie had tried to kill Craig. All the while, the judge stares down at her until eventually June stops talking. The courtroom is silent in the dream and the judge's face begins to distort, narrowing and expanding as though she is chewing with large, inhuman jaws. The judge rises from her seat, her body formless, swimming in all her black robes, and declares June a liar. Staring into the judge's giant face with its grinding jaws, she is at once terrified and mesmerized. *You're a liar!* shouts the judge, until at last June is awake again.

The sky is starless, the birds not yet in song. She can hear her heart thumping in the still, black room. Even her fingers are quivering. Dreyer will put her back on the witness stand this morning. He has a fast mind. She is no match for him. If he believes she was lying about having seen Bobbie that night, he will take her by the neck as a fox will a chicken.

Not even Elstree had been nice. She'd scolded June for stating she'd seen Bobbie the night of the crash, warning her that if it wasn't true she had most certainly broken the law.

She then spent some time coaching June on what to do next.

"Don't add a single new detail," Elstree told her. "Don't admit to anything more than it was your habit to check your daughter. Do you understand? Make it sound like a routine thing, and that you can't remember much. Answer yes or no. This is *not* difficult." She had seemed so exasperated with June. She'd all but rolled her eyes at her.

"I'm sorry," June had kept repeating, though she didn't know what she was sorry for exactly. By stating that she'd seen Bobbie that night, she had made it less likely anyone would believe that Bobbie had been in the car. Why was that wrong?

"The less you say the better," Elstree said. The painted commas of her lashless eyes knit together. "Don't go off script during a cross-examination. You have to stay consistent. I thought we'd agreed on that."

"I didn't mean to make things worse," she'd pleaded.

Now all June wishes for is that she would fall back to sleep. Perhaps she should have a glass of wine. Soon the birds will begin singing and light will flood the room and she'll have missed all opportunity for rest. A glass or two would do it. On the wall behind her dresser are photographs of Bobbie as a little girl. On the night table is a photograph of her and Craig after they were married. She cannot see these things now, but she knows they are there, knows every inch and every detail. She remembers the cross-examination with a similar focus. She tells herself her testimony wasn't exactly a lie. She hadn't really lied on the stand because had she arrived back that night after the hospital and checked, she would certainly have found Bobbie in her bed sleeping. She was sure of this, just as she was sure of the faces she'd memorized in the photographs on her dresser.

She switches on a light. Craig's side of the bed is unoccupied, as usual. These days he sleeps on the couch in the living room or sometimes in what had been Bobbie's room. She knows if she goes downstairs she'll find him there, his bong on the coffee table along with the *TV Guide* and all the spent ash from smoking. He always leaves food out—pizza crusts stacked like ribs, Doritos bags crushed into balls on the floor, cereal boxes with their tops open from where he's taken handfuls from the box. It isn't unusual for him to bring out a pint of ice cream and let it melt over the glass table.

If she were to walk downstairs now, if she were to go to him and tell him she's had a bad dream and ask him to come to bed with her, he would growl like a dog. Actually sit there growling. Then he would say, "That's a negative." And nothing, absolutely nothing else, until she left him alone again.

She knows, too, that if she were to bring a quilt with her and curl up in the armchair beside him, he'd eventually wake and say "Why're you here?," as though she had no right to be in her own living room and there was no value in being close when sleeping.

She goes into the hall. The lights are still on downstairs and she can hear Craig snoring. When he first started sleeping in another room, his snoring was his excuse. He said he didn't want to disturb her. He used to summon her for sex every once in a while. In her chest of drawers are all the red and black negligees, satiny gowns, strappy slips with plunging necklines, none of which she has use for anymore.

She turns on the faucet and sits heavily on the closed toilet seat, squinting into the darkness. She feels the pulse of a headache in the very center of her brow, the weight of her heavy eyelids. She does not turn on any lights. She is aware of the solid band of extra fat around her middle, and yesterday's hair spray making her hair stick out in tufts from her head. The same thought that comes to her every so often springs into her mind once again: She is too old for him. She could never get her body to his liking. For all the dieting and reducing and cinching in of clothes and belts, the effect was never what she'd hoped for. Her skin has stretched out, the texture rippled with stretch marks. Her breasts face down like two dead fish. What she wishes for most, if it were possible to have, is a man who accepts that a woman—that she—will age. A man who accepts that they will both grow old, and for whom she would forgive his own bulging belly or vanished hairline, and from whom she would receive the same measure of grace.

She takes a bath in the dark. It is more pleasant than she would have thought. The water in darkness feels new, as though it could have come from somewhere natural—a river, the ocean. In the dark water, in the veil of quiet, she is able to feel peace.

In her life she has often wished there were someone who could lean over her and tell her what to do next. *Do this, now do this.* A little direction, a little guidance. It occurs to her that there is no "other life" she can create from here. If Craig leaves her or, God forbid, goes to jail, there will be no future to which she can look forward. No attractive direction her life could take. No other, different man. Her life, with all its turns and road signs, has led to this one single point.

Last night, after Craig had fallen asleep on the sofa, she brought a blanket to drape over him. He woke long enough to say, "You did good."

"I lied," was all that she could manage.

"She's the one lying," he said.

June had looked away from Craig, up through the living-room curtains he hadn't bothered to draw, and saw the black silhouettes of trees and a tooth of moon in the sky. She remembered when Bobbie would chase fireflies and make mud cakes and search the window wells for toads, digging gently into the sandy soil where the toads buried themselves to keep cool.

"I will never understand why it has to be like this," she said. She wanted Craig to hug her, but he did not move. "Other families don't have such troubles."

"Here we go again," he said. "It's the witching hour."

There was an abiding absence in her life that she felt more acutely at night and that, however she tried, she could not entirely suppress. But right then, she was not thinking so much about Bobbie's absence as her return, and the fact that she now found herself opposed to Bobbie in a courtroom, of all places, when what she really wanted was for her daughter to visit her like any other daughter might. To be with her, to be part of her.

She had wanted Craig to reach for her or at least open his eyes. The lid of his artificial eye was not able to close naturally like his good eye, and the appearance of an iris made it seem as though he were looking at her when she knew he was not. After a moment, he said, "I'm trying to get a few z's before the hanging. So if you are going to fret about the person tightening the noose, go somewhere else."

She wished he wouldn't speak like that. "That person is my daughter. And they aren't going to hang you," she said.

He yawned. "From the highest tree."

"I don't want to go back in the morning," she told him.

"You have to go. That's the law. And if you don't tell it right they'll believe her."

"I feel like I can't."

"Yes, you can," he said, purposefully. "They're going to put me in jail if you don't go. If you don't tell them exactly like you did yesterday."

"But there really isn't any proof—"

"You're going."

AND THAT WAS how it was. This morning, after her bath, he comes upstairs. He watches as she gets dressed, uses perfume, dabs on concealer, then enough foundation to cover the dark circles under her eyes.

"Do a good job," he says, bringing her a hairbrush.

IN COURT, JUNE cannot decline the Bible that is brought to her by the statuesque black bailiff with his high, dense shoulders and giant hands. She puts her palm across its leather skin and swears to tell the truth. She feels a spreading panic inside her and is desperate not to let this show. She wants the fire alarm to sound, or the lights to go out, or the judge to bang her gavel and dismiss court for any reason at all. Instead Dreyer stands near her with his sheaf of papers while the judge, in her lofty seat, removes her tortoiseshell eyeglasses, polishing them against the sleeve of her robe. The judge has long, well-manicured fingernails that cause her to grip her pen in a peculiar manner. She manages to look both bored and grave at the same time while Dreyer paces four steps one way, then back again, asking questions that clarify some of June's answers of the previous day. She knows Dreyer is just warming up, establishing a relationship with the jury before taking the questions further, deeper. It's like he is opening a wound with a penknife—little stab, little stab—until he is tearing through skin, then muscle, then bone.

Her throat is dry, her lips tight around her teeth. The room is airless and silent except for Dreyer's questions. June looks over and sees Bobbie behind Dreyer's empty chair. She feels drawn to her, yet oddly afraid, too. Afraid of her own daughter. She tries to discern how Bobbie is feeling from the expression on her face, but the girl is now a woman who is skilled at hiding her feelings. Sitting next to Craig at the defense table is Elstree. Elstree's full attention is on the witness stand, and she reminds June of a horse—head high, ears pricked, glossy eyes, staring unblinking in anticipation of near danger.

"Do you remember if it was dark outside or light when you returned from the hospital?" Dreyer is asking.

She does not remember, no. It was so long ago.

"Do you remember if there were lights on in the house or none?"

No, she does not remember.

Dreyer paces, fires a question, paces some more, asks another question. June despairs. How can she continue to answer with nothing other than *I don't remember*? How can she keep this up for minutes, then for hours? She hopes Elstree can see how difficult her job on the stand is. As the questions fly at her, she wants to call out for help—*How do I answer? Now this one, now this?* She wonders why Elstree just sits there without objecting while Dreyer continues with his bullying.

"Can you remember what time it was when you came home from the hospital?" he asks.

She does not know. "Can I have water?" she says.

"It's just here," Dreyer says.

"Where?"

"In front of you."

She can feel drops of perspiration rolling on her skin. She cannot stop herself looking over at Bobbie. She is thirsty. The courtroom waits as she drinks. Finally she puts the cup down, staring out at the giant American bald eagle emblazoned on the wall ahead of her, with its stiff, menacing wings, its eyes that focus outward as though searching the sky for a place to conduct its wrath.

"Do you need me to repeat the question?" Dreyer's voice.

"I don't remember," she says.

The judge shifts out of her boredom and eyes June carefully, then shoots a look at Dreyer.

He says, "Perhaps you need me to repeat the question. Are you aware that your daughter has stated under oath that she was in Mr. Kirtz's car the night of the accident on September seventh?" he says.

June nods. "I heard her," she says. And then, because she knows she has to answer yes or no, she adds, "Yes."

Five minutes more, ten minutes more. She wonders how much longer they can go on. It infuriates her, how the questions keep coming.

"Is there anything you can remember, Mrs. Kirtz, that would suggest Bobbie *had* been in that accident?"

"Anything I can suggest?" She feels almost as though she will begin to cry with frustration. She is supposed to *suggest* Bobbie had been in the car? But then it becomes at once very clear to her: Dreyer has nothing more to say. She sits with this knowledge for a moment before speaking. "No," she says.

Dreyer nods to himself. He has run out of things to ask. He

stands awkwardly, looking at June as though he can't quite believe it, either. There was no further argument, no proof, no clever questions to corner her into a confession. He is done.

June glances at Elstree, who is looking straight toward her, her lips parted as though to speak. Elstree had been right all along. No wonder she'd been so tough in her coaching. She had understood that June need do nothing more than refuse to add to the cross-examination that had taken place yesterday. June's testimony disproves the case against Craig. Bobbie was at home in bed. An eyewitness—her own mother—swears this is the case.

She smiles. She cannot help herself. She almost laughs out loud. How can anyone prove her wrong? She hopes Elstree can see what is happening here, how she has held her own against Dreyer, how she has won.

"Did you notice any unusual behavior from your daughter in the days following September seventh?" Dreyer continues.

"She was fine." This is easy. Just keep saying the same thing over and over.

"Allow me to finish. Inability to sleep, to concentrate, frequent headaches, withdrawal? Any signs of such behavior in your daughter?"

She could see that Elstree was about to object. Possibly, she was going to alert the judge to the way Dreyer was repeating himself.

"Bobbie was her usual self. Just a normal girl," June says.

"Anything that your daughter may have *said* to you during the days after the crash? Or perhaps a comment made by another person?"

June is about to inform Dreyer that there was nothing at all to suggest her daughter had been involved in that collision—no injuries or soiled clothes or signs of trauma—when all at once she remembers something. It is a moment she'd forgotten, or thought she'd forgotten, but that must have stayed hidden inside her for all this time, revealing itself only now.

What she remembers, almost as though it is happening before her, is the night in the hospital when Craig had finally gained enough strength to talk, those first words when he was able to speak. She'd bent her head low to his mouth and heard the croaky whisper after all those days of silence, the very first question on his lips. *What happened to Barbara?* he'd said. *Is Barbara okay?*

The memory alarms her; she is spooked. There on the witness stand, the focal point of everyone in the court, she feels suddenly afraid of what she knows, what she has known all along.

"Oh, oh no—" she begins, then stops herself.

"Mrs. Kirtz?" It is Dreyer.

She looks at his face, his handsome, young, menacing face, and her gaze goes straight through him to where her husband sits in the courtroom, where Craig sits. She wishes she could go to him now and ask him why he'd woken that day, that very first day, and asked about Bobbie, who he had no reason to ask after, who he'd not seen for months as far as June had been aware, and who had not been in the car. She remembers not only that his first words were about Bobbie but also his tone. It hadn't struck her because she had not been familiar with his manner of speaking back then, had not learned yet how to read him. But that night at the hospital when he asked what happened to Bobbie he had sounded conscience-stricken, even afraid. She'd thought it was just the pain he was in, the fear of his own injuries, but it was more than that. She understood this now. He thought he'd killed her daughter.

"If you don't mind answering the question," Dreyer says. She nods, but doesn't speak. Dreyer continues, "Did your daughter or another person say anything that might suggest that Bobbie had been in the car on the seventh of September?"

Her mouth is dry. Her tongue won't work. It's like she has to spit out a whole nest of spiders before, finally, wrenching out "No."

"Your daughter has stated that she had a bruise across the bridge of her nose. Also, that there were many other scratches. Most of the lacerations were able to be concealed, but the one on her face? Do you recall such a thing? A bruise on your daughter's face? I can have the testimony read back to you if that helps."

"No," June says, a little too quickly for it to sound as though she is really giving the question the attention that Dreyer is asking for.

"You are swearing you saw no bruises or cuts or any signs of injury on your child immediately following the night of September seventh?" Dreyer says.

"Yes, I am swearing that," June says. "Nobody could have walked away from that crash."

"Don't concern yourself with the accident right now, Mrs. Kirtz, but just cast your mind back to that time and whether there were any signs of injury—"

"I said there was nothing!" June declares sharply. But everything about her manner suggests she is unsure. She clears her throat, trying to regain some of the bravado she'd felt earlier. Lodged in her thoughts now are the pestering memories of Craig asking after Bobbie when he first woke. It keeps playing out in her head, how he croaked out the words *What happened to Barbara?* Why would he ask that? The memory has unlocked yet another memory and in her mind now she sees Bobbie as a teenager, with her spaghetti arms and large, clear eyes. She's standing in a doorway wearing khaki summer pants that tie at the ankles, striped socks, and a turtleneck. Why is she wearing a turtleneck in the heat? Why is she wearing a hat? June recalls, too, a bruise blooming across the bridge of her nose. She'd asked Bobbie about it and been told it happened at school during PE.

"I don't remember," June says. She glances at Bobbie. She is an elegant woman in her forties, with a slim musculature that she must have inherited from her father. Her hair is honey-colored, piled onto her head rather than draping the length of her back as it once had. Even so, June can see the little girl in her grown daughter. And, too, she can still picture her standing in the doorway in the crazy clothes that were all wrong for the heat wave they'd endured.

Without even drawing a conclusion, June realizes that Bobbie had tried to protect her from knowing. That she had covered herself, hidden any signs of injury, waited for weeks to pass, never allowing her mother to see. This thought, above all others, is what grips June most. For decades she has imagined herself as a victim of Bobbie's capriciousness, of her misadventure, running away as she had. But now, in an instant, she understands this was not the case, had never been the case. Bobbie had done everything she could to shield her.

The moment seizes June, fixing her in the chair. She searches Bobbie's face and wants so much to communicate her new knowledge. *You were there*, she admits silently to her daughter. *You were in that car.*

Now the judge is speaking, but June cannot take in what is being said. Her mind is filled with the thought of her child in that smoking carcass of a car with its crumpled body. It is everything she can do to keep herself still and not run to Bobbie. She cannot hear Dreyer when he responds to the judge, cannot think of anything except Bobbie, who glares at her, who seems to hate her. It is as though all the sound has gone off in the room and she is alone, staring at her daughter whom she has called a liar and whom she lost through her own ignorance, lost long ago.

"Are you going to ask this witness a question?" the judge says to Dreyer.

"No further questions," Dreyer says.

She is free to leave the stand. She can go, but she does not move. She thinks, instead, of how she'd tackled all of Dreyer's questions and had still come out wrong. So wrong, she cannot cope. Cannot. She feels light-headed; she feels weak. She leans to the left and rests her shoulder on the arm of the chair. So this is what fainting feels like, she thinks, like a sudden sleep that comes over you. The room is darkening. Her eyes close. She wonders when she will wake up, and where, and just as she has that thought she realizes that she isn't going to faint after all. She is sweating, and her heart flutters and flips, but she is only having another panic attack. There is nothing wrong with her except the simple understanding that her daughter has been telling the truth and, even worse, that she had tried to do so in years past.

PICK IT CLEAN

It was Saturday morning, early enough so the dew that clouded the corners of her bedroom windows had turned icy and the lawn below was laced with frost. Bobbie huddled in the car with her mother, following a map Craig had sketched on a paper towel, and which she had been instructed not to get wet.

"This is a bad idea," Bobbie said. They were supposed to go to Craig's house and get his clothes. Get more pot, is what Bobbie understood. "I don't want to do this."

"Why is it a bad idea? It's perfectly reasonable for a man to want his own clothes," June said.

Bobbie wore a scratchy olive-colored sweater, jeans with a zipper that wouldn't stay up, her hair folded into a metal clip. "Why do *we* have to go? To his house, I mean. Someone else could do it."

But she already knew. Because he asked for his clothes and records and audio equipment, that was why. Because he wanted them. He'd begun moaning about his things days ago and June agreed at the weekend they would fetch them. Craig said good because the guys he shared the house with were dickwads and jealous of his talents and he needed June to get his stuff before the assholes sold it or stole it.

"We're out here in the freezing cold," Bobbie said, "while he's still sleeping."

"It's *one* morning of our lives. I think we can spare it," June said. She moved the steering wheel around in her fingers, checked her mirrors, then made a great show of driving instead of listening. She didn't know why Bobbie had to be such a whiner. They were only going on a little drive, after all. In the back of the car were empty fruit boxes for packing and the car filled with the smell of bananas and soggy cardboard.

"You had to drive him last night, too," Bobbie said.

"To *work*, Bobbie. The man needs to get to work."

Bobbie flicked the heat on higher, then held up the paper-towel map for June to read. They drove for forty-five minutes, arriving at a decaying house at the end of a long line of similar houses. Craig's neighborhood was full of cars, some slanted onto the sidewalk, some angled halfway onto a lawn. They parked near the house and could see a man at the front door waiting for them. He brushed his hands through his unwashed hair, a phone cord attached somewhere deep inside the house straining across his bare arms. When they walked up the front lawn with their empty boxes he said into the phone, "Aw, shit, they're here now!" To Bobbie and June he said, "Craig sent you people? He sent *you?*"—as though they were ridiculous.

He stood wincing at them like the very sight of them was painful or the brightening day held too much light.

"You must be Craig's housemate," June said in her singsong greeting voice, the tone of which Bobbie thought never appropriate under any circumstances and certainly not now. She watched her mother extend her hand toward the man, who ignored it.

"Your *friend* Craig," the guy began, "hasn't paid his damned rent for months. Now you want me to give you access to the house? No way!"

He crossed his arms, blocking their entrance. He wore a pair of tattered jeans, a digital watch, a "Keep On Truckin'" T-shirt with the big thumb hooked upward, pointing at his beard. The fabric on his jeans was full of cigarette ash and pot resin. His bare toes stuck out from under frayed cuffs. He was about to slam the door when June spoke again.

"I'd like to take care of the rent," she said. She got a checkbook out, her pen ready. "How many months?"

It was extraordinary to Bobbie that June had brought her checkbook, that she had anticipated paying Craig's bills on top of everything else. She felt her chest caving, a terrible dread taking hold. She wondered if Craig had convinced her to do this, and what else he might persuade the woman to pay for, and whether the idea was to drain her mother of the money that Bobbie held and that Craig had convinced himself belonged to him. A thousand dollars, one way or another.

The housemate told them the amount and Bobbie watched as her mother stiffened, then let her pen relax. "I'm sorry," June said. She had a dignity about her that made the next admission more painful than it might otherwise have been. "I can't quite cover the entire amount," she said.

The housemate looked fiercely at them. "So, no money, is that it?" he said. "I'm supposed to let him just walk away like he always does? Because that's what Craig is like, you know. He glides through life and lets everyone else worry about his shit!"

June tried to smile, but the smile twisted on her face. "In point of fact, he's not walking anywhere," she said. "He's had a terrible accident—"

"I know about the accident!" the guy yelled. He made a sweeping motion with one arm, as though dismissing the whole notion. "*Fuck* the accident!"

He stared at them. Bobbie saw the veins in his neck, how his hair was beginning to stand on end with sweat. Finally he let out a long groan and then threw open the door hard so it banged against the wall. "Give me half the money, and then take every stitch of his clothing! Every piece of shit he has!" he shouted.

"Thank you," June said, scribbling the check.

"Mom, no," Bobbie said. She didn't want to give this man any money, or go inside the awful house, or even to stand at its doorstep. She wanted to go home. Now. She wanted to go home and clear Craig out of their house, out of their lives, before something worse and permanent happened.

"Bobbie," June said shooting her an urgent look.

"We can't!" Bobbie said, but June kept walking and Bobbie realized that her mother would go alone into the house, pack every bit of Craig's stuff herself, carry it to the car herself. Do it all, if that was what was required.

So she followed. Meanwhile, the housemate was barking orders. "Leave his stereo in payment! Leave the speakers, too. But all the other crap, get it the hell out!"

Bobbie had never heard a man speak in such a way to her mother. She'd never imagined her mother entering a house like this, either. It occurred to her all over again how the fact of Craig in their lives had opened a door that allowed entry to every ugly creature. The guy kept yelling, nodding his head forward at June as though pecking at her like a bird. Bobbie noticed that he was dirty, his face, his hands. His fingernails were chipped and yellow and his littlest fingernail had grown into a long scoop so that it curled like a talon and yellowed with length. It seemed wrong for a man to take such care to sculpt a fingernail, and she knew he used it to snort, but wondered why someone who could afford cocaine would live as he did and not wash.

She followed her mother through the dark house, feeling vaguely criminal with her load of empty grocery boxes. Her mother asked which was Craig's room, still using the pleasant voice she reserved for customers and doctors and any stranger on whom she wished to make a good impression. Her mother's unceasing politeness, so squandered here.

The housemate pointed to a back room, and they began down the darkening corridor, trying to be careful not to knock against the walls or create any other disturbance. There were rooms here, and rooms upstairs. Bobbie got the idea that there may be others asleep in the house, and so they whispered and were as quiet as they could be on the thinly carpeted floors.

"It's been a lot better since he's been gone!" the guy said. He told them Craig had broken the air conditioner by throwing it out the window in a temper, and they'd had to suffer the heat all summer long. They learned that Craig ate everyone else's food, left the doors unlocked, never changed a lightbulb or cleaned up after himself in the bathroom.

"He's a *hog*, a total dick," the guy said. "He comes across as cool, but he's scum. He siphoned gas from my truck!"

"I'm sorry," June said, as though any of this were her fault.

"And he lost my gas cap, too," he added, "the prick."

"I don't know if you are aware, but it really was a *horrible* accident," June said. "We are lucky that Craig is alive."

She wasn't that much older than the housemate, but something about June's manner, her calm reason, her humanity, made her seem as though she might have been this guy's old aunt. She even looked like an aunt in her work clothes, a plain wool skirt, an open-neck blouse, square-heeled black shoes, big fake pearl clip-on earrings. The pocket on her blouse called out for a badge, and indeed there were pinholes in the cloth from all the times she'd clipped on her name tag. It was ridiculous for her to reason with the housemate, whose eyes were bloodshot from too much partying the night before, and who looked as though he'd never done an honest day's work. No, indeed, not an hour.

"That *sonovabitch*? He *is* an accident!" he said. Bobbie thought perhaps Craig had diddled him out of something more than the rent money. Drugs, a job, a woman, perhaps. She watched him push some crumbs from his blond beard, then wipe his palm across his T-shirt. She noticed now that this guy, too, had the voice of a radio announcer. She knew these voices now, the quality of the tone, the throaty reverb. Behind him, in the living room, was a turntable and giant speakers and more electronic equipment than she'd ever seen. The guy glared at her, then at her mother and said, "Someone should shoot him, you know? Make a better world!"

June reeled back. Her jaw began to work, but she could not form any words. Bobbie looked at her mother in her workaday skirt with its matching low heels, her careful makeup and hair. She thought how her mother had no business in a house like this and no way of answering such a man.

"You need to let us get moving if you want his stuff taken out," Bobbie said.

He turned in a fury to Bobbie. "Oh yeah, little girl?" he said, his voice gaining in volume. But then, all at once, he flicked his hand toward a closed door and said, "That's his. Pick it clean!"

Of course, Bobbie recognized the room, with its single window and its single bed. She'd been in it several times. It smelled like metallic spray paint and scorched dust. Across the mattress were gray blankets, flattened pillows, a crumpled T-shirt, untouched for all the weeks he'd been gone. His clothes spilled from a system of drawers in fake walnut and with broken handles, a collection of jeans and stacks of T-shirts from radio stations across the country and from bands he'd seen. The T-shirts were mostly unworn; some he'd put into plastic bags, some he'd folded into perfect squares.

He had tons of record albums plus two guitars—one electric, one acoustic—and a set of drums stuffed into the closet, accessed by a sliding door. The room was dominated by a desk on which he'd arranged metal baskets containing electronic gear: colorful wire, copper-clad boards, circuit boards, rocker switches, tilt switches, speakers in various stages of development or repair, a microphone capped with a ball of foam around its head.

Having her mother in this room, in this room with her, was too much. She wanted to get out. "Let's just take the important stuff and leave," she said.

"We'll do our best," said June.

"But look at the size of those drums." They were stacked one above the other like tiers of a wedding cake. "They'll never fit in the car anyway."

"He says he needs those. And his stereo, too. We certainly aren't going to leave his stereo for that . . . *person*," June said, nodding her head toward the door.

They made their way back to the car, first with the drums, then with boxes now filled with radio equipment neither of them knew the names of. They dragged along his clothes in green garbage bags. Back and forth, back and forth across the yard. Sections of wire fence had been on the ground so long they were now embedded in the grass, and they stepped carefully around them so as not to trip. Bobbie hooked his headphones around her neck, the giant padded earpieces wagging beneath her chin. She stuffed her coat with all the mail that had been collecting, unopened. She lugged the speakers, then their stands.

At least the housemate had disappeared—that was a mercy—but the brightness of the outdoors contrasted the dark hallway so that they blinked as they went in, hoping not to collide with him inside, and squinted when they came out, carrying as much as possible.

With her mother beside her, Bobbie noticed all the signs of the house's ruin. The air conditioner the housemate had spoken of was indeed tipped on its side out the window, the grass longer near it and weeds growing through its grille. In the living room the curtains were made from single sheets of unhemmed brown cloth that could not be kept open except by wrapping them around a cleverly positioned floor lamp. Bare bulbs, a balding shag carpet. Someone had gotten the idea to take down the wallpaper but given up halfway through. There was a bong behind the sofa and a cage for an animal, or perhaps it was a trap.

She was on her knees by the bed, running her hands beneath it, raking into a pile all the cassette tapes that lay there, when a phone rang from under the bed covers. June and she stared at each other, at first unable to find the phone, and then unable to decide whether to answer it.

"Check if there is a ring in any other part of the house," June said, and Bobbie scrambled up from the carpet and went down the hall. There was another phone in the awful kitchen, an avocado-colored dial phone with a long extension cord, but it was silent.

She felt sure Craig's caller would soon give up, but she could hear the phone continuing to ring and when she returned, she found her mother staring at it as though at a fierce, barking dog.

"What are you doing?" Bobbie said.

June opened her mouth, then closed it again. "Do you think we should answer it?" she whispered.

This was crazy—why did her mother feel she needed to answer another person's phone? "Absolutely not," Bobbie said, but she could read her mother's thoughts, and knew her to be a woman who could not resist a ringing phone or a doorbell or an oven timer.

June took in a breath. "It could be someone . . . important to him."

She meant a girlfriend. Bobbie could tell from the mild panic in her mother's voice.

Bobbie said, "Maybe it's a bill collector. Don't answer."

The ringing persisted, like a person at a front door who has seen you're inside.

"What should we do?" June said.

"Go home."

But her mother could not stop herself. She picked up the phone, holding it lightly, as though she might want to drop it at any second.

"Hello?" June's voice was high and fluttering, a little feather that floated from her mouth.

Bobbie busied herself with the cassettes. She tried to listen to the conversation but June shooed her away, pointing at the closet where there were drumsticks and fans, some sheet music on the floor. She took these things out, then saw a stack of magazines resting on a shelf above the hangers. She brought down a few issues and saw on the cover of the first issue a naked model in tall heels and stockings, her buttocks taking up much of the page. Where her nipples were the editors had placed strategic graphics so that they could not be fully seen—two red stars covering the areolas. Bobbie thumbed through the pile and saw they were all the same type. She put the magazines back where they'd been and fished down some cymbals instead, balancing them on her head like a hat. Soon, she was again trawling across the uneven ground with boxes and knickknacks—a basketball, a desk lamp. She didn't want her mother laboring under the unwieldy boxes.

When she returned, June was making an attempt to fold the bed linen, the phone now put away.

"What did they want?" Bobbie asked. When her mother didn't answer, she added, "The person who called, I mean."

"I don't know," June said, her voice sharp as though Bobbie had asked a rude question.

"Well, you talked to them for a long time," Bobbie said. "I heard—"

"All right, Bobbie. Enough."

They made one last trip to the car. It seemed to Bobbie this was the kind of place where feral cats were poisoned, where anything that got broken stayed broken, and where just occasionally a body might be found. Last time she'd been here, Craig had parked well away so his housemates wouldn't spot her, then checked to see if anyone was home before bringing her inside. She hadn't liked the place then either.

At the car, she told her mother, "I want to go home." Even though Craig was at their home, and it meant returning to him.

June balanced the weight of her boxes on the hood. "But what about the rest of his things?" she said.

A foam mattress, a wooden chair, a desk that couldn't possibly fit. What did her mother think, that they could tie these things to the roof?

"We can come back," Bobbie said, though they both knew that would not be possible. The housemate would throw out what had been left behind. His instructions, which had put her in mind of vultures, were to *pick it clean.*

"Please, Mom." They were standing outside the car, the wind working its way through the trees above them. The car was full; there was no room left to haul a thing.

"I know, I heard you. You want to go home."

The car was warm from sun, but so tightly packed that Bobbie had to sit at an angle and with her knees practically in her face, everything of Craig's surrounding her.

"Who was on the phone?" she asked.

"No one," June said. Bobbie made a face and June said, "Oh, all right! It was a police officer."

Even the word terrified her: *police*.

"What did they want?" Bobbie whispered.

June shook her head. "Apparently information about a fight before the accident. In a motel . . ."

Bobbie didn't hear anything after that. The word *motel* from her mother's mouth felt like an accusation.

"But they just want to ask him a few questions. He hasn't *done* anything!"

Bobbie nodded. She wondered what would happen next. Would the police show up at their door? Ask her questions? Would she have to swear an oath? The thought of talking to a police officer terrified her and she wished they could keep driving, drive far away, that they could escape.

"I'd like you not to mention this to Craig," her mother said. "You won't say anything, will you?"

Bobbie said nothing, not to agree, not to disagree. Instead, she looked out the window at the passing houses.

"He gets very upset about police," June continued. "And we don't want him unhappy."

Of course not. That was the important thing, not to upset Craig or trigger his moods. Bobbie felt a plummeting despair. He was in their house. He brought the police. There would be questions, probes, explanations to be given. It filled her with dread. Finally, reluctantly, as though asking for a tremendous favor, she said, "Do we have to keep him with us?" She almost stopped there, the plea seeming so preposterous given the lengths her mother was willing to go to for Craig. But she carried on anyway. "He is working again now, has his old job back. He could get his own place."

She longed for her mother to answer that of course they didn't have to house Craig, that their home was for themselves and Craig was only there for a short while longer, until he was healed enough to drive himself to work rather than rely on June. She ached for her mother to promise he would go soon, but she felt the way she had as a young child, desiring a particular toy at Christmas, an expensive, luxurious toy, all the while knowing the odds were slim. Even so, she asked, just as she'd asked years back, with a child's heart and hope. When her mother did not answer, she felt a sinking in her chest, and her own inner disciplinarian rising from within her and telling her to stop behaving like this and stop expecting so much.

Minutes later, she began to feel a burning in her stomach that she associated with car sickness, a condition she thought she'd outgrown. At a stoplight, she rolled down the window and stuck her head out to breathe the cool air. She heard the breeze rustling a willow tree that grew messily in a hollow area of ground next to the road. She angled her head, seeing the back of the car, stuffed as it was with all of Craig's things. And with that sight, the weight of his presence in her life pressed against her freshly, as though he had just now discovered her and had set his desire freshly upon her. Nothing could rival his attention, not teachers at school, not her mother, not Dan. The force of it reigned outside the normal domains of school life and home life.

How could she do anything now? After so many incriminating acts and all the time that had passed during which she'd said nothing, how could she speak to her mother of the things that Craig and she had done? How could she warn her mother, and turn her away from him? She knew she had to say something, that this was her last chance. She couldn't bear to confess all that had happened, but there was no other way out. "Mom," she began. She let out a sigh, a wretched sigh loaded with as much meaning as a word and which no word could describe.

"I heard you the first time," her mother said crisply. "You don't like Craig. No need to repeat it."

"It's just that—" She stopped. "The police, that motel—" She willed herself to continue but her voice died inside her even before her mouth closed. It was impossible. If she told her mother she was in that motel room with Craig, everything between them would change. Her mother's opinion of her was like a plant that she tended, keeping it decorous and in flower. It was fully false, yet necessary, and the only way she could continue to be in her mother's presence. How could her mother know any of the truth of what she had done with Craig and then carry on loving her as before? For that is what she wanted, to have things as they would have been if Craig had never existed and had not divided her life into these two halves that must never meet. In future years, she would ask herself why it was that girls like her did not tell their parents, and why they ached with secrets even decades later, and even then felt the impossibility of such a confession. *Because*, she would say helplessly, *just because . . .* And in those years, just as now, she'd keep quiet. Instead of telling her mother what she needed to, she leaned away and spoke out the window, into the bright October morning.

"Will he live with us for long?" she asked miserably.

He would stay for as long as he wished. Bobbie knew this, just as she knew that only a stark and full confession from her would change her mother's mind. She was not willing to pay that price, that great price, no. Her mother, whom she loved, loved an imagined child that she pretended to be. Bobbie would not let her down. She would act as if everything were all right, even though she felt yet another break between them, the distance that severed growing children from their parents and that separated her from her mother now.

The stoplight changed and the car went forward. "For the time being," June said, which might have meant forever, and probably did.

BUS STOP MEETING

Outside the courthouse Bobbie stands nervously on the curb to hail a cab. It takes a while for one to come and all that time she is worried she'll be approached by her mother. Part of her wishes to confront June directly, to tell her she knows that she lied on the stand, that she's seen it twice now and that both times astounded her. She wants to show her the detestable little note that Craig sent to her: *I married her because you would not let me marry you.* What would she make of that? Bobbie wondered. Is it possible that June would imagine Bobbie had invented the note, too?

The sun bears down on her. Finally a taxi arrives. She tells the driver where to go but of course he has no idea where she means—the inn is so out of the way—so she guides him through the first few miles and promises further instructions in a moment. Meanwhile, she closes her eyes. She thinks, I'm tired of all this shit.

The urgency of her feelings gives her a disturbing sense of disorder and wildness; it is as though she has done something for which she should be ashamed, but she cannot imagine what. She has been discredited. Is there anyone who knows what really happened and to whom she does not have to plead to be believed? And then she remembers again the man she has never forgotten: Dan.

Technically, she is not supposed to speak to another witness because to do so could jeopardize both their testimonies. But they've already testified now so perhaps it would be okay. The drive to tell him what happened in court today, to explain what it felt like to sit wordlessly and watch her mother refute her own testimony, is fierce.

Besides, now that she has thought of him, she can think of nothing else.

They have not spoken since they were teenagers. Over the course of recent months, however, she has received three e-mails from Dan. In the first, he explained that he'd found her after much searching and that he hoped she would not be annoyed at him for doing so. There followed a carefully worded, warm paragraph asking how she was, then some information about Craig's arrest, which Dan imagined she already knew about. *I was so sorry to hear that his behavior has continued*, he wrote. *I'd wrongly imagined that your situation with him was unique, not that this would ever excuse it.* His letter was full of formality and apology. She wished she could reach through the computer screen and tell him that Craig was a bastard and let's just get that out in the open quick. Also, that she was immensely glad to hear from him, that she wished she'd had the courage to get in touch with him years ago, but that she'd been too ashamed.

She'd said none of this, of course. Instead, she'd written back just as carefully as he had, crafting the e-mail, then deleting it and starting again. She told him that she was happy to hear from him and that she remained out of touch with her mother and so she had been unaware of the news of Craig's arrest. *Thank you for letting me know*, she had written. *And what a delight to hear from you.* A week or so later, she got a new e-mail, this time to say there had been a police investigation and a raid on Bobbie's childhood home where Craig and her mother still lived. The police had been looking for child pornography but hadn't found any, apparently, and there was some question as to whether Craig had been tipped off. Was she going to be in touch with her mother? Was she going to come back due to all the chaos surrounding Craig's arrest?

She remembers how she typed her reply to Dan several times, changed the wording around, deleting and beginning all over again. It mattered to her. Of all the things she has had to let go of in her life—her home, her only parent, her identity for that matter—the hardest to abandon had been Dan. She typed out the words, *Thank you so much for taking the trouble to write again,* wishing she could say all the other things, which had nothing to do with Craig or her mother but were about how she'd felt about Dan, what he'd meant to her.

She wanted to tell him about her short, hapless marriage to a guy who she'd had no business marrying as she didn't love him the way she knew she was capable of loving. And how, afterward, she'd changed every stick of furniture, painted the walls, torn up the carpets, and gutted the kitchen, remaking the house afresh in his absence, creating a kind of nest for herself to settle into and wait for someone else, maybe even Dan if he'd been present, if he'd been available.

It would have been silly to tell him such a thing—and totally inappropriate. It seemed too awful and comic an admission.

When she heard from him again it was only with regard to the progress of the case. There had been some kind of mistake in the way in which the prosecution was handled. The result was a mistrial. No verdict returned. The girl's family had been devastated; the case had been closed.

The only hope of bringing him to justice would be a separate case, Dan had written. *If a historic case came forward, that is. There must be many of his victims out there.*

Victim. The word didn't settle correctly with her. Even so, she is here. She doesn't know why exactly. Maybe it is to avenge herself, however shallow and deluded that ambition might be. Maybe it is to avenge the young girl who has been Craig's most recent target, if only by allowing her to see that another person had been through the same type of experience with Craig. Or maybe she is here simply because Dan asked her to be. She is going to call him now—hasn't she waited long enough? And anyway, who will know? It isn't as though a court official is listening to her phone calls.

So she dials his number. She hears his voice. "I knew it would be you," he says. "Where are you?"

His voice hasn't changed. Thirty years and he sounds the same. She says, "What if I got changed and we had some dinner together?" She holds her breath, waiting for his answer.

"What *if*?" he laughs. "Just tell me where."

TWO HOURS LATER she is at the bus stop where she'd first run into him all those years ago. The line of stores nearby no longer includes a Kmart, nor resembles the strip mall she remembers. It has transformed into a giant, upmarket indoor mall with a staggering fountain and huge blocky sections with big-name department stores. These days, if a teenager tried to hide here among the flowers the night security staff would spot her. And if a girl tried to get through the great glass entrance hall with nothing on her feet but blood, there would be a guard to escort her out within minutes.

The bus stop looks mostly the same, however. They've traded the thin metallic benches for some candy-colored seats, and the flooring has been updated, but it is enough like it used to be that she finds it easy to remember meeting Dan here. She waits, watching the swoop of headlights as cars pass. At last, a midnight-blue sedan switches its signal light on, then slows coming toward her. Suddenly, she sees Dan behind the wheel.

There is an instant flash of recognition. The flood of anticipation turns at once into something more immediate and visceral. She is flushed, her lips starched, her focus on the man in the car so strong that everything around her fades. She isn't even sure her legs will carry her safely as she walks forward, reaching the door before Dan has a chance to get out, saying his name too loud as though calling him from across a distance. As she climbs in she loses her footing so that she practically falls into the seat beside him.

"Hi." She smiles.

He says her name. He says, "Oh Jesus."

Beside him, she feels every burden float from her. It is as if there is no trial, no lying mother, no Craig.

"It's very good to see you," she says, her words feeling puny, even ridiculous, given the swell of emotion.

They are strangers, but also friends. They know nothing of each other's lives except the very beginnings. What is most astonishing, apart from the fact she can hold in her mind's eye both the boy she knew decades ago and the man before her, is how the air around her seems scented with the summer of 1978, as though those days are present within this one.

The car's interior light fades; the turn signal dings and flashes. Still, he does not drive off. She keeps looking at him, at his face that is at once familiar and so very new. He has become the sort of man who has to shave every day, even twice a day, and whose whiskers ink the skin above his lip. His once overly lean body is a different shape. The shoulders that had seemed bony are now large and full, hard to contain beneath his jacket. Filled out, with a thicker neck and some roundness at his belly, he is solid; the added weight and years give him a presence he'd once lacked. He is magnificent, she thinks. She almost tells him so.

He moves his gaze, taking in the shape of her. She has ditched her court clothes and wears a tunic dress with strappy shoes. Her legs are well-muscled and tanned with California sun. Her toenails are painted pink. In her ears are tiny pearls. "You are lovely," he says. "I feel like an old wreck next to you."

He smiles, then leans over to kiss her hello. Somehow their timing is off and the kiss lands wrongly, not quite on her cheek. They try again, and this time he turns to her and brings her toward him, holding her lightly. "Bobbie," he says again, sounding her name slowly as though learning it for the first time. "I have to touch you to see if you are real."

On the road, he tells her he lives in Bethesda and works as a medical academic, with a specialty in pulmonary disorders. She nods and tries to take in the details, but all she can focus on is how his voice is the same as she remembers, or almost the same. He sounds older but she can hear through the deeper tones that same Dan who'd spoken to her for thousands of hours that long-ago summer.

"What I'd love is to make you dinner but I've got two teenage daughters at home and they won't give us any peace," he says.

"What about your wife?" she says. She might as well get it out there.

"My wife, oh." He raises his hand and flaps his fingers in an imitation of a bird flying skyward. "She's gone."

She isn't sure what to make of the idea the wife is gone. Does he mean gone for a week or for a lifetime?

"We can't eat where I'm staying, either," she says. "The place is booby-trapped. My mother barges in. Also, I think the innkeeper's a spy for my mother. And I think my mother is a spy for him." She means Craig, of course. "You know, Mr. Charming at the defense table," she says, and watches Dan smile.

He drives on, stealing glances at her occasionally. When she catches him, he says, "Can't help it. You look great."

"No, *you* look great."

"*You*," he says. He laughs aloud.

She remembers how they used to joke and she says, "How could I look great when I look nothing like I used to look?"

"You do, you know. Sort of." He gives her hand a squeeze.

"You weren't in court today," she says. "You missed my mother lying on the stand."

Dan nods slowly. "Well, I suppose she would."

"I can't understand it."

"Why not? It makes perfect sense."

"I didn't think she'd actually make stuff up. I never thought of her as a liar." She remembers what Dreyer had said, how parents don't ordinarily lie against their own children. "I wonder if she even recalls all those years ago. Maybe she's just forgotten."

Dan says, "She hasn't forgotten."

"She kept looking at me the whole time, then coming up with these tales. I don't understand the woman," Bobbie says. But of course, if she allows herself to truly imagine what it would be like to be June, she understands completely. That June cannot bear what happened all those years ago is perhaps one of the easiest things to grasp. "I'm really worried we will lose this case," she says.

A moment goes by, and then Dan says, "Did you expect another outcome?"

So Dan thinks the case will be lost. Perhaps he'd always assumed it would be. She lets go a long breath. "Maybe I did, yes. Didn't you?"

"At first. But by the time the trial began, no. Not really."

"It was your idea to begin with. For me to testify, I mean."

"Not because I thought we'd win," Dan says. "I'm sorry if that's why you came all this way. I thought you would want to tell what happened. It doesn't seem right that he should have gotten away with what he did, gotten clean away."

"But if we lose—"

"There's losing, and then there's losing."

She thinks about the girl in the other case, the one that was botched and ended in a mistrial. Her parents have come to court every day since the start of this trial. They huddle nervously together, their grim faces looking around the court as though they are the ones on trial.

"That girl," she says. "I wanted her to know that there is at least one other person in the world who knows she was telling the truth. That whatever happened in that trial, she was believed. I can picture exactly what happened to her, you see."

"What happened?"

"She made a phone call. He kept her on hold while he did a break. They talked through his show; she got flattered. People imagine that girls these days are far more sophisticated than they really are. All he had to do was say the right things and spend a little money. Once she was in the thing, she wouldn't know how to get out. That's the point. He'd have trapped her somehow."

"Go on," Dan says.

"That's it. A very mundane story, really. He'd have convinced her that she was stuck with him. That the whole idea had been hers to begin with. He'd have told her how much risk he was taking, all because he loved her. He'd have told her he was protecting her from other men who would not appreciate her. That she was special and he saw that specialness. He'd say this even as he was taking off her clothes."

"Jesus."

"I'd love to tell her that I understand. I've been on that ride, and it's a difficult one to get off of. Also, that however angry she is now, it will fade as her memory of him will fade. That it doesn't have to touch her. Not really. If she just looks forward, always forward in life, it will not."

Dan nods. Then he reaches across the car and takes her hand again. "You should write her a letter when this is all over. Tell her that, what you just said."

AT THE RESTAURANT they are told they have to wait for a table.

"Good, then we have time for a drink," Dan says.

Behind the bar the bottles are upside down, capped with taps, and gleaming in wild blue-and-yellow light, also reflected in the mirrors. He orders a bourbon.

"Anything else?" The bartender is a young guy with a black goatee and a pointy mustache.

"I'll have a ginger ale," Bobbie says.

"And a whiskey for the lady," Dan tells the bartender. Bobbie laughs. Dan turns toward her, grinning, the blue of the lights making a slash across his face. He says, "Okay, we'll compromise. Not a drink-drink but not a kiddie drink either, okay? Live dangerously."

"Should I?" Bobbie asks the bartender, who smiles a lurid smile and nods his head. She orders a gin and tonic and they find a place in a corner of the bar, waiting for their table.

"I love being here with you," Dan says. As always he is unguarded, stating exactly what he feels as easily as he might mention the weather. She wishes she could be the same.

"The person you remember was just a girl," she says, almost sadly.

He shrugs. "Are we so different than we were before?"

"Is that a serious question?"

He nods.

She says, "I guess I still buy clothes that aren't warm enough. And I still like walking in the woods at night."

"Are you still shy?"

"I was never shy," she says.

"Your most important disclosures were said with your eyes on the ground."

"That was shame, not shyness. And you might have noticed I didn't tell you much."

"There shouldn't have been any shame. It wasn't your fault—"

"That," she says, "makes no difference."

He smiles at her. "You wouldn't even meet my parents."

"Okay, that was shyness. But I did want to meet your mother."

"My mother," he says, shaking his head slowly. "She died. We spread her ashes on the Potomac last winter."

"I'm sorry. And your father?"

"He's ninety. Lots going wrong with him. All his life he treated medicine as though it were a religion. Now he hates doctors."

"Do you remind him that he *is* a doctor?"

Dan laughs, a single loud "ha." Then he says, "I'm not sure he always remembers we're his children."

They are quiet for a moment. They drink and look at each other, and strangely feel perfectly comfortable doing so without speaking. She admires the smile lines around his eyes, his white, slightly uneven teeth, the curly hair that is still in evidence, though graying. Eventually Dan says, "If I met you today for the first time, where do you think it would be?"

"You mean, where do I hang out?"

He nods. "I want to dream up a different intersection for our lives because I am uncomfortable with the real-life one. Actually,

I'm pissed off about it. I feel my first love was taken away from me because of him."

He will not use Craig's name. He has become a man who is very specific about what he believes, what he will do and not do. All the promise he'd shown as a boy has blossomed into an intelligence she can easily detect. But there is also something in Dan that did not used to be present in his youth, a darkness that comes over him at certain times, arriving and disappearing in an instant.

She says, "I would meet you at . . ." She scrunches up her face, deciding. She wants their conversation to become lighter, warmer. For him not to look so broody. "At a dog park," she says, finally.

"A dog park?" He smiles. "Is that a place where you can bring dogs as opposed to all the other parks that are for cats?"

She nods. "Exactly. And I'd see you at the dog park with your . . . hmmm . . . with your Labrador."

"Not a rottweiler?"

"No. Rotties are owned by the people who taught me how to shoot a handgun."

"You know how to shoot a handgun?"

"You bet I do," she says, and she sounds more serious than she'd like.

Dan shrugs. "What kind of dog have you got, then? I mean, in our imagined meeting."

"A beagle," she says. "The story is that I had this beagle, but it died before we met, and these days I come to the dog park the way that mourning widows visit a graveyard."

"And that is where I find you? In the dog park, looking sad and dogless?"

"It's the Labrador that finds me. He's a charitable fellow; he senses my doglessness and does his best to fill in."

"He prefers you, my dog," Dan says. He pretends to be upset by this. "He likes you better than he likes me."

"Don't be ridiculous. He's *your* dog."

"But he sees something in you that is special and he persuades me to ask you out."

They are smiling at each other and she realizes that this is the sort of conversation they used to have all the time, as teenagers.

"And do you need a lot of persuading?" she says.

"No," he says, and finishes his drink in a single long gulp. "None. At. All."

THEY SHARE A bottle of wine over dinner. His glass is always on the wane, so quickly does he drink. She watches him drink and wonders what is going on with him. She can barely eat. She is so distracted by Dan being here, here with her if only for an evening, she doesn't pay attention to the menu and orders randomly. She isn't sure what she's ordered, in fact. Some kind of meat. It might taste delicious if she could taste anything at all. But she is too nervous, though in a most wonderful way.

"You weren't in court when I testified," she says, a little question within the statement. She tries to make it sound like a gentle obser-vation, but she really does want to know.

"Did you look for me?"

"Mmm, yeah, I did," she says. "But I guess you weren't allowed to be there?"

Dan shrugs. "Allowed?"

"Because you were also a witness for the prosecution? I think the DA said—"

He makes a sweeping motion with his hand, waving away any ideas the lawyers might have.

She feels herself hesitate, and then she asks, "Then why weren't you there? Not that you were required to be, of course."

He looks down at his plate, shuffles some food around, then glances up at her again. She sees something unlock inside him. There it is, only for a moment, a small cinder of love still burning from decades past. "I didn't want to hear your story there, in court, with you on the stand, and all those people . . ."

He pauses and she watches him in his cloud of thoughts. He shuts his eyes and when he opens them again, he says, "I didn't like the idea of people prying into your life, however long ago these events took place."

She realizes all at once how little he knows about what Craig actually did to her. She has never told him. That is, she has told him enough and he has guessed quite a bit, of course. Some part of him knows. But they never spoke of the precise facts when they were kids. She could never have brought herself to say the words.

"Do you want me to tell you?" she says. "I don't mind."

"No," he says, resolutely. He tops up her wineglass, fills his own empty one. "What I mean is, I do. I want to hear anything you'd like to tell me, but not here, not now."

She nods. Of course, he is right. Why ruin a perfectly good dinner? She says, "I once told a man I cared about that I'd had this history. I thought he should know. I didn't go into any details, but this man's response . . ." She shakes her head, recalling how the guy had looked up from what he was doing, sharpening a gardening tool above his kitchen sink. She'd been sitting on the countertop in her underwear and a T-shirt, a mug of coffee in her hand. The morning sun was breaking through the clouds and it was beautiful and still, a perfect summer day. She told the man a little about what had happened, this new lover with whom she'd just spent the night, and he'd looked at her with an expression that was half amused, half disgusted, and continued sharpening the blade. "Do you know what he said?" she asks Dan. "He said, 'Wow, you must have been very wild as a teenager.'"

Dan makes a face. "Send him to me. I'll tell him how very wild you weren't."

"I don't talk to him now. I can't even remember his name," she says. But the truth is, she does remember his name and it burns into her even now.

"But you remember what he said."

She nods, thinking how you always hold on to the damaging things people do. "The awful part of it is that I imagine everyone thinks the same way he did. That underneath all the polite nods lies this notion that I was a tramp. That it had to have been my fault."

"That's crazy. You were a kid."

"I know," she says. But she doesn't know, that is the problem. She's never been able to convince herself. She was an especially bright girl. Somehow, being smart ought to have made a difference. And, too, there are those in the world who believe almost any age is old enough. As long as such opinions exist, they hold some sway with her. She doesn't understand why. "I sometimes imagine that I might have done something. Said something—"

"Stop it. That's what rape victims say."

"But it wasn't rape. He didn't have a weapon."

Dan's expression grows dark. There it is again, a cloud of emotion that comes and goes. He leans into the table, looking at her sternly. He says, "He didn't need a weapon."

"Maybe but—"

"All he needed was a little persuasion and a little threat."

"—why couldn't I have said no?"

"Because he made sure you couldn't. And if you haven't put this thing to rest by now, you need help doing so. The sooner the better."

She feels chastened, as though she's just been told off. It triggers a response in her that she does not like, but here she goes, firing back anyway. "Yes, sir," she says. "And I suggest we go together to the therapist's office because whatever is bugging you about your own life shows on your face like a thunderstorm."

She watches Dan as he is suddenly called to attention. He stops eating. He puts down his knife and fork, cups his forehead in his hands for a moment, then says, "I'm sorry. I'm an idiot. I hope you haven't spent all your life so far with idiotic men."

She shakes her head. She hasn't spent her life with any man.

He says, "When we were kids, I thought to myself that as long as we were together, nothing that had happened to you before mattered. That sounds selfish because, of course, it mattered. It mattered to you. But in my naïve way, in my colossal ignorance, I convinced myself that because we loved each other whatever occurred with another man wouldn't have an impact. I'm not saying I ever imagined that I could erase what happened to you, but I thought—I don't know—I thought that I might obscure it with my own feelings for you. Then you left. One day, you weren't on the phone. I couldn't find you. I was a dumb, besotted, teenage boy. I went to your school to look for you. I went to your house and there *he* was—"

She'd had no idea Dan had shown up at the house. She imagines him there in the doorway with Craig staring down at him. *Look, you little shit, what you're after isn't here.*

"But you did make it better," she says. "You made it *so* much better."

"Even if I had made it better," he says, and now she sees it, the source of his discomfort around her, "you still left."

"He was in my house," she says. "I couldn't live like that."

He holds up his hands, as though in surrender. "I know that now. But don't forget that I was also young. I didn't understand anything back then."

"He was in our home and in my mother's bed," she says. "And he was angling for me all the while. It was impossible."

Dan's shoulders slump forward. He puts his elbows on the table, rests his chin in his hands. "But I should have done something."

"What could you have done? You didn't even know where I was."

"I mean, kill him," Dan says.

"Oh that." She laughs. "I almost did kill him, you'll recall, but apparently he's indestructible." She takes a long swallow of wine, reaches across the table, and puts her hand on Dan's arm. He takes her hand, turns it over, kisses her palm. "Do you remember the first time we were together? Every year, when the pumpkins come out, I think of you."

"Of course, I do."

"And do you remember that last time?"

She does.

THE LAST TIME

She rode buses to the McDonald's where Dan worked. In a window seat way in the back, she memorized the periodic table for a chemistry test. Hydrogen. Helium. Lithium. She felt gusts of wind flapping through the windows, looked outside and realized all at once it was Halloween. She could see crowds of trick-or-treaters sweeping through the soft spray of lamplight in their costumes. In the distance, colors of light from firecrackers pierced the sky.

She arrived at the McDonald's as a group of teenagers too old to go house to house came out of the restaurant through the glass doors with burgers in takeout bags. One wore green face paint to look like a corpse. Another wore a rubber mask with blood all down the side. They were shouting to each other, tossing the bag of burgers like it was a football. Meanwhile, a girl in a cat costume balanced drinks in a cardboard holder. Bobbie ducked to the side as they passed, entering the restaurant. She sat in the corner until the other customers were gone, catching glimpses of Dan as he worked behind the counter. It was late; he was closing. The tables had been wiped clean and she could almost hear the emptiness of the machines as one by one they were turned off.

She went up to the counter and called into the back for a cup of coffee. She heard his footsteps, then caught a glimpse of his brown uniform. He had a dishcloth over his shoulder, a set of keys on his belt. He was sweating with the steam of the machines. His hair was a tangle of black curls.

"Can I help you?" he asked, before looking up and seeing it was her. Now his face registered surprise. She heard her name on his lips, heard his laughter. He swept off the uniform cap and wiped the dampness from his brow, then flew over the steel countertop, landing beside her in an instant, his face gleaming. "It's so good to see you! I worry about you in that crazy house."

"It's only crazy half the time now. He's going to work at night."

"But I can't even call you after school!" She could feel the heat coming off him. He wiped his hand across the front of his shirt, then said, "What kind of regime is the guy running that means you can't take phone calls?"

They could hear police sirens outside. A red-and-blue light flashed by the great plates of glass that made up the restaurant's walls, sending blocks of colored light across the floor.

"He'll go, eventually," she said. "Forget about him."

"Wait here. I just have to throw everything into the walk-in."

They headed for his house on foot, him in his brown polyester McDonald's uniform, her wearing his army-issue jacket because she hadn't brought her own. The air was heavy and damp; it smelled of bonfires and flash powder. They saw a bunch of costumed ghosts pile into a car driven by a zombie in a green wig. They heard bottle caps outside a 7-Eleven and thought at first they were pistol shots. As midnight came, the wind churned up, tearing strips of orange crepe paper from decorated porches. Cardboard witches came loose from doorways. Pumpkin candles sputtered their last. They passed flying candy wrappers, torn-off spider legs, a discarded witch hat. The lights inside houses clicked off one by one. It felt as though they were in the afterlife, out among the weary ghosts.

"What if you stay over?" Dan asked. In fact, they hadn't much choice now. She'd arrived on a night bus but she had no intention of going back on one.

"My room is on the ground floor," he said. "My parents are all the way upstairs."

They felt nervous. Nervous they'd get caught in his bedroom. And nervous, too, at having a whole night before them.

His house was as she'd imagined it, one of the yellow mock-Victorians on the hill. His mother had set out a giant basket of pumpkins and squash for Halloween and it was pretty in the moonlight. They skirted around the side and she heard water trickling in the dark and realized there was a pond in the back with a pump that operated a small fountain.

"Did you make all this?" she said, marveling at the rockery with little purple flowers left over from summer still poking out from crevices, and the hebe bushes, lit by tiny bulbs hidden among them. The fountain fed a small pond replete with fish. A wall of rosebushes, their trunks ringed in mulch, separated one part of the garden from another like the walls of a house.

"My mother," Dan said. "She spends all her time out here." Bobbie nodded, as if that made perfect sense, though she'd never imagined that tending a garden would be a serious pursuit for a grown woman. She admired the tidy borders, and the zigzag of stone paths that led to other hidden places. There was even a wooden seat by the pond, so you could watch the fountain break the moon's reflection into a series of concentric circles and listen to the breeze that flowed above in the canopy of an oak. If she hadn't been so cold and so concerned about being seen, she'd have asked if they could sit here for a while.

"Our place is nothing like this," Bobbie said. "It's just trees."

"Trees are nice."

"Which, one by one, fall down."

He laughed at that, and then she saw that it sounded funny and laughed, too.

"That's my window," he said. "Wait here and I'll make sure the coast is clear." He hugged her briefly and felt her shivering. "I won't be long."

When finally she climbed through the window into his bedroom, she was surprised. Not by what she saw but how she felt, peering into his life in so stark a manner. It was a privilege, she understood. He had a nice collection of records, and a turntable neatly tucked into shelves. In a rattan basket were clothes to be washed. The walls were decorated with posters from years back; a set of three track trophies grew dusty on the window ledge above a dozen or more ribbons from field sports. Surrounded by all his things, she felt she'd entered his life fully, and she turned to him with an exclamation on her lips and then could not think of what to say.

"I guess you can run fast," she whispered.

He kissed her, then reached back and turned out the light. He put his finger to his lips to indicate they should undress silently. She watched as he unbuttoned his shirt. Through the darkness she made out the long drop of his torso, the weightless shoulders that seemed to point outward like arrows on a compass. She left her T-shirt and underpants on, he his boxer shorts. He came toward her, took her hand, and when she felt the heat of his chest against her own, she sighed aloud. She could hear music from another room upstairs, the soundtrack to a movie his parents were watching in bed. He put his hand on her lower back, drew her closer to him.

"What do we do if they come in?" she whispered.

He touched her hair, then ran his finger over her brow as he had that day in the bus stop when they'd first met properly. "They won't come in," he said. "They have no interest in checking up on me. Anyway, I've locked the door."

He was right about his parents. They watched their movie and then Bobbie heard their footsteps on the floorboards, then a sound from somewhere in the plumbing as they turned faucets on and off. She and Dan held each other in the single bed, its covers unable to contain them both, and waited until there was silence from his parents' room. At last, she felt the weight of sleep upon the house, and the two of them fully awake within it.

She realized what she was about to do now and understood all at once that she didn't know how. Sex had always been a kind of acquiescence on her part. She had always cooperated what with was asked, but now she was unsure what was being asked. Dan was cautious with her body. He kissed her, then stopped and talked. He nuzzled her neck, put his lips on her breasts, rolled her nipple in his fingers, then glided down the length of her body, laying his cheek against her belly, pausing there for a while as though suddenly struck with a thought.

He was so unhurried she didn't know what she was supposed to do. Sex with him was not a single act, as she'd always experienced it with Craig, but a series of moments. At one point, she wondered if he was waiting for her to do something, to take the lead, so she set into motion, doing the things as Craig had instructed her and which with Craig had been a kind of heartless routine. It was not so now. With Dan, she wanted to offer the things Craig had always just taken from her. She began to move around him, with her hands, her tongue, her lips. She felt his excitement, his thin muscular frame rigid with attention. She felt him hard against her, his pulse thudding against her cheek. But she sensed, too, that something was wrong, caught herself, and stopped. She was scaring him; she saw this clearly. She hadn't realized a guy could be scared.

"What's the matter?" she whispered.

"It's like you went somewhere else."

How did he know this?

"Stay here with me," he whispered, and brought her close to him in what could have been nothing more than a friendly hug. She could feel his heartbeat; she could feel the sweat that rose up like a cloud from them both. He looped his leg around her leg, pressed his shoulder against her shoulder.

"You don't want to?" she said.

She felt his body sink against her, his teeth gently on the rim of her ear. "Of course I do but—"

"You're thinking of him, aren't you?" she said. "Thinking of Craig—"

He sprung back away from her. "No!" he said.

And then she realized it was she who was thinking of Craig,

that he was contaminating the room with his gory face, his deep, sarcastic laugh. Laughing at her, at them, at the puny teenager, at the stupid girl.

"You're fifteen," Dan said like an apology.

That didn't seem so very young to her, perhaps because Craig had been complaining for some time about how ratty she was getting now that she was "older."

"But I've already done everything," she whispered, and then felt her cheeks grow hot.

He said nothing and she squirmed under that silence.

"You're not much older than I am," she said.

"No."

She felt her heart pounding and Craig's voice in her head, calling her a little slut, calling her a bitch.

"I love you," Dan said, speaking into her hair. He then whispered into the blind dark all the sensible explanations for why he felt as he did about sex. "I'm not saying no, just we can't do everything," he said. She could see his eyes shining; she could see his smile, even in the dark.

"Of course not," she said, though she'd assumed they would. She had a diaphragm stuffed into the pocket of her jeans, now on the floor.

He said, "This is making love anyway, isn't it? You and me right now, here. When does sex start and stop?"

It was a remark she would remember and that (she could not know this now) she would repeat to men she had yet to meet in years to come.

"You are right," she said. She wanted to say another thing. That despite how she longed for him, sex was contaminated. It was mostly divorced of feeling. Her body did as it was asked, but to Bobbie it was a little like watching a sea anemone respond to the pressure of a finger. The only thing that felt genuine was kissing, possibly because she hadn't done very much kissing with Craig. And so she kissed Dan, kissed him for a long time.

———

THEY SAW EACH other on Thursday nights because on Friday mornings there was a station meeting that Craig stuck around for after his show. This meant that neither Craig nor June was home early Friday morning, so nobody would miss her. From eleven at night right through until homeroom at school, nobody checked on where she was.

It was their great secret, requiring some stealth, but it wasn't difficult. Dan was the youngest of four children—the others much older than he, now into their twenties—and his parents suffered from what might be called child fatigue. They were relaxed. They didn't worry about an odd noise from Dan's room, or whether he looked particularly tired. This was not because they did not care about him but because the three children before him had all some-how miraculously survived to adulthood, Dan explained. They reckoned their last child would do the same without undue supervision.

When she needed the bathroom at Dan's house they would sneak together down the hallway from his bedroom, Dan being ready to shout out a greeting if his parents were to call out "Dan, is that you?," which they never had. She insisted on being fully dressed even though this meant taking a lot of time just to traverse eight feet of hallway. Moving silently together, fingers entwined, they listened for footsteps, for squeaking floorboards, for opening doors. When at last they reached the bathroom, Dan would turn his back as she peed. Then they made the careful journey back to his bedroom, remembering always to lock the door.

"What would they say if they found me?" she asked once on a stormy November night. The wind was beating the panes of his windows, the roof sounding as though it might blow off. She always hated wind, having grown up in a house surrounded by trees. She worried one would break and crush the house in the middle of the night. She worried about falling branches, too.

"They'd want to know why I never introduced you to them,"

Dan said casually. "I really don't think they'd care that much if you spent the night. My brothers had girls here sometimes. Why can't you meet them anyway? I don't get it."

"I don't want anyone to know. It will ruin it." She didn't believe this was true, not strictly anyway. It was only that if Dan's parents knew then soon her mother would know and that meant Craig would know. And Craig would certainly ruin it. He already knew she was seeing someone, but he couldn't do anything about it. He was still unable to drive and depended on June to get him to work for the midnight shift. One day he would be well and she imagined him tricking her, stalking her in his car, finding out where Dan lived. She could not bear the thought.

"They'd think they you were great," Dan said. "How could they not fall in love with you?"

Easily, she'd thought. Because they weren't in love with her. That was Dan. She could feel it coming from him, that big heart of his enveloping her all the time. She had no idea what she'd done to deserve it. If he loved her, he was mistaken to do so. A simple error in judgment he was bound one day to correct.

She told him it was better this way. She liked how private it was between them. And all the little compromises they made for each other, and what they did in bed together, acts that would never have been enough for Craig but which they attended to with a level of arousal she'd never before experienced and which she could not put into words, though she had tried. She began, *You know when you . . .* and then she described as much as she could muster. *And when you . . .* she said, but found it difficult to finish.

He listened. He added to what she said. It was as open a conversation as she'd ever have about sex, about her feelings about sex, about what two people could do together. Often, later in her life, she would recall how easy it had been with Dan and wonder what kind of crazy trajectory her life was on that the person with whom she'd been most open was her first love, when she was still a girl.

Later that first night, the storm keeping them awake, they sat up in bed. She leaned back into his chest and they watched the power lines sway in the wind.

"In the summer, my parents rent a house at the beach," he said. "Come with us. We'll swim in the ocean every day. At night, we'll lie on the sand and look up at the stars. No time limits. They would love you. And they'd be happy to see me doing something other than reading a book."

"I won't be here this summer," she said. She hadn't thought of this ahead of time, but as she spoke the words she knew them to be true. She told him that she would be leaving. Not forever, not running away in the sense people understood it, but just until her mother got rid of Craig.

"I think this is what it will take," Bobbie said. "I'm going to write her a letter after I'm well away and tell her to make up her mind: Craig or me. I'm not going to live with him. I think he'll leave anyway once I'm gone. I swear he only stays in our house to torment me. So perhaps the whole thing will be easier than I think."

It sounded like a plan that she'd been considering for some time, that she'd thought through, but in fact it had come to her almost as she had spoken it. A part of her wanted to call out, *Don't believe what I'm saying. I am making this up!* But she heard herself speak, heard how convincing she sounded. She would give her mother an ultimatum; Craig would leave and only then would she return.

"After he goes we can be, you know, *normal*," she said. "You and me. You can call me on the phone. That would be something. You can even come over to my house, imagine that!" She sounded confident. She sounded plausible.

"Just give him the money," Dan said. "Please. He says that's what he wants. Give him the money and then maybe he will get out of your life. You can have my car money. Give that to him."

The car he'd been saving for. "No way," she said.

"You pay him a thousand dollars and he'll go—isn't that what he said? So give it to him. What's stopping you? It's a bargain if it means you can live a normal life, surely."

"The money—" she began. How could she explain? Craig would only pocket it. He'd take it and then extract from her more of everything else that she valued. He'd touch her, too. Now that she was with Dan, she could not tolerate that.

But did she *know*, know for sure, that Dan was wrong? She didn't know anything, but she felt it. Craig was like a colossal grinding machine. He'd eat her piece by piece if she tried to outsmart him or buy him off. He'd take her whole and alive.

"Please don't go," Dan said. "You can't. I'm happy, Bobbie. I've never been so happy. If you go, you'll take it all away."

It was too much for her to hear. She knew what he meant. She'd grown to depend on him. Dan was a tonic that made the days bearable. She turned to him, whispered in his ear, then placed her tongue upon the hollow at the back of his neck and bit down gently. She wanted to soak up all of this finally discovered feeling, take in the salt and skin of him, push into the envelopes of his body, and she wanted to remember what it felt like, too, every second of it, because the plan, so haplessly imagined only minutes before, was taking hold of her now. She was leaving. She saw how she'd been leaving for some time, ever since Craig, ever since the invisible surround of his desire had removed her from her own life. First from her mother, then the other kids at school, from everything she would call childhood and would call home, and finally from Dan.

She wanted to tell Dan that the only home she knew now was his body, his voice, the weight of his leg bent over hers, his fingers entwined with hers. That she'd never realized how easy it could be—sex, love, desire. He gave her the comfort she'd once felt lying in her bed in the little house she'd grown up in, in the little patch of the woods where you could look into the trees at night and see a possum, or listen to owls calling to each other, or spy the ragged backside of a raccoon.

"I will miss you awfully. But I will come back," she said. She believed she would come back. A few months would be all it would take, maybe only a few weeks, for surely her mother would choose her over Craig. "I promise."

"Oh," he said, and she felt his sadness in the sigh of that word, then a wave of sorrow. It was as though she had laid the one thing she loved down into a narrow boat, and sent it floating.

"So then," he said. "Well."

One floor up in a hotel in Arlington, light from the streetlamps outside filtering through the curtained window, Dan tells her he is going to do a fingertip search to find all the familiar places of her body, the freckles and moles she'd had as a teenager. She leans back on the bed and laughs as he moves down her torso in the dim light of the motel room.

His touch is at once familiar and completely new to her, though how he lingers, and pauses, and talks every so often is the same. He says, "Here, this. I remember," and traces an appendectomy scar. He finds a mole on her calf and says, "Gotcha!" He holds her feet in his hands, kisses her toes then all the way up. "Here, I am not sure," he says. He licks the crease of her thigh, then inward. "I don't recall exactly—"

She laughs, and he rolls her on top of him, his hands coming to a rest on her thighs. "Why can't this be a very long, slow night?" he says. He has to return to his girls in a couple of hours. "I'm too old to make love quickly."

She laughs. "You were always slow, if I remember. It's a quality I've come to appreciate."

She likes how he wears his hair, the front pushed up and away from his brow. She likes that she can see his smile, even in the dark room.

He lifts her up higher on his chest. "I used to hate watching you slither away through my window because it meant a whole week would pass before I saw you again. And here we are in the same situation—well, almost."

They are quiet now, moving quietly, too. The headlights of passing cars throw blocks of shifting light across the ceiling. The air-conditioning in the little room clicks on. For some time, longer than planned, they engage in the splendid peaceable process of making love, still with the curious stop-start manner that she remembers, and with a graceful quality as though in a dream.

Afterward, still entwined, he asks her how come she never called him after she left, why she did not contact him again.

"I'd have done anything for you," he says, speaking into her hair.

"I was in a horrible place," she says. "Not physically horrible, though yes. I mean, I was just a mess. You didn't want to be near someone like me."

"But that's *all* I wanted."

She can feel him right up next to her, the fold of his body cocooning her. It is a loss she cannot think too much about: that she might have had this man near her all these years but has not. That his teenage daughters might just as easily have been theirs. "You had better things to do, important things—"

"I might have been able to help you."

"I wanted you to live your life. I didn't want you to worry about me."

"That's exactly what I did. I worried."

"Don't be cross."

He draws back from her, taking in her shape, her breasts, the neat line of hair low on her belly. "Look at you," he says.

She remembers the early years after she left home. She'd been lonely, that was true, but remarkably calm about her circumstances. Her worst winter was when she worked in a canning factory and all her clothes smelled like fish. One summer in Delaware, working in a camper van that had been converted to a mobile restaurant selling fried clams, clam bellies, and whole lobsters, she got a bracelet of burn marks on her wrist from the fry oil. She missed school more than anything, and the sorts of kids you meet who are still in school. For a brief, intolerable time she stopped believing her life would ever get better.

"I imagined you were really happy and that was why you didn't come back," Dan says.

She almost laughs. "Once in a while I thought of killing myself but only in the mildest, most comforting of manners, a kind of get-out clause I never intended to exercise."

"Oh Jesus."

"It wasn't the way you are thinking."

She heard him take in a breath. Then he said, "Yes, it was."

How can she explain to him that thoughts of suicide had not required desperate sadness as much as it had a condition of non-feeling, no emotion at all? Killing herself would have been like walking into a swamp, deeper and deeper into the sucking mud, until there was no returning. It had not been something she wanted or didn't want. She'd had no idea how much trouble she was in until later.

"Would you ever live in Maryland again?" he says. "If I gave you a very good reason."

It occurs to her to ask about his estranged wife, but it wouldn't make any difference in her answer, so she says, "I can't. It would be impossible for me to live here again."

She hears his sigh, solid and audible in the darkness. She can feel his despair in all his loose muscles and sense his thoughts racing toward some other conclusion than the obvious one, that they will disappear back into their own lives.

"I have a practice here," he says, as though this is the worst, most onerous piece of news he could deliver. "And an NIH post."

"Surely these are good things?"

"If they are good, then why do I feel so dug-in? Tell me that. Why do I feel so stuck?"

She thinks about this, lying in his arms. Then she says, "Because you've never had any real trouble. You're just bored. Boredom is easy to fix with any imagination." It comes out quickly and sounds critical. "Sorry," she says.

"Don't be sorry. I think you might be right. Tell me, though, how does that feel?"

"You mean real trouble?"

"Yes."

"Like you are an animal that is being hunted," she says. "Like you've been run to ground."

He nods in the darkness, considering this. "Like someone is going to kill you?"

"Killing is one possibility. There are others."

"Did you ever worry he would kill you?"

"No."

"Did you think he might hurt you?"

"No," she says, lying.

RUN TO GROUND

■ ■ ■ *1978*

Early on, when Craig first came to live with them, she wondered whether he was having sex with her mother. She said nothing about this—not to Dan, not to anyone. She chased away the thought but it came back, parking itself inside her head.

June was plump and motherly. These were traits that she'd heard Craig speak against many times. He'd once told Bobbie that being a mother ruined a woman's vagina for sex, that it was too stretched to be of much use. This had disturbed her because she could not imagine a happy marriage between a man with his perfectly intact body and a woman whose weary sexual parts could no longer satisfy him after their firstborn, but now she hoped it meant he'd leave her mother alone.

June was also overweight and Craig insisted upon women with slender torsos and long legs. Svelte, nubile. He spoke these words as though they lent sophistication to his observations, pronouncing the word *nubile* in a lurid way. He felt himself to be a better judge of the female form than others. He talked about the shape of a woman's ass in the same manner that a wine connoisseur might speak of bouquet or finish. There were heart-shaped butts (good) and beetle butts (bad). He had *standards*. He had *minimum conditions*.

What Bobbie discovered eventually was that Craig's conditions were difficult to meet if a woman were even halfway through her teenage years. Craig held in high esteem the shape she'd had as a thirteen-year-old. *That was perfect*, he'd told her, remembering the year he'd met her, before they'd begun having sex. *Though you are still good now*, he'd admitted, sitting on the mattress and turning her around slowly, judging her from all sides. He wanted her hips to be confined and neat. They could not be so big that they were *breeder's hips*. He needed the stomach to be taut and smooth, *like the inside of the arm*. Hair needed to have gloss and be long (always long) and straight and flowing; the face should be bland and simple, the cookie-cutter face of a doll. She'd worried about this, believing she only had a few good years before becoming tainted by her condition, that of being female, of being somehow reduced because she could no longer look like a child and have the shape of a child.

For all her fretting over these past matters—Craig's requirements, his carping and exactitude regarding which women were fuckable and which were unfuckable—she was not able to feel any comfort from her mother's failure to come up to Craig's "standards." Despite everything he'd said about women with round figures and wobbly bellies and character-filled faces no longer wrapped in the pleasant vanilla beauty of youth, he was doing something with her mother she could not bring herself to imagine. At night, in the house now decorated with Thanksgiving colors, as the year came closer to an end, she'd hear the noises—not those from her mother but those from him. He would groan and call out and she knew that he did this on purpose, not out of pleasure but to show her that he had won. Her mother was his, as she was his.

SHE PREPARED HER escape. She folded two pairs of jeans into a duffel bag, added a week's worth of underwear, several shirts and sweaters. She tucked into her bag a little porcelain set of bears her mother had once given her, a father bear, mother bear, and baby bear glued onto a piece of gold cardboard and protected by clear plastic. It seemed too large a decision and not really her own to make—whether she would leave on this day or that—so she prepared almost daily for what she knew would happen soon. She put in one thing—a book, a bracelet, a bathing suit—then took out another, changed her mind about a sweater, added heavy socks. She removed the bears (in case they became broken during transit), then put them back (in case they became lost over time in the house). Thought about which hairbrush, what shoes.

She lay awake at night, every night the same, a sea of worry rising with the moon. She could hear her mother. She could hear Craig. During the day she was distracted, her brain zipping along at so great a speed that none of her thoughts were useful. There were times when the world seemed clouded, as during certain evenings in summer when a combination of hot dust and dying light dulls the atmosphere to a haze. In such a state, she'd taken a math test, suddenly forgetting the formula for the area of a trapezium and what to do with an exponent when dividing. She hadn't even attempted the word problems: *If a train leaves St. Louis at 10:06, traveling at 82 mph . . .* And when she came out of the exam, pressing her fingers to her temples and holding them there, she'd looked down the long corridor of the school hall and seen her classmates as though from behind a distorting glass. She'd thought then—she really had— that she had to leave, to run away, that tonight might be the night. Because some part of her had already gone.

Who could she tell about the sex and the sounds and the whole preposterous existence? She asked herself this question all the time. She might be able to tell a stranger, but then the stranger would tell someone she knew, and probably tell her mother. So she told no one, not even Dan. She kept the duffel bag hidden behind a board in her bedroom wall. Stuck into the trunk of a tree in her front yard was the money. She had everything ready.

In her night table were biographies she'd borrowed from the library, and she thought she had to return these books before she left. Meanwhile, she read how Helen Keller brushed her fingers over paper and learned to read, how a young Winston Churchill escaped capture by soldiers by climbing a high wall, then crossed the desert with a pistol and a pair of sturdy shoes. What interested her was how you get from here to there, how one moved across the rough and dangerous landscape of life to higher ground. What do you take with you, she wanted to ask, and what do you leave behind? And when—this is what she wanted to know—when do you do the actual leaving?

AND THEN ONE DAY she had her answer. She came home from school on a stormy afternoon and Craig was waiting for her. As she approached the front step, he pushed the door open and there he was, standing on the oval rug in the hall, leaning on his crutches, his body filling the entrance. She felt for the first time that the house belonged to him and that she was entering his home. He pulled her indoors with a quick jerk, his face alive with anger. She flew forward, dropping her books on the rug.

"You really did fucking lose it, didn't you?" he said. His body arched away. He was standing at his full height, his bad leg angled to the side, balancing his weight against the door and on the crutch beneath his arm.

"I don't know what you're talking about." She was trying to pick up her notebook without letting all the papers fall loose of the three-ring binder that had opened.

"The money," he said, his face suddenly inches from her own. "I've torn this place apart and it isn't here! You really did lose it, didn't you?"

"I don't—I don't know what—"

"Where is it? If you haven't lost it, tell me where the hell it is."

"Don't you remember? I gave it to you! I gave you it all!"

He breathed out a heavy sigh, swung his head toward her like a snake, and said, "Oh Jesus, do I remember! I remember how we tore through the state trying to get the damned money back before my show. I remember having to drive like a stunt man! I remember thinking you were so stupid you'd leave five hundred bucks in a room! I remember all of it, Barbara! You took that money out of the goddamned car and walked off, leaving me for dead! You got the whole grand! You've hidden it somewhere, so where the hell is it?"

The contents of the hall closet were strewn across the wooden floor. Jackets, windbreakers, dusty shoes, a tangle of scarves, a long-outgrown winter coat. She looked into the living room and saw the chaos there, too, evidence of Craig's searching. Drawers hung open, papers her mother kept in a bureau scattered across the floor, books pulled from the shelves, their pages thumbed through in case she'd placed the bills inside.

She could imagine the kitchen, where the contents of the messy cupboards would be in heaps on the countertops, and where every cereal box and coffee can would have been scrutinized. Had he toppled the linen closet, searching for the money inside all their clean sheets? Had he turned over the mattresses? Gone through all her clothes?

"What's the matter, Barbara? Can't you remember where you put it?"

He tapped her head hard with his finger and she suddenly remembered a film he'd had her watch starring Marlon Brando and a bewildered young actress. Brando's character had hit the girl with the heel of a shoe while she was naked in a bath. *I wouldn't do that to you*, Craig had said as she gazed wretchedly at the film. He was making a point about his gentleness. *I wouldn't rap your skull with a shoe.* Years later, she would remember *Last Tango in Paris* all over again, but for different reasons. She would wonder what had been wrong in the 1970s that such a film could have existed, with Maria Schneider being only nineteen in real life. With Brando being deep into his forties. Why did the public not protest such a thing? It had been a terrible time, the '70s. At least a terrible time for girls like her.

"Is this how you treat me?" Craig was saying. "Stealing? Does it never occur to you, Barbara, that *you* broke up with *me*. You never had to say it, but I felt it. I felt it here!" He slammed his fist across his chest. "I felt it right here!" he said again, and hit himself harder.

"You broke up with me, left me for dead, and now you just sit there and smile!"

"I'm not smiling."

He grabbed her arm and squeezed. "Get my money and we'll be friends, okay? Sound like a deal? We'll be pals."

"Let go of me."

"I'll let go of you all right! You don't mean a thing to me!"

He squeezed her arm harder. Then he suddenly dropped his hold.

She rushed up to her room, praying he wouldn't follow. She began to put away all the clothes strewn on the floor from his searching, and her mattress and sheets and jewelry box and all the things he'd rifled through in her closet. She was shaking, not with fear as much as with adrenaline. She pushed socks into drawers, books into shelves. She thought, *Forget it, I am going.*

It was decided. She'd leave all this crap behind and get gone.

And then, there he was again, standing in the doorway. When she turned to look, he came toward her, leaning on his crutches. She noticed once again how tall he was and how much space he took up and how his shirt sleeves never fit, pulling up before meeting his big wrists.

He swung on his crutches, crossing the room. The naked half of his face with its absent eye loomed a foot above her. The expressionless landscape of his face made it difficult for her to read.

"I'm feeling like we need to sort things between us." He spoke calmly, slowly. "We used to be so close."

She felt the blood rising to her neck, then her throat, now her face.

"I got a present for you," he said.

She thought how nobody was home; nobody would be home soon; nobody was outside; nobody would hear.

"What's the matter, don't you want a present? It's a peace gesture."

She was holding a pair of jeans she'd intended to change into.

She stood still, clutching the jeans to her chest. He guided her wrist to one side and lifted them away. She felt a flutter of panic. Behind him, through the open door, was the narrow hall and a flight of steps. She saw that he was looking down the V-neck of her blouse, with its plastic snap buttons and the western design that was in style at her school. She thought she might be able to get out of the bedroom and downstairs. She could rush out the door and from there keep running. She wished she'd hidden the duffel bag she'd so carefully packed somewhere outside under a tarp instead of in her bedroom. She wished she'd left the night before.

She gauged that his newly mended arm could not yet take too much pressure; she judged the angle of his stance and saw he was still favoring his right leg, too. He could not get quickly down the chipped brick steps to the yard, then over the clumpy, wet ground. If she were to run, he would not catch her. But she wouldn't run, and they both knew that.

"Don't you want the present?" he said again. He was breathing near her. The injury to his face had done something to his sinuses. She could hear the air moving through his nostrils and the gentle rumbling inside that reminded her of an animal's slow, deep respiration. Where the eye had been was the dark hole she'd grown used to, loose skin. Nerve damage meant that the entire side of his face had eroded inward a fraction of an inch.

"Open your hands," he said to her now. "Close your eyes and open your hands."

She put her hands out, shivering. He stared hard at her breasts and she angled her elbow across her chest.

"Close your eyes," he said again.

She could tell by the sound of the wind and the sudden drop in the house's temperature that the front door had been left open. She could run straight through, she thought, but she couldn't imagine how to get around him now that he was so close. And so she stood still. Then, finally, she fluttered her eyes closed and wondered if he would touch her breasts and that would be her "present."

To her surprise, she felt the weight of a little box in her palm. A gust of wind howled through the hall downstairs. She heard Craig make a sound like a grunt and realized he was laughing.

She opened her eyes. The box was an egg carton, split down the middle so it was now a half-dozen box. On the top, Craig had drawn on the cardboard in ballpoint pen a picture of a little ribbon and bow.

"Open it," he said, as though talking about a jewelry box with a ring inside.

She slid her thumb to the cardboard tab to lift the lid. It seemed to her that there really were eggs inside; she felt the weight of them in the hollows of the box, and she wondered if they were chocolate eggs and how he'd have managed to find chocolate eggs in November.

She heard her voice around her before she realized it was her own light, girlish scream. Inside the carton, lined up in the manner of grocery store eggs, were half a dozen glass eyes. They stared up at her as though they were living things, extracted from a still-warm body and placed in the carton like something out of a horror film. She began backing away, the carton still in her hand, and as she moved the eyes began to rattle inside the hollows in which they sat, and she lost her footing and banged her head on the closet door and the eyes dropped onto the floor and rolled. She could hear them, jigging across the floorboards. She could hear her heart pounding in her ears. Just then, the wind changed, slamming the front door shut, and the whole house seemed to darken and go quiet.

"Barbara!" Her name like a thunderclap, his voice rising. "I wanted you to help me pick one. Now look what you've done!"

She leaned against the wall, standing on the tips of her toes as the eyes rolled across the bare floor. Her heart drummed against her ribs. Her hands, over her face as though to protect herself, dampened with sweat. "Oh God!" she said. "Oh God, oh God . . ."

The eyes were samples, each one carefully painted to correspond with an existing eye. Intricate, with a kind of taxidermy beauty to them, they were whole and exact. Craig was to choose one, apparently, to be his new eye.

"What is the matter with you?" he said. He seemed genuinely perplexed, shocked even, by her fear, by her revulsion. "Are you going to pick them up for me now that you've nearly broken them all?"

It was impossible; she could do no such thing. The idea of touching one appalled her, as though Craig were asking her to touch some part of him inside his own head, to reach into his empty socket and touch where the eye had once been. But the notion that they were still on the floor, temporarily resting by a leg of her bed, or the baseboard, but at any moment able to roll again, horrified her, too.

"Do you know what an oculist is?" Craig asked her. She shook her head. He said, "You give him money and he makes you an eye. An eye like one of these. You know what I need so that I can get him to make me an eye?" She didn't answer, so he went on. "Do you know what he wants in return for one of these nice eyes?"

She shook her head.

"*Money.* The same as I need to move out and get my own place. Isn't that what you want, Barbara? For me to have my own place? That way, we don't have to hide from your mother and sneak around."

So it was back to that. He wasn't done with her. He'd said he was, but no.

"I need my *money,*" he continued. She felt his fingers on her cheek. She smelled the sulfur from matches he had struck, a little burn to the fingernail. "I'd love to have a nice-looking face. It could never be as nice as yours—"

"I don't have your money," she said, and her voice seemed to sink to the floor.

"Don't lie, it'll make your nose grow long," he said, and took her nose between two fingers. "What I need you to do right now, Barbara, is pick up what you've thrown everywhere, these valuable things that you've chucked on the floor. And then tell me where the money is. Would you do that for me, Barbara? Give me back my money so I can get an eye?" he asked in his sweetest voice. It was so easy to believe he only wanted what was due him: his own money, an artificial eye.

"I . . . don't—" she began, her words two gusts of breath.

He gave her nose a little tweak. "You don't *what*, Barbara?"

"*Have* it," she said. "I don't have it." Her shoulders were shaking now. "I don't have any of your damned money. Your goddamned money!"

"There's no use crying about facts, Barbara. You have it. The only money you have is my money."

She forced herself to stop crying; she stood straight in front of Craig with her shoulders back, her fists clenched. "It was left in the car!"

He shook his head. "The police say no."

"Then they are lying!"

Craig dropped his hand and took in a deep breath, considering this. "Maybe," he said. "But I think you are lying."

"Fuck you," she said.

"Dirty little mouth." He breathed out audibly. "You gave me *half* what you really had—just five hundred—when you thought you could get away with that. And then, when I was dying in the car you stole all of it back, didn't you? That, little darling, was a much bigger fuck-you than anything you can say now."

"It wasn't your money!"

"I paid for the motel. *I* paid for the room."

"The police took it!"

"Oh, if you hadn't stolen it, they would have. They'd have taken it all right, which is why I'm not mad at you. You saved it. You did a good thing to keep it from the cops. But now it's time to give it back." He moved toward her. She could feel his breath on her. She could smell his skin. "I'm not mad at you, Barbara. You did a good job, an admirable job. I might have done the same. Tell you what, why don't I give you a little reward for that? Give me back my money, and I'll give you a reward. Say, a hundred bucks. A hundred is a lot for a girl. You could even run away with it. That's what you are planning isn't it? To run away?"

She stood with her mouth open. She wondered how long he'd known her plan.

"Oh, yeah, that's what girls like you do, isn't it? Run away? Blow truckers? See if I care. Be a whore for truckers if that floats your boat."

She could feel his anger like a cushion of fire between them. She wondered if he would hit her and decided that if he tried to, she would push away his crutches. She would topple him.

"I'm being very nice, really," he said gently. "A lot of people wouldn't be so nice. People do crazy things for money."

"No," she said, as though fending off the next thing. What was coming now. What she knew was already on its way.

"You read about it in the papers," he said.

She stared at the floor. She heard a voice in her head: *When do you leave? You leave now.*

He said, "You give me back my money and we will be friends again." A pause, a long sigh from him. "You know I still love you, don't you? But I can't abide a woman who steals from me. I can't put up with that kind of shit."

"I don't have it," she said, and then she heard the roar rise within him, the anger almost like a thing outside of him, swirling between them, circling her. She knew that if she tried to run, he would grab her, and whatever invisible barrier had prevented him touching her would have been broken and she would be his. But she did not move. He did not touch her. She did not give him the money, nor look out the window to the tree where the jam jar of bills was hidden, nor down to the floor where the eyes lay, staring up, staring into the corners of the room, at her, at them both.

A THOUSAND DOLLARS

D riving back to the inn, the little hotel room where they'd made love now miles behind them, Dan says, "What are you going to do about tomorrow?"

"You mean, if I get called back to the stand? Dreyer doesn't think I will be."

"They will ask about when we were young, what we did in bed together. They will try to make it look as though you were 'loose.' A wayward teen, all that kind of thing. Not that it should matter to you."

"Is that what they asked you? How much did you tell them?"

He takes her hand. "As little as possible."

"I don't remember that there was a great deal of actual sex between us."

"There wasn't," he says decisively. "No."

"Whatever we were doing together—you and I—how is that relevant to what Craig did to me?"

"It isn't relevant."

"So, what is the point of—" She has to stop herself.

"No point. What I am trying to say is that the questions will be geared up to discredit you."

They swing into the long gravel driveway of the inn. The pebbles crunch and pop beneath the tires. "My mother has already done that," she says. A security light pops on and he angles the car so that it does not shine in their eyes. "We're going to lose, aren't we?" she says, a flat statement.

He picks up her hand, turns it over, presses her palm to his face. He says, "Probably."

"I still think we did the right thing, though. Do you?"

"Absolutely," he says. "Whatever happens, I think you did the right thing. For this girl, especially. She'll know that someone else took him on. That has to help her."

He begins kissing her. He holds her as close to him as he can in the car, then says, "I wish so much had been different." Then, a little later, he says, "Let me know if I can persuade you to live here. It's about time I started waking up with you. I'm willing to beg."

She laughs. Another thing she always loved about Dan, how little guile he had, how impossible he found it to conceal his feelings.

"I might let you beg a little," she says.

"When can I begin?"

"Tomorrow night. Let's—"

"—have dinner at my house," he interrupts. "Come meet my kids."

And she agrees. Though she is crazy—she knows she is crazy—there is no other answer but yes.

A SMALL SECURITY light flicks on as she steps toward the front door. It takes her three tries with the ridiculous, ornate door key she's been given, but finally she works it out, then turns toward Dan and gives him a little wave before pushing the heavy door inward. The hallway smells of cedar and fire ash and some kind of insect spray. She hears Dan's car back slowly down the drive, and she thinks she feels his reluctance to leave even in how slowly the car pulls away.

Would she live here again? She cannot. And it feels to her not a choice but a law of physics. She cannot live in the place in which it all happened. She cannot live near her mother, much less Craig. But there is another truth, and this one is harder for her to fathom though it feels equally true. She has loved Dan all her life. There had been a moment earlier in the evening, when they stood in front of the mirror in the hotel, looking at each other naked, him behind her, his arm across her middle, and she'd thought how easy it would have been to marry him, to have been the mother to those girls who now apparently miss their real mother, who has gone to another man, another state, claiming Dan had not loved her enough.

It's just after midnight. The house is quiet except for the ticking of the grandfather clock. The security lights disappear all at once, leaving her to find her way by moonlight up the staircase. A line of nightlights in the hallway guide her to her room, and she believes she has navigated safely and without disturbing anyone, until she opens the door of her bedroom.

She knows at once that someone is inside. The door is locked but the bedclothes, which before had been made with precision—with the sheets folded back just so and a chocolate coin left for her on the covers—are crumpled. She stands at the doorway, checks the room number, considers calling for Mrs. Campbell, then, insanely, takes a step inside. She breathes in steamy air from the bath. The air contains a floral scent and she knows at once that it is June.

"Mother," she says. No answer. "This is ridiculous! You can't just let yourself in here."

She kicks her shoes off, drops onto the bed. "Good job in court today," she says. "You sounded convincing even to me."

She hears some water sloshing in the tub. She imagines her mother in there among the frothy bubbles, ducking her head underwater, refusing to hear. "You can't stay here, by the way," she calls. "I'm calling a cab. You're going home."

Still no answer and now Bobbie is spooked. She steps toward the bathroom with its bright, unforgiving light. Another step and she can push open the door a little further. She has a moment in which she wonders if somehow she's walked into the wrong room. She sees the edge of the tub. She sees a surface of crisp bubbles in the bathwater. She smells the soapy mist. At last, she knows who is there.

He is spread out in the bath like a walrus on the sand. He knew where she'd been staying all along, has been waiting for her here, perhaps all night.

"Hi Barbara," he says.

She does not scream or run from the room or take any of the actions she ought to take. She sees his neck poking out from the bubbles, his big head leaning against the end of the bath. A foot rests at the other end, the skin of his hairy stomach skimming the water's surface. Later she will ask herself why she did nothing, said nothing, and she will tell herself this absolute truth: because some part of her always knew he'd come.

"You are late tonight," he says.

"Get out," she says. She finds it difficult to make the words. "Get out or I'll kill you."

"Oooh, harsh. She'll *kill* me. Look how the lady talks."

She goes into the bedroom, then out into the hall. She thinks she cannot stay in the hall without waking people. Later she will think how silly it was to worry about waking people when that was exactly what she needed to do. Wake them up, wake them all up.

She comes back into the bedroom and paces from one end to the other.

"I can't hurt you," she hears him say. "I'm a naked man in a bath for chrissake."

"Get out *now*," she tells him.

"It's your own fault I'm here. You've upset your mother. She's thrown me out of the house. And now I've got nowhere else to go."

There could be only one reason for June to throw him out: her mother believes her, she knows she was in the car, knows everything else, too.

Bobbie says, "I doubt that very much."

"She did. She's gone nuts."

"I don't believe you."

"She got one of your dad's old billhook knives—"

Her father. Thirty years, and his tools are still in the shed, just as his photograph (she imagines) is still on the mantel above the fireplace.

"—and she said she'd take my dick off if I didn't get out. So I left. She'd have done it, too. She was drunk, see. You don't know this about your mother but she's a stinking drunk—"

She stops pacing and stands unsteadily just outside the bathroom; she doesn't dare look inside again but speaks into the doorframe. "How did you get in here?"

"—and she's much worse since you disappeared, missy. Much worse. You might one day ask yourself why you did this to your own mother. June was a decent person. Before you left she was a nice woman."

She knows this already, the contrast between what her mother had been and what she has become. She says, "I'm calling the police. Stick around and you'll end up with yet another charge against you."

"I won't have any charges. Case dismissed."

She hears the words *case dismissed*. How could that be? She stands in the doorframe now, staring at Craig in the bath with all his smugness, his showing off, and tells him he is full of shit. "You're a liar," she says. "You lie to everyone and you're lying now."

"I swear," he says, holding up his right hand. "This thing is over. I was hoping it wouldn't get to the stage of *whatshisface*, that dick of a boyfriend of yours, offering his two cents, but it did. As if he had any idea what was going on. He has no idea what we meant to each other." He breathes in deeply, then adds, "My lawyer was going to call you back as a witness—a hostile witness. You like how that sounds? You seem pretty damned hostile, that's for sure. How do you like the idea you'd be a witness on my side? I think it's pretty cool."

He knows how she feels about it, that she hates it, that she hates him. "Calling me back when?" she says.

He shakes his head, leans forward in the bath, pulls some toilet paper off the roll, then blows his nose with it. "She says she's pretty sure that won't happen now. You're off the hook. Apparently she doesn't even need you to win the case. What do you think of my lawyer anyway? Being bald and all? I call her Baldilocks behind her back—"

"You're an idiot," she says. She watches as he shrugs, then tosses the used paper into the toilet basketball-style.

"Baldilocks says we'll all be dismissed tomorrow morning at nine o'clock, like schoolkids. That's the rumor anyway. You've come a long way for nothing if what you wanted was my ass."

She wants to tell him he is wrong, but he may not be wrong.

"There's not enough evidence to continue," Craig says. "But your mother is under some very odd impressions. She thinks I'm guilty."

"You *are* guilty."

"Guilty of what? You liked it."

She almost attacks him now. She feels her hands moving, searching for an object to throw.

"I don't know what you think you are staging here, Barbara. And it won't work anyway."

What she was *staging*? She steps from the doorway into the bathroom. "I'm not talking to you. I'm going outside, into the hall, and you have two minutes to get your clothes on and get out of here—"

Suddenly, he stands. The water spilling noisily to the edges of the bath and over onto the floor, a squeaking sound as his heel twists against the enamel. She sees his broad body, the roll of fat circling below his waist like a wobbly ledge. His thighs, his long arms, the pads of fat on his chest that gather beneath each armpit. And his penis. He touches it now, drawing attention to it. She sees the wine-colored mark at the very tip which might have been a birthmark. She sees his hand working away.

She is backing into the bedroom as he comes toward her. His body is immense, in motion, red with the heat of the water. He is striding toward her, bursting forward in long steps, water cascading from him like a bear shaking off the spray of the river. The air is wet and full of the innocent scent of shampoo and in a flash he is there on the woolen rug beside the bed, reaching for her. She tucks her chin down toward her chest, but it isn't her neck he grasps but her hair. With a single, strong tug he seems to pull her straight off her feet onto the bed, where he covers her body with his body, her mouth with his hand.

He says, "You can lie in court all you want but I know what happened and *you* know what happened!" His weight pins her body in place, his knee digging into her thigh. Her hair is an anchor she cannot defy, nor can she make much of a sound with his hand over her mouth, his arm across her neck. "We had a love affair, Barbara. You *loved* me. And you *wanted* sex with me."

Her eyes are blurry but she can see his face hovering above her. She can feel his cock pressed against her, hardening.

"You used to sit on my face and let me lick you. Do you remember? And you came, too. Don't think I couldn't tell. I felt you come right up against my tongue."

She saw his tongue now. He'd stuck it out, was curling the tip of it.

"So stop lying, Barbara. Lying to your mother. Lying to the world, when all the time you wanted me as much as I wanted you."

He is fully erect. But she is still clothed. Panty hose, underpants, shoes. He will have to loosen his grasp to get all that off her. She wants to scream, to shout out, to wake up the place. But she can't make a sound, not to shout or even to whisper, with his hand clasped just so.

"You think I want to fuck you, don't you?" he says. When she says nothing, he angles his head, the expression on his face as though he's waiting for an answer.

She doesn't understand how he expects her to speak, or what he wants her to say, or why.

He presses into her. Her leg is turning numb. Her face, beneath his open palm, feels small and fragile. Her teeth press painfully against the inside of her lips. She has an ache in her jaw where he is pushing it up against her ear. The cartilage beneath her nose is like a ledge of crumbling gravel. The back of her earring has already pushed a hole into the skin at the base of her skull.

"You think I want to fuck you right now, don't you? But I can fuck anyone I want," he says. She listens to him breathe, in, out, in, out. Then he says, "I'm not going to fuck you. Why would I? You're hardly that nubile young thing I remember."

She can feel him pressing his erection against her, a steady heartbeat at the top of her thigh. He says, "I don't even *want* to fuck you, but if you scream, I might hurt you."

She feels her breasts being squashed beneath his arm. "We had a future," he is saying. "I was going to marry you. And how did you thank me? Left me to die in a car. Stole my money. Is that love to you, Barbara?"

She can feel his hand move beneath her dress. She tells herself, *Do something now!* But she's afraid to move, afraid not to move. She tries to scream but it is only a shrill noise, a kind of stuttering bird-like sound that comes from deep inside her throat.

"And then you left altogether didn't you? Off to *realize* yourself, or whatever it is that young girls do. Be a flower that fully opens."

Suddenly her mind fills with all the crap he used to do to her, how pain had always been part of that last effort he made while having sex, the final minute or two before he came. *Turn over, turn like this, bend your knees.* He'd fuck her up the ass and tell her to sit in the bath afterward until it stopped hurting. He'd tell her that his problem was having such a large dick.

"We could have been something," he is saying. "You and me, Barbara. We were always meant to be—"

She tries to speak. Against all the violence, she manages finally. "Craig," she says, because she knows this is what he has longed to hear from her. His name in her mouth. "Just wait a minute, okay?" She is amazed by how calm she sounds, how her tone is so unlike how she feels. She realizes her voice is that of her childhood self, the little girl he took week after week, the Barbara he invented and thought he knew. "I've got your money," she says. "I brought it all the way from California. Let me give it to you."

He is suddenly still, listening. She continues, "A thousand dollars. Don't tell me you don't remember. It's yours. It's there, in that closet thing. The wardrobe. If you look, you'll see."

She watches his face, so close above her. She feels him loosen his grip a little. "You brought me my grand?" he says, his voice slurring with desire. "Why would you do that?"

"It was yours—"

"You've got me in court! In front of the whole fucking world. Now you're saying you brought a thousand dollars for me. Is it really that you're hoping I'm dumb enough to get up and go look for money that doesn't exist?"

She doesn't have an answer and she watches as his good eye hardens onto her.

"I don't want your money anymore," she says. "It brought me bad luck. I've had a bad life, Craig, and I think the money is cursed. Like the Hope Diamond. Remember when you told me about that? About the Hope Diamond? How it brought bad luck?"

He doesn't move at all, but he says, "I know about the Hope Diamond."

"You told me that it was cursed. Do you remember?"

"Yeah."

"Well, that money cursed me. My whole life."

He nods slowly, as though this makes sense. She can tell that he likes to hear how nothing has gone right for her since leaving him.

"That money is my Hope Diamond," she says.

She hears him breathing again, that strange nasal whistle that has stuck with him since the accident. Finally he says, "I could have guessed as much." She feels an easing on her thigh, but the leg is frozen from his weight. If she tries to bend her knee, she won't be able to.

"Get it," he says, and pulls her up from the bed. "Get the money." He twists her arm around her back. She stumbles, her shoulder wrenched backward, one of her shoes gone, the numb leg unable to hold her weight.

"I can't stand properly," she says.

"Yes you can," he tells her.

"My leg is numb."

"Bullshit," he says. He pushes her back onto the bed, then goes to the wardrobe himself. "Where?" he says, throwing open the mahogany doors.

"At the top. On the right-hand side in the back," she tells him. She works her toes hard, trying to get the blood flowing there and regain some strength in her leg. Meanwhile he leans into the wardrobe, cocking his head so he can see.

"Back where?" he says.

"Under that striped blanket." She remembers there was a blanket, but she can't remember much else. She hopes she has enough time now, that he doesn't give up immediately and turn to her.

"Do you see a blanket?" she says. She tests her leg and realizes she can now bend her knee. She slips off her remaining shoe, saying, "It should be right there."

"Yeah, I got it."

She waits for him to feel around under the blanket, to push deeper for the money. By the time he realizes there is no money, it is too late. He turns back with a new head of fury, but she has already got the stem of the bedside lamp in her hand. She brings the pewter base of it up against the back of his skull with every ounce of strength she can muster. She feels the sharp, square base against his skull, hears the terrible thud.

He collapses in a series of motions, like a dying horse. First his knees cave beneath him, then he kneels on the rug with a thud. His shoulders swing toward the left and draw him up and sideways, so that the rest of him topples. She wonders if the noise of his falling will bring Mrs. Campbell, but even as she has this thought, Craig is suddenly silent and still, lying on his left side, the back of his head bleeding onto the pretty wool rug. The room still smells of soap, the windows fogged from the long, hot bath. She reaches over to feel for a pulse at his neck. She wonders if this time she really has killed him. But there it is, the steady, slow beat of his pulse. He is still alive. She sits on the bed looking down at him, wondering how long before he'll wake up and realize what she's done.

LEAVING 1978, LEAVING NOW

She fished the money down from the tree's hollow nest and left on a night in 1978, wearing a duck-down coat, a pair of leg warmers, and the desert boots she'd bought at Kmart. She had a Christmas scarf that would serve against the cold but also allow her to wrap it around her face to hide if she had to (she would not have to hide; she would discover that nobody pays much attention to a teenage girl in train stations and at bus stops).

She crossed a dried cornfield, bare in the approaching winter, the sound of her shoes on the choppy ground like she was stepping on shells. In the distance, a forgotten string of foil pie plates tied onto a faceless scarecrow waved in the breeze. Overhead, dark clouds mushroomed in the great expanse of sky, threatening rain. She reached another road, where a succession of hills reminded her of a roller coaster, and there she walked along, counting her steps to a hundred, then counting again, seeing how long she could kick a stone and have it still stay on the road, then finding another stone.

She wished more than anything she could say goodbye to Dan, and that she didn't have to say goodbye at all. She found a phone booth outside a post office and rang him.

"I called time," she said. Calling time was what they named her running away, as though a terrible game had been taking place.

She could hear Dan's voice, thick with emotion. "I wish I could do something for you," he said. "I wish you'd come live here."

She could not allow herself to imagine what it might be like to stay with Dan, to stay safe with him. His parents had no idea she even existed. She'd insisted he not tell them for the same reason that she refused to let him know where she was going now. It was for his own good. She understood this as fact. He had plans for his life that needed his full attention. He had a good and decent life ahead of him that she did not wish to interrupt.

He said, "I want at least to imagine you wherever you go, in a particular city. Where are you going? At least tell me that."

"New York. I'll send my mother a letter from there, an explanation. Then I'll move on."

"Okay, but—"

She told him to hang on and wait. He'd see her again, possibly very soon. Her mother would rid herself of Craig. Or else Craig would get bored and go.

She got to town and bought a Slurpee from the 7-Eleven. She walked. The temperature stayed reasonably warm, the clouds holding in the heat of the earth. Decorative lights in a garden center lit up trees and she realized with a start that it would soon be Thanksgiving. She felt her house pulling her, like a tide that took her in, telling her to go home and prepare for the holidays. Roast a turkey, carve a pumpkin, get out the good candles, the tall glasses, the gravy boat. Her mother and she had always celebrated holidays with care. They ironed the linen, made centerpieces for the table. Her mother had done such things easily, teaching her daughter the traditions she herself had been brought up with. Before Craig.

She grew tired but whenever she thought of stopping she thought of Craig lying in her mother's bed, stewing in his anger, conjuring his plans.

She sat down on a painted stone outside a house with a long driveway and a mailbox angled like a scythe on the end of a bent pole. She imagined her father with her, or who she imagined her father might have been, because in all honesty she could not recall him fully. For many years she would wish someone could have helped her figure out these knotty little bits of life, in which there is no right thing to do but only a series of wrong and worse to choose from.

She wished she had a companion to walk with. Wouldn't it be great to have a dog tagging along? The two of them would set out to find their fortune as characters do in fairy tales.

A car rumbled down the road toward her. She looked at her feet, caked with mud. She wiped her chin on her shoulder. The car passed her, but she could hear the tires pop along the stony edge of the road, and the slowing engine, and she saw that it was stopping for her. The inside lights were on and she could see a pair of eyes looking at her from the rearview mirror. She glanced away, hoping the driver would head off again, but instead she heard the engine dying and then a door opening and shutting. The driver was a tall girl wearing a pink tracksuit. Long neck, long torso, long arms that she crossed in front of her to hold together the sides of her unzipped sweatshirt.

"Don't be worried," the girl called to her. "I'm not a highway robber or anything." The wind carried her voice away, but Bobbie heard and waited until she got close. The temperature was now dropping, the night becoming a little more punishing as the wind lifted the dampness of the ground. She watched the girl walk toward her. She watched the electrical wires shiver between poles. The girl looked cold, exposed as she was by the open road. "We're lost," she said. "Maybe you can help?"

She was a high-school debater, with a car full of other kids. They were looking, as she put it, "for the state of Virginia."

"The whole state?" Bobbie said.

"Well, part of it anyway. The bit near D.C. What's it called? Arlington."

"That's easy," said Bobbie.

"Hey, she knows the way!" the girl called to her friends.

It was an old sedan with an AM radio and Pennsylvania plates. The kids were giddy with exhaustion, having driven all day, drinking Cokes and eating Fritos and arguing about the evidence they were going to present at the debate. Three guys and the girl in pink.

"You drive me and I'll show you," Bobbie said. She explained, and drew a map for them on a pad of lined paper they had in the car. She asked them to drop her off so she could get a bus over the 14th Street Bridge to Union Station.

"I'm going to visit my grandmother," she explained.

"I'll take you," the girl said. She was a big athlete of a girl who it was easy to imagine turned her attention to all games, including those of the mind, like debating.

Bobbie gave them a fake name and told them she was from Virginia. When they got to Union Station, a rush of regret seized her, a feeling of homesickness and loss. She wished she was going with these guys and not to the train. It felt suddenly as though she were being kicked out, sent off into the wilderness while they stayed by a warm hearth.

"What were you doing all the way back there?" one of the boys asked.

"I was with my boyfriend," Bobbie said, as though this was a secret.

"Oooh," said the girl. "Cool."

The wind was picking up now. Bobbie saw traffic lights bobbing on their wires, and the horizontal shadows of the swaying trees. The flagpoles at Union Station strained.

The girl looked out into the night, at the traffic along Massachusetts Avenue, the flags like sails, the lamps glowing on their iron stalks "This is such a beautiful city," she said. "I wish we didn't have to leave so soon."

"It's a great city," Bobbie said. "I'll never leave it."

She waved goodbye and disappeared into Union Station with its ornate vaulted ceiling, its rush of people, the smell of America somehow contained inside its walls. She bought a ticket to New York, like so many thousands of girls who bought a ticket and hoped it would work out okay. In the vast and echoing station, she watched the departures board, and when finally her train was called, she drifted downstairs amid a crowd of other people and became a New Yorker. Money hidden in her socks, in her bra, in her bag, in her shoes.

AND TONIGHT IS not so different, she realizes. She steps out of the inn and into the wild, damp air of rural Maryland. She is surrounded by a beautiful darkness that feels thrilling to her. She looks up at the sky where stars are multiplying above the steep roof of the inn. Then across to the emptiness beyond, where hidden in darkness is a beautiful field. She wonders whether Craig had been lying when he said that his case was being dismissed. She thinks of the girl whose case had been botched. She decides to be in touch with the girl. She will tell her how difficult it can be to prove the truth. She will tell her that it wasn't her fault.

She might have found herself back on the road, walking as she had all those years ago when she'd had to stop and pick grit out of her heels. Part of her would have enjoyed walking tonight. She thinks she could walk for hours. But there is no need. In her hand are Craig's car keys and there, hidden behind a honeysuckle, its bumper edging the inn's pretty stone wall, is his shining car. It's an old Mustang Coupe, with a long nose and a lot of chrome, the little horse emblem galloping across its grille. She unlocks the door and drops into the driver's seat, smelling at once that familiar scent of marijuana she always associated with Craig.

She eases the Mustang out of the driveway, the headlights off until she has circled away from the inn. The car is so low it feels like sitting on the ground. She brings the windows down, letting the night in, steering easily through the empty lanes and finding beautiful the dense forest and its canopy of trees above her. If she knew where Dan lived, she'd go to him now. She'd tell him that while she can't live in Maryland, they could still find a way. *Let's do that*, she'd say. *Let's try.*

She doesn't know if he will ever come to California, but she wants him to understand that he is welcome. Her house is set up on a hill. At night she listens to the creaking groan of sail rigging in the harbor. She wishes Dan could be with her, listening to the same sounds, feeling the same breeze. There had been a moment during their lovemaking—the memory of which seems far off, days or weeks even, not hours ago—when she'd felt him move inside her and recalled all over again how decades ago she had longed for him after she'd left home. How she'd dreamed of him from the seats of Greyhound buses and hostel mattresses, how she had felt a hunger as real as any just to hear his voice.

Driving to the airport, she admires the sky, the beautiful city in the distance. She listens to a classical station, Chopin's Nocturnes under a high, bright moon. The roads are calm, the air cool. Even the airport seems peaceful at this hour. At Dulles, she parks the Mustang in a state of such egregious violation she is sure it will be towed. But just in case nothing worse happens to the car, she keys it, too, a nice five-foot scar up its middle.

Inside the terminal, she sends Dan a text. "Where I live you can look out over the lights of the marina at night. Come see me there. XX." She then texts everyone she can think of involved in the court case, telling them that she will return and testify, if needed, and will do whatever they ask. For now, however, she is taking a little holiday.

"Someone might want to scrape Craig off the floor," she writes. "I hit him when he attacked me. Please encourage him to file a suit. Tell him it would be a pleasure to see him again in court."

She boards the first plane out at dawn, paying three times the normal fare, handing over her credit card without hesitation. She imagines Dan. She wonders if this is truly the end of their story. And then she feels her phone vibrate in her pocket. She answers, and it is him. She should have known.

"What the hell happened?" he says. "Are you all right?"

She tells him she is fine, that she's getting on a plane. These facts, said as though they were the answers to what he wants to know, sound cold even to her. She sounds like a robot, she thinks.

But he is not fooled. "You are not fine," he says.

"I'm okay."

"Don't get on the plane. Please. Let me come get you."

They are still boarding. Mostly businesspeople with their brief-cases and their suits. She doesn't have any luggage. Outside a streak of light tells her it is sunrise. If she wanted to, she could walk straight off the plane, back into the terminal, down the escalators.

"I'll be okay," she tells him.

"I'm sure you will be."

"I thought I'd get out of here for a little while."

"Hmm," he says, evenly. "I've heard that before."

"I'll come back."

"No," he says. "You won't. Your memory will tie me to all the ugliness of that bastard and you won't come back. It's not fair, but I can't blame you."

She thinks he may be right. "How do you know?" she asks.

"I don't. I don't know anything except I want to see you right now."

But he does know. She thinks that even though he hasn't seen her in all this time, there is an important part of her that he under-stands, knows by instinct and feel, knows through a private conver-sation taking place in their hearts. "I don't associate you with him," she says.

He says, "Go downstairs and have a coffee and wait for me. I'll come get you. I'll come right now."

She thinks about that, how easy it would be.

"I'll make you glad you changed your mind," he says.

He is joking, she thinks. He is acting as though he is making a big play for her, but it is pretend. It must be. "Really?" She laughs.

"Yes," he says, seriously. "Let me try."

His voice is different from how she's ever heard it. Or perhaps she is different. Much of what happens between two people is com-plicated for her. Sex, definitely (she loves it and hates it and wants it and needs it and hates it and wants it and loves it . . .). Her ability to bond with a person (she wants him, she doesn't know what she wants, she says please stay close, don't get too close, love me, don't love me, stay with me a little, stay with me a lot . . .).

All that seems such nonsense now.

She stands. She walks against the tide of people coming through the narrow aisle between seats. She has to apologize to everyone. "Sorry," she says, over and over. Into the phone she says, "Okay, I'm doing it."

She feels as though she is about to jump off the plane like a skydiver. She feels she is about to jump from the plane and fly. She shows her boarding pass again to the stewardess and explains there has been a change.

Into the phone, to Dan, she says, "Are you still there?"

"Of course. Are you really getting off that plane?"

"Yes. Yes, I am."

"I'm getting in the car right now."

She thinks about Dan. Grabbing his car keys, his wallet, scribbling a note for his girls.

There are things she wants to understand. About how he loves her when she carries such shame. How it is possible. She believes he must have doubts, doubts about her character, her integrity. She imagines there are things he will want to know. It had been easier before the trial. It had been easier to say nothing to anyone. She is afraid he will ask her how it began. And for a moment, imagining how she will owe him an explanation, she almost turns around again. She almost runs.

"Do I have to tell you?" she says into the phone. "Do I have to tell you . . . everything?"

There is a hesitation, then he says, "No." He sounds confused. "I don't know what you are talking about. Tell me what?"

"About how it began. With him. Do I have to tell you that story? Just say."

She is on the ramp that connects the plane to the terminal. In a few moments, they will close the doors and the flight will depart. A steward stands at the door, looking as though he is trying to figure out what she is doing. She makes a gesture to him as though she is leaving, and she thinks she is leaving, too. She hopes so.

"None of that matters," Dan says. "Why do you think that matters? No, you don't have to say a word."

She enters the terminal, almost vacant at this early hour. The windows are filled with a red sunrise. The escalators glide empty up and down. The boarding gate has corduroy ropes across it now; she has to duck under them.

"Where are you?" she asks him. "Where are you right now?"

"In the car."

"I'm going to tell you," she says, walking fast back through the terminal.

"Tell me what?"

"How it began."

"*Now?* Don't."

"I want to. Hang on."

She drops into a seat at the end of a long line of interlocking chairs. There is nobody around and no reason not to tell him. Plus, over the phone is better. A little distance might help.

"I rang him at the station one night. He'd given me a T-shirt at a promo some weeks before. He'd told me to call him, so I did."

She describes to him the first time Craig picked her up in his car, how she watched him drive and thought how cool it was to be in a car with a guy who could drive. She tells him about the first kiss, and that she'd never been kissed so it was new and interesting. She'd thought it a good idea that he could teach her how to kiss so that when she met another guy, a boy she liked, she'd know what to do. It had not occurred to her she would have to kiss him from then on whenever he asked, or that she was obligated to see him. But she was obligated. And she became locked into him—she felt unable to escape—once they began with sex.

"One night, I let him take my shirt off. We were on a blanket under some pine trees. I was being bitten by mosquitoes but I let him take it off anyway." She imagines Dan asking why. Why had she taken off her shirt? He does not say any such thing but she answers as though he has. "Because it was the next thing to do, you know? And once I took my shirt off, everything had to come off. I hadn't understood, you see. That if you play an adult game, if you are having grown-up sex, you don't go just so far and turn back. You have to keep going."

Craig had covered her almost immediately, his chest in her face. What she'd thought then was how difficult it would be for the mosquitoes to get her. They'd bite him instead.

"It felt like sandpaper," she says. "When he was inside me, I mean—"

"Oh Jesus," says Dan.

"—the first time, anyway."

Sex with Craig had been awful but instructive. At the time, she told herself that it was good to know how, even if she didn't like it. That it was important. Now she curls herself into the hard airport chair, holding the phone as close as she can to her mouth. She says, "I could name every part, knew what muscles were used. It was science. I was interested in this weird scientific way. I must have been crazy."

He tells her she wasn't crazy. Not then. Not now.

"More?" she asks.

"No. Yes. What I mean is, I don't need to hear more. I think you feel you have to tell me, though."

She'd liked that he was so tall. A big man but playful. He would take her to amusement parks and bowling alleys and the movies. He would send her secret messages over the radio that she had to figure out. Sometimes it would be the first word in a series of song titles. Sometimes, the message was in the lyrics. He'd just blurt out a hello over the air and it was for her. Only her.

"I could have anything I wanted," she says, remembering how in those days a tub of popcorn would seem such a prize. "And the way he fussed over me. I mistook it for something else. I just didn't understand."

"Of course not," Dan says.

"I didn't like him, not like you imagine. And he wasn't attractive, as such. But he was so powerful, you know? I was impressed by the fact of him, like when you see a zoo animal in the wild. He was immense and mystifying." She stops suddenly, worried she has made him sound better than he was. "But I hated him. Not at first, but over the weeks and months. Because I didn't want what he wanted. I mean, I put up with it, you know? He figured that out. I was a girl who didn't like sex. In his mind there were only two types and I was that type. Later it occurred to him that it wasn't just the sex, it was him. I didn't like him. That's when he got nasty."

What she does not explain is why she could not stop. Couldn't stop him. Couldn't stop herself. Everything that happened with Craig had to remain concealed, hidden, brushed away. To keep it from being known, to prevent it spilling out into the rest of her life, she had been willing to do anything. Anything at all, even continue with it.

She tries to stop herself thinking too much. She finds it difficult to regulate her breathing. "I never once said no to him. Do you understand? But I didn't agree, either." She swallows hard. She wishes she had some water. She says, "Until that last night with him, the crash night. We had sex in the motel, but I was ready to say no after that. From then on. I was going to handle it; I was going to walk away. I think I was. But then I crashed that damned car. If I hadn't done that, he'd never have hooked up with my mom. He'd never have come to the house and—"

She can't bear to think about the rest. All the possibilities. That she might have lived in that house surrounded by trees, lived with her mother, been a child a little longer.

She listens for Dan's response. He seems to be struggling to say anything at all. Then he says, "I understand. But I don't agree with your conclusion. You don't think you were complicit, do you? That you were"—he hesitates, then continues—"that you were responsible?"

She sighs. "I don't know. I don't know if I feel responsible, but when I think about the girl in that other court case, I know that she wasn't responsible."

"Where are you?" he says. She tells him where and then she closes her eyes. She hasn't slept in what feels like forever, but the tiredness she feels isn't from that. It's from everything else, the great weight of her history, a history that still makes her feel both absurd and unclean. She is holding the phone but no longer talking into it. She is not sure if she is asleep or awake, until at last she opens her eyes fully and there is Dan in the seat beside her. His hair messed up, his face dark with a morning beard. Shoes, no socks. Jeans, no belt. His watch strap sticks out of his front pocket. His keys are in his hand.

He smiles. "I didn't want to wake you," he says.

She doesn't ask him how long he has been sitting there but unfolds herself stiffly from the chair. He takes her hand and she follows him out of the terminal to where the morning is now brightening, the traffic making its fury of noise. He puts his arm around her; they don't speak. In the car, he leans toward her and hugs her for a long while. Then he says, "I should tell you that your mother called me."

"June?" It sounds almost impossible. "I didn't think she knew who you were."

"She knows who I am all right. She called the house phone."

Bobbie is on the front seat beside him, angled so she is facing him as he describes how June woke him up, looking for her.

He says, "That's how I learned what happened. That you and Craig had a fight—"

"It wasn't a fight," she says. "Anyway, how could she have known?"

"You must have texted her, too."

"I don't even know her cell number," she says. She sighs. "Craig woke up and called her."

"She thought you were with me." He takes her hand. "She wanted me to tell you that she's glad you're safe. I didn't know what was going on, so I called you. And thank God, too, or else you'd be up there now," he says, pointing to the sky.

Dan puts the key into the ignition and she says, "Wait." She wants to stay here just a moment longer. She knows that on the other side of this car journey there will be phone calls and people she needs to see. The police, for one. "Let's just sit a few more minutes," she says. Then she says, "So I guess he's not dead."

Dan smiles. "Just as well."

For a moment she thinks what it would mean for Craig to be dead. She wonders if she would feel better. That with his death all the awful history would lift away, disappear. Sitting in the car with Dan, and for a long time to come, she believes that this is how it works, that one's history dies with the people who made it.

BUT SHE IS wrong. Years later, Craig will lie on a sweaty hospital mattress with cancer all through what is left of his stomach, and metastases spreading across his lungs, unable to breathe or move. For days and weeks he will remain miserably still and it won't change a thing. His death, when it comes, will not help her. Nor will it take anything from her. It will not close the thoughts that trample her mind. Death, she discovers, is no ending for anyone but the dying. Craig's death cannot put to rest a single part of her own past, cannot unstick or shift or move a thing. That is her work.

But she does not know this yet. Sitting in the car with Dan, she might have been convinced that hurting another human can help ease one's own pain. Anyway, Craig's death is many years away. Closer, in only a few years to come, she will hold her mother's hand as she is dying. She will answer June's plea to be forgiven without hesitation. *Of course*, she will say, as though it is her privilege to forgive, or as though there is nothing to forgive at all. She will say, *Mom, oh, Mom, you were so lovely to me.*

And for that moment, with her mother's delicate hand in her own, she may even feel that this had been the case. That her mother had been solid and loving and protective, that nothing had ever occurred to disrupt their happy union. It is not difficult for her to take such a burden off her mother, to relieve June. In fact, it is easy for her. She was always such a clever girl, such a talented woman.

She can cope with anything. She has lived a beautiful life, despite all that has happened. She has lost nothing, not even Dan, who will wait for her outside the hospice room as her mother's heart struggles. To shoulder her mother's guilt is no task at all. *You were good. You were perfect*, she will whisper. She will hope her mother hears her, and that she believes her. Because nothing changes between those who have truly loved, however deep the injuries. She will say it again to be sure. *I love you.* She will rage not against her mother's death but against what her mother might carry into it. She cannot let her mother feel unloved or unloving. She is not so ruined inside that she will allow her mother to suffer thoughts about which she can do nothing, or allow June to take into the afterlife the terror of regret.

Acknowledgments

I'd like to thank Drake Johnson, who gave me a crash course on court-rooms and who has been so supportive of this novel, and Mark Meredith, who helped me think things through. Thank you to my friends and readers: Hope Resor Bruens, Lisa Hinsley, Sergei Boissier, as well as Liz Goldenberg, who reminded me (among other things) of the geography of my childhood home. I am very grateful for Paul Sweeten's valuable attention to the manuscript. I am incredibly grateful to Lettice Franklin at Fourth Estate in the United Kingdom. Susan Estelle Jansen always causes me to write more truly and was an essential reader of early drafts. I could not have done without the thoughtful, sound advice of my editor, Nan Talese, to whom I am grateful for the work not only on this novel, but on so many before it. Finally, I've dedicated the book to my daughter, Imo, who keeps me current and makes me think.

A Note About the Author

Marti Leimbach is the author of several novels, including the international bestseller *Dying Young*, which was made into a major motion picture starring Julia Roberts; *Daniel Isn't Talking*; and *The Man from Saigon*. She lives in England and teaches in Oxford University's creative writing program.

A Note About the Type

The text of this book was set in Garamond No. 3. It is not a true copy of any of the designs of Claude Garamond (ca. 1480–1561), but an adaptation that probably owes as much to the designs of Jean Jannon, a Protestant printer in Sedan in the early seventeenth century, who had worked with Garamond's romans earlier in Paris. This particular version is based on an adaptation by Morris Fuller Benton.